To Barbara Zir

March 2009 –

Thank you for your support and for joining the people of the Ship Hector on their journey Toward the Horizon!

Jeanne Mac Gregor Lah

Toward the Horizon

By

Jeanne MacGregor Lahn

International Standard Book Number 13: 978-1-60452-021-7
International Standard Book Number 10: 1-60452-021-3

Library of Congress Control Number: [on order]

BluewaterPress LLC
2220 CR 210 W Ste 108 #132
Jacksonville, FL 32559
http://bluewaterpress.com

This book may be purchased online at -

http://www.bluewaterpress.com/horizon
or through
amazon.com

Cover Art
by

Dave MacIntosh

David MacIntosh is a full time, self taught artist who found inspiration in pictorial books featuring the works of the early European painters. Building on this early influence he has developed a uniquely recognizable and appealing "Old World" style that is reminiscent of the early "Masters of Light". For many years while showing his work in Halifax area galleries he concentrated mainly on marine themes, but now produces quality work in other areas as well (primarily portraiture, landscape and historical). To date, his oil paintings hang in many private, corporate, education and museum settings locally and abroad.

Although David does not consider himself to be a wildlife painter, he has to his credit three Canadian Wildlife Conservation Stamps, P.E.I. 1996 and N.B. 1997 (national program), the third presents the Atlantic Waterfowl Celebration that takes place in Sackville, N.B., this event has in the past received the Governor General's Award of Excellence. The images used for these stamps were taken from commissioned works he completed for well known photographer Sherman Hines, who also for a time received some art instruction from David during family visits to his home in the Windsor, Nova Scotia area.

At present, during the summer season David is the resident artist at the Hector Heritage Quay in Pictou. His images are used for almost all material promoting this very popular tourist destination (brochures, guides, posters, sea chests, labels, etc.). A new look for the cover of Donald MacKay's popular book "Scotland Farewell", almost 1/3 of the content of the award winning documentary "New Beginnings" and a design for the large stone Ship Hector Foundation donor monument were also recently completed.

In addition to the permanent display he is creating for the Town of Pictou which documents the history of the arrival of the first Celtic immigrants and present ship "Hector" reconstruction, David can also be credited with creating images for two other Nova Scotian tall ships, the "Pictou Castle" for Captain Dan Morland, Lunenburg, N.S. , and museum paintings of the "Avon Spirit", a top sailed schooner built near Windsor N.S. under the supervision of Vice Admiral (ret.) Hugh MacNEil. Hugh also recently asked David to do a portrait of Admiral Leonard Warren Murray who commanded the North Western Atlantic Allied Forces during World War 2. The finished portrait is prominently displayed at navel command headquarters in Halifax. This earned David a personal invitation from the Navy's supreme commander to it's unveiling and the image appears in a publication "In Peril on the Sea" by Donald E. Graves. His portraits, which are incredibly life like are in great demand by many individuals from both the private and professional sectors.

Recently, his work, which over the years has been used on just about everything from magnets to murals appeared on the cover of Stanley Spicer's "Age of Sail", Master Shipbuilders of the Maritimes. Many of the images that were created for the Avon River Heritage Museum also appear within the publication. David also has been given the honor of being in the company of some of the most accomplished artists in Canada, past and present, in "above and Beyond", a history of J.R. Shaw's Family in Life and Business.

David was the original official artist for the R.C.M.P. Adopt a Library, Literacy Program.

This novel is dedicated to my dearly departed grandmothers…
May we always remember our past while we continue to strive for our future.

Ruth (Billy) MacGregor Ramaley, the first woman in the family to graduate with a Bachelor's Degree in Journalism and my childhood best friend. It was because of her that I explored our Scottish heritage and discovered this remarkable story.

&

Bernadette Johnson Sorlie, the grandma who loved little children so very much. She always had lemonade, Jell-o, cookies and a warm hug waiting for every child or grandchild that might drop in for a visit. I like to think she is still watching over us.

✦ ✦ ✦

I would also like to thank my mother for the valuable gift of her time spent teaching me to read and love books as a child and for always encouraging me to write.
I am so grateful to my father for his gifts of stoicism, laughter and courage. I miss you.

✦ ✦ ✦

I love and thank my husband, Eugene, beyond measure for his patience and his support.

I love and thank my children for teaching me about life, hope and unconditional love.

Last, but never least, I thank my dear friend and faithful proofreader, Bonnie Corcoran.

Without all of my wonderful family and friends this story might never have been written.

Jeanne MacGregor Lahn
November 2007

Toward the Horizon

This story pays homage to the courageous immigrants of the Ship Hector on their fateful trip from Scotland to Nova Scotia in the summer of 1773. Although the following novel is based on actual events, the characterizations are fictional.

Jeanne MacGregor Lahn

Chapter One

Loch Broom, Scotland: Spring 1773

ugh McLeod leaned heavily on his gnarled pine walking stick as he prayed silently above the grave of his beloved wife, Flora. She was buried in the family burial plot, behind the old kirk on the hill. He stood with his back to the sea, ignoring the beauty of Loch Broom where it emptied into the Minch over his left shoulder. Beyond that, the rugged Northwestern coast of the Highlands held back the sea on either side of the mouth of Loch Broom. Teasing ocean breezes tugged at his whitening red hair, whipping stray strands from its loosely tied knot into his careworn face.

His prayer ended, he opened his eyes. Tears welled up and slid free, first from one eye and then the other, tracking down his cheeks to drip off the chiseled granite of his jaw and fall onto the earth which his Flora lay beneath. Despite his age and his disfigured leg, he was still a huge and imposing figure with all of the fierce features of his Norse and Celtic ancestors.

"Oh, Flora, my dear one, it's glad I am tha' you didna live ta see wha' has come aboot," he spoke in his thundering Highland voice. "And yet, here I stand, selfishly longing to take comfort in your arms. I know not, what is ta become of us."

He paused to swipe at his face with one huge hand, annoyed to find the moisture there. "Our eldest, Hugh... I ken he resides there with you and the good Lord, but now 'tis only our son, David, and this auld wreck you see before you that are left to provide for the bairns and their mithers." He shifted his weight from one leg to the other with a slight grimace as pain shot through his crippled left leg. An echo of the saber that had pierced it long ago rang against the bone. "Achh, spending me life a soldierin' has ill equipped me for such a task!" His mind wandered back through the mist of years past.

He had been a young man during the bloody Jacobite rebellion thirty years past and he and many from his clan had been a part of that final doomed battle on Culloden Moor. The door to Scotland's freedom had closed firmly on that blood drenched day. Those few of his clan that had survived the ghastly slaughter under the English leader, Cromartie, had struggled home in defeat, only to find the war following them to their once peaceful coastal and loch side homes. In the hellish decade that had followed, he had occasion to be sincerely glad that he'd at least known the satisfaction of killing some of William Cumberland's English troops. They had shown no conscience and given no quarter during the murdering, raping and burning that had been done during Scotland's long despairing years after the English victory.

Despite few able-bodied men left alive, the troops had come to burn and loot the surrounding areas. While Hugh was trying to protect his home, his thigh had been run through by a British saber, just above his left knee. He and the other men and most of the older boys of the village and countryside had been marched off to prison. The English soldiers took those that had served at Culloden and even those who had not, along with any lad over twelve-years-old, to thoroughly quell thoughts of further Scottish rebellion.

His wound had festered off and on for most of the first year of his captivity. At one point, only his massive size and his ferocious temper had prevented the prison doctor from lopping off his leg with one of his wicked looking little saws. By sheer willpower alone he had survived, but the scarring that ensued had left him with a permanent limp from his stiffened left knee. The only thought that had sustained him through those dark years was his tenacious desire to return home to his wife, Flora, and their young sons, Young Hugh and David.

Flora had been luckier than most women were after Culloden. Their home was near the coast and her family ties were strong in the outer islands. She and their two boys had sought refuge on the McOulachan isles with some of her kin and they had been spared the post war atrocities inflicted on many of the mainlanders by "Butcher" Billy Cumberland and his troops.

After several long years in prison, Hugh and his fellow Scots prisoners were given the choice of deportation to the Americas as indentured servants, or enlistment in the Highland regiments of the English Army. Many family men chose to fight for the English, and with their oaths of allegiances sworn, they prevented any further persecution of their families at home. It also paid wages that were nearly non-existent in those days from any other source, especially after so many English nobles had been granted large tracts of land after their victory. This money the soldiers earned could be sent home to their kin and was often the deciding difference between life and death for their loved ones. Choosing to enlist also allowed the men to keep alive the hope of seeing their family between military campaigns, where deportation would not.

For Hugh, there had seemed no other option. With his crippled leg, the labors of fishing he had been raised to would be difficult at best. His lack of balance aboard a fishing boat could endanger others; but he could still fight as well as ever. He had swallowed his pride painfully and sworn the hated oath of allegiance to the very army that had imprisoned and crippled him.

Hugh drew a shaky breath and stood a little taller. "Ah, Flora.... Forgive me, my love," he said, with a sigh. "I am acting like an auld fool feeling sorry for me self! We have borne sa much already; surely we will bear up ta this as well. Sleep well, mo mhurninn, my love!" Feeling somewhat comforted just for having talked to her he turned and began to limp away, leaning heavily on his cane. He made his way with difficulty along the narrow path that wound down across the rock-strewn hillside below the kirk.

A lone golden eagle screamed as it circled effortlessly overhead hunting small prey. A short way downhill Hugh paused on a stony ledge to watch it and rest his aching leg. The magnificent bird needed only an occasionally flap of its great wings, as it skillfully rode the currents of air that rushed uphill from the loch. Suddenly, the eagle angled sharply toward earth, drawing its great wings into its body in order to speed up its steep dive. Hugh squinted, trying in vain to see any movement on the ground below. In the blink of an eye, the eagle snatched up what looked like some unfortunate rodent in its lethal talons. A few powerful strokes of its wings later and the eagle soared toward its mountaintop aerie with its prize.

Hugh watched the lone eagle go, admiring its strength and beauty. He felt it was a good omen and took comfort in the thought that it was. He would, with the good Lord's help, find a way to provide for his own. He continued on in his labored way, hitching down the mountainside with his walking stick supporting him when his leg threatened to fail him.

By the time he reached the cluster of homes above the small fishing village of Ullapool, it was mid-afternoon. Several small boats were bobbing on the bay of Loch Broom, but most were still out in the Minch seeking the salmon, trout, and herring that were gathering near the mouth of the Broom after leaving their winter homes out in the Atlantic. Soon, most of the salmon would move up the loch, seeking the rivers and streams of their birth. Once there, they would spawn the new generation and then die, completing their circle of life.

Hugh walked past several cottages as he made his way to the home where he lived with his eldest son's widow, Janet. Their neighbor, Molly McKenzie, was stirring woolens with a pole as she dyed them in a great steaming cauldron outside her cottage. She glanced up as he approached and smiled, her blue eyes sparkling with good humor when she recognized him. "Good day ta ya, Hugh McLeod, been up to the auld kirk to see Flora again, have ye?"

"Good day ta ya, Mistress McKenzie, aye, I have. And a fine day for the hike it was, too," He answered, bowing to her as he passed. The rich animal smell of boiling wool drifted on the breeze. On the hills behind the house, her youngest boy, Colin, and her daughter, Elspa, could be seen herding their few sheep along, like willful little white clouds floating upon the green hillside.

"Give Maggie and Janet me best!" Maggie added, with a flap of a work reddened hand in his direction before he was too far gone.

"Aye, I wull, and mine ta your John!" He shouted back, waving back with a hand that was nearly as gnarled as his old walking stick.

A little further down the path he came to Dougald McLeod's place, where no one was about to greet him but their skinny barking dogs. He patted their furry heads to shush them as he continued on his way. He was just passing the widow Murray's place when she came bustling out the door with a worried looking lad at her heels. She nearly collided with him and he steadied her with one huge hand, as the startled lad ran right into her ample rear end. "What has got you in such a swivet then, A bhoireanaich?" Hugh asked, hiding a smile.

"Oh! I b-beg your pardon, Hugh!" She stammered, turning a gimlet eye on the boy at her rear, who hurriedly stepped back a pace, flushing hotly as he did so. "I'm on my way ta see ta young Abigail. Her time has come and the babe is in some hurry to be born!" The freckled lad with her shifted nervously from foot to foot and tugged impatiently at her sleeve. "Aye, Adam! If you will pardon us, we mun be on our way." The round little midwife rushed downhill in a flurry of skirts and disappeared around a bend, half dragged by the frightened lad.

Hugh shook his head and chuckled softly to himself, thinking of his own nervousness when his mother was birthing his little sister. As if it would matter one way or the other what he did! It was something men could only helplessly wait through, praying all would be well. He had waited through the long agonizing hours of his Flora's labors and then again through his daughter-in-laws', as well. No matter how skilled he had become at fighting, he knew there was little he could do to defend his women from the mysterious inner dangers of childbirth. A few minutes later, he passed the small cottage of Abigail and Christopher Murray. He muttered a prayer for her and the bairn's safe delivery and crossed himself, as her tormented groans could be heard coming from inside.

Off the well worn path and around another small hill, he arrived home to see one of his concerns skipping toward the cottage with grasses scattered through her red hair and across her homespun skirt and disheveled shift. In one hand she carried a somewhat wilted bouquet of wildflowers. Her mother, Janet, appeared at the door with little Finlay on her hip. Spotting her daughter, she put her other hand on her free hip, her mouth pursed in obvious irritation. "Elspeth Rose McLeod! Just where ha' ya been all this time then? I sent ya ta look for your grandfather, did I no?"

Looking at the ground in embarrassment, Elspeth still came forward to courageously stand before her mother. The small bouquet hung at her side, now forgotten. "I'm sorry, Mither," She began, "But, I...."

Hugh cleared his throat to interrupt as he came into view and to the rescue of his small granddaughter. "I'm here, Janet, and sa she did find me," He said, with a sly wink over at Elspeth. Startled at first, Elspeth quickly realized she might be saved from a scolding and her grin broke, like sunlight as the rain clouds fled.

"I picked these for you, Mama," she added, belatedly offering the limp little bouquet to Janet.

"Oh! How pretty they are, Elspeth!" Janet relented, as she smelled the early spring wildflowers. Her irritation evaporated as she inhaled their sweet smell. "Well, it's sorry I am then, lass, and thank you for these pretties!"

Little Finley reached out with chubby fingers toward the flowers his mother held. "Pah!" He exclaimed, his other arm whirling with excitement. "Pah, mah!"

Elspeth giggled and grabbed his excited little hands in hers. "He said they are pretty, Mama! Did ya hear it?"

Janet laughed too. "Aye, I think he did!"

Hugh laid his walking stick against the wall and reached out for the little boy. Finlay stretched both his little arms eagerly toward his Grandfather, clinging to him as readily as he did to his mother. Hugh sat down on the wooden bench outside their house, arranging his stiff leg as comfortably as possible and then held the boy up high. "Of course he did! That's me fine wee laddie," He crooned. "Sharp he is, like a wise wee owl."

Finlay squealed with pleasure as his grandfather swung him through the air as if he were flying. Hugh put him on his good knee and began jostling him as he always did. "Ride your pony, me wee little owl, ride him!" Finlay bubbled with laughter and in between the chuckles his eyes grew wide, looking exactly like the little owl his grandfather had said he resembled.

"Father, could ya mind him?" Janet asked. "I should go and milk the goats. I hear them bleating from here." She ducked inside with the flowers and rushed right back out.

"Of course I wull Janet, I could use a spot of rest, meself. Be on your way then, I will sit with the bairns." As Janet disappeared over the rise, he patted the bench next to him with a grin, inviting Elspeth to join him.

"Oh, Grandfather!" Elspeth said, as her mother disappeared. "Thank you for telling Mama I found ya! But isn't it like tellin' a lie?" She asked, soberly.

"Well now, lassie, ya were out looking for me, aye?"

"Yes, Grandfather, but I didna find ya!"

"Aye lassie, ya did! Just as I was coming ta hame, why there you were! And if you were admiring the flowers on the way, well tha's why the good Lord put them there. 'Tis no a sin ta admire and love God's handiwork! Besides, I canna sit by watching me only granddaughter be punished because I am myself gone too long up the ben!"

Hugh patted her flaming, sun warmed hair. She leaned in and hugged him close. "Taing, Grandda," she sighed. "I didna mean ta be gone sa long either, but it was such a fine day! And the flowers are a-springin' up everywhere! Besides, I kent ye were on the mountain with Granny Flora and wanted ta be alone."

Hugh hugged her back. "Ah, lassie, ya ken me sa well. You are much like your Granny Flora." His throat tightened for a moment, thinking how much his wife would have loved this little girl, having never had a daughter of her own.

"Best run along now and help your mither. The men will be ashore soon and there is mun yet ta do afore supper."

"Aye, Grandfather," she said, and scampered off to find Janet.

Hugh stood up and scanned the loch trying to spy his son Davy's fishing dory. They wouldn't likely come in until sunset, after they had used every precious minute of daylight. Often these days, they could be seen mooring by lamplight. After the too recent loss of his son, Young Hugh, his men and their boat to the unpredictable sea, Hugh couldn't loosen the knot of fear in his gut every time his remaining son, Davy, went out with Elspeth's older brother, Willie. He sent another plea to the heavens, that Davy would not widow his wife Maggie, as his Hugh had widowed Janet. "And may the Lord watch ower your big brother, Willie," he said softly to the little boy.

"Weee!" Finlay said clearly, pointing out to the boats.

"Yes, my fine Finlay! Willie is oot there!" Hugh agreed with a laugh, pointing to the boats down on Loch Broom. "He is on a boat! Can ya say 'boat' then?"

"Bo!" Finlay shrieked with glee.

Hugh laughed and tossed the boy in the air, deftly catching him as he fell. "What a fine wee fellow ya are, me wise wee owl!"

The old man and the toddler both laughed joyously as they enjoyed the pleasure of each other's company. One head glowed like warm silver and the other like copper fire under the lazy afternoon sun. Soon the family would gather to greet the returning men and have supper, but for now this golden time was theirs alone.

Chapter Two

Eastern Shores of Loch Katrine, Scotland: Spring 1773

The sun's dying rays stretched long and soft across the late afternoon air, lighting James' path into the foothills of the Trossach Mountains. Despite the rapidly setting sun James felt reluctant to return home with the meager catch he had managed to snare. He had hunted for many miles around, sitting patiently near game trails for hours, hoping to bag a deer or at least a fat grouse for his family's support. He looked down at the puny rabbit and squirrel he had in their stead and sighed. He thought of his wife, Mary Katrine's smiling face. Somehow, no matter how poor the hunting or fishing was she always made it into something that would satisfy all. She seemed to work magic stretching their provisions with soups and stews.

He paused only a moment before jumping across the small, icy burn that flowed through the greening glen. Thoughts of the winter past swiftly wiped the last vestiges of a smile from his face. His sister-in-law, Ann, had died slowly before their eyes, failing to thrive again after the birth of her tiny twin sons, William and Alex. James secretly believed that she had died of a broken heart as well, having lost her husband, William, only a month before their twins' birth. William had died of a strange wasting sickness that had come on during Ann's pregnancy. They had done their best to nurse him back from his illness, but all their efforts had failed and William had not lived to see his twin sons be born.

James ground his teeth, feeling the hopeless rage of being unable to provide better for his growing family. In addition to his and Mary's four youngsters, there were now the twins to care for as well. Orphaned as they were, James and Mary had no choice but to raise them as their own. Food was the scarcest commodity of all in the Highlands just now; the only thing scarcer was hope. The only reason that the twins had lived at all was because of his beloved Mary. She had given birth several months before Ann, to their little Alasdair, and had milk enough to nurse all three babes after Ann's death. But he was worried about Mary and hoped she could continue until the bairns were weaned. All the nursing and caring of so many babes at once was beginning to take a noticeable toll on her. The fragile looking flesh around her large brown eyes was smudged dark with fatigue, her young forehead was creased with worry and she had grown very thin. There was a deep sadness in her that James could not name, despite the fact that the three babes thrived and grew, and it worried him.

James could hear dogs barking and the shrieks and shouts of children at play as he rounded the last bend of the winding footpath. Several youngsters were scuffling around in the dirt with their feet, trying to kick about a small bundle of rags that had been wound into a rather lopsided ball. There were small groups of children standing off to either side yelling encouragement to their friends. The village dogs had joined the fray, thinking it great fun to try to steal the ball and make the children chase them instead, which they often did.

Little Lizzie, only three-years-old, tried in vain to push into the rabble and join the play. Her older sister, Katy, pushed her gently away from the others, "Gwa' Lizzie! You're too little ta play! Don' be naughty, aye?"

Always precocious, Lizzie scowled in frustration, her little bottom lip pursed into a pout she pushed at one big dog that bumped into her. "Gwa', goggie!" she screeched in her shrill, little voice. "Bad, Gog!" she added as the dog hung his head and retreated in defeat. Lizzie folded her arms and with satisfaction gleaming in her eyes, watched one of the few creatures that would obey her, skulk away.

James laughed at this little outburst as he approached. Within seconds, he was surrounded by squeals of, "Da! Uncle James! Mr. McDonald!" The dogs added their barking to the din until it was nearly impossible to distinguish one voice from another. The dogs pawed and whined their greetings to him, rolling over to present their bellies as he patted them. They sniffed politely at the game hanging from his belt with inquiring noses. The children performed a similar excited dance around him as he patted each one on the head or laid his hand on a bony shoulder of one of the older lads. "Well, my wee Lizzie," he said scooping up her warm little body, "sa it's too little ya are agin, aye? Well tha' wull be remedied soon enough I'm thinkin'."

Seven-year-old Katy looked up at him worriedly with her mother's shining brown eyes. "I didna want her ta be hurt, Da! Ya told me ta watch out for her and so I did."

Her earnest little face looked so serious, that he reached out and yanked gently at the curl on the tip of one shiny black braid. "Aye, Katy, and a fine job ya did too!" He kneeled down to include her in a hug with her little sister. "Both my girls look right as rain!" He buried his face against their small heads for a moment, one red head, and one black. After a moment, he lifted them both off the ground in a warm embrace as he breathed in their sunny grassy scents.

Ten-year-old Andrew appeared at James' elbow, eyeing the rabbit and squirrel tied to a strap of leather thong around his waist. "Shall I clean those and bring them ta Mother for you then, Da? She'll be waitin' on ya." His nimble fingers were already working at the knot in the thong before James could answer.

"Aye, lad and hurry now, its late I am with them too. I had ta wait a long, long time before I spotted even that wee squirrel. Even the trout seem ta be scarce in the burns, after such a bitter winter." James put the girls down and stood up.

"Were there no deer ta be seen, even in the forest then, Mr. McDonald, sir?" One of the older lads, asked. Hope wavered on the skinny lad's face.

"I walked nearly ta Achray and back, Hamish, and nary a bitty bird ta keep me company, let alone a deer!" Seeing the boys' crestfallen faces, he added, "but, take heart; there is always tomorrow, lads!"

"Young Angus," James called to a red haired lad with a pubescent sheen of fuzz on his cheeks, "did you and your Da ha' any luck on your sealg ta the north today, then?"

"Aye, sir, only twa' auld grouse though; good only for the soup pot, I expect." Eyeing James' rabbit and squirrel as Andrew finished untying them, he smiled. "That's a fine catch ya have there, too, sir! We'll all et some hot broth tonight."

"Aye, we will at tha'." James said. He watched with a smile as Andrew took the game to the chopping block next to the house. Angus, Hamish and several other MacGregor youngsters tagged along at his heels to watch, jostling for the best position. James watched the boy walk away, feeling warm with pride. His dark auburn hair looked very like his own, with just a bit of curl, like his mother's shining black locks. He was small, but already growing long of bone and showing the promise of the man he would one day become.

The other lads his age respected him and were always eager to watch him show off his prowess with a knife. He could already dress game or clean a fish almost as well as James could, in spite of his young age, and he wasted none of the precious meat. He could whittle a piece of wood into any imaginable shape or animal and often enjoyed making gifts of his work. Andrew's natural gift with a blade had already earned him the nickname, Sgian Dubh, or black knife, among his friends. It was also due to Mary's brother, Ian, whom he resembled and who had also borne that nickname in his youth. Ian had spent nearly as much time with Andrew as James had, teaching him the many uses of the small sock knife and larger knives as he matured.

James glanced to the east at the scarlet glow of the setting sun as it reflected off the upper slopes of Ben An. Happy to be home, his heart squeezed tight and then expanded to take in the sight and commit it to memory. The glen itself already lay deep in plum shadows. It was still early in the season and it would be full dark soon. He shivered, a nameless fear suddenly gripping his heart. "Get you now ta your evening' chores, you wee beasties! I must go and greet my wife before she starts ta worrit for me," he said, shooing them off with pretend gruffness.

All the children scampered away to their own family's fire, confident that if the McDonalds had meat, they would share around what broth they could that night to every needy hearth.

James stepped through his own humble doorway and went inside. Sgian had been right. Mary already had a large pot of savory smelling herb broth bubbling over the fire just waiting for some meat to be added. She sat by the fire in the willow rocker he had made for her, with one of the twins snuggled comfortably in each arm. Next to her, lay little Alasdair bundled up in his withy basket and already sound asleep. She smiled at him, "Whist! I finally got them all ta sleep," she whispered.

Gently James reached down to take one of the small bundles from her as she rose from her chair, carefully holding the other. He put the babe in a larger basket next to the fire and she placed the other, with his head facing the other direction, to nestle alongside each other in the same basket. Mary stretched her burdened back with an arching stretch and then put an arm around James' back. They watched all three babes in the firelight for a few moments. Little Willie made small sucking noises, as if dreaming of still nursing and they chuckled. Alasdair stirred a little, so they backed away quietly, in order not to wake them.

James drew Mary into his arms and among the shadows of the room, they fashioned a greeting all their own. Mary's soft lips were as warm as always, but he could feel how tired she was. She leaned into him as they kissed and he was very nearly holding her full weight. Their lips parted and he stared into the dark depths of her eyes in the flickering firelight. "Ah, this is sa hard for ya, my love. I want sa badly ta make life a wee bit better for us all," he whispered to her. His large brown hands smoothed back the shiny midnight curls that escaped their pinning around her sweet face as he stared into her wistful brown eyes.

"Acch, we are doin' just fine dear," she scolded, "and a far cry better than most! We've a roof o'er our heads, good health and each other. God shall provide the rest."

"Well, the good book says, 'the Lord helps those that help themselves' my dear heart. Although, I think we've been doin' plenty enough on our own side of the matter! I'm just wondering when our Lord will remember us and get around ta doing his share of the helpin' is all."

"Why James Andrew Campbell McDonald, don't ya be mocking the Lord that way! 'Tis bad luck and a sin at that!" Mary said, her cheeks turning a healthier shade of pink, as she teased him. "I won't have it in this house!" She stamped her small foot on the packed earth floor and crossed her arms across her chest defiantly.

"God forgive me, then! I meant no disrespect ta the Lord.... or to you," he added, playfully pulling her to him again. "I ken that the Lord wull forgive me, sa wha' aboot you, my sweet Mary?" He leaned in and nipped lightly along the side of her neck until she giggled and squirmed in his arms.

"Stop that," she gasped, wriggling in his grasp. "We'll wake the bairns!"

He grinned, loosened his hold on her, placed a quick kiss on her brow, and then stepped over to stir the fire. He knelt to block the sleeping infants from errant sparks with his body as he turned the smoldering chunks of peat over with a stick. Meanwhile, Mary retrieved their wooden quaichs, tied a few dried roseships, some dried chamomile, and a pinch of their precious tea leaves into a small piece of cloth and dropped the little bundle neatly into the tea kettle to steep.

James smiled and pulled his whiskey flask out of his breast pocket and poured a small splash into each quaich that awaited the brewed tea. "Have a wee nip before we add the tea, my dear; it warms the bones. Not that mine need be warmer, but yours surely do!" He winked mischievously and handed hers to her.

"James!" She admonished, but she said it with a smile. "You can be such a wicked, wicked man! But I must be wicked as well, because I love ya dearly, my own." They had a few precious moments of quiet with each other, sipping and listening to the hiss and pop of the slow burning fire before the hurly-burly of their bairns tumbled through the doorway.

Little Lizzie was leading the way through the door at a run, squealing, "Mama! Mama! I helped!"

"Whist, hush you now!" Mary scolded. In the commotion Alasdair woke and began fussing.

The twins squirmed and threatened to wake as well, before Lizzie quieted herself. Lizzie rushed worriedly to Mary's side and patted and stroked the twins and Alasdair, trying to soothe them with her little hands. "Baby sleepy, shhh," Lizzie said, imitating Mary's motherly comforting tones. With peace in the room again, partially thanks to Lizzie's anxious ministrations, the babes drifted back to sleep.

Sgian handed his mother the nicely skinned and cleaned rabbit and squirrel, which she promptly pounded flat with her maul and deftly cut into pieces. She efficiently added every morsel to the already boiling vegetables and water and then added the brewed tea to the remaining whiskey in her and James' quaichs.

Katy handed her the small pail of milk she had been able to get from their skinny little highland cow. "That's a good, lassie," her mother said softly. "Let's make a bit of oatcake, aye?" She smiled down at Katy, as she pushed back her sleeves.

Katy smiled back at her mother lovingly. "Yes, Mama, "she replied, as she pushed back her own small sleeves to help.

"I can help!" Lizzie chimed, stirring from her place by the twins' basket.

"Whist," her mother reminded her, with a nod toward the babes. "Ya are helping, lassie! You're tending the babes should they wake. And a great help ya are too! Now, hush."

"Aye, Mama, "Lizzie whispered obediently. Taking her task most seriously, she bent down to examine her tiny charges with a small worried scowl which comically imitated a little old woman. Satisfied that they were going back to sleep, she sat down between the two baskets.

James chuckled softly and patted her small head. Sgian sidled up to the table, eyeing James' whiskey flask with interest. "Is whiskey tasty, Da?" Sgian asked, as he leaned in curiously and sniffed loudly, "it doesna smell very tasty!" He wrinkled his nose as he drew away.

"Well now, to a wee laddie, no it doesna, but I am no a wee laddie, aye?" He added with a wink. He finished his whiskey-laced tea with an exaggerated flourish and smacked his lips for effect.

"I am no a wee laddie, Da!" Sgian exclaimed indignantly.

"Nay my lad, your a fine, braw, lad" James quickly responded, having no wish to offend his eldest son. James scratched his beard thoughtfully and glanced at Mary. "Weel, if your mither has no objections.... you may have a taste. But mind me, just a taste!" He cautioned. "If a man has too much whiskey afore his full height and wits have come ta him, he'll go saft in the heid."

Nodding seriously, Sgian warily picked up the artfully decorated flask that he knew was a prized possession of James. With a confirming glance to his mother, who wore a mysterious little smile, he slowly raised it to his lips. His throat bobbed with the first greedy swallow, but he quickly pulled the flask from his lips with a grimace. His eyes grew quite round and began to water as he gasped for air. "Da," he finally croaked, "how can ya drink it?" He wiped the back of his hand across his mouth and quickly handed the flask back as though his hand burned from it, "'tis filthy fire in me mouth!"

James and Mary held back their laughter, so as not to be unkind, but a warm look passed briefly between them. "Well laddie, it's as well ya don' yet like it. You still ha' a bit of growing to do, aye? The flavor gets better with age.... like a woman!" He added with a playful wink.

"James!" Mary said, reproving him gently.

"Tis a good bit of advice, my love, and the truth, as well," James retorted, with a grin and a decisive nod.

Sgian glanced from the flask to his mother, looking doubtful as to the truth of his father's words. He drew in a deep breath and coughed again, ending in another grimace. "If tha' is true Father, then I shall marrit the oldest lass I can find!" Sgian said vehemently.

Mary and James laughed heartily at this, but were quickly admonished by Lizzie. "Mama, Da, the babes!" She whispered fiercely. They guiltily stifled their laughter and looked away from each other to prevent further outbursts.

Mary and Katy finished patting together the oatcakes, placed them in a hot pan over the fire, then set out the rest of the quaichs to be dipped into the stew pot for their suppers. The children had all washed up before coming in, knowing that their mother would have ushered them right back out, if they had not. James ducked out to do his own washing in the cold little burn. He rubbed his hands and face vigorously with the icy mountain water and then stood up, briskly shaking the water off. He stared up at the star sprinkled sky for a few moments, letting the last glistening droplets of water drip from his beard and fingertips.

He drew in a deep breath, paying silent homage to the beauty of the newborn evening. In every direction the valley was lost in darkness. Faint, contented, family noises were all that could be heard and they mingled prettily with the song of the bubbling burn. Ben An's snow-capped peak still shone in the soft darkness, as if lit from within by the memory of the sun's fiery kiss. As he walked back to their cottage, he could see the early stars as they appeared over Loch Katrine to the west. The horizon was still rimmed with jeweled tones that shimmering alongside silvery water and golden sky, reflecting in a way that made the line between water and sky difficult to distinguish.

Despite the ethereal beauty in front of him, James knew a feeling of profound emptiness. This was no longer the Scotland of his forefathers. Scotland's defeated rebellion against England thirty years prior had changed its fate forever. Harsh English rule, greedy landowners, and the long occupation by armies of soldiers had reduced her remaining people, her native and domestic animals, even the very ground under their feet to a barren and poverty stricken condition.

The McDonalds and their tenant farmer kin were no longer welcome with these new landowners. They were seen as a burden and an impediment to improving the lands, grazing animals and increasing the lord's profits. Not only that, they were often falsely accused of any criminal activity in neighboring regions and constantly persecuted. To live to see another day was more of a challenge now than it had ever been before. Instead of life getting easier as time went by, it was getting harder with each passing year to provide for his family and starvation had become a common fact of life. For a father, it was an aching fear that haunted him mercilessly and one he felt helpless to remedy. James rearranged his face, hoping to hide his deepest fears from his family as he went back in to rejoin them at the fire.

Chapter Three

Town of Blantyre, Scotland: Spring 1773

ane Forbes absentmindedly drummed a tattoo with her fingernails on the bottom of the china saucer she held. The tea was starting to cool in her cup and still her mother had not come in from the garden to join her. She picked up the letter she had been staring at since it had arrived and sighed. It was clearly addressed to her mother, Mrs. Mary Jane Forbes. Jane would not dare to open it herself, despite knowing her entire future likely rested upon its contents. Glaring at her uncle's seal in frustration, she slapped it back on the table. She was past all patience and was rising to go and drag her mother away from her beloved flowerbeds, when she suddenly appeared at the door of the sitting room. "Oh, there you are, Mother! I was just coming to fetch you. Your tea is getting cold," Jane said, nervously sitting back down on the settee.

"Is that what you're all a flutter about then? My tea may get cold?" Mary teased, with a smile. Their one remaining servant, Gwyneth, had come to tell her of the letter's arrival a quarter of an hour before. But she had stayed out in her garden to collect her thoughts the best way she knew how, by weeding and plucking while the whirlwind in her mind calmed itself in the simplicity of labor. She quickly patted her graying light brown hair by habit, with barely a passing glance at the large oval mirror on the wall, to assure that its heavy coils were still properly in place before she gracefully crossed the room toward her daughter.

"Mother, I sent Gwenny to tell you that the letter from Uncle George had arrived quite some time ago and...." Jane began to protest, half rising again from her chair.

"Hush now, lassie, I was only finishing the task I had begun. I had to put the flowers in water and wash the garden grime off my face and hands now, didn't I? A task worth doing is worth doing well; remember that, lassie. Now then, let me have the letter, dearie." Mary held out her freshly scrubbed hand for the letter as she took her seat next to Jane. She broke the familiar wax seal with a quick flick of her thumbnail and opened the letter with her usual brisk efficiency. A portrait drawn on heavy stock fell out of the letter and she placed it face down on her lap for now. Not wishing to keep her daughter in suspense any longer, she began to read the letter out loud:

"My Dearest Mary,

It is with a greatly relieved mind that I write to you this day. An agreeable proposition has been presented to me, which I now propose to you. My dear friend and colleague, Mr. Martin McCain has a son, Colin Charles, who is of marrying age. He is desirous of a match and has agreed to let his family make inquiries seeking said match from eligible young ladies in Scotland. He is an educated man, raised by respectable folk of some means, who are all of good character. He is occupied within their family mercantile business and is at present living overseas, establishing trade routes within the Americas."

"The Americas!" Jane interrupted, with dismay.

"Now Jane let me finish!" Mary said, laying a calming hand on her daughter's arm. She took a small sip of her tea and made a grim gesture of distaste at its cool temperature. She returned the teacup to its saucer and resumed reading the letter.

"Not only does he wish a suitable young woman of good family name, which is uncommon in the Americas, he is most agreeable in the matter of caring for her widowed mother, as well. As I have known Mr. McCain and his family for many years, I believe this to be the most suitable arrangement that can be obtained for my beloved niece and you, my only sister, as well as a fine solution to your present situation. As much as I will dislike being separated from you, I can rest assured that you will both be maintained in comfort and well treated by a family that is well known to me.

So that Jane will know that I have given due consideration to her happiness, I have enclosed a small portrait of the young man in question. She can see for herself that he is a handsome and kindly looking young man, aside from all of his suitable character, financial, and family considerations. Please reply with an answer to their proposal, as soon as you are able, so that marriage contracts and travel to the Americas may be arranged.

> *With all my love,*
> *Your dutiful brother,*
> *George Danforth."*

Mary laid the letter aside and looked at the young man's portrait with interest.

Unable to wait any longer to see her possible future husband, Jane jumped up to lean over her mother and peer at his picture. Her heart paused for just a moment and then began to beat faster as she saw that her uncle had indeed been most correct in calling him handsome.

He looked to be four or maybe five years her senior, with kind dark eyes set below a wide intelligent brow crowned with longish dark hair. He had somewhat of a boy's face yet, smooth skinned and slightly plump in the cheeks, giving his entire face a look of general happiness and geniality, despite the serious pose. His mouth, though, was what really caught her attention and admiration. He wore a fashionably trimmed moustache over lips whose edges were so sharply defined and beautifully arched that they almost looked feminine.

Jane smiled at the picture and then smiled at her mother, flushing prettily. "He's beautiful, Mother. I had no idea Uncle George had such a fine eye for men! Perhaps, he has missed his calling and should be a matchmaker. Saracene should no doubt seek his services, forthwith!" Jane giggled.

Mary smiled and stifled her own laughter. "Jane! That's a perfectly awful thing to say!" She scolded. "Saracene Meadows is a dear friend to you!"

"Well I don't mean to disparage Sara, Mother. But you have seen her last two choices of beau! Her taste in men leaves much to be desired, I should think."

"Well, nevertheless, it is a poor comment from a true friend and quite beneath you," Mary added, a little more sharply.

"I'm sorry, Mother! I don't mean to be unkind. It's just that Sara and I have grown up dreaming of our future husbands and planning such lovely families. I just can't bear to think of her married to someone like Hector Boughton, Ughh!"

"Well, I have to say I thought him a most disagreeable fellow also, what with his distasteful snuff habit and his pompous airs. But, he comes from a good border family with connections to the nobility," Mary said. "Not a terribly good looking fellow, I must admit, but it is a match that her family approves of."

"I would rather die an old maid than to wed the likes of him," Jane scoffed.

"Well, and mayhap Saracene would rather wed the likes of him, than be forced to live so far away in the Americas with all the dangers that abound there?" Mary asked bluntly, as she raised one long eyebrow, contemplating her daughter's attitude. She eyed Jane speculatively, trying to gauge her daughter's true reaction to the matter at hand.

Jane glanced up quickly at her mother's serious tone; then her blue eyes darkened with realization, losing some of their luster and cheer. Frowning a little, she said, "To be sure, the thought of leaving Scotland and going to the Americas is disconcerting, at best. I hadn't thought about moving so far away. Or to such a wild place," She added, looking down at the portrait she held with a worried scowl. "But, everything else is as I had always hoped for," she sighed. "And you and I would have each other, as always!" She added, looking back up at her mother. She left the unasked question lingering in her eyes and behind her words, hanging between them like an unshed tear.

Mary patted her hand reassuringly, and folded it between her own. "Yes, dear we will have each other, whatever may come. As you know, there is nothing for me here now that your father is gone. I don't wish to be a burden to you, but this is almost as much a chance for me as it is for you, since they agree to my accompanying you."

Jane scowl was replaced by a brightening smile. "Well, let's take the chance then, Mother! Let Lavinia have Father's estate, as she has such a burning desire for it, then. You will come with me and we will make our own home. It will be as fine as this is, one day. Finer even, because it will truly be ours." She said, with a flap of her hand indicating the lovely house around them. Jane kneeled before her mother in a rustle of skirts, grasped her mother's hands and raised them to her lips, kissing them soundly, "I promise that we will, Mother!"

Mary gazed down into her daughter's earnest blue eyes and felt a great weight of worry lift from her chest. Her husband, Duncan's, older sister, Lavinia, had been putting increasing pressure on Mary to turn over the estate. It was the family manor and by a provision of Duncan's father's will, now belonged to Duncan's sister Lavinia, rather than to Duncan's heirs after his death. Mary, being Scottish by birth, had not been a favored choice for her husband to make in the first place. And being women, neither she nor Jane could claim the estate. She found they were quite alone, as the English in-laws sided with Lavinia to keep the estate in their family.

Mary and Jane had been left with little in the world beyond their own personal possessions, a small maintenance sum and their good family name. They had been invited to stay with Lavinia, but clearly as guests. The thought of staying on, with Duncan's designing younger sister playing mistress of the manor while looking down her nose at them, was more than Mary felt she could bear. There were very few choices left, but Mary still wanted her daughter to be happily wed more than anything else. "Are you quite certain, my dear? We could wait for another match, if you have any doubt at all."

Jane shook her head firmly, her dark blonde mass of braids sliding slightly, from the motion. "No, Mother. This is what I wish to do." She looked down at Colin's portrait again and smiled at the sparkle the artist had captured in his eyes. She thought that he looked like a very kind man. "I am quite sure of it," she asserted with a nod.

Mary exhaled loudly, as the lightness in her chest spread. She drew her only daughter into a warm embrace. "Well then, it's decided. I trust your Uncle George as to the young man's character and family. And you seem to find him.... agreeable," she said smiling and drawing back to look questioningly into her daughter's eyes again.

Jane nodded firmly and then with a shy smile, returned to staring at the portrait of her soon to be husband, her eyes shining. "Mrs. Colin McCain.... Jane Isobel McCain," she mumbled, getting lost at once in girlish daydreams.

"It is settled then. I will reply at once, so that George may draw up the marriage contracts and begin arrangements for our travel." Mary left her daughter to her romantic daydreams and walked slowly to her own bed chamber to ponder how she wished to sketch the framework of their future into the pen strokes of her reply.

Chapter Four

Greenock, on the Firth of Clyde: Spring 1773

Ian MacGregor walked away from the Crossroads public house reading one of the broadsheets that had recently been posted around Greenock. He paused to carefully pack the saddlebags on his small highland pony with the bread he had purchased for his trip home. He carefully folded the post and put it in his pocket, pulled his cap down firmly and nodded goodbye to a few of the men he had become acquainted with from the docks. He made his way in the opposite direction through the throng of people and wagons. They jostled their way past Ian and towards the docks and the waiting ships, like spring salmon in a hurry to spawn.

He pulled the copy of the broadsheet out of his ragged jacket and re-read it again. Maybe it was the answer he had hoped for. And then again, he could perish in such a treacherous ocean crossing and it might all be for naught. He was unsure, yet still excited. There was a great deal to consider.

"But by God, if it were true...." He muttered to himself. Free passage across the Atlantic to Alba Nuadh; the new Scotland! The chance to own land again, free and clear, just for the farming of it. To hunt and farm a plentiful and by all accounts bountiful land and also have provisions for that crucial first year. Wasn't that worth such a terrible risk? His mind raced with his tumbling thoughts. He thought that it was surely worth the risk, but he was not sure his sister and brother-in-law would agree; especially now, with all the bairns to care for after Ann's and William's deaths. He could not, in good conscience, go without them and leave

James to provide for them all alone. But he thought there was a good chance that if he told them about the offer that they would wish to go.

If it weren't for his brother Alex, they would none of them even have a place to lay their heads, as it was. Ian's and Mary's older brother, Alex MacGregor, had kindly given them the use of the small crofts in the valley they lived in, in return for their help at harvest, planting and any other time a need arose for sheer manpower at the MacGregor farm. They owed a debt of gratitude to Alex, but he, Mary, and her James would much prefer to work their own land. The farm here would always belong to someone else. They had no hope at all of obtaining land to call their own in Scotland.

Ian lived alone in a small cot that could not support a wife and bairns. He could not stay where he was and ever have much hope of marrying, with so very little to offer. It wasn't that he had someone in mind at the moment, but he dreamed of a pretty wife and family. Most of all, he dreamed of his own land. Across the ocean lay that chance, gleaming like a rainbow of promise, land to farm and to pass on to his children, after he was gone.

Ian wanted nothing so much as this chance to make a life. Starvation and cold need not trouble his family, as long as he could work and hunt a more bountiful earth. He imagined he was there already walking the farmlands and forests. To see oats waving in the fields and kine and sheep grazing lush, green grass would be a miracle. "Aye, a risk worth taking, it is. God, give me the words to convince my family of this opportunity," he said, softly to himself.

A passing woman looked at him strangely as he muttered to himself. She looked hastily away when he caught her eye and picked up her skirts to walk even faster. "Oh, aye," he said out loud. "Now I be a dafty too." Only slightly wobbly from the whiskey he had recently consumed, he touched the brim of his hat and gave a slightly ironic bow toward the woman when she glanced back fearfully. He grinned as she hastened to a run and he continued on his way down the narrow lane leading his pony.

Ian had come to Greenock after hearing that there was work to be had on the docks again. He had even been willing to ship out as a deckhand, despite his lack of any experience. It had been yet another disappointment and now he must trek home, with but a shilling left in his worn out pocket. Inexperienced labor was being turned away, as even the experienced men were hungry for work. If you did not have a friend or kin to put in a word for you, there was simply no work to be had. They hired their own before hiring a skinny highlander with no experience. The only other work available to him was soldiering and he knew that he could never bring himself to do that, not after all that the English had done to his family over the years.

The resentment toward the English was generations deep in the MacGregor clan. It had only been sixty-odd years since his cousin, Rob Roy, had been alive to lead the English on many a merry chase. Now Ian and his kin were not even allowed to use the name MacGregor, since it had been proscribed, or they risked going to prison. It had been many, many years now since their clan had held their traditional lands. The Campbell's now held most of that land, thanks to their alliances with the English over the years. The MacGregor clan was scattered and in ruins, for which he blamed the English Crown. Ian would rather be dead than soldier for them.

Ian turned onto the road that ran southeast out of Greenock and gently turned his pony's nose in that direction with his rope bridle. The sturdy little pony balked a bit until he gave his customary "tchaa" and a little leg to encourage it. He planned to travel back the way he had come - through Port Glasgow, around the eastern shore of the Firth of Clyde and then continue north along the eastern shore of Loch Lomond. He would follow the lakes and valleys east from Lomond toward his home on Loch Katrine. It was another full two days past Loch Lomond on foot to Loch Katrine, on one of the rough paths that snaked through the Scottish Highlands.

Unconsciously, he picked up his pace, letting his mind flow ahead in the mile-eating way of the highland man that he was. He would be walking on the last half of the journey, as he had on coming, to spare his little pony. For now, he rested and enjoyed the ride as his mind turned over the details from the broad sheet he carried.

Ian reached Port Glasgow late in the evening. He would have preferred to sleep in the forest outside of town, but he felt that he should check here again for work before giving up entirely. This town wasn't half the size of Greenock, but it boasted a bustling harbor. The public houses and rooming houses near the harbor were a good place to start. Aware as he was of the dangerous nature of harbor towns, he stopped a moment to check the blade at his waist and the smaller sgian dubh in his stocking. He would be ready if anyone wanted to trouble him.

When Ian was a lad, his Uncle Andrew had taken it upon himself to train his nephew in the art of hand to hand combat. His uncle Andrew had been renowned from Aberfoyle to Balquiddar for his speed and

agility with a knife. It had earned him the nickname of Black Knife, or
Sgian Dubh. It was a name that Ian had carried in his youth, as well, and
it was for him that Ian's own nephew, younger Andrew, was nicknamed.
Older Andrew had many a time taken an armed man down that attacked
him, with only his sock knife, his speed, agility and his quick wits. Those
who underestimated him soon suffered scars to remember him by. After
his uncle Andrew had trained him as a boy, the same could be said of Ian
himself. Ian had taken it upon himself to pass on these same skills to his
own nephew after the elder Andrew had died.

Near the busy docks he spotted a tavern with the dubious name of
The Dowsing Kine. Several watermen stood about the door and two were
in a rough scuffle on the ground nearby. The man on top reared back and
smashed the other fellow in the nose with a tremendous crack and the
unfortunate fellow underneath him went quite still, knocked out cold and
nose likely broken. The man on top clumsily climbed off him and cheerily
grabbed his mug of ale off a nearby bench and polished it off, wiping his
mouth with the back of one of his grubby sleeves.

Feeling it a good time to interrupt, Ian hailed the fellow. "That was
most impressive, sir. Could I beg a moment of your time?"

The man turned his dark eyes to Ian and scowled. "What is it then?
Want your turn at me, do ye?"

"Nay sir, I ask only any news ya may ha' of a captain looking for a
crew, or a warehouse needin' a strong back?"

The man scratched his greasy head and then his unkempt beard
thoughtfully, making it stand out, like a bushy hedge. "Can't say as I
have... at least not for green hands," he answered, looking Ian up and
down doubtfully.

Ian nodded his head reluctantly. It was plain to anyone that he was
no sailor. He wore his dark hair long with small plaits on each side, in the
traditional highland way. He sported only the tanned skin of a farmer,
not that of a bronze skinned waterman. He was tall, lean, and suffering
from slight malnutrition from the harsh winter past. "Aye, sir, 'tis true
I've no experience, but I'm a verra hard worker."

"Sorry, mate! There is nothing hereabouts for the likes of a teuchter,
like you, except me," the man sneered, stepping closer and raising his
fists in invitation.

Ian's hand itched to grab his blade and carve up this rude man's grin
and teach him a lesson or two in manners, but he could ill afford to end up
in gaol again. The last time he had been incarcerated it had nearly killed

him. He was in no shape to tolerate it after a hard winter. Ian looked the man over from his greasy hair and tarred pigtail, insolently down his filthy clothes to his rough shoes. His muscles tensed in preparation to fight, despite his wishes. This man just wasn't worth it. "Dinna fash yourself, then, I'll be on my way." He touched his hat carelessly, just a hair's breadth from being rude, and then did likewise to the other men. "Gentlemen," he said, sarcastically, no longer unable to conceal his anger.

All the men grumbled and stepped toward Ian menacingly.

Just as he was turning away, but wary and expecting to be jumped from behind, a local blowzabella sauntered out of the public house. She sized up the situation in an instant and put on a pretty pout as she swayed past Ian and approached the group of men. "Now then, are none o' you lads goin' ta buy me a pint? I'm gettin' sa bored," She sighed, as she smoothed her hands slowly down her bodice, showing off her ample figure suggestively. "Mebbe I shall go ta hame," she fawned, placing herself directly in front of Ian and smiling a secret smile, as she swished her rear end suggestively toward the belligerent sailors.

The fighting man stepped up immediately taking her bait and puffed up, like a toad, both sure of himself and full of arrogance. "Surely, I will lass. If'n you want to put that sweet arse on my lap, that is," He said, his eyes pinned to the skirts over her posterior.

"Now wait just a minute, Tom!" said a smaller companion. "I was just aboot to buy Mabby a pint my own self."

Tom grinned menacingly. "And sure as you'll have to get through me then. Would you like to have a go then, Rob?" He snarled back at him.

Rob flamed red, but clamped his mouth shut prudently. He had no wish to have his nose rearranged by Tom Mandler. He had seen the result of his anger often enough and his eyes flitted unconsciously to the man still prostrate in the dirt, nose bleeding profusely.

Forgotten in the brewing excitement, Ian started to go, but not before he caught a mischievous wink from the woman, Mabby. She knew that she had interrupted what would have been a rare stramash and was obviously enjoying her power over these men immensely. Ian grinned and tipped his hat respectfully to her as he turned to leave, chuckling as he went.

Mabby squealed as Tom obviously pinched her backside and chased her as she ran playfully back through the dark doorway she had emerged from.

Shaking his head and still chuckling at the woman's antics, Ian moved on to the other public houses that were lined up and down the narrow street, asking now and again if anyone had work for eager hands. He learned a few new colorful insults he had not heard before and got into a minor scuffle with a would-be thief over his pony, but he found no luck with any of the dockside public houses or shops. Nor any from the draymen he questioned, who frequented the docks looking to haul loads. Not wishing to sleep on the docks with only one eye closed, he rode out of Port Glasgow and through the night on the road for home. He had been searching for work for a fortnight and he was out of both money and patience. It was time to head for home.

Chapter Five

Ullapool, on Loch Broom, Scotland: Spring 1773

Situated as it was, on a natural harbor, Ullapool had seen booming growth in its fishing industry. Many of the boats came from Scotland and England, but some came from as far away as Ireland and Scandinavia to ply the rich waters of the bay and the outer islands. This was not of any benefit to the local fishermen, despite the collective skills of many generations. Their small dipping nets could not compete with the big luggers from the south, nor the efficient fishermen from the north and it kept the price of herring down for what they were able to catch.

Davy McLeod tied off his small boat and began filling a small sack with the herring they had netted. It wasn't enough to sell this time, but it was enough for their families to eat for a few days. He culled out about half of the catch and put it in two separate sacks for his two crewmen.

Alan, the older of the two brothers reached out for both sacks and then handed one to Geordie. "When are we goin' oot again then, Davy?" Alan asked.

David looked up at the northwestern sky, a pale blue streaked with pink mare's tails. "Looks like rain coming on the morrow ta me, lads. We'll see how saft it is in the morning, aye? If she is just a drizzle, we'll go. If not...." he shrugged, indicating the sacks they held, "then best make her last the days."

The men nodded glumly and went their separate ways, two to the left, along the busy road to town and two to the right, along the northeastern hills of the harbor. Davy walked along with his nephew, James William.

He could not help but to notice Willie's lack of interest and he put a hand on the lad's shoulder. Since his brother, Hugh's death, he had been trying to coax the lad out of his silence. He knew it was hard on the lad, not having his Da around. At twelve, he wasn't yet a man, but he was now responsible for his mother, Janet, and his younger sister and brother. Davy felt frustration at not being able to break through the lad's obvious grief.

He came to his own cottage first and poured out less than half of the herring into a bowl on a bench outside the door. He twisted the top of the sack shut over the rest and handed it to Willie. "Here ya are lad; bring this hame ta your mither and Grandda. Ya did a fine day's work! And tell her what I said aboot the rain tomorrow, aye?"

Willie gave him the ghost of a smile, nodded slightly in acknowledgement of his uncle's words. He then turned slowly and somberly toward home.

Davy shook his head sadly as the lad walked away. He wished things were different. He wished it every day when he saw his nephew's sad blue eyes looking out across the bluer water. He knew he was longing for the father that was taken from him by the sea, but he could not fathom what else he saw in the depths of the boy's eyes, but he was not doing well. His wife, Mary Margaret, came to the door with their young Alex at her breast and watched Willie walk away. Davy picked up the wooden bowl and sat wearily on the bench. "Ah, Maggie, I feel so useless ta the lad."

Maggie squeezed his shoulder as she stood beside him, patting him reassuringly. "There now, my love. Ya ken ya ha' done well by the boy. Why, if it werena for you, who would teach him ta fish the noo?"

"But he doesna love it, like his Da did. I see him looking at the farms we pass with a fierce longing. I ken he wants to be a yeoman, and mebbe raise some sheep or some kine. He is of the land, not of the sea."

"Well and people can change, my dove," she said gently.

"Aye, but can a horse turn into a fish?"

"Well, you ken what Auld Granny would ha' said." Maggie said, with mischief gleaming in her green eyes.

He groaned sarcastically at being subjected to yet another of her Auld Granny stories.

"Oh hush now," she said laughing. "Auld Granny did say as tha' kelpies were made tha' verra way. A horse or young woman that came ta the shore alone could be turned into a water horse by another. And why then they mun swim away ta live wit' the fishes forevermore."

Davy laughed at his wife's earnest attempt to cheer him and she joined him.

Little Alex released his mother's nipple with an audible pop, as his parent's laughter distracted him from his meal. He smiled a toothless, milk-rimmed smile up at his father.

"Well, maybe wee Alex wants ta be a fishy as well? Yes, my little silver darlin'," he cooed to him. "Would ya like ta be a wee fishy then?" he asked the babe, while tickling his chubby belly. "Or mebbe a kelpie?"

Alex giggled and pumped his small fist up and down with glee. Still a wee babe over the winter, Alex was relatively healthy from a diet of his mother's milk, unlike the rest of them, who had come through a harsh winter of dried fish and goat cheese and had grown thin.

Davy gazed out to where the sloping point of land jutted out into the loch, just past the town of Ullapool. His eyes often rested there. Named, Dead Man's Point, it served as a grim reminder of leaving the protection of port and heading down the loch and out to sea. Often during that winter past, the storms had been so nasty that many larger vessels had come to port, to hide in the sheltering arms of Loch Broom. Smaller boats, like Davy's, had no chance at all against the fury of the North Atlantic, where the winter seas often swelled to staggering heights. He knew from harsh experience what that was like. He could all too well remember the vicious storm which had taken his brother, Hugh, and his mates down into the dark depths.

Alex had been taking advantage of his father's distraction to pull his large index finger gradually toward his eager mouth. Leaning forward as far as his swaddling allowed, he chewed experimentally on his father's finger.

"Ouch!" Davy said, startled out of his reverie, "this wee fishy bites!" He pulled his finger from Alex's grip to examine it. "And he has teeth too!"

Maggie grimaced. "Aye, tha' he does. He has just aboot chewed me raw this day, the wee ratten!" Maggie exclaimed, rubbing her breasts, gingerly. "I can scarce bear ta have my shift touch my bosom today, let alone lace my bodice. He has two new teeth starting the noo. Here! You take this fishy and I will take those fishies," she said, taking the bowl of herring from him and deftly passing him the baby.

Davy placed Alex up on his shoulder and patted him a bit. Soon he was rewarded with a satisfied belch from the little body. Cradling his head in one big palm and his round bottom in the other, he put the boy in his lap facing him. He studied the fascinating and subtle blending of Maggie's features and his own that made up this new and unique face. He had his mother's green eyes, but instead of her dark blonde curls, he had his father's dark locks. The nose and chin were also like his own, but set between them, he had his mother's plump kissable lips. He bent down, gave the baby a smacking kiss on those lips and then for good measure blew noisily on his round little tummy too. Alex chuckled with laughter and drew his knees up, curling his little toes up with pleasure.

"A bhalaich," Davy cooed to the babe. "You look more like a silkie than a kelpie or a fishy to me." He moved his fingers through the soft dark waves starting on the small head and smiled. He leaned in and blew again on Alex's tummy and made the baby squeal with laughter. A small trickle of spit-up ran out of his mouth and Davy expertly sat him up, wiping at his mouth with his trailing drapes. "Now don' be a'wastin' your supper now, lad, or your Mum will scold the both of us."

The baby looked at him with round solemn eyes and then began to hiccup. He leaned him on his shoulder and patted his back again urgently and wiped off a little more milk-tinged spittle. "Mum, mum, mum," the boy chanted, as he patted him.

"That's right, lad. Mum, mum, mum. Mum will spank your bum!" He laughed.

"Bum, bum, hic, bum," muttered little Alex, matching the rhythm of his flailing arms.

Davy laughed out loud and placed the baby back down on his lap between his knees. "Well aren't we the chatty fellow today, me wee fishy!"

"Umm, hic, mum." Alex replied.

"Let us check on the goats, my lad," he said, popping him in his basket that sat just inside the door. "Maggie, I am taking wee Alex with me oot back ta check on the goats."

"All right man, take the pail with you and I'll finish here," she called, as she deftly scaled the herring to prepare them for frying over the hot fire.

Davy and little Alex disappeared out the door and around the back toward the small pen that housed their two goats. The goats had been given as dowry to the young couple when they wed and they were much appreciated for their milk and the cheese they could make because of it. It had seen them through the lean winter months.

He set the baby's basket next to the pen, close enough for the babe to see them and far enough away that the goats could not chew on his swaddling or the withy basket. Little Alex began blowing excited bubbles as soon as he saw the goats, his chubby arms churning in his excitement. "Da-ga-bla!" He babbled.

Davy entered the pen and shut the wooden bar behind him. Both goats bleated with excitement and crowded him. "There now lassies," he cooed, as he patted their sleek heads. They were both nearly bursting to be milked, since they had weaned their babes. The kids had been promised to Hugh and Janet and had been taken to them during the winter. Alex and Maggie had been diligent about their daily milking to keep them flowing.

"Naaa!" They cried to Davy.

"Aaah!" Alex yelled from his basket.

Davy chuckled as he pulled the milking stool under him and reached for the larger of the two, Abby. He put the bucket beneath her bag, put his forehead against her warm flank, and began to milk her. The rhythmic hiss into the pail soon became soothing and it was no time at all before it was the smaller goat, Ana's turn. Davy kept his face turned to the fence where his little boy watched happily from his basket, his green eyes round with wonder.

Davy could see beyond him, to the deep blue-green bay of Loch Broom. The sun was setting in golden splendor behind the cliffs beyond Ullapool. The oranges and yellows melted together into warm wispy arms that stretched east, as if reaching for the embrace of the darkness that approached behind him. Golden light from the setting sun touched every surface with a gilt edge. Behind his son's head a nimbus of warmth spread out from his son's curls, like a halo.

Davy stared westward, transfixed at the magical view before him, knowing the minutes were short before all the brilliant color turned to the hushed purples and lead grays of twilight. With the goat's both now content, he just sat still watching, as if by moving he might break the spell. Fairy time, the old folks called it, that bit of time between darkness and light when the light itself seemed alive and aware. The distant mountains across Loch Broom shone as if carved of warm pure gold. Down near the water and to his right, the town of Ullapool now lay in shadow below and it twinkled here and there with lamp and candlelight.

In a rebellious blush of warm colors the sun sank behind the mountains, outlining their dark edges in fierce relief against the lighter sky. Davy watched the sunset, seeming a golden carved man himself, as the babe stared up at him in silent awe. And then the magic time was gone, as quickly as it had come. Shadows settled around the curves of the land and the nearby hollows began to pool with darkness. Davy sighed, feeling somehow blessed and renewed. He thought of his mother, recalling how she had called this time of day the gloaming and he smiled to himself. It seemed a most appropriate description to him. A way of describing a great change as it occurred, like a birth or a death. He sent a small prayer up for the repose of her soul as he glanced up the ben to where she lay. Then he picked up the baby's basket in one hand and the pail in the other and went down to Maggie and his supper.

The babe was subdued that evening and Davy and Maggie had a quiet meal of fried herring, as Alex chewed thoughtfully on a piece of teething leather or simply stared at his parents. A warm fire crackled on the hearth and a peace settled over them, as the stars gradually appeared. After little Alex fell asleep, his parents sat together companionably for a while, she sewing a tear in his coat, and he working on a piece of oak that he had earmarked as the curved seat of a rocking chair for Maggie. He rasped over the surface, carving deeply into the wood and smiled to himself, thinking of her shapely bottom sitting on it someday soon.

"What are you grinning about, Davy? You look like the Donas himself a' grinning there!" She laughed, as her needle flashed in and out.

"Why your fine plump arse, m'dearie, that's all!"

"Why Davy, and in front of the lad too!" Maggie scolded, smiling despite herself.

"Well and isna he the proof of tha'," he teased, waving toward the sleeping infant.

"Aye, and if you say so," she demurred.

A warm look passed between them, as they both thought of the approach of bed and the fiery heat of each other's arms.

"I do," Davy said, holding her gaze, "and I always wull."

"Well then," Maggie said her green eyes glowing in the light of the humble rush lights. She put away her sewing and rose. Then she moved the babe's basket, so that a stray spark from the slow burning peat would not ignite in his wrappings. Maggie walked toward the bed, slowly undressing as she walked. When she reached it, her naked skin glowed like the moon against the dark sky and she lay down slowly, a mischievous grin lighting her face as she beckoned to him.

Transfixed as he was by the beauty before him, Davy realized he was gripping the piece of wood hard enough to turn his fingers purple and he quickly put it down, rising off the bench as he did so. Slowly and deliberately he walked over to his wife. He lay down and took her gently into his arms, breathing in her complicated smells of baby, wool and milk. Her green eyes glowed up at him, like seawater in the sunlight. They had always reminded him of the sea that he loved so much. Clear green, with a touch of watery blue, they were as deep and mesmerizing as any ocean he could imagine. He stared down and down into their depths, remembering how they had pierced right through him when they had first met. They still did.

He pulled her closer and slowly they began to move in an age old rhythm that matched their beating hearts. They made love on the little bed, the warmth between them kindling into an aura of heat and love wrapped warmly in the peace of the gradually fading firelight.

Chapter Six

Loch Katrine, Scotland - Spring 1773

Mary Katrine McDonald had been awake with the babes since before dawn. Willie and Alex were both cutting teeth and she had stolen away before the light filled the valley to wash her face and her aching breasts with the cool mountain water from the bubbling burn. After her absolutions, she stayed crouched by the burn, taking these few treasured moments to be alone. The glow behind her and the ben grew with each passing moment and Mary speculated about the reddish glow to the morning sky that usually preceded a storm.

Footsteps and movement on the path behind her startled her out of her daydreaming and she moved quickly to adjust her bodice laces and then turned around to peer into the forest. In the misty morning light, a man and a small horse appeared out of the trees. She recognized the profile and a smile lit her face. "Ian!" She cried, already running up the burn toward the trees to meet him.

"Hullo, my sister!" Ian tiredly responded. He hugged her hard, and then he let the pony have his head to drink from the little stream. Ian also knelt and took long, thirsty handfuls and then splashed his face and neck. Refreshed, he looked his sister over critically. Fatigue clung to her like an old worn out coat.

"You look nearly as tired as I feel, lass. How goes it with you?"

"Achh," Mary said, shrugging it off, "'tis teething babes is all. Doona worrit yourself aboot it! I wish ta know how things are with ya. I take it ya had no luck in Greenock then, since you are here the noo?"

"Nay, they are only hiring their own and strange lads with no experience are none too welcome!"

"Well, and so you are hame," Mary sighed, secretly glad her brother had not left them to venture off alone on some ship. "Let me get back ta my hearth and I will give ya some hot food." She hooked her arm through his and began to pull him toward the cottage.

"Wait! There is something I must show ya first," Ian said, stopping her. He pulled the broadsheet from Greenock out of his sporran and carefully unfolded it. "I wish ta speak with James aboot this, but I would like ya ta have your say in the matter, afore I do."

Mary took the paper from him and slowly began to read it, her eyes growing wider with each line she read.

"I willna show it ta James if you are set against it, Mary," he quickly assured her. "But I plan ta go on my ain if ya doona."

"Is it true then? Free passage and free land?" Mary questioned excitedly.

"Yes, I checked wit' the harbormaster at Greenock and it is the talk of the town. There is sa much land in the New World tha' they will give it away ta any man what can work it! James, I, and the lads when they are grown would all ha' our verra own land. Think of it, mo' nighean bahn!"

"I intend to do just that, mo' brathair, but over a bowl of porridge. 'Tis a lot to ponder and there are the bairns to think aboot. I need time ta think aboot all it could mean and wrap my heid around it. Come along!" she ordered, gripping his arm again.

Encouraged by the speculative look in his sister's dark eyes and the thought of hot porridge, he gladly let her pull him along to the McDonald's cot.

When they reached the little cottage, they found James amid the morning throng of children, holding small Alasdair who was awake and hungrily complaining.

"There you are, my dearest," James said, the relief evident in his voice. "Ian!" He exclaimed seeing him enter behind her. "You've returned to us then, man?"

"Yes, I am come hame," he said while clapping his brother-in-law on the back. Little Alasdair fussed and Ian reached for him. "Here, let me take the wee laddie."

James gratefully handed over the infant and then whisked the rest of the brood outside to wash up. "Taing, Ian. I'll speak with you directly then," he said, as he was pulled out the door by the always persistent Lizzie.

Ian nodded and glanced at his sister. She had her back to him while she added handfuls of oats to the boiling water for the morning's porridge. Ian would wait until she spoke to him first, before telling James his news. He then turned his attention to the baby on his lap who was staring back at him with comically fierce attention. "Well, hullo my nephew and how is Alasdair Ian this fine morning?" The ripe smell of a dirty clout rose from the infant as if in answer. "Oh, ho, so that is your main complaint then, eh, lad?" He walked over to the bed with the babe and grabbed a clean clout as he passed, from the double row of them hung to dry by the fire. "Let Uncle Ian set ya ta rights!" He announced confidently.

Freshly diapered and stomach temporarily forgotten, the baby cooed as Ian returned to the table with him. "A bhalaich, your Uncle Ian loves you too," he said, stopping to blow bubbly sounds against the little fist he held. "Let your mither get porridge for the rest of us and it wull be your ain turn for breakfast."

After a glance to be sure the twins were still sleeping, Mary put the pot into the middle of the table and then laid a small loaf of day old bread on the table and sliced it thin. The family began to file back into the cottage, each grabbing a piece of bread and dipping it into the pot of porridge as they passed. Katy came in with a pail of milk and this was passed around as well. Contented murmurings of thanks passed back and forth with the sounds of chewing and swallowing. As the pot emptied, young Sgian stared hungrily at the remainders. Mary noticed it and said, "take that last bit Sgian, you are a growing lad and ya took a small share ta begin with."

Sgian nodded and gratefully wiped up the last bits that clung to the sides of the pot with the remaining crust of bread. "Thank you, Mither; the food is especially grand today."

Mary laughed. "That would be a fine compliment, did ya not say it each and every day that I make your breakfast!"

"Yes, Mama," Sgian said, grinning as he swallowed. "Shall I help ya clear the table then?"

"Nay, be off with you! Go and do your chores and then ya can play with your sisters. I wull clean up breakfast and then I mun feed Alasdair," she said, eying the squirming bundle on Ian's lap.

Sgian began helping despite his mother's protests and took the pot and pail, intending to scrub them clean in the nearby burn. He stopped at the door. "My little brother needs his strength too," he said grinning. "I'll clear up and you can feed 'im."

Mary smiled at her boy and in a rare glimpse, saw through to the man he would one day become and was pleased. "Off with ya then," she said smiling at him gratefully. She turned to Ian as Sgian left and relieved him of his wiggling handful, "you too, Ian. I'm sure tha' James could use help cutting the peats and I can handle this wee one my ain self."

She settled into the rocking chair with Alasdair as the house quieted down and put him to her breast. He clamped on at once and she felt the familiar pull and tingle of her milk as it let down in response to the infant's demanding suckling. Mary held a quaich under her other breast to thriftily catch the now flowing milk, in order to not waste a drop. Later, it could be fed to one of the twins by dipping a rag into it for them to suck on. With so many hungry mouths in their house she had to use all the means at her wits disposal to keep them all content and fed.

She rocked gently in the chair in the age-old rhythm of motherhood and relaxed as the baby nursed. She took the quiet time to think about what Ian had brought back from his trip to Greenock. A great chance for them all seemed to be only an ocean away.

"Only an ocean," she muttered ruefully. That was the crux of her concern. She felt barely able to meet her family's growing needs here in the land of her birth, let alone in a strange land. And above all of that, there was a good chance that they may not all be able to survive the perilous journey aboard ship, especially the babes. Ocean crossings were known to be terribly dangerous and uncomfortable even for adults. She shuddered at the thought of not just one, but three nursing babes to try to bring safely to land. The other three children, although older, were also at great risk. The thought of losing any one of her precious children filled her with a paralyzing fear.

And yet, what lay ahead for them here in Scotland? She mused. All that was left to them was a life of tenant farming and scratching for a meager living, forever just one step ahead of starvation. Land ownership would always remain just a distant dream. But in the New World, by all accounts, the land was fertile and green and the hunting and fishing were fabled to be beyond compare, like the Scotland the old ones wistfully told stories about.

Gone were the days of highland plenty, gone with so many of her clan and kin. To this day, her family name of MacGregor was still proscribed; so, she had been called Mary Katrine Campbell, despite being a MacGregor. She had been named after her famous clansman, Rob Roy's less famous wife and the loch where she herself had been born and still resided. Using the Campbell surname was a trick Rob and other MacGregors had sometimes employed.

The use of their name had meant death to the user for many a year now. She had never in her life been able to use her MacGregor surname and now she was married and a McDonald. She thought of her own poor folks long dead and the many siblings she had lost to war, starvation and disease in the nearly thirty years since Culloden. It made her sad to think of herself and her brothers, Alex and Ian, being all that was left of her mother's twelve children. Would a chancy ocean crossing reduce her number of children even more cruelly? Could she bear to even take any chance at all? Mary wondered.

James she knew well, as well as she knew her own soul. He would stand by her either way, but she knew that in his heart he was longing for more, much more than the nearly barren slopes and forests of Scotland had left to offer. Mary thought of her James growing old and weary, beaten down by time and his lot in life, and having to watch his sons and daughters suffer the same fate. Could she bear that as payment for their not taking this risk?

Staring down at his innocent eyes and little stub of a nose, Mary felt her stomach flutter and sicken at the empty thought of losing her little Alasdair. His glowing skin was flushed and well fed and he had begun to fall asleep, sucking very softly by instinct alone and no longer in earnest. She stared across the room at the little withy basket that held the adopted twins nestled together.

She had been there with James' own brother during his sickness and then watched in helpless horror as her good-sister Ann had slipped away despite all her efforts. Toward the end of Ann's illness and with the awareness of her approaching death, she had spoken privately to Mary and James. Ann had begged them to care for her infant sons with all of a mother's anguish and despair. Tears welled in Mary's eyes as she remembered the broken look that had been in Ann's eyes. Her conflicting emotions had been both beautiful and horrible to behold.

One of the twins began to squirm in waking, as if hearing an echo of her sad thoughts about their mother. She shuddered and Alasdair's lips let go of her with an abrupt snap of skin. As if waking from a dream the answer came clear to her. They would go, they had to. If James thought it wasn't too foolhardy they would go - bairns and all. Hope was what helped her decide. Here there was none left for them.

Mary was terrified of the ocean voyage, but the hopes and dreams of all of them, including those they would leave behind forever were a great deal more powerful. The possibilities that lay at the end of the journey outweighed the fear of the journey itself. She stood with decision and put Alasdair in his basket. Never one for letting the men make all the decisions, she would speak to James herself when the men returned to the house. She felt both exhilarated and frightened at the thought of the journey to come, but she had been taught to quell her fears from an early age and continue to always push forward. She would certainly not stop now, not when fate had dropped this chance for more at their feet.

Chapter Seven

Port of Greenock, Scotland - early summer 1773

Mr. John Ross stood on the dock watching the Hector's provisions being loaded. Burdened men plodded up and down the gangways and large casks swung overhead on booms. He had completed the job that Mr. Pagan, the owner of the vessel, had hired him for, by recruiting its load of immigrants bound for Pictou in Alba Nuadh, the New Scotland. Only nine adults and some children were boarding in Greenock. The remaining one-hundred-seventy-eight passengers, nearly half of them children, were booked to board the ship during the next week to the north in Ullapool, on Loch Broom.

Finding people willing to leave the troubled shores of Scotland had proved to be no great difficulty. Most of the people he had recruited were poor tenant families with few prospects. For them, the chance to own land was a great persuasion. Most could never hope to have a place where they were any more than tenants by any other means than what he was offering to them. This offer was nothing short of a miracle for most people, especially coupled with the tempting allure of freedom.

In the Americas they would be free to wear their tartan, speak their native Gaelic - sing and dance to the piper's songs of their heritage and all else that the English now forbade. They were not even required to pay for their passage. It was offered in return for settling this wild land belonging to Mr. Pagan and his partners. They also were promised a farm of their own on this land and provisions for that critical first year just for the settling of it. It was the best offer that Mr. Ross felt he had offered to anyone in all his years as an agent. He had even found two well paying customers that would not be settling there, but merely needed transportation to the New World.

All that remained for him to do was to see the few passengers settled on board in Greenock and then accompany the ship to Ullapool to finish loading its remaining passengers. It had been week's since he had been home to Ullapool and he was anxious to complete his mission and return there. Captain John Spiers would then be in charge of completing the ocean voyage when the Hector set sail from Ullapool.

The captain and the ship itself were the only thing that bothered Mr. Ross. He eyed the man in question as he paced the decks barking orders to his men. He wore his black hair in a greasy pigtail that hung from beneath his cap. Years of ocean going had tanned his skin to a dark brown, with splotches of pink here and there on his face and hands where the years of sun had scorched his skin until it had peeled again and again. Captain Spiers had sharp blue eyes that lay in waiting predatorily, within a permanent squint. Those eyes were what bothered Mr. Ross the most about the man. They were just as blue, cold, and merciless as the sea before a storm.

The Hector, itself, also worried him. She was a lumbering old two hundred-ton berthen, Dutch flute cargo ship, with a square stern capped by a row of somber windows. The old ship had a rounded squat shape and was better suited to carrying cargo than passengers. She wasn't outfitted for speed, lacked even a head for the comfort of her passengers and crew and also suffered from a fair amount of rot. The Hector was obviously well past her prime.

Captain Spiers along with her owner, Mr. Pagan, had insisted that she was seaworthy and sound. To her credit, she had made many trips across the ocean carrying both cargo and immigrants safely to the Americas and back again. She did sit well in the water and her dark hull was freshly painted to match the sleek, dark water below her, as much as her upper rail, stern and bow were painted a cheerful blue to match the sky above. The details and trim around windows and rails boasted a sunny yellow color that contrasted nicely on the blue. But examining the Hector in person, Mr. Ross found himself more than a little worried about his brother Alex and his family, who would be among the passengers boarding a few days hence in Loch Broom.

While Mr. Ross was worrying, a carriage pulled up to the dock with the clatter of hooves and wooden wheels on cobbled stones announcing its arrival. A young woman stepped out when the driver hopped down to open the carriage door. She was wearing a small grey hat perched fashionably askew high atop a pile of blonde curls that was held precariously in place by pins studded with lovely pearls. The beautiful young woman touched her hand to her hat to make sure it was secure in the stiff harbor breeze and then stepped down lightly, merely touching the tips of the driver's fingers for balance. The driver smiled a mainly toothless and thoroughly besotted smile at her and tipped his hat as she smiled at him. She glanced about shyly, like a snail peering out of its shell, but she quickly spied Mr. Ross, whom her uncle had described very well.

"Excuse me, sir! Are you Mr. Ross, and is this the Hector?" She asked.

"Why yes, it is. And you must be Miss Forbes?" John Ross answered, as he walked briskly down the gangplank to meet the lovely young lady.

Some of the tension left the girl's face and she smiled a dazzling smile at him. "Why yes, I am. I don't believe we have had the pleasure?"

"I am sorry my dear, I am Mr. Jonathan Ross, ship's agent, at your service." Mr. Ross bowed gracefully, one leg extended toward her in a polite courtly fashion. "And your mother... is she not with you?" He asked, peering past her at the empty carriage.

"Of course," she nodded seeing the direction of his gaze. "My mother will be joining me very soon. She will arrive with the next coach, as she had some last minute errands," Jane replied. "Perhaps you would be so kind as to escort me to our quarters?"

"It would be my pleasure, Miss Forbes," He said, drawing her arm through the crook of his offered one. Being one of the few paying customers, and a lovely young lady, Mr. Ross felt she deserved his personal attention.

The driver began unloading her bags and she allowed herself to be led down the dock. As they appraised the ship, it became very obvious that it was in poor shape. There were large cracks in many of the planks, many of the sails were sporting patches and the rails had been mended with odd boards in many places.

"You are quite sure that this is the Hector, Mr. Ross? I hadn't expected it to be so...." She trailed off, indicating the looming hulk before them with a casual wave.

"Yes, well," John Ross said, coughing politely, to cover his embarrassment. "She is most seaworthy and her crew is quite experienced, I can assure you. You and your mother also have the best accommodations on the ship, after the captain, of course. Allow me to lead the way."

Jane watched him with sharp eyes as he went first onto the swaying boards of the gangway. A blonde charmer with a light step, he could not conceal the doubt in his voice or the guilty hunch to his shoulders. He turned around to offer her his hand and she followed quickly matching her steps to the swaying rhythm beneath her feet.

Mr. Ross took her satchel and then hailed the first passing seaman and pressed him into loading the remainder of her luggage on board. The burly redheaded man ignored him until a glance rewarded him with one of Jane's sunny smiles. He grinned, despite himself, and quickly about-faced and moved to obey.

Mr. Ross led her up to the rear deck and to a small door off a short dank hall. He opened the door for her and indicated that she should enter. He remained outside the door holding her bag like a gentleman. "If you like, you can refresh yourself here and then you can meet your mother on deck perhaps?" He did his best to be polite and stepped back as far as the cramped hall would allow.

Jane stepped past him and over the threshold and found herself immediately in the middle of a tiny chamber. Two tiny berths were stacked atop each other to her right, a small wardrobe with a basin was directly ahead, and two tall windows made up the wall to her left. Jane quietly looked around the little room, a small finger of fear touching her heart, as she realized she would be sharing this cramped and musty room with her Mother for the next two months. And more than that, they would be at the mercy of the sea and her moods. Jane swallowed determined to be brave and took the satchel from Mr. Ross, pushing it hastily onto the top berth. "I believe I shall wait for my mother on deck after all," she said, softly.

Mr. Ross cleared his throat. "Yes, yes! Of course, you should!" He led her back out of the small hall and down the steps of the rear platform to the main deck.

Jane gratefully breathed in huge gulps of fresh air as she emerged on deck. The port smells were not a great improvement on the cabin, but she felt a little better out in the breeze.

From the road another carriage pulled in and came to a stop. Her mother, Mary Jane Forbes, stepped down from the carriage, her hoop skirts waving to and fro, like a church bell from her descent, as she raised a parasol to cover her fair skin from the sun. Jane smiled as she saw her, at once comforted by her mother's unchanging properness. She knew she would be scolded once again, as soon as her mother saw that she was without her own parasol, but she even welcomed that rather than think about the rising fear in her breast. When her mother looked around with confusion in her eyes Jane called to her, waving frantically from the railing.

Spotting her, Mary Jane spoke quickly with the driver and then strode purposefully toward the Hector. The driver nodded and followed her with the first of her many bags and towing her trunk, then put them down at the foot of the gangway to better help her aboard.

"There we are, careful now," Mr. Ross said as the ship dipped toward the dock on a rogue wave. He reached for Mrs. Forbes as soon as she neared the deck and grasped her hand, pulling her the rest of the way onboard.

"Goodness," Mary Jane exclaimed as she landed on her feet after rocking back the other direction.

"Yes, Mistress, it takes some getting used to," the driver remarked, landing beside her. More sailors bustling about necessitated them moving aside as introductions between Mr. Ross and Mrs. Forbes were quickly concluded.

Jane led the way back to the stern and their small cabin and Mr. Ross remained topside supervising the loading of their belongings from the two carriages. When they reached the tiny cabin, Jane opened the door for her mother and let the accommodations speak for themselves.

"Oh, dear," Mrs. Forbes exclaimed, "I had no idea!"

"Is this really the best Uncle Danforth could arrange, Mother?" Jane asked quietly.

"Unless we want to wait another month, he said that this is the only ship going anywhere near Boston. We have to meet up with Mr. McCain and the next ship in Nova Scotia in order to get to Boston from there. We could wait a month hence and get a ship directly to Boston." Her mother said doubtfully, eying the room with distaste.

"Really, Mother, I don't wish to wait so long to be settled, now that it has been decided. If this is how we must get there, then so be it."

"Well, my dear, let's set ourselves to cleaning this cabin then. Perhaps we can make it more tolerable. I seriously doubt it has seen a wash bucket in quite some time," she said, while drawing a gloved finger through the grime on the basin. "I will go on deck and try to rescue some of our linens out of that trunk before they stow it. We will have clean sheets and a clean cabin tonight, at the very least."

"I will see if I can get someone to fetch me some water and some rags and get started," Jane answered.

✦ ✦ ✦

James and Mary McDonald arrived at the ship in a sagging wagon loaded past capacity with assorted bundles and their six children. Ian was bringing up the rear on his pony. All three infants were sleeping peacefully in their baskets after being lulled for days by the rocking of the wagon. The older McDonald children were quiet and wide-eyed with awe. They had never seen anything like the bustling docks around them.

"Is that our ship then, Da?" Sgian asked.

"Ship! Ship!" shrieked Lizzie.

"Whist, Lizzie! We don't want to wake the babes now, do we?" Her mother reminded her.

Alarmed, Lizzie checked the baskets over with a critical motherly eye. "They are sleeping, Mama," she whispered, relieved.

Katy leaned against her mother for protection. Overwhelmed by all the noise and activity, she remained as quiet as a mouse.

"This is our ship," James replied, noting the name across the stern. "This is the boat we will cross the big ocean in! Now, let's everyone lend a hand and take wha' they can carry. Ian and I must speak to the agent and then we will help ya finish."

Ian spotted Mr. Ross on deck ordering the loading of some trunks and parcels. "There is the man himself, James," He said, indicating the thin blonde gentleman on the deck of the ship.

They boarded the Hector and spoke with him for a few moments, their shirt sleeves flapping in the stiff breeze off the Firth of Clyde. He checked them off the roster he carried and then shook the men's hands hurriedly. They were back at the wagon in a matter of minutes.

"All set!" James declared. "We begin boarding the noo. Mary, why don't ya go ahead first with the twins, and let Katy watch wee Alasdair for a moment."

"Me too, Da, me too!" Lizzie protested. "I am a big girl too!"

"Yes that ya are. You stay and help your sister with Alasdair then," he answered, seeing Katy's alarm at the thought of being left alone.

With a satisfied nod, Lizzie moved closer to Katy and glanced into the babe's basket to check on their charge.

James pulled Mary aside as she climbed out and he handed her the twins' basket. "Find a corner spot near the ladder ta the hold. We should get more fresh air for the bairns there." He stared into her eyes, meaningfully. She knew he meant for them to be able to get out quickly also, should the worst happen. Mary shuddered, trying not to think about the long confinement ahead for them all.

They had talked to the children before they left their home on Loch Katrine. They had done their best to make it seem a grand adventure rather than the ordeal they knew it would be. The only one who seemed nervous about the trip was Katy. She had always been wise for her age and she had picked up on nervous cues from the adults, despite their being careful. Lizzie and her brother, Sgian, were both more excited than frightened.

Mary glanced at her daughters. Lizzie was bouncing up and down and Katy just stared silently up at the ship, looking terrified. "Stay put and mind your sister, Lizzie, and I wull be back. Are you all right, Katy?"

"Yes, Mama," she answered, her face pale and her dark eyes perfectly round with fear. She had never been so far from her home and now the ship loomed above them.

"Yes, Mama," Lizzie mimicked beside her.

James, Sgian, and Ian began to unload the wagon. Ian would need time to sell it and the ponies to one of the teamsters on shore, before they embarked. They would need the small sum they could get for them when they reached their destination.

Mary climbed the gangway with the help of one of the sailors and was shown the way to the passenger hold. She climbed down the short, slanted steps that more closely resembled a ladder and had the twins' heavy basket handed down to her when she neared the bottom.

Mary stood still for a minute, letting her eyes get accustomed to the gloom. She was glad that she had traded some of her embroidery for lots of candles in town. She did not intend to spend weeks at sea in complete darkness.

The smell reached her first, one of unwashed bodies and human excrement, along with a sickly damp smell she couldn't identify. As her eyes adjusted to the light, she was dismayed to see the size of the hold that they would have to share with so many others. Mary estimated that you could fit two of the cottages at home in here, end to end, and no more. Pulling a hanky out of her pocket to cover her nose and mouth and checking the light blanket over the twins she quickly explored the small area all the way back to the bulkhead, which housed the huge water casks but no head for the convenience of the passengers. Sailors bustled by her, groaning under the weight of huge casks and bundles that they were loading into the stern compartment. Rats ran about under their feet, disturbed from their hiding places. Mary shivered with revulsion, thinking about them being in such close proximity to her and her family. She pushed the thought away, seeing nothing to be done about it.

Choosing an area near the entrance to the hold, but out of the way, she spit onto her hanky and scrubbed an area on the grimy deck before reluctantly placing the babes' basket down on the planks. With a sigh, she realized she would have to clean their entire area before allowing her family to bed there. Checking one last time to be sure the twins were sleeping, she climbed back on deck to retrieve the girls, little Alasdair, and some seawater in her largest bucket in order to scrub with. She immediately checked the babes' basket when she returned to assure herself that no rats had climbed in with them.

By the time the men began to come aboard with their belongings she had nearly half of the small area she had claimed scrubbed, making the cleaned planks noticeably lighter than the surrounding area. The babe's baskets were on the clean area and under the direction of their mother the little girls helped sort bundles onto that area as the men came down with them. Ian came down with her precious spinning wheel and she had him hang it on a sturdy spike that came through the hull near the ceiling, so it would be out of their way.

"This entire hold should be scrubbed," Mary remarked to James during one of his many trips back and forth to fetch her fresh seawater. "Sickness wull fester here and make us ill!" She looked around the hold in mounting dismay and stopped for a moments rest and to tuck a stray black curl back under her mobcap.

"Well, doona fret dearest. As soon as we get our things aboard, Sgian and I wull help you do just that. The smell canna be at all good for the bairns," he agreed.

"It isna all tha' good for us either," Ian remarked, his nose scrunched up in disgust, as he set down a particularly large bundle of bedding.

"Taing, Ian. I must wash up myself before one of the babes wakes up for a feeding whilst I be covered with this filth. Achhh!" Mary growled with disgust on her face as she looked down at her own grimy hands and then displayed them to Ian with distaste.

As if he were called, little Alasdair started fussing from his basket.

"Aye and there ya are!" She answered, throwing down the scrub rag in a splatter. "Girls, tend the babes, I'll be back straight away." She left on the run to quickly go and wash and retrieve yet another bucket of sea water.

"There, there, baby!" Lizzie cooed, as Katy rocked the basket.

Little Alasdair sucked noisily on his fist and finding it unsatisfactory began to wail in earnest. Katy quickly picked him up and jostled him against her shoulder, while patting his small back to comfort him. Lizzie checked the twins with a worried little scowl, but they were still sleeping soundly, despite Alasdair's hungry cries and the ship's commotion.

James, Ian, and Sgian came back with another load of baggage including Mary's rocking chair which had been disassembled into pieces and placed in a sack. Mary was right behind them as they came down the ladder. She took the crying Alasdair from Katy and sat down to nurse him. She only let him nurse on one side, in case the twins woke also, but he seemed replete and went right back to sleep. Being so young, he spent a great deal of time sleeping, much to Mary's relief. She thanked God silently for his being such a good baby and kissed one rosy cheek affectionately as she replaced him in his basket.

The men finished the final loading of the remainder of their possessions and Ian left to conclude the pre-planned sale of their small cow, and their wagon and horses.

Under Mary's direction, Sgian and James both pitched in to help scrub the filthy planking beneath their feet. Mary insisted that Sgian borrow a mop from one of the deckhands, so that he would not be on his hands and knees in the grime.

As they were working, a male passenger came down the ladder slowly. Two small legs were busily churning away near his backside. Reaching the floor, he hastily put down the squirming child he had been carrying, like a sack of meal under one arm.

"Run then, ye wee rascal, since you're a mind to!" He remarked irritably. The child hit the boards running and ran in a small arc, but stopped when he noticed the two girls by the baskets.

He put his small grubby fingers in his mouth uncertainly, staring at them wide eyed, and then ran back to cling to his father's leg, like a little crab.

The tall, thin man also slightly resembled a crab, with his long legs and arms looking ungainly as he stood partially crouched over, due to the low ceiling in the hold. He blinked, trying to adjust to the dull light below decks. He saw the little girls first, and then James stepped into the circle of light by the ladder. The man smiled then and extended his hand to James in greeting.

James grasped his outstretched hand firmly and smiled back. "I am James McDonald, at your service, and this is my family," he said, while making a sweep of his hand to indicate his family nearby. "My wife Mary and her brother Ian," James said, as they appeared next to him in the small square of sunlight from above. "And my eldest lad, Sgian, then Katy, Lizzie, and the babes Alasdair, William and Alex."

"Yes, well, very pleased ta meet you all, I am sure. What a large and lovely family you have! My name is George Morrison, and this is my lad, Hector." Hector still clung tightly to his father's leg and merely stared at them all, fingers still firmly in his mouth.

Mary approached, looking up the ladder hopefully. "And your wife, sir, what is her name?"

A brief look of pain crossed Mr. Morrison's face and he cleared his throat before speaking. "My wife's name was Rose, missus, and she went to the Lord this winter past. Hector here is all I have left of her." He tousled the little boy's longish blonde hair affectionately, as he visibly choked back tears.

"Oh, I am sa sorry! I didna think before asking. What a terrible loss for you!" Mary answered, dismayed that she had asked and caused the man pain.

"Thank you, missus that is kind of ya. It is quite all right. How could you ha' known?" he asked with a resigned shrug of his shoulders.

Lizzie had crept closer during their conversation and stared openly back at Hector as he stared at them with all the fingers of one small hand still stuffed nervously into his mouth. "Your name is Hector, like our boaty?" She asked him boldly.

Hector turned his face into his father's leg and shyly refused to look at her. "Yes, child, his name is Hector. Like the ship, but no relation," Mr. Morrison joked, with a wink toward James. "I hate ta beg a favor sa soon after our introductions, but perhaps your missus and children would keep an eye on my Hector for a short time, so I might collect our things?"

"Of course, I can help ya carry if you wish, Mr. Morrison, and you can return the favor by helping us finish mucking oot this filthy hold," James answered, grinning.

Mr. Morrison smiled. "Agreed, and please call me George," he said with another dazzling smile. His somewhat homely and solemn face was transformed into a very handsome one when his radiant smile broke free.

Hector reluctantly let go of his father, and with a shy smile took Lizzie's outstretched hand and followed her to their corner. The men returned in a matter of minutes with a small satchel and two clinking, clanking sacks. James looked at the sacks curiously, as he set one of them down with a jangling thump.

"My tools," George said in explanation. "I am a joiner by trade and these tools are mine and Hectors means of support. Now then," he said, wrinkling his nose and rolling up his sleeves. "If you wull give me a rag, we shall have this dank place clean in no time a'tall."

Several other young men arrived while they worked and after a bit of urging from Mary, they also leant their hands to help finish. All together, five single men had arrived to join them on the Hector. As they were finishing scrubbing the last of the boards, the ladder creaked announcing another passenger. Two small shoes and a skirt hem appeared at the top of the ladder and began a timid descent.

One of the men, who had introduced himself as John, went quickly to help her down. When she reached the bottom it was obvious to all that the woman was in an advanced state of pregnancy. She thanked the man meekly and looked around at the rest of them, blinking like a cat in the gloom. A large bundle suddenly thumped down beside her from above, startling her.

Mary approached her and introduced herself immediately. Obviously, pleased by another woman's presence, the young woman smiled gratefully at her. "Oh I am so pleased to meet you, Mistress! I am Jane Gibson."

Not wishing to repeat her earlier blunder over George's missing wife, Mary remained silent about the whereabouts of her husband or kin. She invited her to make her pallet next to her own family's and brought her over for introductions. It came up in conversation that she was not a widow, but a wife going to join her husband who had apparently gone on ahead of her to Nova Scotia to scout the area.

"So, you are traveling alone then?" Mary asked gently. "There was no one who could ha' come with you?" She eyed Jane's swollen abdomen with meaning.

"Oh aye, my brother Charles is coming. He is bringing the rest of our things from the dock the noo. But not to worry," Jane replied, patting her round belly, "I have counted the days most carefully and we should reach shore long afore I am due ta deliver this bairn. Four weeks afore it, at least!" she added, nodding emphatically.

Knowing how unpredictable birthing could be, and gauging the size of the young woman's belly, Mary had some doubts as to the timing of the crossing, but she prudently kept her fears to herself.

"All aboard?" The call from above came, just as Jane's brother Charles scrambled down the ladder with another bundle.

Wanting to watch as the ship embarked, everyone scrambled to grab children and go topside to find a spot at the rail out of the way of the busy sailors. The harbor was full of all sizes of ships coming and going in the noonday glare as they departed. The water twinkled cheerily in the sunlight as the Hector's prow cut through the shining surface of the water. The passengers gathered around the rail near the bow and chattered excitedly, as the ship was towed by two smaller boats out into the Firth of Clyde.

The ship rode smoothly behind her escorts on the calm, sparkling waters. They passed by smaller fishing boats coming in with their catch and the children waved happily at each of their fellow sailors below on the water. Not being tall enough to reach the rail, Lizzie and Hector peered through the uprights at the passing boats, their little arms and waving hands were all that could likely be seen from below.

When they reached the mouth of the harbor the two small escort boats detached the towing lines and Captain Spiers gave the wheelman orders to turn west and barked to the men to drop the sails. He supervised the prompt completion of his orders from the squared off rear platform at the stern of the ship as the Hector steered in front of the wind.

"Ahhh!" The passengers said collectively when the ship shuddered as the sails filled with air and the ship began to collect herself with a groan. The waves snapped briskly against the hull as the Hector sliced through the water picking up speed. It became a little rougher out on the Firth as they turned south past the curve of land west of Greenock. The ship maneuvered into the prevailing winds and rode the swells diagonally, flying along on a stiff breeze. Shore birds wheeled overhead, screeching at each other as they circled the ship.

Lizzie and Hector were clapping and screeching with delight along with them, while the older children, Katy and Sgian, merely stared with wonder.

James put his arm around Mary and smiled at her. "We are off to the New Scotland, my dearest," he said, eyes brimming with unshed tears.

"And may God keep watch over us," Mary replied, crossing herself. She was more than a little nervous about the ocean crossing, but she knew there was little she could do, but make things comfortable for her family. Their feet had left the shores of their beloved homeland and the course toward their future had been set. Resolutely, Mary turned away from the green shores of her homeland and returned to the hold with her family.

Chapter Eight

Loch Broom, Scotland, July of 1773

Old Hugh McLeod was excited, he had to admit it. He was more excited than he had been since the fighting days of his youth. His remaining son, Davy, had come up from Ullapool several weeks ago with the news of the Hector and the incredible offer.

Hugh had been reluctant to begin with, worrying about leaving the graves of his wife and son with no one to visit or to tend them. But eventually he realized it would be much harder to bear the separation from his living kin who chose to go, especially his beloved grandchildren.

It had only taken a day of discussion for his family to agree to the move. Tales of the rich, fish-filled waters of Alba Nuadh had reached their little corner of the world. There was so little left to give up and they were well accustomed to hardships.

Hugh had taken a day or two more to think it through and then decided to go with them and do what he could to help them make a new home. His place was still among the living. His mind was also eased somewhat that the Widow Murray had agreed to tend the family graves for them in trade for some of their furnishings and the two young goats that Davy had given him. He trusted her to keep her promise, as she and Flora had been close friends.

He shaded his eyes to look out across the harbor and at the same time heard his grandson, Willie, cry out. "There she is, there she is... the Hector!" Hugh spotted her now, sailing around the point of Ullapool, her sails being raised up and tied off on the yardarms of all three masts by swarming seamen. The transformation in Willie, since the voyage had been decided on, had been remarkable. Seeing his liveliness restored in a way that had not been present since his father's boat had gone down, made Old Hugh glad in his heart for this opportunity.

The harbormaster's boats were already rowing out to meet the Hector and tow her into port. His daughter-in-law, Janet, came up beside them with her other two children. Elspeth and the nearly two-year-old Finlay watched the ship come into harbor in silence. Young Willie, still excited, called out to Davy and Maggie, "hurry, you have ta come and see her!"

Maggie came out of their cottage first, carrying little Alex's basket, with a large bundle over her back. Davy came out close behind her carrying a similar load, but leading the two goats by ropes. It was he who had insisted that no one bring more than they could carry comfortably. He was well aware of the space constraints aboard an ocean going vessel, having seen them so often. But Maggie had stood firm on the matter of the goats. "Their milk will help sustain us on the voyage," she had said, "and they can eat the ship's refuse!" So he had finally agreed.

"Boa-t!" Finlay hollered, his little arm pin wheeling restlessly.

Elspeth came to stand between her mother and her grandfather and patted Finlay encouragingly. "Yes, Finlay, It is our boat! Do ya want ta take a ride on the big boat?"

"Boa-t! Boa-t! Boa-t!" He chanted.

Hugh laughed, reached out to take him from Janet and then looked around at his family. "Wull, my dear ones, this wise wee owl is ready, how aboot the rest of ya?"

Twelve-year-old Willie answered eagerly, "Oh, aye! I canna wait ta see the New World!" Willie had been the most willing to make the voyage after hearing about the land offer. Davy had also been eager, after having heard tales for many years of the grand fishing to be had there; but it was Willie's dream to farm his own land that had really set him afire. Davy wanted this more for his nephew and his own son, than for himself. It promised more than they could ever hope to have here.

The women had been more reserved about the idea, what with all the children at risk. But they were also both well aware of the limited options left to their men folk and children, were they to remain in Scotland. Landless and with no hope of restoring the old clans to their glory, the future was now bleak in their homeland.

Everyone nodded in wordless agreement and picked up their sacks. It was time to go. Elspeth took one last, longing look at her beloved hills strewn with flowers and saw her mother and grandfather do the same. Elspeth had her mother help her to press some of her favorite flowers, weeds, and thistle blooms in the family Bible and it resided now in the small sack on her shoulder. It comforted her to know that a small piece of Scotland would be coming with her.

The group moved downhill toward the harbor slowly, children and goats in tow. All across the hill, other family groups could be seen, doing the same. Many were leaving the Highlands to make this journey. Spurred on by the hope of something better, the groups gradually converged on the harbor, where many other families already waited near the pier. Some had wagons or pony carts, but the majority just had what they carried on their backs. Many small boats also plied the loch to deliver passengers from further up Loch Broom. Fear pinched faces turned to each other in solemn greeting as the larger group assembled, although even for these folks, the growing excitement was contagious.

"Hoy there, Murray!" Hugh called out to a couple with three older children. Standing tall above most of the throng, Hugh was spotting many of his friends and neighbors in the crowd. "And McKay," He called, waving to a large family group nearby, "so, you are taking the offer as well, aye?" William McKay, the piper, nodded back to Hugh as he stood proudly next to his wife Margaret, their four sons and a fair haired lass. Hugh was comforted that at least some of the people from his hometown would be among them once they reached the unknown of the New World.

Many of those around them talked in animated voices about the voyage to come. Many seemed in an upbeat mood and were happy to be there. A few here and there seemed genuinely frightened. They stood off by themselves, pale faced and wide eyed, staring at the ship as it docked, as if it were a monster about to devour them.

There was a small group of passengers standing on deck to greet the newcomers and one of them was waving frantically to someone in the crowd. Hugh recognized him as John Patterson and by leaning on his cane and standing on tiptoe to look around he could see the blonde heads of his wife Ann and their daughter, Rebecca. Hugh had heard from his son Davy that John had gone to Greenock to sell his boat and by the grin on his face, all must have gone well. Davy himself had sold his share of the boat to his more than willing partners, Alan and Geordie.

Davy was also hailing friends and fellow fishermen from the area as the throng surged toward the arriving ship. Hugh saw him patting the back of his friend Davy Urquhart and his lovely new bride, Christian.

Being of a mind not to lose any of his brood in the mass of people, Hugh gathered them in closer. Maggie looked especially pale, so he slung his small sack under one arm and took the basket containing little Alex from her. She smiled gratefully up at him and stretched her back, cracking it audibly, even in the noisy crowd. He did a quick headcount and made sure that his other three grandchildren were next to him, where he had a better chance of preventing their being jostled overly much. The goats bleated in protest to the growing crowd and he drew them in closer, as well.

The ship was quickly tied up to the long pier and several sailors opened a gate in the rail and began to slide the gangway over the side toward the pier. Ullapool harbor had a deep enough inlet to allow for the big ships to dock, rather than anchor out in the bay. A fierce-eyed, weathered looking man placed himself at the gate next to a tall man wearing a tri-cornered hat over blonde curls. "Order, let's have some order here!" He growled above the din. The crowd quickly grew quiet in response. "I am Captain Spiers and this, as many of you may know, is John Ross, the ship's agent. In a single line and in family groups, I want you all to board in an orderly fashion, first giving Mr. Ross your full names and relationships as you pass. There is plenty of time, as I don't plan on embarking until the evening tide out. Welcome aboard the Hector," he said blandly, and abruptly turned his back on the crowd.

Somewhat more subdued, the first family group walked up the slightly swaying gangway to the ship's deck.

There was movement and murmuring to Hugh's left, in the crowd. It parted to reveal Rob Innes, Janet's father, with a bundle under one arm and a determined look upon his weathered face.

"Da," Janet exclaimed in surprise, "what are ya doin' here?"

"Why, I am coming with you, lass. You and the bairns are all I ha' left and I still be young enough to be up ta the challenge," Rob answered glaring round at Hugh, ten years his senior, daring him to challenge this logic.

Hugh was surprised, but quickly regained his composure. "Welcome to you, Rob. We wull need all the hands we can get oncet we land." Hugh extended his hand in friendship.

Surprised to have received none of the expected argument from the senior McLeod, Rob hesitated a moment and then a big, toothy grin broke across his face. He grasped Hugh's hand and shook it. "Taing, McLeod."

Janet hugged her father fiercely, her face beaming with a happiness it had not previously shown. "Oh Da, thank you! I despised the thought of leaving ya behind!"

"Wull, not ta worry now, lass. I am coming with ya. How could I live with no seeing my grandchildren again, I asked myself? And I found that I couldna!" He chucked Finlay under the chin and smiled, tears leaving wet tracks down the landscape of his careworn face.

The crowd surged forward again, as the line up the gangway kept moving. A few older children ran wild through the group, causing screeches and scolding as they conducted their mischief. The chattering amongst the family groups continued, like lively birds being social, as they moved steadily although slowly forward toward the gangway.

James, Ian, and Sgian stood on deck watching the last of the passengers board. The women had stayed below to guard their corner of the hold from any would be usurpers. Lizzie had put up quite a fuss about it, wanting to be a "big girl" and go on deck with her Da. Finally she had been subdued, but still she pouted below.

Fascinated with every aspect of the ship, Sgian leaned over the railing gawking at the newcomers. He felt like a seasoned sailor already, having had four days on board before these newest passengers arrived. He leaned so far over trying to see well, that his Uncle Ian had been obliged at one point to grab him by the collar and haul him backwards to prevent his falling overboard.

George Morrison had arrived on deck to join the other men just in time to witness this near mishap and chuckled to himself. He caught a sharp glance from young Sgian, and not wishing to embarrass the lad, he quickly composed himself and promptly turned his laugh to a cough.

"Where is wee Hector?" James asked.

"Your wife and daughters were kind enough ta mind him for a spell, so I thought I would come see the new arrivals," George answered. "She said as she had 'said her goodbyes to Scotland in Greenock, she wouldna be doin' it again here.'"

James smiled to himself. That was his Mary all right. Once her pretty head was made up about something, she stuck to it. He thought to himself. It was the MacGregor in her; they were all just as stubborn as the rocks in the field, but as loyal as any you would want on your side in a fight. "Aye, tha' would be my Mary," he said out loud to George, still smiling.

The sun hovered low over the water making the water look dark red, like blood. Gazing at it, Ian said, "You know what they say, 'red sky at night is a sailors delight.'"

"Is that so? Well then, I guess we are in for fair weather on the morrow then. That's a blessing!" George remarked.

A passing sailor paused as he heard Ian's voice and gave him a rude shove, as he passed. "You, agin. Here mooching around for work again is you?"

Ian recognized the voice and turned slowly toward it, drawing himself up taller. "Indeed I am not. I am a passenger on this ship."

"Are ya then? Should ha' guessed it," he sniffed. "You've joined the rest of the idjuts on this here trip."

"Who're you calling an idjut, clot-heid?" George asked, stepping closer menacingly.

"If I were addressing you," Tom Mandler sneered, "you would know it!"

Ian put a restraining hand on George and spoke again. "Why don't you go about your work, sailor, before I report you to your captain?" Ian remarked sarcastically.

Angered to a shade of red that matched the western skies, Tom Mandler fumed. He poked his finger sharply into Ian's chest. "Listen up, mate! Lots o' things can happen on an ocean voyage. You'd best watch yourself. Your friends canna be with you all o' the time," he added with a glare round at the men. He turned on his heel and stormed away.

"What was tha' all about then, Ian?" James asked, as he relaxed the fists he had unconsciously had clenched at his side.

"Oh, I sort of met the fellow outside a tavern in Greenock and we had words. He is naught but horse dung, doona worrit about him."

"Words, was it? Seems as though he could make this trip rough for you, A charaid," James persisted. "That type of fellow rarely gives up on a fight."

"Aye, I'll be careful of him. And he had best be careful of me, as well!"

"And me, as well," Sgian piped in. The men turned to him for the first time in the conversation to find him with his small knife drawn and ready in his hand.

"Sgian, put tha' away this minute! You will stay oot of it, ya hear?" His father scolded, quickly hiding the small knife. "I doona wish to reach the New World, only to watch my eldest son shit himself on the gallows for murder!" James hissed.

"Yes Da," Sgian replied, obediently replacing his knife in his sock. He was not called Sgian for nothing. He glanced at his Uncle Ian and saw a small proud smile playing on his face. One sharp look from James wiped the smile from Ian's face immediately.

Grateful for a distraction, Ian said, "Now would ya look at tha'," and pointed past their shoulders to a man on the pier who was approaching the ship at a run, bagpipes honking noisily at his side.

The sun hung low and pregnant with orange light as Hugh McLeod leaned against the rail of the Hector. He was getting his last look at Scotland and he knew it. Many folks were on deck strolling back and forth, or doing much the same that he was. The raucous atmosphere was gone, replaced by a melancholy that tugged at his heart. The tide would be going out soon and they would sail away from Scotland forever, toward the Americas and hopefully toward better lives.

He stared for a long time up the hill toward the old kirk. He had made his last visit to the graves of his wife and son, but he still felt incomplete. "Goodbye Flora, my love," he whispered. "I shall miss you so." Hugh bowed his head and said a short prayer for the good Lord to keep his beloved Flora and his son, Hugh William, in his arms until the day he could join them. Several large tears dripped down his strong chin and splattered onto the railing.

Sailors were still busy on deck, checking ropes, riggings, block and tackle and giving final tugs on the knots holding the excess cargo on deck. At the last minute, his son Davy joined him on deck, quietly laying a comforting hand on his father's arm.

"All aboard?" The final cry came from the stern.

Just as they were about to pull in the gangplank, a man came running down the pier, his squeaking and squawking bagpipe under one arm and a bundle under the other. "Wait! Hoy there, and wait," he cried above the idly honking pipes.

The sailors stopped and the man quickly boarded, the gangway coming up behind him with a final thud. John Ross had already departed and so no one was there to welcome him.

"Thank you, lads," he said politely to the sailors. Then he dropped his pack, but not his beloved pipes, and leaned forward to catch his breath while panting heavily.

Interested, Hugh approached the small round man and introduced himself. "You just made it, sir! I am Hugh McLeod, and you are?"

"I am Colin Campbell. Or perhaps I can use my birth name now," he said with a glint in his eye. "I am Colin Donald MacGregor, at your service sir," the barrel-chested man said, dropping into a courtly bow.

Hugh had at first been tense and frowning. Now he relaxed. He had been slightly suspicious when the man said his name was Campbell, but now that his true name was revealed, he relaxed. Many of the Campbells were friends of the English and had been the McLeod's enemies, since long before Hugh's time. MacGregors however, were a completely different story. They were good people for the most part although landless, nameless and occasionally lawless, they had persevered much hardship. Many had taken the names of their mothers to avoid prosecution for using their prohibited birth name. Others had simply taken the name of their enemies, the Campbell's, in defiance of the Crown, as English soldiers tended to be much friendlier to a Campbell than a MacGregor. "A piper, are ye?" Hugh asked, pointing to the now silent pipes.

"Aye," Colin answered, patting the bagpipe fondly, making it hoot softly like a living creature.

Several people down below on the pier frowned up at the piper. No one wanted to be nearby if any English soldiers should happen by. The penalty for playing the bagpipes was still death, if you were caught. The English considered them an instrument of war and therefore banned their use.

James, Ian, George and Sgian approached the group. "Well, you can play as soon as we're out of harbor, man. They'll be no English oot where we are goin'! I, for one, shall enjoy hearing the pipes say goodbye to these green shores for the last time," Ian said, clapping the man on the back. "And a fellow MacGregor too, welcome, man!"

"We also have another piper on board, name of McKay. I'll introduce you proper like, as soon as I see him," Old Hugh said, looking around.

The ship shuddered and groaned as the pilot boats pulled her away from the pier. Many more teary passengers had now come on deck to say goodbye to their beloved Scotland. As they came around Dead Man's Point, the small lead boats detached and returned to Ullapool. The ship's dinghy was pulled in and the tide began her pull on the Hector from the mouth of the Broom and out to the North Sea, beyond.

With the flapping sails and the water whisking on the hull for accompaniment, the piper tuned up and began to play a mournful tune. Hugh recognized it as Farewell to the lasses of Mon Tay and he smiled to himself, remembering dancing to that tune at his wedding. A tug on his sleeve announced the arrival of his own bonny wee lassie and he drew Elspeth warmly into his embrace. Willie stood nearby and edged closer.

"Say goodbye to Scotland lads and lassie, but remember her always, Cuimhnich!" Hugh said, choking on his own emotion.

"I will Grandda, I will never forget, Cuimhnich!" Elspeth raised her little fist up over her little mob cap, red curls escaping to shine in the sun along with her tears, every bit as defiant as she was herself. Her brother William stood beside them. More excited than melancholy, he whooped out loud. "Goodbye, Ullapool! We are off!"

The small fist fell, as the silver head and the smaller red head leaned into each other and watched as one. William, now quiet, watched the green hills capped in golden light recede, finally realizing he would likely never see his birthplace again. Their beloved Ullapool, gilded from the setting sun on the hills above and nestled close to the water below, slipped slowly out of sight behind the point. The piper solemnly played another outlawed tune in a solemn farewell tribute to the beloved hills and shores of their native land. The music from the pipes echoed back to them across the water, as if another piper answered MacGregor from the receding shore.

Chapter Nine

Captain and Crew

aptain John Spiers stood in his place on the bridge barking orders to his helmsman and the sailors aloft in the perilous riggings. They were just rounding Dead Man's Point and he wanted to catch the light southerly breeze and get the Hector out of Loch Broom with the quickening tide. Now that they were on their way, he focused his attention on the task at hand. His sharp blue eyes flashed back and forth, searching for any unfortunate seaman who was not doing his share of the labor.

His eyes quickly found his cabin boy, Nate. He was standing idly near the bow of the ship watching the sunset-tinged water slide past, as the great bow of the ship sliced the waves in two. "Nate!" He bellowed. "Shag your arse back here!"

Startled, the boy quickly looked up and met his captain's eyes across the ship. "Aye, coming right away, sir!" He called. He scuttled up to the rear deck and with no small amount of courage, placed himself squarely in front of his fierce looking captain.

The captain glowered down at him. He was a good-looking blonde lad of about thirteen or fourteen-years-old, who was just beginning to show signs of the man he would someday be. He was an obedient cabin boy, even if taken with too much daydreaming, but he needed far more correction than the captain felt was normal for a boy his age. "Don't you have enough duties, lad?" Without waiting for him to answer, he said, "No, I thought not! Go aft and check on Mrs. Forbes and her daughter to see if they require anything. Then get you to the hold and make sure that all is well there."

Nate nodded briskly and took off at a run for the rear door to the two small cabins at the rear of the ship. He knocked on the door to his right and then jumped back when a pretty young woman opened it almost immediately.

"Yes?" She asked.

"Good day to you, mistress," Nate said, quickly removing his cap. "The captain wishes to know if you require anything, as we are headed oot to sea, the noo."

She stepped back into the small cabin and grabbed a basin filled with a nasty substance that Nate recognized all too well and handed it to him. "You can empty this overboard for me, if you would? I have made dozens of trips these last few days and my mother shall require it again shortly." She brushed a damp curl out of her eyes with the back of her hand and sighed.

"What's amiss then? Has she got the ague?" He peeped in curiously, to see an older woman with a sickly pallor lying on the lower berth.

"I sincerely wish that were it, but no. She has been like this since we first set sail from Greenock. She seemed fine while we were docked today and now she has gone over to it again."

"Ah, she is seasick then," Nate said, nodding knowingly. "But we arena even out on the big swells yet! Near the coast, as we ha' been, has been fairly smooth sailing."

The woman on the berth groaned at this ill news.

"You'd best go empty the basin and get it right back here!" Jane said, glowering at him and hurriedly pushing him out the door.

"Yes, Miss," he said and beat a hasty retreat, his bare feet pounding down the steps. He reached the railing and flung the contents far over the side, his nose wrinkling in distaste as the breeze carried the sour smell of vomit right back to him. He rushed back, gagging, and sincerely hoped he would not be asked to do this too often.

The cabin door still stood open and as the first of the real ocean swells hit them, the lady on the bunk sat up to signal frantically for the basin as he returned. Just in time, she got the basin under her and terrible retching sounds emerged over the large rim. Jane helped hold the basin and looked up at Nate, as she teetered tiredly, back and forth. "I am afraid you may have to do the same again. I need to rest for a moment. Er, what is your name, boy?"

"So sorry, Miss," he said sincerely, feeling sorry for her and wishing he had known of their misery earlier. "I am Nate, the cabin boy, at your service." He bowed and then stood a little taller, obviously proud of his position.

"Very pleased to meet you Nate," Jane said with a grim smile. "I think we shall become fast friends." The awful retching having stopped, she again handed him the noxious half full basin to empty, with her pretty brow raised in question.

"Yes, Miss!" he answered. Having done his duty again as quickly as possible, he returned to the cabin. "I can get some biscuit for your mother, Miss. Tha's wha' is wanted for seasickness. And doona let her drink anything, anything at all, until she stops the retching."

"Please call me Jane. And when might we expect that to be, Nate?" Jane asked with a rueful smile.

"Oh, not ta worry, mistress! Those that get the seasickness usually get their wame calmed down in a week or so. I've never heard of anyone dyin' of it, as awful as it is, Miss," he added apologetically, with a nod to poor Mrs. Forbes prone figure. "I must go and check on the passengers in the hold and report ta the captain, but then I will come back straight away with the biscuit."

"Thank you, Nate! We will be here," Jane said, her voice dripping with irony.

The first person that Nate spied as he landed in the murky hold below was young Sgian McDonald. The two stared at each other for a full minute and then Nate introduced himself, boasting in his young voice.

"I am Nate, the cabin boy and right hand of Captain Spiers, who is the captain of this here ship!" He added, in case this boy did not know his captain.

"And I am Andrew McDonald," he answered. "But you can call me Sgian Dubh," Sgian answered, puffing up with equally boyish self-importance, "because, I am well known for my hand with a blade."

"Indeed," Nate answered more respectfully. "You had best keep tha' last bit ta yourself," he added, whispering close to Sgian Dubh's face. "The captain is none too fond of people creeping 'round his ship with knives."

The two boys glared into each other's eyes for a few moments sizing each other up and then they both started to laugh.

Nate realized immediately that he liked this short dark-haired lad, and he looked forward to the possibility of a new friend.

Sgian also liked this gangly, blonde, older lad and patted him on the back. "You're no going to tell him then are you?"

"Nah," Nate answered, with a grin, "not unless ya stick me wit it!"

Both the boys doubled up with laughter at their private joke and ended up slapping each other on the back as they guffawed and jostled each other boyishly.

"Who is in charge down here, then?" Nate asked after he caught his breath.

"Come on. I will introduce you to my Da. We were the first ones on board at Greenock, so folks seem ta come to him as their leader," Sgian said proudly.

James was standing between a very portly man who held a set of bagpipes idly under his arm, and a pretty dark haired woman with a baby on her hip. "Well and my Mary is glad ta have some MacGregors on board, especially a piper," he was saying. "'Twill make the trip more enjoyable to be sure," he added, with a wink in Mary's direction.

Sgian pulled at his arm, as soon as he was done speaking, and introduced Nate.

"At your service, Sir," Nate addressed him, bowing with a flourish. "The captain wishes ta know if anything is amiss here or if all is well among the passengers here below."

"Many are still settling in, lad, but all seems well sa far," James answered, with a glance around, "other than a few with weak wames that seem not to take to the sea verra well that is."

Nate nodded knowing what he meant all too well. "It is cleaner down here than I last remember it," Nate said as he looked around. Even with all these passengers in such close quarters, it smelled much better than it had, when they had unloaded their last passengers in Greenock, as well. "Whose doin' was tha'?"

"That would be my wife, Mary McDonald," he answered, proudly introducing the woman at his side. "She took it upon herself ta organize us as soon as we arrived on board in Greenock. We were a regular cleaning army, we were!"

"Well done!" Nate exclaimed, trying to sniff unobtrusively. "I shall let the captain know of your industry, Mistress!"

"Thank you, Nate. My mother always said that 'Cleanliness was next ta Godliness.'" Mary greeted him with a sweet smile and a soft hand on his bony shoulder.

"Yes, Mistress," Nate replied, tardily removing his cap, and staring at her spellbound. She reminded him sharply of his own petite mother, lost to him for a few years now. Her hair had been blonde like his own, not dark like Mary's, but other than that, they could have been twins. Feeling suddenly uncomfortable he said, "Well if there is aught that you need, just send for me and I will come as quick as I am able."

Mary nodded, smiling and turned away to let the men finish talking.

Nate stared after her longingly for a few moments and then quickly gathered his wits to explain the daily rationing of biscuits and water and the Sunday meal of dried beef. "The captain is strict aboot such matters and will brook no disobedience concerning food and water. Oh, and the ale is for the sailors only. It is always promised as part of their wages, ya see."

"Not ta worrit, we wull keep order here," James replied.

"Well, if there is nothing else I can do, sirs, I will be off now. I ha' a sick passenger in the stern cabin tha' needs me and a captain ta report ta," Nate said.

Reminded of his own seasick people, he asked Nate to bring them down a bit of biscuit, as well, when he could slip away. "And thank you, Nate, we shall call on you," James replied with nod.

"I'll take my leave then," Nate replied formally. He pulled Sgian with him toward the ladder. In an aside he said, "Meet me on the port side of the deck, up near the bow, just after dark and I will show ya somethin' grand!" His eyes sparkled with excitement.

Sgian nodded in agreement and Nate nimbly climbed back up the ladder to attend the Captain and poor Mrs. Forbes.

Jane tucked some stray strands of hair back under her cap and straightened it. She had hoped, after the day in port, that her mother was finished being ill. It had been a miserable time alone with her, since sailing from Greenock. Jane had carried the basin filled with vomit out to the rail a few more times and now they were down to just the wrenching heaving with little emesis. She wet a rag from the small bit of water in her pitcher and bathed her mother's sweating face. Her mother groaned again. Hastily, Jane poured another splash of water on the rag and then turned again to try to wipe away her mother's ghastly green pallor. She kept up a nervous chatter, although her mother was rarely responding to her, other than to groan dramatically from time to time. "Now Mother, really. I cannot understand why you are so ill and I am not! I feel right as rain! Surely, you must feel better soon."

"I shall never feel myself again. I fear I shall surely die!" Mary Jane rolled in agony in the small berth.

A rap at the door announced Nate's return with the biscuit.

"Here you are, Miss!" He exclaimed, breathing hard from running. Nate held the biscuits out to her like a rare delicacy. As Jane took one, he exclaimed, "Now ha' her nibble at it slowly and if after a quarter hour there is nay vomiting, then have her go at it again. And no water, mind! If she canna bears it, then you wait a bit before you start again at the nibbling and so on, until she is better."

"Thank you, Nate!" Jane answered gratefully. "And could you, er.... wait around for a short time?"

"Yes Miss," Nate answered, with a sigh. I would gladly do her bidding all day, he thought. He watched her lovely profile as she attended her mother with elegant hands and wondered idly if anyone ever said no to her about anything.

Jane broke off a small piece of the hard biscuit and brought it to her mother's mouth. "Here we are!" Jane spoke in such a perfect imitation of her mother's cajoling from her childhood, that Mary Jane had to smile weakly. She nibbled a small corner and then gingerly swallowed. Then she sat with a thoughtful look on her face and tried another nibble.

Jane watched her expectantly as she kept nibbling. A long swell lifted the ship fore to aft and Mary Jane stopped nibbling and began paling again.

Nate returned with the basin just in time as Mary Jane expelled her attempt, violently. He sighed loudly. "Well Miss, just keep doin' what you're a doin' and she will come 'round."

"I certainly hope so, Nate! I don't know how much more of this she can take!"

Nate knew that she could, indeed, take a lot more from having seen men do so for weeks, but he kept that to himself for now. Better to just see how it went with her.

"I will empty the basin for you again and then be on my way Miss," Nate said. "I have many other duties you see," he boasted. He hopped anxiously from one foot to the other as the dinner bell rang.

Jane smiled, despite herself. "Oh, of course, and we wouldn't want to keep you from them! We can manage here now, thanks to your biscuit remedy. I am grateful for the reprieve too," she said handing him the basin.

Nate flushed at the compliment and then rushed out again with the hated basin.

Chapter Ten

Aboard the Hector

The stars were out in all their glittering glory and the full moon floated high in the sky by the time Nate found the time to slip away from the captain. He met Clancy, the man at the forward crow's nest, as he was climbing down. A new man that Nate didn't know scurried up the mast to take his place. "Hoy there, Clancy!" Nate called softly.

"Aye, 'tis you there, Nate!" Clancy answered quietly, spying him immediately on the dark deck. "Out for your evenin' stroll?" Clancy knew well what Nate was up to. He had seen him do it nearly every clear night at sea since he had joined the Hector's crew.

"Aye, Clancy, I'm just out for a stroll." Nate answered, peering around in the shadows. A movement behind Clancy caught his eye and pinpointed where his new friend, Sgian, was still waiting in hiding. "Have a good night, then, Clancy!" He said hurriedly.

"You too, laddie, you too!" Clancy's teeth flashed in the darkness as he smiled in passing.

Nate leaned over the rail, looking deep into the inky waves as they passed. A flicker of light on wet skin eventually showed him what he was looking for. With another quick glance around, he spoke softly into the dark. "Come on out, Sgian. This is wha' I wanted ta show ya."

Sgian joined him silently at the rail, straining his eyes to see what Nate pointed toward. Then a shiny dark hump rose above the waves and a noise hissed into the night air, like the gas escaping the body cavity when you poked at a long dead carcass. The huge hump and long fin quickly slid forward and disappeared under the waves, only to be replaced by another, and yet another, each blowing out air upon surfacing. The moonlight glimmered wetly on their strange slick hides.

"What be they? Sea monsters?" Sgian asked in an excited whisper.

"Very like! They be sea beasts called whales. They oft swim alongside the ship, once we get oot ta deeper waters. I like ta watch them." He paused, staring thoughtfully off into the moonlit night. "I oft times wonder wha' they think of us. Maybe they think the ship is another of their kind?"

"Wha' is the blowing noise they make? Are they talkin'?" Sgian asked.

"No. I don't think so that is. I was told 'tis the sound they make as they surface ta breathe," Nate answered. "Listen and you'll hear them trying ta talk."

Sgian waited in silence straining to hear something above the flapping sails and the slapping waves. A deep, mournful, wail suddenly echoed across the water. It was quickly answered with another, just like it. Reverberating calls then rang back and forth in the dark water, even from under the ship. They were oddly sad and musical, reminding him of bagpipes. Sgian felt his skin wrinkle into gooseflesh as he listened to their eerie underwater conversation.

Staring at the huge hulks sliding by their ship in majestic arches, Sgian wondered out loud if they would attack the ship and then wished he had not thought of it, as his heart began to pound.

"Aye, well, I ha' heard tell of them doin' so," Nate answered. "And surely, they are large enough ta do it, but those were whalers that were tied up ta them and trying ta kill them, ya ken. Most ships sailing by seem ta have nothing ta fear from them."

"They are magnificent!" Sgian sighed, finally finding a use for one of the many large words his mother was always trying to teach him.

Nate smiled to himself and said, "I thought ya would fancy them. I had hoped they would come tonight."

Both boys stared silently into the moonlit sea beyond the hull, watching the huge ship sized bodies slide wetly by, as the Hector kept pace with them. Their mournful calls surrounded the ship like a haunting lullaby. The sound of water sluicing away from the slice of the bow through the waves reminded the boys of their own vulnerability and seemed to accompany the whale's lonely cries into the night.

Sgian slowly became fascinated by a strange sparkling glow that seemed to come from just below the waves. A watery, but bright green light seemed to shimmer from somewhere below the waves. "What are those lights under the sea then, Nate?" He finally asked, breaking their silence.

"Some sort of underwater fairies, I imagine. They come sometimes with yon beasts when I ha' seen them before. Sometimes, it just glows all alone trailing behind us as if to mark our passage."

"Do you see them often?" A male voice asked from the darkness beside them.

Both boys jumped, but it was Sgian who challenged him. "Who's there?"

Another young boy about their age stepped out of the shadows beside them. "I am James William McLeod," he answered. "But people call me Willie. I didna mean ta be spyin'," he added quickly. "I was sittin' here alone 'til both of you came, wondering what it was my own self. I ha' fished with my father and my uncle me whole life and ne'er seen aught like it."

All three boys sized each other up tensely in the darkness for a moment or two. Nate had seen this boy earlier. He had been quietly exploring the ship since they had set sail out of Loch Broom, but he had not tried to talk with him yet.

"It only happens oot in the deep waters after sunset," Nate finally answered him. "Fishing is best done near the coast, aye?"

"Aye, tha's true enough," Willie agreed. "So do ya see yon water fairies often then?" He persisted.

"Well, as I said, they travel often with the whales, but not always together like." "The whales doona come every night," Nate added thoughtfully, "seems most likely when we are nearer to land, than it is when we be a few weeks oot. I ha' never seen the fairies up close, mind, only their wee lamplights."

Willie nodded and edged closer to the two others. "So who are you, then?" He asked, peering curiously at their faces that showed clearly in the moonlight.

This time Sgian answered first. "I am Andrew McDonald, but I am called Sgian Dubh."

"Because he is quick with a knife!" Nate whispered emphatically, just in case the new boy was the fighting kind. "And I am Nate, cabin boy for Captain Spiers," he added importantly.

"Pleased ta meet ya," Willie said with genuine respect. "Do ya mind if I stay and watch them wit' ya?"

"Nay, not a'tall," Nate answered gesturing generously to the empty rail next to them. "Just mind that ya stay quiet or we wull be in for it!" He hissed, with a quick glance around at the shadowy deck. Most of the sailors were below decks in their berth. They ran a skeleton crew at night, since they sailed so much slower, but Nate did not want to get caught idling here on deck or he would get his ears boxed, at the very least. He tried not to think about the worst that could happen to him.

The boys watched the oddly sparkling waves silently, waiting for the eventual sighting of the huge slippery bodies among the waves. The hiss of air coming out of the surfacing whales mirrored the sound of the surprised inhales of the boys, as they spotted each of the great beasts that seemed nearly close enough to touch. The moon traced a magical path between her and the Hector as it rose higher into the starry night sky. Gradually, the whales moved farther and farther from the ship, seeming to follow the glow of the fairies' lamps. Their echoing cries faded away with them, until they were just a distant moaning and whistling, coming back to the boys occasionally across the inky star-sprinkled water.

The spell broken, Nate was nervous to get back to his duties before he was missed. The boys whispered their good nights and all three agreed to meet there again the following evening. Sgian and his new friend Willie crept quietly back toward the hold and the chatter and music that rose from its depths. It sounded as though the passengers were having a ceilidh below decks this first night. Nate hesitated only a moment, wishing fiercely that he could go with them, and then sighed and walked quickly in the opposite direction. As he tiptoed toward the Captain's quarters, he hoped with all his might that he had not been missed yet.

No one paid any attention as Willie and Sgian crept down the ladder and into the smoky depths of the hold. All eyes were on the pipers, McKay and MacGregor, as their chubby reddened faces puffed life into their bagpipes. The hold was crowded with families, all having claimed a very small piece of the hold's floorboards to call their own. Some were perched rather precariously on the outer edges, where the deck sloped sharply upward toward the blackened beams of the deck above, but where it was also less cramped. Many youngsters were sitting down in front of the pipers, in a rough semi-circle, an eager audience to this loud high pitched music.

Sgian sidled closer to his father and tugged at his sleeve. "Da, are we having a ceilidh?"

"A bhalaich, here you are then!" James replied. "Aye, I suppose 'tis. Where ha' you been then, laddie, off exploring?" He asked with a grin.

"Aye, Father," Sgian answered excitedly. He began to tell him about the whales, "you willna believe..." After a small nudge from behind him, he caught himself and politely introduced his new friend instead. "Oh, and this is Willie McLeod, from Ullapool."

James stood silent for a moment and then smiled and took the boys outstretched hand in his own. "William is a fine name, lad. 'Twas my brother's name, may he rest in peace," he added crossing himself quickly. "And where are your people then?"

Willie looked around a moment in the dull lamplight thinking of his own dead father and shivered. Then he spotted the rest of the McLeods. "Oh, they are just there, sir." He said, pointing out the McLeod family.

"Achh, just so," James replied, following Willie's pointed finger with his eyes. There were two goats squeezed into the family group and several adults and children. James recognized Hugh and David. "I met those men earlier. And which one is your Da then, laddie?"

Willie braced himself, stood a little taller, swallowed and answered, "my Father died at sea when a storm took his boat. We are fishermen from Ullapool. I am the man of my family now. With Grand Da's, and my mither's help, tha' is." He pointed to a big, grizzled looking, old man, seated next to a much younger red haired woman that closely resembled Willie. "And my Uncle Davy and his wife Maggie, they are just there," he said moving his finger slightly, toward the family group by the two goats.

James groaned inwardly for asking the lad and forcing him to remember things that were obviously painful. "Now I am the one who is sorry for askin'." He patted his shoulder and said, "But a fine young man ya are and a great help ta your mither too, I'd wager!"

Colin MacGregor was just finishing a rather sad lament and many women were wiping tears from their faces and even a few of the men were surreptitiously blowing their noses. Wishing to break the solemn mood, James McDonald walked over to William McKay and leaned in to whisper something to him. The piper suddenly beamed from ear to ear, and without ever releasing the pipe from his mouth, he nodded toward a clear space between him and the half circle of children and then nodded to MacGregor, the other piper, to follow his lead.

James retrieved a charred stick from a nearby cook pot, strode back into the semi-circle and then drew a cross with it on the wooden floor. As they had no swords to cross, the drawn cross would have to serve in their stead for the sword dance. Then he strode back to his family group, held his hand out to his wife Mary, and bowed grandly to her. "Would you do me the honor of dancing for us, milady, and give blessing ta our crossing?"

Mary blushed prettily and smiled at him. Sword dancing was a special talent of hers and she enjoyed it immensely. She rose and dipped into a saucy curtsey and handed him the bundled bairn in her arms, as she passed him in a whoosh of gathered skirts. Sword dancing used to be done by the maids to bless the men's swords before battle and it was a truly beautiful thing to behold.

"Watch this!" Sgian said proudly, as he poked his new friend Willie in the ribs with his elbow.

Willie had just made eye contact with his Grand Da and was waving to him. The surprise poke in the ribs caught him off guard and he bent over slightly to guard them. After a frosty glare at Sgian, he looked back toward his family. His Grand 'Da threw him a quick wink acknowledging that he saw him and then all eyes were on the small lithe figure of Mary McDonald preparing to dance.

Mary stood in one corner of the cross and placed one foot behind the other, on point. She then raised one arm above her head like a graceful swan's neck, with the other arm curved, like she was holding a babe; except low across her belly as if she were framing herself between the two. No one spoke and an expectant silence filled the hold.

Unnoticed by all, Nate had returned. After finding the Captain already in his berth, the call of the music had proved too tempting and he was watching now through the open hatch above. A few of his fellow sailors that took turns sleeping on the deck, also sat nearby awake and listening. He held his breath as he watched Mary. Then the music began and as she started to move he let it out in a wistful sigh.

Colin MacGregor joined William McKay in the lively lilt, and Mary stood with her hands now straight down at her sides, with her skirts raised just enough so all could see her trim ankles and small bare feet. She made elegant kicking motions, and small steps up and down, pointing one small foot occasionally, this way or that way, across a bar of the cross or in front of the other foot. The footwork was quick and complex, but it perfectly matched the complicated rhythms of the music. Her small feet flew back and forth and up and down, flexing then pointing, as her upper body remained rigidly posed, her face smiling. Then she turned slightly and gracefully continued on, repeating the same movements perfectly again, in the next corner of the cross. Back and forth, she danced, her dark eyes snapping with joy, some of her dark curls falling free of their bindings to float around her bouncing form.

She was now moving faster and faster with each trip around the quarters she completed, keeping up with the ever quickening tempo of the pipers. Her small feet were now flying across the floorboards as they danced. She seemed to be almost floating above her skirts, serene and smiling, but her small feet were nearly a blur below. James began to clap in time to her steps, and others quickly joined in, until nearly everyone was clapping rhythmically. Someone on the other side of the pipers began beating a bodhran in time with the tune and another began playing a flute. People crowded closer to watch shouting encouragement and praise.

Mary reached up without pausing and tucked an errant curl away from her now sweating face. The clapping was now constant as she made yet another circuit of the quarters around the cross. This time around, her feet were a pale blur, she danced so fast. Mouths hung agape among the children who were watching enraptured. In a swirl of skirts and dark hair, she suddenly stopped dead, with the last note of music still hanging in the air to come echoing back from beyond the ship. She stood posed as she had begun, her dark head bowed for a moment as she took in large gulps of air. Then the crowd exploded into cheers and applause.

Still panting, Mary threw her head back and beamed at the crowd, then dipped into a brief curtsey. She motioned to her daughters to join her. Katy hesitated near the bairns' baskets, but Lizzie was excited and already on her feet pulling on Katy's arm. She stood up, blushing and bowing her head shyly, letting Lizzie lead her out onto the floor. The crowd backed up a little to make room for them and they grasped the waiting hands of their mother. Katy and her mother had done this dozens of times, and Lizzie had happily joined them as soon as she could walk, so all three knew exactly what to do. They let go of each other's hands and put them down at their sides. Facing their mother who stood across from them in the opposite quarter, they each claimed a quarter and began to match her steps in a dance resembling the one that Mary had just performed alone. Always staying opposite of her, they stood side by side, small legs pointing and flexing in perfect unison. Slowly at first, they circled, all three stepping deftly in and out of the sections formed by the cross and returning to point.

Little girls nearby watched these slower steps carefully, and then stood and began to mimic them as best they could. A few older girls and women joined them too and as the music slowly sped up, the floor filled with dancing women and girls, all laughing and prancing over imaginary swords. The many small feet beat on the floorboards, in time to the clapping of the crowd and the quickening series of measures from the bagpipes. Skirts spun and long hair sprung free from caps and pins into whirling dervishes all twirling around each other. As the music came faster and faster, gasping women and girls dropped out one by one, laughing and panting as they fell into the waiting arms of their husbands or fathers.

Willie saw his Aunt Maggie stay with them for a long time and then she finally stopped, collapsing into his Uncle Davy, laughing with delight. Old Hugh was chuckling and grinning next to them and he promptly thumped her on the back in approval.

Finally, only Mary and her girls were left. They made one last fiendishly quick circle around the "swords" and then stopped, instantly still, on cue to the music. James rushed out to gather them all into his embrace, as the applause once again soared from the crowd. He swept Katy up in one arm and pulled Mary close in the other, squeezing Lizzie between them all. As soon as he let go, Lizzie was hopping up and down excitedly on her dusty little feet, eager for him to pick her up. He bent to pick her up, giving her a loud kiss on the cheek as he did so. Lizzie squealed and buried her head in his neck, causing those nearby to laugh and cheer even louder. They made their way back over to their family group as one, being thumped and pummeled with excited hands from those wishing to touch them and absorb some of the night's magic. Amid exuberant praise from others as they still clapped for them, the McDonalds sat down.

Ian and Sgian embraced them as they returned and Willie quietly left them to go back to the McLeod's. The noise was so great that all three babes were now awake and squalling, so the celebration was short lived. James and Katy each took a twin and Mary ducked into the shadows near the hull with them, Alasdair in her arms, to try to calm them down. "A leannan," Mary crooned to him, as she sat down and rocked him on her shoulder. Lizzie cuddled up next to her, placing her small red head on her lap.

"Whist, now. Whist!" Katy and James each whispered to the twin they held. A soft look passed between father and daughter at that moment, acknowledging the love they felt for one another and for these squirming bundles they both held. Sgian and Ian sat below them, neatly boxing in the space between the rest of the passengers and the hull of the ship.

The confines of the hold and the ship's rocking made it impossible to lay down very well, so people either sat huddled together leaning on one another or took turns laying and standing to rest. Others were also struggling with overtired children and fussing babes. Ian and Sgian shared out a blanket and wrapped it around them as they sat down back to back, leaning against each other. James shook out two woolen blankets and covered his brood as they snuggled together.

Next to them were Jane Gibson and her brother Charles. She lay down in the corner for the night, her back creaking ominously, as she reclined her heavy belly. Charles sat next to her, up against the beamed ceiling, spreading a blanket across them both as he sat watching over her protectively.

George Morrison lay down, with his knees bent, in the small space between the McDonald's and the ladder to the hold. With his tyke, Hector, already sleeping on his chest, he pulled his jacket up and over them both. He stared through the open hatch at the swaying stars above as he drew in a long, shaky breath. He despised being cooped up in the hold, but he got some small measure of relief by being right beneath the ladder leading out.

Around them in the hold other families were also settling in for the night, making what space they could on the damp and crowded boards, often just cuddling close together in a heap. There was still some laughing and chatter, but it was subdued now by the quiet needs of all the bairns that were trying to go to sleep.

Colin, after a brief glance around and a small shrug, lay down where he stood, deftly unpinning his tartan and wrapping it around himself. Using his softly honking bagpipes as a headrest, he rolled towards the storage area of the hold and went quickly to sleep in the manner of a Highlander out in the heather. To the delight of the nearby children, he could be heard snoring loudly after just a few minutes, his bagpipes mewling softly in a matching rhythm.

William McKay returned to the waiting embraces of his own family. His wife was still panting from her own dancing and his sons took turns clapping him on the back for playing so well that night. McKay carefully put his precious pipes in a sack that he placed near his head and between him and two of his sons. His wife lay beside him and the two younger boys behind her. A young blonde girl curled up at their back.

One by one, the few lamps were turned down, candles were blown out and the hold slowly faded into darkness. The gentle slap of water against the hull, combined with the motion of the waves, created a womb-like effect. With the illusion of safety and the quiet swaying and the stresses of the day behind them, many people seemed to find it easy to slide into sleep. Peace settled quickly on the jumbled group of passengers, and those that did not fall asleep right away, at least found the quiet restful.

Near Old Hugh, Willie curled up opposite his mother, Janet, under their quilt. Elspeth and Finlay were curled up in the warm pocket between them, Finlay already sleeping soundly. Old Hugh sat near them, wrapped in his tattered yellow and black tartan with a faint red stripe in the pattern. It was the McLeod tartan that had only recently been unpacked after its many years of hiding. Ever the soldier, he had placed himself between the next family and theirs protectively, leaving his son Davy, Maggie, and little Alex on the other side to flank Janet and her three children.

From where he sat against his uncle Ian, Sgian could see the moon clearly through the hatch of the hold. He saw a small form rise and then stand in silhouette in front of the moon. Then the dim shape ran his hand back through his hair, to get it out of his face, in a familiar motion. Sgian had seen his new friend, Nate, do exactly that several times just this night. Sadness welled up in his heart for the cabin boy, who had been watching their fun all alone from above.

Nate stood up slowly and walked back toward the stern and the captain's quarters, where he made his bed on the floor alone. Before he climbed to the stern platform, he stopped by the railing when he felt wetness on his face. He put one hand on the railing and with the other hand he swiped at his eyes. He had not cried in several years and it surprised him that he would now. The resemblances between Mary McDonald and his mother had wakened old ghosts. It made him long for her now, in a way that he had not for some time, until his insides ached.

Staring out at the moonlit ocean, he sent up a silent prayer to her, longing for the comfort of her touch. He stared for a long time into the shining face of the moon and fancied he could see her face there smiling down at him, like she used to. With an annoyed shake of his head he flung off the lingering tears and then scrubbed hastily at his face with his sleeve, squinting into the shadows. He had no wish to have one of his fellow sailors spot him sobbing at the moon, or he would never hear the end of the teasing he would get from them. Seeing no one about, he climbed the steps to the stern and tiptoed across to the cabins at the stern of the ship.

Seeing a crack of light beneath the Forbes' cabin door, he stopped there before going to his own rest. Very, very softly, he tapped on the door.

Jane opened it just a crack and peeped out at him. "Yes?" She whispered sleepily.

"Sorry ta disturb ya Miss," Nate said softly, politely averting his eyes. "I was just wonderin' if your mother is feeling better the noo?"

Jane smiled tiredly. "Yes, she has finally stopped retching and is sleeping. Thank you for all your help with her." Jane stifled a yawn. "I am going to get some sleep now myself. And you should too," she added with a tired smile. "Goodnight, Nate!"

"Yes'm," Nate answered as the door creaked shut. Guilt weighed upon him as he tiptoed toward the captain's door. He should have checked on them earlier in the trip and maybe saved them some days of misery. It was his duty. Not only that, but he was well acquainted with being new on a ship, sick and scared. He vowed that he would be more attentive to them from now on. He tiptoed across the cabin and curled up in his place on the floor, by the Captain's berth, as quietly as he possibly could. He breathed a small sigh of relief, thinking he had successfully avoided the Captain's wrath.

"Boy!" The Captain barked suddenly from his berth. "What have you been up to, with your sneaking about?"

Startled, Nate stammered to answer him. "I-I-I was just checking on the passengers sir!"

"By all that whining racket of those damnable pipes from below, even I could tell that they were fine, lad!" Silence swelled into fear in the small cabin, thick and stifling. "Try again!" Captain Spiers barked at him.

Waiting for the blow that was sure to come, Nate cringed, and quickly spoke again, hoping to satisfy his captain's anger before he got going. "I was bringing biscuit 'round and I saw some whales, sir. So, I watched them for a bit."

A booted foot came out of the dark and caught him square in the back. "You were shirking your duties! That's what I thought!" The boot returned with a couple of well aimed parting kicks and then stopped abruptly. "Do it again and I'll have ya dragged in the sea for a while, like the useless wee poolie ya are!" Captain Spiers snarled menacingly at him from the darkness.

Shuddering with fear, Nate mumbled, "yes sir," and curled into a small ball, he pulled his jacket collar up over his ears. He barely breathed waiting to see if there was anymore that would be said or done to him. Hurting and humiliated, between his aching back and his fear that the kicking would start again, it was a long time before the comfort of sleep would find him.

He lay curled up like a snail, thinking about his mother again and how different things might have been had she lived. As his fear turned to anger and rose, he also wondered about how his life might have been, if this hateful man lying nearby were not his father. Captain Spiers had, on occasion, stopped at home to visit his wife and son between his voyages. Infrequent as these stops were, Nate had never really known what sort of man his father was. He would sometimes bring gifts, sometimes even nice ones, and he had always been good to Nate back then.

However, the only gift he had brought to the family on his last visit to them was the smallpox that had killed his mother and his baby sister. Nate had spent six long months trying to survive alone, before his father had come home again. When Captain Spiers had returned he said little about his dead mother and sister, he simply took Nate with him when he left, making him his new cabin boy. Nearly three years had gone by since that fateful day.

At first he had been so excited. Adventure on the high seas and a real position at his young age, seemed to Nate the only good outcome of his bad situation. And then the real nightmare began.

It seemed nothing he did was ever good enough for his moody father. A beating became the eventual outcome of nearly every scolding he received. In his shock and fresh grief for his family, it did not occur to him, at first, that it was not his own mistakes that brought about the frequent beatings. He soon learned that almost anything could and did set his father's temper off, especially if he had been drinking. He usually just tried his best to stay out of his father's way so that he would not find fault with him. Experience had taught him that if he did not, he would live to regret it. Afterwards, his father was always very nice to him and actually treated him better than usual - at least for a few days.

After a time, it had grown into a routine. He found he could not even enjoy any of the good times with his father, without the lingering dread of the inevitable escalation to the next beating that was to come. Now, after seeing other families up close, during the four ocean crossings he had now made, he knew that it was not really his fault. He knew that he was not the horrible boy that he had at first believed that he was. The thought that his father was just plain mean had at first been hard to swallow. But he soon learned that some men just seemed to be made in such a way that violence was an acceptable and desirable solution to all their conflicts. Nate had seen several among his fellow sailors and previous passengers. Some even seemed to relish it. Sometimes, even some women seemed to have a taste for it. Nate felt sick when he thought of some of the things that he had seen these last years.

The severity of the beating never seemed to have as much to do with what someone actually did wrong, as it did the beater's own temper. Nate had seen kids do some awful things on board and receive only a wishy-washy tongue lashing, while others were constantly humiliated with the cruelest punishments after only a mild lapse of manners. He did not understand this disparity in human nature and it was a shock to him, each time it occurred. His own mother, while being strict, had never treated him or his sister in such a way. She had never punished them more severely than a quick slap on the bum for doing something dangerous.

Despite his increasing love for the sea, after a few years being in such close quarters with his father, Captain Spiers, it had grown nearly unbearable. His fantasies more and more often involved stealing away at the next port they docked in. He was frightened to be alone in the world, but he was becoming even more frightened of what would happen to him if he stayed with his father.

The beatings had turned increasingly ugly lately. When Captain Spiers was getting ready to strike him, he would get a shine to his eyes and a certain set to his jaw, that was a warning of what was to come. Then during the worst of the blows, an unnatural expression of glee would rise on his features and he could not be stopped then, until Nate's blood flowed. Sometimes, Nate felt sure that he would be beaten to death, long before he could ever find the courage to run away from the Hector and his unloving father.

His father; the thought sickened him. You would hardly ken we are related by how he treats me, Nate thought. As the deck below him pitched slightly back and forth, it rocked him as a mother rocked a babe in her arms. He laid thinking for what seemed a very long time. Finally, merciful sleep took him away to where neither boot, nor any harsh words could reach him. His young body finally relaxed as he slid into his dreams.

Chapter Eleven

The Voyage

George Morrison walked the length of the deck and back, wearing a scowl that was deeply etched into his already gaunt and solemn face. Katy McDonald had offered to watch over his son, Hector, as he slept this morning and George had eagerly agreed. He was depressed and shaken by what the day to day life on board the Hector had proved to be like. The reality was much worse than he had imagined.

He had climbed his way out of the darkness of the hold squinting, his eyes adjusting gradually to the light. The red morning sun burned his eyes. He felt a bit like a damp clam, peeping out of its shell, but he also felt freer than he had in days. Being confined in the dank, smelly, below decks with an active toddler had strained his patience to its limits. He drew long grateful breaths of the exhilarating salty air as he paced the Hector's weathered boards and stretched the cramped muscles of his long legs.

They were only eighteen days out of Ullapool. It was mid-July and it was warm and comfortable up on deck. It was bone-chilling and damp in the hold at night, but during the day the heat from the sun baked the wood of the old ship, and the passengers' sweating blended with the natural moisture in the hold and made the air steamy with humidity. George had felt he was drowning a few times in his sleep and woken in a panic, thrashing about to find he was still in the same clammy hold. The constant presence of rats, especially at night, had also become extremely troublesome for everyone on board. Many was the night he had awakened to shrieks from one of the passengers or one of the rodents chewing on his blanket or crawling across him or little Hector. It seemed that no matter how many were killed, there were always more.

The drastic changes in temperature and the constant humidity were also making many people sick, and most of the children had runny noses and coughs. The crowded dirty living conditions added another pungent odor that layered on top of the moist wood smell, making the hold more dank and swampy than any moor he had ever experienced in Scotland. Sometimes, he felt sure he would suffocate long before they ever reached dry land. With another month to go onboard, he was already wondering how he would bear it for even another week. He sighed, realizing that at least he only had one small boy to care for. As difficult as that had proven to be, many on board were dealing with so much more than he was.

Poor Mary McDonald had six bairns, with three not yet weaned. George had become very close to the family during these last few weeks that they had been together aboard the Hector. He saw daily what a supreme effort it took Mary to juggle the care and feeding of her babes. Ian and James took constant turns caring for them, and the older children were also a big help, but it was only Mary herself that could provide the life giving milk to the three babes. The small woman had become noticeably more tired and drained looking in the last week or so. She was already quite different than the lively little woman that he had seen dance with such spirit on the first night of their voyage.

Watching her with growing desperation, James had begun to try adding the hard biscuit they all ate to the twins' diet in addition to their nursing. He tried to feed it to them crushed at first, and then dampened with water, each with varying success. After a few days, he found that the hard version seemed most appealing to them. Taking as long as it did for them to chew, it served as some entertainment for the teething babes, as well.

It wasn't nearly as appealing to the adults in that form. After it was dampened by their gnawing, the long strings of biscuit filled drool dripped constantly from the babes' mouths and onto their caregivers. The McDonalds and most of their surrounding neighbors and new friends were dirty, stained, and rumpled already, but the biscuit drool added yet another layer of crusted filth and misery. Alex's, William's, and Alasdair's biscuits had left their mark everywhere, as the babes were passed around daily to the nearest available pair of hands.

The biscuit drool had been nicknamed "the crud" by those who wore it. George was covered in the crusty muck himself, from Hector chewing the biscuits. The half-chewed crud that dripped from little mouths and fists had become as much a way of life below, as had the necessary chamber pots that had the nasty habit of overturning during the larger sea swells. He ran his hands through his hair and found a tangled mess. He patted his growing beard, feeling crusted over whorls and wild tufts everywhere there too. He glanced down at his once snowy white sark and saw that it had become a stained, smelly and thoroughly disreputable rag.

A passing sailor gave him a critical once over with one thick eyebrow raised in amusement, then chuckled to himself as he went about his duties. George glared at the man and continued to glare at his sweat stained back as he went about his work. To be mocked by one of these greasy sailors, George knew he must really be a fright to look at. He realized there was nothing to be done about it in any case and sighed as he returned to his pacing. There was barely enough water on the ship to last the voyage, and the daily rations were barely enough to keep everyone aboard from dying of thirst, let alone enough to wash with.

A sudden thought struck him. The women had devised a clever method of washing the bairns' dirty clouts and some of their dirtier clothing. They tied them securely around the middle with heavy string, threw them over the rail, and then dragged them through the churning seawater alongside the Hector. After being wrung out and then returned to the sea a few times, the garments were mostly clean. Older children were then employed to help take turns standing on deck and holding the wet, flapping garments over their head to dry them in the breeze.

Captain Spiers became irritated with the laundry business early on and had ordered that only a few of the passengers be allowed on deck for this laundry "nonsense" at any given time. The rest of the clouts and clothing that could not be dried above, had to be hung to dry on make-shift lines that were strung all over the hold from the beams below decks. With the humidity and stagnant air below, nothing ever seemed to dry completely. This added dampness and the occasional drips from above, had not improved the swamp like atmosphere, or the hot and heavy tempers of the cramped passengers. The very air in the hold was now pregnant and uncomfortable spurring arguments from the most minor annoyances. Small squabbles and even outright fistfights had become a daily issue also.

George had wisely trained his little Hector to piss into a pot a month before sailing from Greenock, and had no clouts to worry about. But his own sark desperately needed a wash and he had no wish to impose on one of the women to wash his clothes for him. Purposefully, he marched to the rail and peeled the filthy sark off of his upper torso with distaste. He fished around in the sporran that he always wore at his waist, deciding he would use the women's method and just wash the filthy thing himself. Finding a good length of string inside, among a jumble of other objects and coins, he tied his sark around the middle with it. Wrapping the other end of string securely around his palm, he dangled the sark over the railing and down into the ship's wake. It took more strength than he would have thought to keep a hold on the wet garment as it twirled in the ship's wake. He was amazed that women and children had been performing this task and his respect for the women grew.

After a few minutes, he raised the wet sark back out of the water and up over the rail. He used the wet sark to scrub vigorously at his face, hair, armpits, and beard. Then he lowered the sark back into the water and let it swish through the passing waves for a few more minutes. After he retrieved it a final time, he squeezed out the excess water and held it out past the railing. It snapped briskly in the passing breeze, echoing the sound of the sails snapping above his head.

While George stood bare-chested, holding his sark to dry in the wind, James climbed out of the hold, blinking blindly, like a mole in the unaccustomed brightness. "Over here, man!" George called to him.

James turned toward the voice and shaded his brow from the glare, until he spotted George by the opposite rail. Once he saw him, he walked slowly over, gingerly shaking out his cramped arms and legs as he came.

"What's amiss then?" George asked nervously.

"Achhh, 'tis naught amiss, I just wished to join ya in your breather, now tha' the twins be both asleep," James answered. "Your Hector is still sleeping too," he added.

Relieved that he need not go below just yet, George relaxed and smiled. Returning his attention to the drying of his sark, George again breathed deeply of the fresh ocean air. James leaned out over the rail upwind of him, breathing audibly in appreciation, allowing a fine spray off the sea to hit his face when they crested a wave. George moved slightly behind him to take advantage of James body to block the sea mists from re-wetting his drying sark. They were making good speed in strong winds, and the ship danced up and down the moderate swells. There wasn't a cloud in the massive stretch of sky and the sun and wind burned on George's shoulders, pleasantly evaporating the slick of moisture from his skin as well.

The peaceful moment was cut short when a strong gust of wind hit the Hector as she mounted another wave. Startled, George grasped the rail to catch himself and momentarily lost his grip on his fluttering sark. It flapped madly out of his hands and off into the sky, twisting and reaching past them in the wind like some strange sea bird, to fly quickly out of sight behind them. He dashed toward the stern chasing it and up onto the rear deck just in time to see it smack into the swells behind the ship and quickly sink from the surface, swallowed whole by the sea.

"Blast it ta hell!" George cursed, as he slammed his palms into the rear railing. "And me best sark too!"

James had run behind him and now he joined George at the rail. "I'm thinking tha' sounds as if ya own another and tha' is good news," he answered, patting him on the back sympathetically.

"Oh, aye, I do." George answered with a sigh. "But 'tis a work sark, and worn thin for all tha'. The one sinking in yonder waves was the last of the fine shirts my wife had sewn for me. I guess I should ha' kept it packed away, but her hands had touched it last and so I've been wearing it since Greenock; for good luck, I guess," he added, with a ghost of a grin. He slapped the rails again in disgust. "Bloody hell!" he cried.

James squeezed his shoulder awhile and then let his hand drop. "It's sorry I am that you lost it then, man," thinking of the loss of loving deeds from his deceased wife, more than the more immediate loss of the sark. George had not spoken of his dead wife since he had boarded the Hector. Even then, all he had mentioned was that her name was Rose and that she had died that winter past.

George stood at the stern rail, clutching it so tight that his big knuckles gleamed white in the sun, as he stared blindly at the ship's wake. Tears quivered at the edges of his eyelids, ready to overflow. James glanced around them, but the only person near enough to hear was the cabin boy, Nate, whose slim back was to them as he swabbed the upper deck. The first mate, Dewey, was at the Hector's wheel and likely out of earshot in the wind. James leaned on the rail beside George and waited patiently for him to gather the words that he sensed he was trying to form.

"Ah, James, A charaid," he finally said with a sigh. "I've said naught to ya of my beloved, my Rose." His voice cracked while speaking her name, but he took a deep breath and kept talking. "It was November, and a saft and most miserable night, it was. Rosie was due to bear our second bairn and the birthin' pains had started early that morn. I didna send for the midwife until she was well along, as she had delivered Hector with nay trouble and she said it wasna necessary. The thought that it may ha' helped her if I had, will haunt me to me grave." He stopped, wiped at the tears that had spilled over, collected his emotions for a minute and then continued his tale.

"She was in terrible pain by the time Dora, the midwife, got there and was writhing on the bed. Hector was upset by her screams, so I took the lad and myself off to finish a cupboard I was making for a customer. Well, before too long, Dora came oot to get me and tells me the babe was breech and she needed my help to try to turn it 'round. I couldna leave Hector alone outside, so I grabbed some wood scraps and set him in the pantry to play with them, but my thoughts were mainly for my Rosie.

She was obviously in a bad way and I smoothed her hair off of her sweating face as I moved to her side to help. Dora stood on the other side of Rosie and instructed me to push up on her belly on the bottom right, as she pushed on the top left to try to rotate the child clockwise as it lay in her belly. I can still hear her screams when I close my eyes." He stopped talking and covered his mouth for a moment, as he shuddered in private horror.

"Something shifted after a few attempts and we felt her stomach relax as something let go inside. It seemed as though we had been successful, as her pains came faster and harder then. The blood flowed from her like a river stream then and still the child didna come. Rose could no longer bear down without help so Dora straddled her and pushed on the top of her belly with each birth spasm, and I held her feet and pushed back against her. At last we could see the top of the heid. Rosie gave one more great effort as we pushed and the head finally popped free. It was an awful bluish color; not at all as it had been when Hector was born.

Dora wiped the infant's face and nose and told Rosie ta push again, but my Rose had already left us. Dora freed the bairn, but by the time my son was born he was obviously dead too. Covered in his mother's blood, we took turns rubbing the wee lad and blindly hanging him upside down. I held my Rosie trying to talk her back from the beyond. Both Dora and I sobbed, frantically trying ta get him or her ta draw a breath. Just one breath," he finished softly.

George stopped and turned his back to the sea. He looked James in the eye, his own eyes wet and red, but finally less reserved. "I lost everything but our Hector that night and I canna be sure of that either. I realized the boy was standing open mouthed behind me, his little eyes glazed over, after his mother and brother died. I pulled him to me to shield his view, but it was too late, much too late. I ha' no notion how long he was there and he hasna spoken of her since. We stayed silently in that house for a fortnight after the burial, neither of us alive in any real way. When I ventured oot with him, I saw the broadsheets about the Hector and her offer. I saw it as a sign from God that the name was the same as that of my laddie. I decided to leave that house and its sad memories behind us, before it consumed us both. I havena wanted to look back, or think on it since."

James glanced past George and saw Nate, no longer moving, just staring at George with a look of pity on his face and tears shining in his eyes. Obviously, he had heard most of their very private conversation. James cocked one eyebrow at him in mute question and glared meaningfully. Nate blushed and turned quickly away returning to his work. James glanced back at George who had followed his gaze.

"Privacy of any kind is scarce aboard this ship," George said to James, with a dismissive shrug. He wiped his eyes roughly with his bare arm, and took in a shuddering breath, the worst of his raw emotions now spent.

"It's sorry I am for your losses, A charaid. I am honored that you chose to share your story with me. But you still have a part of your wife, you know? Your boy, Hector, as you said. For my Mary and me, we left Scotland to escape the slower death of working unforgiving ground and hunting for skittish rare game, whilst the big English landowners got fat off the meat of our children and of us. We lost my brother and sister-in-law last year and the twins are now ours ta raise as we can, along with our own four. But we try ta see it as a blessing, rather than a burden. When they are older, we will have more hands to help us do the work of building new lives. And of course, on the hope that if God's will was that we are ta work ourselves ta death, it will at least be on our ain land tha' could be left to our ain children, and not some feeble English nobleman."

"Thank you, friend James. I am feeling better just for repeating the whole thing out loud, somehow, and I am grateful that it was ta you that I spoke of it. I canna put into words the thanks and blessings I feel, having a friend like you on board. Not ta mention, the help your womenfolk ha' blessed us with. I think without you all, I would go quite mad before reaching Pictou."

George tried to stifle a chill, but James sharp eyes missed nothing. He laid an arm across his friend's shoulders and suggested they go below to get George's other sark. George shuddered and then sighed and smiled at James with renewed vigor in his eyes. "Aye, things will be all right, if I don' freeze my arse off and end up wi' the ague tha' is!"

James laughed and patted him on the back and then led the way back to the dreaded ladder to the hold. He smiled to himself, thinking how much it transformed his friend George's face when he had smiled. He sent up a silent prayer that George's life could be renewed someday, when some lass saw one of those smiles and made it her mission to make them less rare.

Nate still felt the sting of his shame for listening to the men's conversation, but he also felt a new respect for these men who had done what he so wished to do himself; leave a place of unhappiness behind and forge a new life. A plan began to form in his mind as he finished his swabbing and moved on to the lower decks. Maybe their destination was a way out and maybe, just maybe, a new chance for himself. He would jump ship when the Hector sailed away from Pictou. He had several weeks to work it all out, but for the first time in a long time he began whistling as he worked, a gleam of hope shining like stars in his boyish eyes.

Jane Forbes and her mother Mary Jane were also out strolling on the deck that crimson-skied morning. Jane's mother had finally stopped being seasick and was eating a little bit and keeping it down. She was still pale and looked weak and drained, having lost a few stone in weight. Jane hoped a turn or two around the deck would do her some good. By the time they had made it three times around, Mary Jane was tired, so Jane tucked her back into her bunk with some cold tea and biscuits.

Mary Jane had told Jane to stop worrying and fussing over her, so she left her mother to sleep. Feeling restless, Jane went back out on deck alone. She found a quiet spot between two barrels and sat down on the deck idly watching the water surge by. She was soon distracted by the drama surrounding the two men chasing the shirt up to the back rail. They could not see her across the aft of the ship, but if she leaned forward, she could see them. She could also hear them as George started to cry and she felt like an awful eavesdropper. But feeling it would be more embarrassing for them all if she stood up suddenly to return to her cabin, she remained where she was. Nate was slowly swabbing the upper deck nearby, but he could not yet see her.

As she listened, she could not help herself from being pulled into George's sad story. After a time, the men left and returned to the hold below. Nate spotted her then as he drew closer. She was startled when she saw him looking and her small hand flew to her breast to slow her booming heart. But he only smiled and held a finger to his lips briefly, discreetly returning to his work as if he had not seen her.

Red-faced and feeling guilty, she found she could not contain her curiosity and began nonchalantly strolling toward the open hatch to the hold. A few sailors leered impolitely at her as she walked by, but none dared stop her. She stayed near the hold, pretending to examine her shoe and overheard a great deal of what Mary was telling James. Horrified, she was unable to break away until she saw Captain Spiers approaching. Quickly she stood and closed the distance between them, to distract his attention away from the hold for now.

"Is everything all right? He asked, frowning.

"Oh, my shoe, that is all. Silly thing came loose on me, but it is fine now." She took his offered arm in hers and kept his momentum moving away from the hold.

"Would you care to take a few turns around the deck with me?" He asked, smiling politely.

"But of course!" She answered as she smiled what she hoped was her prettiest smile. She had no wish for him to be anywhere close to the hold where he might catch wind of the dangerous secrets she knew it contained.

Standing a little straighter he nodded graciously, flattered by her attentions. He led her away to walk the deck of his ship.

Mary McDonald met the two men as they descended into the hold and merely gave George a curious look, seeing his bare torso. Anxious to talk to James, she pulled him aside immediately as George went to look for a sark. Mary told him quietly that some of the older folks and the bairns were now showing the ominous signs of bloody flux and it was spreading quickly. Everyone had become loose from the diet and the travel, but some were worsening to the vomiting and bloody diarrhea characteristic of this more serious and potentially deadly disease. Alarmed women had been quietly showing the contents of their family's chamber pots to Mary all morning, before bringing them up for emptying into the sea. After she consulted with Maggie and Janet McLeod and some of the other Ullapool women whose men were used to sea travel, they had guessed it was the beginning of the bloody flux, known to healers as dysentery.

Dysentery being a quickly spreading disease and with it still being early in the voyage, this was bad news. They had acted quickly. Families were already trying their best to cordon off the ill into the sick area that had been hastily thrown together by the women in the rear storage area. It consisted of just blankets as partitions and what extra bedding they could scratch together. Family members were taking turns trying to give water to and care for their own ill. Janet said it was best if the bloody flux folk were only given water and no food for now. It was the best they could do to try and help. They planned to keep them in the cargo area at the rear of the hold, hoping to keep the sickness contained and suspend having to notify the captain.

Stories had circulated for years of ship captains tossing ill passengers off into the sea, to keep such diseases from spreading. It made little difference if they were still alive or not. Their main concern was containing the disease and maintaining the crew to complete the voyage. Not one of them felt like testing captain Spiers view on this matter just yet. From what had been seen so far, it seemed likely he would be of a mind to subscribe to that manner of dealing with the outbreak of illness.

To make matters worse, some of the children were showing the frightening red spots with blisters atop them and the runny nose and fever that indicated the pox to anyone who had seen it before. Mary's eyes filled with tears as she recited a list of about eight children including their own Lizzie, one of their twins Alex, Maggie McLeod's small son Alex, Janet McLeod's son Finlay, George's son Hector, two of the Murray children, and Becky Patterson. All eight had developed the characteristic little red blisters.

James took her tired little frame in his arms and closed his eyes in silent prayer for the sick ones and for her, because he knew she would work tirelessly to save as many as possible no matter what he said. He told her he would be right back and went to tell George about Hector. Then they went together to see their children in the makeshift infirmary.

The pox victims were separated by only a thin blanket partition from the bloody flux victims and they spotted Lizzie's dark red hair, which looked unsettlingly like blood in the gloom. She lay sandwiched between Hector and the basket containing small Alex. A lantern was lit and hanging from a beam in the corner, and it was obvious that all three children wore the telltale spots of pox on their soft little cheeks and bare arms. Lizzie woke up and smiled at the men in a diminished version of her normal beaming face. "Hector and I are taking care of Alex until Mama comes back." She raised herself up weakly and satisfied at the sight of Alex's little sleeping face, she lay back down. "I am sa itchy, but Mama said I mustna scratch or I will scar. What does scar mean, Da?"

James smiled at her constant curiosity, even when ill. He sat down and let her rest her little head in his lap, stroking her hair as he answered. "Weel love, it means ta leave a mark that will ne'er go away. She doesna want you ta mess up your pretty wee face, aye?"

"Well, can I at least scratch my bum?" she whispered. "I doona care about scars... back there!"

James laughed out loud in spite of the circumstances. "Lizzie my girl, do as your Ma says, as I don't want ta see scars on your little bum either, the next time I have ta spank it!" He teased and tickled her which made her giggle and squirm. They smiled at each other in a loving moment and then he asked her if she was thirsty. George had already drawn a ladle of water from a nearby pail and had given a little to Hector as he talked to him and soothed him. James took the dipper and scooped up a half scoop, hoping to convince Lizzie to drink it all. She did, but had to stop and cough twice. Little Alex woke nearby and began crying right away. Lizzie groggily rocked his basket, while James went to fetch Mary to try to nurse him.

Mary came back at once and tried with limited success to get Alex to nurse a little. His little nose was so clogged that he had to stop after several gulps to breathe. Exhausted from his efforts to feed with a clogged nose, he soon fell back into a restless sleep. James noticed Mary carefully wiping her breast before pulling her shift up over it and asked her about it. "Janet McLeod told me her Granny said to wipe her bosoms with water and a few drops of clove oil after feeding a sick child, before feeding a well one to prevent the spread of sickness. I am trying it to protect William and Alasdair. Luckily, that Janet McLeod has a few medicinals such as tha' with her." She looked into his eyes and shrugged. "I thought it important ta try, tha's all."

"Aye, my love, that it is," James answered quietly. "And bless Janet for telling you so." He looked over to the basket where Janet's little Finlay lay, also sick with pox. His mother, Janet, was looking up at James. Unable to not overhear their conversation, she nodded to him gravely before looking back down at her little Finlay. She whispered loud enough for him to hear, that her father-in-law, Old Hugh, was one of the ones on the other side of the thin blanket, afflicted with bloody flux. Her head tilted toward the floor with meaning and her small hand could be seen resting in his larger rough one as it reached under the draped barrier, offering her comfort the only way that he could. Maggie sat nearby, leaning against the planks and holding her only son, Alex, who was also showing the dreaded red spots. Despair and illness had begun to creep onto the Hector, as silent and deadly as fog on a calm sea.

Above decks there was nothing calm about the sea as the crew was busy dealing with a sudden squall that had blown up. They had no time to even wonder about those below decks, all but one. As Nate slid around the wet deck taking barked orders from every direction, he wished again with all his heart to be a part of the families below. He had seen the warmth and liveliness there, despite the terrible crowding and squalid conditions. It made him realize ever more painfully what his own life lacked.

Chapter Twelve

Sickness and Death

Old Hugh, the most unlikely of all, was the first to get past his bout with the horrible bloody flux. He had been weakened, but he was undefeated. Within a few days he was even helping out with the care of the others still afflicted. He was also the first to notice the unused portions of the biscuit and water rations that were not being used by the poor souls that were sick. He began saving them, like a squirrel saving nuts for winter, knowing that every morsel and drop might be needed later.

On the last night of Hugh's illness, he had a dream of his beloved, Flora. He had heard her calling him to the upper deck of the Hector, so he rose from his sickbed and climbed the ladder to the deck. She stood facing him, a few feet away at the rail, her white wedding skirts billowing in the night breeze, like the sails above. She was young again and as beautiful as the day they had wed. He went into her arms and felt the years melt away in a moment. He felt stronger and fitter than he had in many a year and he let tears of joy run unchecked down his face. He loosened his hold on her and looked deeply into her dark eyes, filling both big hands with her long red hair, as he gently held her lovely face. "Flora? Is it really you? Am I dead then?" He choked.

"Hugh, 'tis really me, but you arena dead; you are dreaming, mo luaidh. I've come to tell you something because you wull live and you mun listen, or more wull die than are already doomed."

"Who is doomed? Please.... not our grandchildren?" He said, choking on his rising fears.

She looked out to sea, as if listening for a moment, "I canna say for sure, my Hugh, the bairns on board are in grave danger, but tha' is already done. I need you ta listen on another matter the noo. I want you ta put aside any food tha' goes uneaten, or water tha' may be wasted. Waste nothing and save all for what is coming. You mun do this straight away. I'm in the way of knowing tha' many will perish if you doona do this. Tha' is all I can tell you before I mun go."

"No, Flora, please doona go! I am sa very lonely without you," Hugh cried, holding her closer.

"And I have been lonely for you, my only. But I mun go and you know I must." She smiled sadly and then kissed him long and lovingly full on his lips. "We will be together again," she whispered, "but later, mo luaidh. No mere ocean shall keep us apart. I will wait for you until the end of time, my love, until the end of time." She disappeared like smoke in his arms, but he heard her say from far away, "Remember, my love, remember when ya wake."

Hugh opened his eyes an instant later and was still on his pallet in the sickroom and not on deck after all. He could still feel the touch of her skin and smell her hair on his hands. It had been many years since he had woken up hard and wanting her, but he was now. He kept his hands to his face as he softly began to sob in the early light. He lay there until all traces of her smells were gone and the fever of wanting her had passed, then he sat up and wiped at his face. His innards still felt empty and bruised and he was sweating, but he could feel the worst of the illness had past. Hugh vowed before he rose from his pallet, that he would not forget a single word that Flora had given him as her loving gift, anymore than he could forget that last sweet kiss before she had vanished.

But for now it was time for the living, and to see what might be done for them as best he could, especially the little ones.

After several days, the bloody flux took its first victim, a girl named Janet Fraser, aged eleven-years-old. When her mother tried to rouse her for some weak tea that morning, she saw that the poor girl had passed in the night. Janet's mother's grieving wails woke the hold and her husband jumped up in a panic clambering clumsily over people to get to her and silence her keening cries.

Old Hugh had been right nearby giving water to Old Archibald Chisholm, as he seemed to be recovering also and quickly went to Janet's mother's side. "Jean Fraser, isn't it Missus?" He asked the wailing woman.

She looked up at Hugh with some confusion in her eyes, but nodded and quieted down as her husband arrived at her side to place a comforting hand on her shoulder. "I am Jean Fraser, aye, but I doona believe I know you?"

"I am Hugh McLeod, Mistress," he said with a polite bow. "I just thought ya might need some assistance." He looked up at the man at her shoulder, whose eyes were shining with wetness, staring down at their once beautiful child, who now lay motionless and curled up from the pain. Her motionless body stained with vomit, blood and filth.

The man closed his eyes briefly and then opened them on Hugh. "Thank you sir, we will be glad of the help. My name is Kenneth Fraser. My wife should tend our son William here, whilst you and I take care of Janet." His voice cracked when he said his dead daughter's name out loud.

Hugh glanced over a few feet to a boy of about thirteen who resembled his sister and his parents, but lay sleeping and whey faced. Hugh could not stop himself from watching until he saw the lad's chest rise and fall in breath, and then he drew an uneasy breath.

"No!" Jean shouted suddenly, startling them all. "I will gather some of the women folk and we wull prepare her for a proper Christian burial! She is a maid and no man's eyes or his hands should see or touch her or do such work. I willna have it!"

"Aye, that is fine, that is best." Hugh said immediately, soothing the alarmed woman. "I will fetch some of my 'ain womenfolk straightaway, whilst I speak ta your husband."

Jean barely nodded as her tearful gaze remained fixed on her daughter while the two men walked out of the partition together. Hugh stopped to tell Elspeth to quietly fetch her mother and auntie and have them see to Jean and Janet Fraser. Then they walked over to the ladder and began quietly climbing up.

"What's amiss then?" Hugh jumped as the quiet voice spoke out of the gloom, just over his left shoulder. Hugh peered into the gloom, as a face appeared next to the ladder. He recognized James McDonald. He had noticed how others trusted him and went to him with their problems, so he motioned quietly for him to follow as well. It was a gray somber morning with the storm from the night before having tired itself out until only a light mist fell out of the sky. The somber gray waters were nearly indistinguishable from the gloomy gray of the cloudy skies above them.

The ship was barely making way, as they climbed out of the hold and walked quietly over to the rail.

Old Hugh looked around to be sure they were alone then cleared his throat and began to speak quietly, as the three heads leaned together. "It's sorry I am for your loss man. My women will help your Jean with your Janet and prepare her for burial, sa doona worrit there. What I wanted ta talk ta you aboot is the burial. We darena tell the Captain yet, aye? Lest we risk all the sick being thrown overboard, before some can get well! And bein' at sea, why we canna do anything but a burial at sea for the pur' lass." Hugh waited a few moments letting what he said sink in, hoping that Kenneth Fraser would come to see it as the best answer on his own, so it would be easier to bear.

Kenneth stared out to sea for a long time and then his head dropped in defeat and he sighed. "I understand what ya mean, man. The best we can do is ta put the pur lassie's body owerboard under cover of night, so's we can mebbe avoid anyone's notice." Tears spilled over and down the man's cheeks and he closed his eyes and gripped the rail tighter.

"I think we mun do tha', aye," said Old Hugh. "But I think we can do it one better and have a quiet service and a poetic benediction if you will, before her burial at sea. Do ya think your wife will be able ta bear it ta be done in such a manner? She mun realize we canna hide her body on board 'til we reach land for a proper burial. Many would die as a result of trying it."

"Aye, she willna wish ta risk our lad." He looked to the skies and pleaded tearfully, "Dear God, help us! We will both have ta bear it. There is nay other way. My cousins, Jane Gibson and her brother Charles Fraser should be told, as we are kin."

James had stayed quiet up until now, picking up the thread of the problem from their conversation. "I think ya chose wisely and bravely Mr. Fraser. I am James McDonald. I only hope I can be as brave as you, should I lose one of my ain. You may count on my help and my discretion, and when all has been done for your daughter I will help bear her body ta the sea." He patted this new man on the back feeling an instant kinship, with his own family also in such similar peril.

"Well I had thought my bairns old enough not ta fear the crossing owermuch, ya ken?" He looked at both men and said, "What a bloody fool I was."

A sailor approached from the rear, so all three men nodded to him, pretending to have just been out on deck for air. Quickly they made ready to go back into the hold and climbed back down. When they got to the bottom, they were met by a curious Ian, Sgian and Katy, who had been wakened by their comings and goings. James stopped and quickly whispered a shortened version of what was happening and asked them to stay put for now. He would go alone to talk to Mary, who was in with the pox-ridden children.

Kenneth headed toward the other side of the blanket partition, stepping over still sleeping bodies, his head hanging dejectedly with the knowledge of what he would have to tell his Jean. He prayed that she would be reasonable.

Old Hugh hovered near the ladder for a moment before descending, enjoying a few last breaths of briny air. In silence, he watched the seabirds dive into the sea for fish and then dance into the air with their prize, while others wheeled overhead chasing them through the masts screaming for their share. Then he wiped his sleeve across his face and prepared himself to go see to the babes with the pox, since their mothers would be busy helping Jean with her Janet. James was filling his teary wife in on the details and Hugh looked away when she saw him watching. He turned from her in shame, as if her tears were his very own fault.

In the gloom, he could see wee Alex and little Finlay as they lay near the McDonald bairns in their baskets. A pockmarked, but industrious wee red-headed little mite of about four or five-years-old seemed to be in charge of the brood and was taking turns softly swaying each of the three baskets in turn. An old soldier himself, he recognized a General when he saw one and this little fireball was just that. A blonde boy who was even younger was taking orders from the redheaded girl, but scowling ferociously at her as he did so.

She, in her turn, would glare right back with a look on her face to curdle milk, and say "Hector!" pointing and stamping her tiny foot, scowling until he obeyed. Hugh watched this in amusement for a few blessed moments, thinking how much she reminded him of his granddaughter, Elspeth, as she had been just a few years ago. Then he went over to relieve the little girl, before she and Hector came to blows.

"Weel now, you seem to be doing just fine here lassie, but I must properly introduce myself, before I take ower these wee laddies from ya. I am Old Hugh McLeod, and these two laddies are me grandsons, Alexander," he said touching one basket, "and Finlay," he said touching the older toddler.

"Pleased ta meet ya, sir," Lizzie answered. "I am Elizabeth Mary McDonald," she said precociously, "but you can call me Lizzie; everybody does. I already ken the bairns too. We've all been in here such a long time." She yawned and sat down, trying her best not to think of scratching and unconsciously squirming because of it. "My little brother is named Alex too. He has a twin!" She exclaimed, with an expectant look that begged a reaction from him.

"Oh my," Hugh exclaimed. "I see! So, he has a brother tha' is the same as him? Same age and all, I mean."

"Aye," Lizzie nodded knowingly, "some people canna tells them apart, but Mama, Katy, and I always can. His twin, William, has a mark on his bum and Alex doesna! When ya change their clouts, ya can tell. Here, I'll show ya. " Before Hugh could stop her, she began to pick up the legs of little Alex to expose his bum and just then, Mary returned from speaking with her James, still wiping at her tears.

"Lizzie!" She scolded, in a quiet hiss. "If tha' child is sleeping, then leave off him! What in creation are ya aboot ta do anyway?"

"Mama, I...." She began to explain.

But, Old Hugh stepped in immediately, by standing and introducing himself with a courteous bow and a sly wink toward Lizzie. "Achh, doona be angry at the lassie. Lizzie here was just showing me how well she is taking care of my grandsons for me. And I am most appreciative o' her efforts, when the lass is obviously feelin' sa poorly herself."

Mary smiled, but she was not so easily fooled. She looked Lizzie in the eye and asked her directly, "was tha' the way of it then?"

Lizzie gulped, and so did Old Hugh, recognizing the superior officer of a higher rank. "Weel Mama, I was doin' just as Old Hugh here says, when I started talking aboot the twins and their marks tha' tell them apart. I thought I might show him that little Alex doesna ha' one."

Mary's scowl quirked into an amused smile, despite herself and she turned to introduce herself to Old Hugh in order to hide it. "It is kind o' ya to help with the babes and the older folk. There are just too many sick and too many more fearful of the sickness that canna or willna help." She shook her head, wondering at those that refused to help their own.

"Are you not worrit yourself aboot getting the pox, Mistress?" Hugh asked.

"No, I had it when I was a lassie, so it's no likely I'll get it again. Now your little Finlay here looks like he may be oot of the woods the noo and his Ma says he is nursing better. But I am still worrit about your Alex," she added more seriously. "He is far too quiet and won't take anything to eat or drink, other than some weak suckling with his mother. I've my own two here, and you can see Miss Lizzie is getting better already," she smiled wryly and indicated the little girl with her head. "As for Hector, our friend George's bairn, 'tis still too early to tell, but my own wee Alex is no doin' well a'tall." She picked the child up gently and he hung listless in her arms, covered with oozing red blisters. I'm nursing three and he is no takin' his share, that canna go on much longer for either of us."

"Now we have the added burden in here of the three Murray children, two of the Ross', two of the McKenzie's, Becky Patterson, and Charles Mathewson, along with some bairns that are getting very little care," she said with a sweep of her small arm. "Their folks are all dealing with their other children too between caring for these. I know they are all frightened of a'catchin' it themselves, or their other children a catchin' it. I am frightened too, but we mun ha' more help!"

Tears filled her eyes and she quickly tried to hide them, as she sat down on the floor to try to nurse her Alex with limited success. The boy seemed listless, and seemed to have trouble swallowing with his runny nose causing frequent pauses, but he nursed a little and then after a bit of weak crying he fell right back to sleep in her arms. Mary looked up at Hugh with tears tracking down her face and then carefully laid Alex back in his basket near Lizzie, who crooned softly to him and rocked his basket gently.

Hugh picked up his own little Alex, since he knew his ma was busy with the dead girl. As his Alex started to cry Hugh began softly singing an old Scottish song. All the children's eyes were soon on him as he sang, gently rocking the wee babe in his arms, letting the seas help him along. He sat down by little Finlay and laid a hand on him too as he sang. He sang very softly at first, just so those nearest him could hear.

"Hi! says the blackbird, a sittin' on a chair,
Once I courted a lady fair;
She proved fickle and turned her back,
and ever since then I be dressed in black.

Hi! says the blue-jay as she flew,
If I was a young man I'd have two;
If one proved fickle and chanced for to go,
I'd have a new string for my bow.

Hi! says the little leather winged bat,
I will tell you the reason that,
The reason that I fly in the night,
is because I lost my heart's delight.

Hi! says the little mourning dove,
I'll tell you how to gain her love;
Court her night and court her day,
ne'er give her time to say, oh nay."

Mary smiled at him, and pulled little Lizzie and Hector onto her lap as she sat. Many of the other children in the room were paying closer attention. Hugh noticed that some even tried weakly to sit up and move closer, so he began to sing a little louder.

"Hi! says the woodpecker sittin' on a fence,
once I courted a handsome wench;
She proved fickle and from me fled,
and ever since then my head's been red.

Hi! says the owl with eyes so big,
if I had a hen I would feed like a pig;
But here I sit on my frozen stake,
which causes my poor heart to ache.

Hi! says the swallow, sittin' in a barn,
courting, I think, is no harm.
I pick my wings and sit up straight
and hope every young man will choose him a mate.

Hi! says the hawk unto the crow,
if you ain't black than I doona know,
Ever since old Adam was born,
you been accused of stealin' corn!

Hi! says the crow unto the hawk,
I understand your great big talk;
You'd like to pounce and catch a hen,
but I hope the farmer will shoot you then!

Hi! says the robin, with a little squirm,
I wish I had a great big worm;
I would fly away into my nest;
I have a wife and I think tha's best!"

Mary and the children laughed and begged old Hugh for more. Mary looked around feeling her despair lift a little, to see so many of the sick children smiling or sitting up. She joined in the chorus of "More, more," and Old Hugh gave in easily.

"Weel," he said closing one eye and scratching his head as he thought. "Do any of ya ken Aiken Drum? I need help wi' tha' one ya see." He put the sleeping Alex in his basket and pulled little Finlay onto his lap, since he was now wide-awake.

"Oh! I do, I do," chimed in a half dozen voices.

"Weel all right then... unless you'd rather hear another one?" He teased.

"Aiken Drum! Aiken Drum!" The children confirmed. Lizzie was hopping up and down on her knees, like a mad rabbit now, all thoughts of scratching gone for the moment.

Hugh cleared his throat comically for a long time, until the children giggled and then started into the song in his clear baritone.

"There once was a man lived in the moon,
lived in the moon, lived in the moon,
There was a man lived in the moon,
and his name was Aiken Drum."

Most of the older children joined him at the chorus.

"And he played upon a ladle,
a ladle, a ladle,
and he played upon a ladle,
and his name was Aiken Drum!"

Hugh picked up the tune again.

"And his hat was made of good cream cheese,
of good cream cheese, of good cream cheese,
and his hat was made of good cream cheese,
and his name was Aiken Drum."

More children joined him into the remembered chorus,

> *"And he played upon a ladle,*
> *a ladle, a ladle,*
> *and he played upon a ladle,*
> *and his name was Aiken Drum!"*

Hugh began again.

> *"And his coat was made of good roast beef,*
> *of good roast beef, of good roast beef,*
> *and his coat was made of good roast beef,*
> *and his name was Aiken Drum.*

Now even the littler children knew the chorus and they all chimed in, Lizzie even dancing around as she chanted along with everyone.

> *"And he played upon a ladle,*
> *a ladle, a ladle,*
> *and he played upon a ladle,*
> *and his name was Aiken Drum!"*

> *"And his buttons made of penny loaves,*
> *of penny loaves, of penny loaves,*
> *and his buttons made of penny loaves,*
> *and his name was Aiken Drum."*

The bairns joyfully joined in with their chorus again.

> *"And he played upon a ladle,*
> *a ladle, a ladle,*
> *and he played upon a ladle,*
> *and his name was Aiken Drum!"*

Hugh finished the last verse with a funny face and kept glancing down at his own bare legs sticking out from under his kilt and shaking his head, making everyone laugh.

"And his breeches were made of haggis bags,
of haggis bags, of haggis bags,
and his breeches were made of haggis bags,"

he paused for a moment holding the last note, and everyone chimed in,
"And.... his name was Aiken Drum!"

The children repeated the chorus one more time with great spirit and then the ones nearby begged for more, but Old Hugh had to put them off for later, worried as he was about the doings in the next room and the burial to be planned. He set little Finlay down by Mary and promised her that he would be back very soon and bring more lasses with him to help. He promised the children that he would sing with them all later, if they all drank their water, tried some biscuit and obeyed Mary.

He stepped out of the blanket partition and went to the one next door. Not knowing what to do, he cleared his throat, and then said, "It is Old Hugh, is all well that I can come in the noo?"

His daughter-in-law, Janet, parted the curtain and whispered that they were finished. She and Maggie, the dead girl's ma, and the other women who had helped, were busy wiping and cleaning their hands and arms with a cloth. Hugh recognized by odor, his Janet's precious clove oil and some of his precious whiskey. His daughter-in-law was a fine herb woman and had some knowledge as a healer. She had served as midwife on several successful births back home. Hugh told Janet that she and Maggie were both needed next door with their bairns and they left right away. Another clanswoman nodded politely to him and then left. Only Kenneth, Jean, and their son were there now; other than the sad cloth bound bundle that lay before them. His own son, Davy, came in behind him, along with James and Mary McDonald. They all waited respectfully until the grieving couple was ready to acknowledge them.

Their other child, William, was awake now and sat grieving with his parents over his sister's wrapped body. Finally Kenneth Fraser turned to face them, his eyes red, but now swollen and dry. He thanked them for all their help as he had thanked the women when they had left. "I am afraid I doona ken a priest on board, and the captain usually presides over such matters. I am at a loss what ta do?" His wife Jean began to cry harder again and he reached back to put a comforting hand on her shoulder. Kenneth looked around helplessly at the rest of his kin that had gathered near the partition, who merely questioned each other's faces silently.

Old Hugh coughed nervously and then spoke up. "I am no preacher, but being an old soldier, I have been present at many unusual burials and forced goodbyes. It says in the Good Book tha' anyone can act as the Lord's servant, if the need arises. Since I am one of the elder members of the passengers, I would be honored if you would allow me ta act in place of a priest and lead us in prayer and give the poetic benediction."

Kenneth and Jean Fraser looked into each other's eyes for a moment and then she nodded. Kenneth raised his face to Hugh again and said, "Yes, sir, that'll do just fine."

Hugh cleared his throat and pulled his tattered Bible from inside his coat. He went to the Frasers and knelt by their side near the wrapped head of young Janet. He opened his Bible to the letters of Saint Paul, 1 Thessalonians 4:13 and began to read:

"But we do not want you to be uninformed, brothers, about those who have fallen asleep, so that you may not grieve as others do who have no hope. For since we believe that Jesus died and rose again, even so, through Jesus, God will bring with him those who have died. For this we declare to you by the word of the Lord, that we who are alive, who are left until the coming of the Lord, will by no means precede those who have died. For the Lord himself, with a cry of command, with the archangel's call and with the sound of the trumpet, will descend from heaven, and the dead in Christ will rise first. Then we who are alive, who are left, will be caught up in the clouds together with them to meet the Lord in the air; and so we will be with the Lord forever. Therefore, encourage one another with these words." Hugh stopped for a moment and wiped at his own eyes, then he placed one hand upon the dead girl and made the sign of the cross over her.

He spoke in Latin, "Janet Fraser, May the Lord bless thee and keep thee, may the Lord cause his light to shine upon thee, may the Lord lift up his countenance upon thee and grant you peace." He finished the poetic benediction, by reciting it again in their native Gaelic tongue after the Latin and then a third time in English. All was quiet other than some soft weeping from Janet's parents, her brother William and their kin.

"Tonight we will do the burial." He addressed them all. "Wait for my signal. It will be you and I," he said squeezing Kenneth's shoulder, "and James here, and my son Davy who will help with the burial. Mistress Fraser," he said, addressing Jean, "I hope tha' you find we have done right by your dearly departed daughter and tha' you may find your peace in it."

She slowly raised her head to meet his eyes with her own tearful ones. "I thank you from the bottom of me heart, Hugh McLeod, for all you ha' done for us and for our dear Janet. I ken she is with our Lord now and is delivered safe into his arms. All else matters naught ta me after this moment. We will go on, because we must." She smiled weakly at her son and husband beside her, and their kin standing near the doorway. "Her soul is at peace the noo, whether she is in land or sea and I ken we will be reunited someday; thank you for reminding me of tha' and more."

Hugh lifted her hand and impulsively kissed it. His own tears fell on the back of her hand as he let go and they lay glistening on the back of her small hand in the gloom, tracking across the dirt there. "Milady," he choked, and left them all as quickly as he could.

Everyone but the Frasers left. The very pregnant Jane Gibson had dared not stay and risk disease herself, so she left immediately, after having hovered nervously near the partition during the small service. The others all went back to tending their own ill, feeling an odd mixture of hope and fear, as a result of the spiritually uplifting service. The harsh reality of all the ill that were still lying in their makeshift sickrooms forced everyone to turn their thoughts again toward the living.

Hugh went back into the poxed area and searched for his kin in the gloom. Mary McDonald was with her bairns and trying again to nurse her little Alex. James was nearby with Lizzie and Hector, amusing them with a story. These two seemed to Old Hugh to be getting better, but then he reminded himself that you could never be sure with the pox.

His own daughter-in-laws were also trying to nurse their bairns and Janet seemed to be having success with Finlay, as he was noisily drinking. Maggie however, was cajoling and trying as best she could, but wee Alex just kept weakly turning his head away. Hugh's son, Davy, had come back to them and he sat next to her. Hugh dropped his old frame down next to Davy clumsily because of his leg. "How is wee Alex doin', lad?"

Davy looked briefly at his pale son covered in angry red spots, which were obvious even in this dim light, and then back at his father. "Not well a'tall, Father. Not verra well a'tall," he answered softly. "He hasna nursed now since yesterday either and he seems verra weak. Maggie even tried some goat's milk from Ana soaked into a rag and he wouldna suckle it. I want to stay with Maggie and the babe tonight, but you can call on me when 'tis time for the other matter." There were too many other little ears lying nearby to speak of what had happened that day and what would have to happen that night.

Old Hugh nodded and sat resting for a while, looking around at the little ones and the sick older children too. He wondered how many, and if any, would survive with so much of the voyage still ahead. Some of the women, who were caring for their children, now bore the angry red spots as well, although the children were by far the sickest. He closed his eyes in silent prayer. Please Lord, watch over us and doona take any more of these fine lads and lasses, if it be your will. Amen. His head lolled and he fell into an uneasy sleep where he sat near his children and grandchildren.

He woke from his nap a while later, to a small commotion next to him and nearby weeping. He also had the vague sense of having just been with his Flora again. He shook his head to clear it, only to find his Davy on his knees next to a prostrate and sobbing Maggie who was cradling their little Alex as he limply lay on the boards in his wrappings. Like hearing an evil echo, he turned his head toward more weeping, and this time it was Mary and James crying over their wee Alex. Mary was upright but curled over the babe's wee body and rocking back and forth as she wept. James glanced up at Hugh, saw him looking, and shook his head. Two babes had not made it through this already accursed day.

As quickly as he could, Hugh slid over to Davy and Maggie's side and whispered to his son. Davy slowly shook his head as tears dropped down on his wife and the child she held close as she lay. "We have lost a McLeod this day, Father." Then he broke down completely, lying over both his sobbing shaking woman and their dead son, weeping loudly. Old Hugh looked over at Janet, who was just putting a pink faced Finlay in his basket. Catching his eye, she quickly slid closer to the group and put Maggie's head on her lap, stroking her hair softly, as she also silently wept for her precious little nephew. Old Hugh placed his large gnarled hand on his son, his own tears already tracking a ragged course down his chiseled face.

Over in the McDonald's group, James was trying to comfort his Mary, and little Lizzie was holding Hector's hand and crying also. "Poor, poor Alex!" Hugh heard her say several times, knowing it was for her own Alex, but feeling it was partly for theirs too. They all wept as quietly as they could, realization creeping in, that they should alarm as few people as possible. Death and panic were sailing among them now. People nearby were already taking notice and holding their own sick children closer, crying and praying silently in an age old plea for this plague to pass them over.

After a while, Hugh shakily stood, and went over to the McDonalds and offered his condolences about losing their Alex, as he also told them of their own Alex's passing. He looked deep into James eyes to see what strength was there, and satisfied with what he saw, he quietly told them they would handle these babes in the same fashion they had the girl this morning and all three would be buried tonight at sea.

James nodded and drew a shaky breath to calm himself, then turned to address the people in the sickroom. "Today we have lost some of our children, but many more remain. We must keep our wits and our silence for now, lest the remaining sick become victims of the captain's wrath and are given ower to the sea. 'Tis common for a captain ta order the sick thrown overboard before the entire ship is taken with the pox and canna make port. We are hoping ta avoid this, by keeping our silence. Join with us now in this pact ta save our remaining bairns." Many gasped and fear-stricken women clutched their children even tighter in mounting horror.

James quickly spoke again, "We'll conduct ourselves in as civilized a manner as possible and nurse as many back to health as we can. But there is only one way ta honor our dead and keep our remaining wee ones safe. We must have secret services, which Hugh McLeod here is prepared ta do in place of a priest," He glanced at Hugh, who nodded solemnly. "We must have the burials at sea. There is no other way ta protect the remaining sick, keep panic from the other passengers, keep it from the captain and still give peace ta our bairns."

His strong voice wavered on that last word and he took a moment to collect himself. "Maybe the pipers can play some farewell tunes tonight, as our caithris. May God be with us all as we struggle through this together. If any of you should need help in any manner, please speak quietly to either Hugh McLeod here, or myself, James McDonald." He bowed slightly to the now quiet group and turned back to Hugh, whispering, "Can you do this for the dead? Or is it too much to bear, bein' you've lost your own grandson this day?"

"I can and I wull," Hugh answered steadfastly. "I am no priest, but if I can give some comfort ta the families of the departed, then tha' is what I mun do. Maybe tha' is the reason why the good Lord has seen fit ta keep me on this earth sa long." His pain etched face betrayed his thoughts; that it had already been too long and he had seen much more death than a person should.

He bent down to caress Mary's shoulder as a father would and she looked up at him tearful, but clear-eyed. "Thank you, and may God bless you and yours for what you are doing."

She pulled the sobbing Lizzie into a one armed hug, trying to shush her and said to her, "Wee Alex is with God now, and God takes good care of his own, old or young. But God has left the care of the living ta us now, hasn't he?" Mary lifted Lizzie's little chin to look into her eyes. Lizzie nodded, tears still running down her marked, but healing face. "I want you ta keep special watch over Hector for us, as we get little Alex ready for God. Do you suppose you can do tha' for me, lassie?"

"Is it my fault Mama?" Lizzie burst out. "I tried ta watch him, Mama, I tried sa hard!"

"Oh no, my girl," Mary said, pulling her into her embrace, "you've done well! You have done sa well. He was just too sick and it was just his time and tha' is all. I couldna stop it either. The pox was just too much for his wee body."

Lizzie nodded and wiped her eyes with a strength usually reserved for one much older than she. After laying her small hand on Alex for a moment, she took a deep shuddering breath and then grabbed Hector by the hand. They went over in the corner to play with some blocks that George Morrison had cleverly fashioned for them, from an old scrap board he had found in the hold.

James went out to get George who was again up on deck taking a breather, before having to take care of Hector again. He motioned for Ian to follow. Once alone on deck, he told them quickly and quietly of the deteriorating situation below decks. They would be needed tonight also, since now they were now sneaking three bodies up to the sea for burial, not just one.

Sgian, sensing there was trouble, had snuck up the ladder behind his father and overheard all that was said. When James turned to go below, he saw his pale shocked face as he stood listening on the upper slats of the ladder. He quickly went to him and grabbed him by the shoulders before he fell, and ushered him back down into the hold with George and Ian right on his heels. "How much did ya hear, laddie?"

"Enough, Da, more than enough." Tears began to spill down his cheeks and he wiped at them angrily and glanced around with some embarrassment. "Poor wee Alex!"

James patted him on the shoulder and pulled him into a brief hug, which Sgian broke first. "I think we shall need the help of the cabin boy, my friend, Nate," he said, manfully trying to get past the raw emotion, but looking none in the eye. "He can make sure we arena seen this night and he is friendly with the fellow that mans the crow's nest at early eve."

James glanced up at Ian and he nodded, but he had to ask anyway. "Are you sure ya can trust this lad, son? It is a matter of great importance that the captain not find us out."

Sgian looked him in the eye and stood taller, wiping manfully at the last of his tears and said, "Yes, Father. I would trust him with my life."

James glanced up at the trap to the hold and the steadily lowering sun and then back to his son. "All right then, go you and fetch him. Quick and quiet mind you, and tell him we need the bow area clear of all eyes and ears just after dark ta do the burials. Hurry now!"

Sgian stopped at the ladder. "I would like Willie McLeod ta come wit' me, Da."

James turned and motioned to Willie who was watching them intently, a little ways away. He quickly scrambled over people to be next to them. "Go with Sgian, lad. He will explain all, when you find Nate." The boys rushed up the ladder together and disappeared from their sight. James stopped to talk briefly with Katy, who was alone right now with Alasdair and Alex's twin, William. Both babes seemed fine and were sleeping, but she kept rocking them anyway. Tears rolled from her dark eyes as she stared straight at her father. She knew by his face what he was likely to say. One of her siblings had died and she was afraid to hear it.

James did not want to leave Katy alone, but his Mary needed him and so did the others. Much needed to be done before nightfall. He quickly told her of what had happened, and reassured her that she was a huge help with her little brothers right now. He kissed Katy's cheek tenderly and ran a hand across her dark head, hoping that she and the babes would find comfort in each other.

Maggie had already begun washing down their Alex. She and Davy hugged him and said tearful goodbyes. Both of them stared for a long time at his beautiful little face that was such a perfect blending of their own. Davy reached out finally and gently closed his little green eyes forever and began to sob harder. Then Maggie quietly wrapped him in the blanket she had made for him before he was born and paused to kiss his forehead, before covering his little face. She did not utter a word during the entire process, not even to her husband, Davy. They both sat huddled together grieving, hugging as a little family for the very last time.

Hugh stood nearby waiting with Janet, her father Robert and Finlay as they all grieved for the little boy. He knew time was short, but he had no wish to hurry any of them as they mourned. It was difficult enough to say their goodbyes.

When James returned, he and Mary went through the same heart wrenching process and prepared their little Alex in the same manner. Ian and George tried to help in any way they could. Ian stood by his sister Mary's side, stroking her dark hair softly, while she cleaned poor little Alex in her lap. George played with Lizzie and Hector to distract them. James sat in front of Mary and quietly asked for her and his good-sister Ann and his brother, William's, forgiveness. He had never felt more of a failure as he did right now, looking at the small ruined little boy that they had taken as their own on a deathbed promise. He wept openly, no longer able to keep his tears at bay.

Mary shushed him and tried to smile shakily at him, through her tears. "We've done our best, and there is no better than that, my love. Ann and William ken that. And wee William is fine. If he hasna gotten sick by now, he willna." Other nearby parents with sick children politely turned their backs to give the grieving their privacy, but also held their own children even closer, praying silently that they would be spared.

After washing the babe and swaddling him in clean wrappings, they each kissed the head of the baby and wrapped his face. James knelt, head bowed, for a few more moments and then his head came slowly up, finally able to face his wife and meet her heartsick gaze.

Sgian hissed from the other side of the ratty blanket partition and James quickly stood and went over to hear him say that all would be ready above. James told the boys to go and get their sisters, and to leave the babes in the care of their neighbors, Jane Gibson and Charles Fraser. Robert, Janet's father, overheard this and offered to watch all the babes and goats while the funerals were conducted in the sickroom. James and Mary nodded gratefully, unable to speak.

Elspeth and Katy were at the door quickly with the boys. They were told to stay near the blanket at a little distance, to protect them as much as could be from the sickness that was an unwelcome guest among them. James nodded to Old Hugh and he stepped out of the shadows and began the prayers and then finished with the poetic benediction over each little body, just as he had with Janet Fraser. The girls returned tearfully to the well babies and the goats, and the boys and men made ready to carry the bodies up on deck.

Sgian stuck his head out of the hold and saw Nate's shadow nearby. With the hand signals they had quickly worked out earlier, Sgian opened and closed his fist. Nate responded with the same signal to say that all was ready. The five men with their sad burdens quickly climbed the ladder and stopped to adjust their eyes in the dim moonlight. Nate came to their side and then led the way. Old Hugh stood near the hold opening, his eyes squinting in the starlight to try to keep watch for movement from the stern.

The five crept towards the starboard side of the ship's bow and stopped under the forward yardarm, and behind the nets. Nate nodded again and Kenneth, George, and Ian dropped their larger body overboard, flinching at the loud splash it made as it hit the waves. Davy hesitated only a moment, then quickly stepped forward alongside James and they dropped their smaller bundles into the sea at the same time. The tiny splashes that they made seemed all the more heart wrenching for their smallness and the seeming insignificance among the vast ocean of sounds.

They all crept quickly back down the ship, following Nate, who led them without a stumble over ropes and obstacles in the dark. They stopped near the hold as Nate watched and listened. Old Hugh made a soft yawning sound, which meant it was all clear, and Nate waved them on to the hold opening where Old Hugh stood in the shadows. All of them climbed down and Nate shut the grate to the hold over them, staring grimly down at James and then he disappeared silently into the night.

Janet was standing by in the sickroom, insisting that all the parents and bearers wash their hands in her new freshly oiled rag. She had already had Mary do her breasts again, before nursing her two babes that were well, and Lizzie's little hands as well. She also told them the good news that Willie Fraser seemed to be better and could now keep down food and water, as well as Old Archibald Chisholm. With the flux clearing, only a few more sick remained in that area, and they seemed to be improving. The bad news was that three more children had come down with the pox that evening, so the newly cleared space was sorely needed for more of the sick children.

Davy left right away, to go to his Maggie who was seeking solace with her goats and young Elspeth. Ian went back to his family's place to be with the other two babes and Katy and Sgian. Kenneth also separated from them and went to comfort his wife and see to their son. No one felt much like talking.

The other men - Old Hugh, George, and James stood there looking around at all the sick, scared faces and the desperate pleading in their parents' eyes. Old Hugh wondered just how many more times they would be asked to bear the dead to the sea again. Maggie McLeod's empty place had already been filled by Abigail Murray, with her infant daughter, Margaret, and her youngest boy, Adam.

Janet McLeod with her Finlay moved over to settle in by Mary McDonald, Lizzie, and Hector, now that Maggie was gone to her grief and her goats. Hugh walked over to put a comforting hand on Abigail's head and got a weak smile from her. Then he walked over to sit the night through with Janet and Finlay.

James sat by his Mary and Lizzie and George squeezed his large frame in at the back of the group and took his Hector on his lap. All was quiet, even in the other room, as the deaths had brought fear home to them all. There was nothing else to say and nothing else to do, other than hold the ones they loved and pray for both the living and the dead to be delivered to a better place.

Nate hurried back to the rail and watched the blurry bundles in the water until they disappeared. Tears welled up out of his soft heart and he found himself crying for the lost children, yet frightening himself with his longing to be with them and have done with his fate. As he reached the stern, before it rose to the rear deck, he saw the fairy lights and smiled through his tears. Maybe the fairies would let these unlucky little ones live under the sea, in the paradises he often imagined there? It made him feel a little better to see the lights on this night and at this place and it gave him some comfort. He wondered if he should tell Mary McDonald about it. He had been wishing for an excuse to see her fair face, during these last dark days, and he thought she would somehow understand how he felt about the fairy lights and the dead children.

Up near the cabins, on the stern deck, Jane Forbes intercepted Nate. She had been waiting in the shadows after watching the goings on, and now she pulled him urgently back down onto the main deck away from any listening ears.

"So, it's true? We've great illness below?" She whispered, but stared at him openly, demanding an answer. She pulled her cloak tighter around her as the fear of the truth she had seen for herself, turned her bones to ice.

Nate didn't say anything at first and spent a long time looking around for anyone about. Then trusting his gut, he told her quickly of the sad doings that night and of the many sick below.

"I watched the men come up with the small bundles and drop them into the sea." She choked, beginning to cry. "They were the children, weren't they?"

"Yes'm, they were. But you canna tell the captain!" Nate pleaded, in a whisper. "There is great danger that he would throw the living sick overboard. I have seen it done before ta protect the ship and its passengers!"

Jane clapped her hand over her mouth in horror. Such an atrocity had never even entered her mind. "Don't worry, Nate. I shall never tell!" She walked to the rail to catch her breath and clutched it for a moment digging in her nails. Her guts rolled with the revulsion she felt for this Captain Spiers. "I may wish to know more from time to time and I want to be of help, so please be honest with me always. Please believe that I am your friend. If a distraction is needed, or help below, or anything at all you can count on me. Please let me know straight away!"

Surprised, Nate took her by the hand and looked into her pretty eyes rimmed with her unshed tears and earnestly told her, "I will, Miss, I promise." He knew this young lady meant every word and he was glad of her help and sympathy.

Below them, the pipers were playing soft laments on their pipes. No words were said to give away the happenings below, but the notes still lay heavy on the hearts of all who heard them.

Chapter Thirteen

"Yea, Though I Walk Through the Valley...."

Jane and her mother, Mary Jane, were out strolling on the deck the next morning. Low gray clouds scurried past the ship as a chilly mist fell from them. "Is it just my imagination, Mother, or does it grow colder each day?"

"No, it isn't your imagination, dearie, I feel it too," Mary Jane answered, pulling her shawl tighter about her neck. "This wet dampness is worse on my bones than the worst winter at home."

"Would you like to go back to the cabin, Mother?" Jane asked, concerned.

"No, dearie, the walking helps get the creaks out. When I feel like going in, I will let you know. You needn't fuss over me anymore, really! I feel much more myself these last days," she answered crankily.

They just walked for a few more minutes in silence, and then Mary Jane spoke again. "I am sorry for being a crabby old woman, daughter. Please forgive my outburst. It is just such a misery, this ocean travel, so much more so than ever I expected! And my feelings are muddled about being such a burden to you and your new husband, now that it is about to happen."

Jane rolled her eyes skyward. She had been hearing this refrain all too often lately, and was getting quite tired of it. "Mother, we have been over this many times already. You will not be a burden, unless you keep referring to yourself as such, each and every day!" With a grunt of disgust she aimed a kick at a rat that sat near the rail and sent him sailing into the dark waters.

They walked again in silence and as the cold rain started to come down as sleet, they pulled their shawls up over their heads, but kept right on walking around the Hector's deck. Her mother again broke the silence first. "I'm sorry, Jane. I hadn't realized I was saying it out loud so often. I have had nothing else to think about as we get closer to our new home."

Jane put her arm around her mother's shoulder. "Don't you know what a comfort it is, to have you with me?" She asked her, with a kindly shake. "Why, I should be so frightened by now that I would be out of my wits, were I alone on this journey never to see you again!"

"You, frightened?" Her mother chuckled. "Why, I have never seen such bravery as I have always seen in you! Why you never even wanted to play with dolls and sew quietly in the house, like most girl children. Oh no! Not you! You were out playing with the boys and climbing trees and swimming in the duck pond and all manner of un-ladylike behavior. For which I was oft chided by your Father and Lavinia!" She added with an obviously proud smile.

"Oh, Mother. Was I really such a terrible child?" Jane asked, with a mischievous grin.

"No! I never said you were terrible, and I defended you often! I told your Father and also the prim Miss Lavinia," she sneered, "that you would turn into a fine lady one day and one with great strong spirit. And my, but you have! Now you are on your way to a husband who is a fine match and with whom you will have a secure life. I always knew it would be so, from day one."

"Ah yes," Jane laughed, "your story of how I was a smart girl even when I was a mere babe!"

"But you were! You looked straight at me when I first held you on the day of your birth. I remember thinking that your eyes were so grown-up looking! Then you looked around at your surroundings, and at all of us, almost as if you were already thinking about a future that would be better than that which you were born to."

Jane stopped to hug her mother for the gift of that story, and her mother's pride that shone brightly through it all. Though she had told and retold it hundreds of times over the years, Jane still enjoyed watching her face as she told it. As she was letting go, she noticed Nate over her mother's shoulder, near the hold again. He was speaking seriously with two of the boys who stood there, obviously nervous that no one overheard their conversation. They all warily stopped talking as soon as another sailor passed and until he was past them a good, long ways, which only confirmed her fears.

Without even thinking about it, Jane glanced around herself to make sure no sailor seemed to be noticing the boys during their work. All hands seemed to be busy with the riggings and sails and many were starting to slide around a little, so they were concentrating on the quickly icing decks, not on the boys.

Her heart jumped a little when she spied Captain Spiers near the wheelman. He was staring straight at Nate. She had heard enough of the muffled beatings going on across the hall at night to have a good idea of the true nature of Captain Spiers. He did not allow Nate to do anything but work onboard or he was beaten. He was treated more like a slave than a sailor.

She turned her Mother suddenly and made straight for the stern and Captain Spiers. "Let us go and have a word with the captain while we are out and about walking, Mother."

Startled at the quick turnabout and the even quicker pace her daughter was setting, Mary Jane merely said, "All right," and let herself be pulled along the slippery deck by her headstrong daughter.

Jane pushed her Mother up ahead of her, to catch her if a swell made her stumble on the stair, and then she pushed ahead again towing her directly toward their squinty eyed captain. "Well good day to you Captain Spiers! Don't you look dashing standing here overseeing our great ship's progress," Jane fawned, as she curtsied prettily. "Do you not agree, Mother?"

Mary Jane looked back at her daughter like she was slightly mad for a mere second and then recovering, she turned to the captain herself and dropped into an elegant curtsey. She had no idea what her daughter was up to, but she knew her well enough to go along. She took his offered hand as she rose and was grateful for his assistance in rising, with her joints creaking as she did so. "My, yes, you cut quite the handsome figure here at your helm! How do you manage the ship in such dreadful weather?" Mary Jane asked, as she took his offered arm.

The captain stood a little taller from their flattery, but answered, "Surely, such fine ladies as your selves have no wish to hear the technical details of a mariner?"

"On the contrary," Jane answered quickly. "That is, if you're not too busy, sir." She said, smiling coyly.

"But, of course not, it would be my honor to escort you," Captain Spiers answered, removing his hat and revealing his thin, greasy black hair, as he bowed to them both.

Doing a marvelous job of hiding her distaste for him, Jane said, "I would love to hear how these great sails above us are chosen to be pulled up and down according to the weather we are having!" Jane exclaimed, flapping one hand like a mad seabird. Jane hoped he would think her dense and charming, as was fashionable for women these days.

Captain Spiers took each lady by the arm and walked to the other side of the ship's bridge, as Jane had hoped he would, and began to explain first the riggings and then the function of each sail in its different positions. She pretended to listen with the utmost attentiveness, occasionally sneaking a protective glance past the captain toward the boys by the hold as they continued to talk. She kept his back to the hold and continued to ask inane questions whenever he seemed to be ready to turn back around.

This went on for several minutes, until the boys shook hands quickly and Nate walked away, as the two boys went back below. Nate's eyes immediately went to the bridge, searching for Captain Spiers and spotted him with his back turned talking to Jane and her mother. Jane risked a quick wink to him, while the captain leaned forward to demonstrate some block and tackle and explain to them about the great sea anchor that came from the ship's stern. Nate flashed a bright smile of thanks back at her and then he quickly made himself scarce. He scurried to the other side of the ship towards the bow, to help roll up the freezing ropes that lay slack across the deck.

Captain Spiers was almost finished with his explanations, but Jane was getting so tired of listening to him drone on, that she suddenly leaned forward to her mother and said, "are you all right, Mother?"

"What, well I..." Mary Jane stammered, caught by surprise.

"Oh, dear, you look very peaked all of a sudden! I should not have you out in such weather this long! Forgive me, Mother. I am a dreadful daughter! Maybe you should go and rest?" Jane squeezed her hand to make her point clear.

"Oh well, yes, but I hadn't wanted to interrupt such an interesting orator and mention anything," she replied demurely. She had quickly caught on to Jane's game and played along, pinching her face dramatically, as if in pain.

"I am terribly sorry to cut this short, Captain Spiers, but I think I should really take my mother in to lie down, straight away!" Jane added for emphasis.

"Surely!" Captain Spiers replied, eyeing Mary Jane with concern. "I certainly think that is best. We can continue the lesson at another time?" He asked, staring openly at Jane.

"Oh yes, to be sure! I would simply adore that! Another time, then?" she agreed, flirtatiously. She was already moving away from him toward their cabin leading her mother.

"Another time," Captain Spiers answered, tipping his hat slightly to her. He watched her sway away with her mother and lecherously took in her build from behind. A very pretty woman, he had tried not to think on her much, since she was betrothed and a paying passenger. But as she had begun to show some interest, he began to wonder a great deal more about her, in ways that a gentleman should not.

Shaking himself from his lecherous daydreams, his sharp eyes scanned the decks for Nate and found him at last, working hard up near the bow as he should be. Anything of importance that the boys below may have told Nate, he felt confident he could beat out of him later. His eyes were too sharp to have missed their discussion.

Captain Spiers knew the boy was coming to despise him for the beatings, but still he felt justified in his reasons for doing so. He also felt justified that he needed to work the boy hard, since he was responsible for making the boy a man now. He brooked no laziness from any of his crew in any case. If he were to treat Nate any differently than the other sailors, they would take notice and wonder. He also did not feel enough for the boy to wish it known publicly that he was his son. That would imply a permanent responsibility and that was something that the captain did not want. He never had. He had done well by always taking care to think only of himself and his ship first. Nothing would ever change in that regard. Besides, he liked to keep his options open. The boy was proving more trouble than he was worth lately and he felt that he might soon want to be rid of him, permanently.

Back in their tiny cabin, Mary Jane whirled around on her daughter, shut the door behind them, and pulled her by the hand over to her berth. "Now please tell me, young lady, what in heaven's name that was all about?"

Jane quietly explained what she had seen and heard lately around the ship and what she knew about the cabin boy, Nate. Mary Jane sat with both hands over her mouth, a typical reaction of hers to something that shocked her. She shook her head, wondering, and then whispered worriedly, "How many are sick do you suppose?"

Jane shook her head. "I don't know, but I saw three children's bodies being given quick burials at sea, just last night. Nate expressed his wish to me that no one is told, or Captain Spiers could possibly throw the rest of the sick overboard alive, in order to save the rest of us. Nate told me that Captain Spiers has done it before. Can you imagine the barbarity?"

"I also know that boy is beaten nearly every night, so Lord knows what may be done to him, should the captain discover that this involves him too. He seems to be helping the passengers below, and just a while ago I saw him talking to two other lads near the hold and they all looked much too serious for boys that age, so I know there is more trouble below. That is why I was trying so hard to distract our captain."

"Well, that explains your behavior. I knew you were up to something, but all that flirtatiousness from a betrothed woman! It could be greatly misunderstood, you know. Especially, when your own mother was wondering if you had gone daft. This captain is not a man to be toyed with; he is obviously ruthless, with no scruples whatsoever!" She shook her head to try to clear the horrible mental images from her mind.

Jane smiled weakly at her. "I know, Mother. But I had to distract him from Nate, if I could, and flattering that monster is all I could think of." She got up and paced the few steps back and forth across the cabin a few times. "Don't worry Mother, I have you here with me, and I hope I could call on some of the male passengers, if things turned.... well.... if things became sordid." She stopped and took her mother's face in both of her hands. "I must help below, if I can. It must be simply awful. And I will be very, very careful about the captain." She got up and began pacing again. "I have thought of a way to help. And if I am lucky, even with the captain's permission, as well."

"And just how do you propose to accomplish that?" Her mother asked.

"Well, you know we have all of my old primers and embroidery in one of the trunks? I think I could ask him if I might go below, on the pretense of giving some of the children some schooling and some needlework lessons. I will tell him I am bored. Surely, he would not refuse me that? And I would actually do some of that too, but for now I merely want to help the sick in any way I can. I had the pox already when I was young, remember? It was when that awful Hector Boughton kept hanging around and then he took sick with it and so did several of the neighboring children, including me. You stitched my sleeves closed so I could not scratch myself and make scars, remember?"

Mary Jane smiled a little smile tinged with fear. "Aye, I remember. And I also remember thinking I would lose you, but you recovered nicely. But, what does this have to do with anything you propose?"

"Well Mother, I have heard it said that once you have had the pox and beaten it, you probably wouldn't catch it again."

"Probably?" Her Mother asked, wide-eyed. "I have heard this also, but you would risk our future on this probability?"

"Yes, Mother, I am sorry, but I would! Even if I were to take sick; I overcame it before and I can overcome it again. I'll not rest idle on this ship, having tea and biscuits each day, while there are sick and dying children to be cared for below. I simply cannot!" She threw her hands up in exasperation and turned to stare out at the ship's wake. She shivered, thinking about the little bodies that now lay so far behind them in the sea.

Quietly, her mother stared at her, her thoughts unreadable, and then she said, "Jane if you must do this thing, then I want to help also. I know I am too frail just yet, but in a week or so I can help you below and keep from dying of boredom myself." She circled her arms around Jane from behind her and held her close. "In the meantime, I can keep our captain away from the hold area as much as possible. Maybe we can get your Nate to retrieve a few other things from our trunks that I think may prove to be useful." Mary Jane stared at her, meaningfully.

Jane understood exactly what her mother meant and hugged her mother gratefully until there were tears in both of their eyes. It was decided. They would at least try to do what they could. Jane felt even more love for her mother at that moment, than at any other time that she could remember. She knew what a great risk it was to reveal their type of healing. People had been burned at the stake for much less in the New World in the not so distant past.

Her mother took Jane's face into her hands and looked deeply and sincerely into her eyes. "Just promise me, that you will be very careful! You know there are those that see the old healing arts as witchcraft and then you and I would lose all. Everything! I could not bear that!"

"I will be careful, Mother, I promise," Jane answered, hugging her again.

"I am going to go out and ask Captain Spiers about it, right away! Will you please come with me? I have no wish to be alone with him; I do not trust him."

Her mother was already grabbing her cloak again and said, "Of course, let's go immediately! Since I am still ill he won't detain you too long with questions," she said, the old sparkle of mischief returning to her eyes and warming her limbs into action.

Sgian and Willie came clambering back down the hold, climbing over people as politely as they could. They went to the hanging blanket door and peered in, looking for James and Hugh. The room was full to capacity with sick children and worried adults. Willie spotted his grandfather first, with his gray hair and beard standing out in the semi-darkness, and waved to him. Hugh handed little Finlay back to Janet while she sat talking to George. Hugh tugged on James' sleeve, as he walked by interrupting his play with Hector and Lizzie. The boys had seen Mary on their way through the hold. She had waved at them tiredly, while she was nursing one of her remaining bairns.

Hugh and James came close to the boys making a tight circle in a bare spot and asked them if all would again be ready up on deck tonight, for the other two children who had died overnight. Two of the McKenzie's four children, little Elspa and the youngest McKenzie lad, Colin, had both died during high fevers very early that morning. Poor Molly McKenzie had been out of her wits with grief after losing them. Now she sat silently and stared straight ahead. She and Janet McLeod had worked tirelessly through the night bathing their hot little bodies with cool water, trying to break the fever that finally overwhelmed them. Molly's laughing chatter and the usual twinkle in her blue eyes was replaced by an empty, dead gray as she sat alone in eerie silence next to the wrapped bodies of her two youngest children. Her husband John came in behind the men, and they told him quickly of their plan.

He hung his head, a tear sliding down his nose. "I ha' already told the older lads tha' their brother and sister were gone, and tha' was hard enough." He wiped a sleeve carelessly over his eyes and took a deep breath. "Noo if ya wull excuse me, I mun go an' tell my Molly what we mun do the noo." John and Molly both spoke English with the heavy highland brogue that came from further northeast, where they and their kin were from. It had grown even heavier with Gaelic slang because of John's grief and its sound aptly mirrored the sorrow of them all.

The men and the boys nodded in silence and Old Hugh's eyes burned, his tears threatening to overflow as he watched John carefully approach Molly and the two still little bodies. He had seen them just a few weeks ago it seemed. Although, in some ways it seemed many years had passed, since they had been running joyously on the green hills above Ullapool chasing their wooly sheep. Now he tried to steel himself to read the services that would commend their souls to God forever, just a day after losing their own wee Alex. He was used to giving quick services on battlefields in his younger days, but doing it for all these bairns was nearly more than even he could bear. He felt sick of heart. But he had promised, so he would do it as long as it was necessary. And every single morning and every single night, he prayed with all his heart for an end to it.

Suddenly, Abigail Murray let out a wail and Janet was by her in an instant. Janet unwrapped the babe's blankets and tried for a few minutes to vigorously massage the infant and encourage her to breathe, but the life was gone from Abigail Murray's tiny three-month-old bairn, Margaret. Janet hung her head in defeat and pulled Abigail close into an embrace. Both women's shoulders shook with helpless emotion, as they kneeled together over the naked, spot riddled and now lifeless infant.

Old Hugh hung his head. "So that'll be three tonight again James, three more bairns," He said angrily, as he wiped his eyes roughly, as if they were to blame for his having seen so much death.

James looked around with Hugh. All around them in the room, frightened parents and older children were crying. Hope was quickly fading in the room, like the light on a cloudy day. And hope was what they needed desperately at this point. People were close to panic and everyone was afraid of the horrid red spots and the death that threatened with them.

"Lord, help us!" Hugh muttered, with a sigh. Suddenly, he became aware of some very persistent person trying to get his attention from behind. He turned to find the source of the tugging at his coat and all the throat clearing that was going on behind him and the curtain. He parted it to have a look and to everyone's surprise, in walked a young blonde woman with striking blue eyes who was tall enough to have to hunch slightly to avoid the ceiling, as did most of the men. To Old Hugh her eyes looked like sapphires even in the gloom. Her face was somber, yet she still had a girlish look about her, that he could see. She was obviously well dressed and upper class. When she smiled at them hopefully, her smile lit up the room.

The two boys recognized her, because of being told all about her from Nate.

Sgian bravely spoke up first. "You are the woman traveling with her mother back in the cabin, aren't ya miss? Miss Forbes, Aye?" Their eyes were lit up with boyish interest.

"Yes, I am. But you may call me Jane," she said smiling warmly at them both, and shaking their hands in turn. "I am afraid that you have me at disadvantage, young sirs, since Nate has only told me a little bit about you both. But you must be Sgian and Willie, am I right?"

Delighted and speechless that she knew their names, both boys nodded emphatically.

"Well then. Perhaps, you can introduce me to your father, Sgian? And I was told that I must also speak with a gentleman called Old Hugh?" She looked to both older men with one pretty raised eyebrow, assuming correctly that it was these sharp-eyed men she sought.

"I am Hugh McLeod," Hugh said first, bowing to her in a courtly fashion, "and this is Sgian's father, James McDonald." James also bowed to her, but stood coolly distant for now. He bore some obvious distrust on his face. She could only assume that it had more to do with personal experiences that had not endeared him to the upper classes, especially the English, and not her personally that gave him this aloofness.

"And Willie here, he is me grandson. How can we be of service to you, Miss?" Hugh asked smiling at her in a way that he hoped was encouraging to her.

"Well, it is a rather long story, but between what I have overheard near the hold on my daily walks round the deck, and what my friend Nate tells me, we have a problem onboard. Pox, I am guessing, by what I can see?" Her bright eyes were everywhere at once, taking it all in.

James face became even stonier, but Old Hugh persisted. He had a good feeling about this lassie and despite her obvious upper class English looks; he thought he saw some Scottish good sense and more than a few secrets in her blue eyes too. "You are right aboot that, Miss and we just lost three more bairns this very day. Just, how exactly do you propose ta help us though? If ya don' mind me askin' o' course?"

"Not at all," she replied. "I have Captain Spiers permission to help with reading and to teach needlework to any willing children, which I fully intend to do. But first," she paused trying to word it right. "I merely wish to help with the care of your ill."

Janet had come over to see what was going on and she stood by her father-in-law, curious, but quietly waiting to see what would happen.

"And beggin' your pardon, Miss, how do you propose doin' tha'?" James interrupted.

"Well, with these few simples that we brought with us, to begin with." Jane smiled a triumphant smile, opening one of the large schoolbooks she carried to reveal hidden caches in the back filled with small packets of herbs and bottles of potions. "And with these," she said as she lifted the top layer of cloth and flosses back on her large needlework basket to reveal some shortbreads and some biscuit that she had been squirreling away, from the tea that they were served daily in their cabin. There were even some dried fruits and several odd looking roots that the men could not identify.

Janet gasped at the rich outlay of medicinals, reaching out unconsciously for the larger bottle she hoped was opium. She quickly pulled her hand back ashamed, but Jane took the bottle out of the cleverly carved out space in the book and put it firmly into Janet's hands in invitation. Janet uncorked it, sniffed it cautiously and then smiled broadly for the first time in many days. "My name is Janet McLeod. I think you'll be verra welcome here, Miss...?"

"Forbes," Jane answered quickly, "but please, call me Jane."

Janet quickly glanced over the rest of the revealed herbs and whatnots and then dragged Jane abruptly past the shocked men and over to her corner by Finlay. She wanted to quickly take inventory of the things Jane had brought and think how best to use them. It was a king's ransom of herbs and medicines, the likes of which Janet had never seen all in one place, other than an apothecary's shop. She raised her voice a little and told James to fetch his Mary to come to them as soon as she was done nursing.

"I can see you are also a healer?" Jane asked carefully in an aside.

"Aye and it takes one to ken one, I always say," Jane said with a knowing smile. They understood each other immediately and nothing else needed to be said about the dangerous nature of their talents. Healing by women and devil worship were still thought of as one and the same, by many of the churches and also by the ignorant public at large. The two women started chatting quietly, but excitedly about several options for the fevers and the itching and ignored the men completely.

James closed his now wide open mouth and swung around to look at Old Hugh, with one brow raised, an unspoken but irritated question in his eyes.

Hugh just stood there smiling with a twinkle in his eyes and patted James on the shoulder reassuringly. "I think our miracle has just arrived. Don' worry, if'n Janet trusts her and me ain gut agrees, well 'tis all right then. You heard her! Go and get Mary, man!"

Not totally trusting this English looking woman himself, he did trust Old Hugh's judgment; so he left, ushering the boys out with him, to go and fetch Mary. "You two lads go and see what can be done for the McKenzie lads, all right?" James asked, seeing the two of them huddled together forlornly, up toward the bow. "They're from Ullapool; do you ken them Willie?"

"Aye sir, I do. Come on, Sgian." They began the slow scrambling process to cross all the people and reach the sad-eyed McKenzie boys.

James climbed over to Mary and began quickly, but quietly, filling her in on the new arrival and Janet's apparent excitement. "She asked ya ta come directly. Are you finished there wi' Alasdair and William?"

"Aye, William is asleep and Alasdair is just aboot." With an audible pop, she released herself from Alasdair and then handed him to his father as she rose to leave. James put Alasdair over his big shoulder until he heard several small belches, and then the little body relaxed against him again in sleep. He carefully laid the lad in his basket and watched him for a few moments in precious slumber. He felt a curious mixture of both relief and guilty love in his heart that the pox had not taken his youngest son, at least not yet.

He looked over at Katy, who was sitting dejectedly against the curved hull of the ship watching him. He squeezed through their belongings and slid up to sit next to her. Feeling even guiltier for not paying much attention to his eldest daughter, during these battles for the younger ones, he put a loving arm around her shoulder. "It's sorry I am, that ya ha' been sa alone these last few days. We ha' been busy wha' with the death of wee Alex and all tha' has happened. You do ken your mother and I ha' been busy trying ta save all those we can and bury those we canna?"

"Aye, Da, I do." She leaned her dark, silky head against him, and he held her close for a moment, just father and daughter.

"Well, what is it then, A leannan?"

"Why do the wee ones have to die Da? Why would God want that? They werena bad and little Alex hardly ever fussed. They havena even had a chance ta live yet!" She broke down and he held her, stroking her dark head and letting her just cry out her sorrows for a while, as he crooned to her softly in Gaelic. "A leannan.... a bheanachd.... mo cridheachan."

After a bit, she started to quiet down to just sniffles and the occasional shuddering breath. He continued to hold her and then he took a deep breath and began to speak to her. "This is no what God wants, my dearest, 'tis the way of this world, not of heavenly things. God put us on this earth with free will. The will ta choose how and where we live and wha' we do with our lives." James paused to think.

"Only the strong can survive all the perils of this world. Some just don' get that far, aye? But, when tha' does happen and any one of us tha' believes in Him is lost; the angels weep in heaven, as does the Lord himself. The souls of the dead are borne safely ta His loving arms ta live in peace forever more."

"But, what about wee Alex, Da, and the other babe? Surely, they are too young ta believe in our Lord?" Katy asked, her breathing still hitching from crying so hard.

"Ah, but these wee ones are not required to believe, my precious one. None are. They are His already. God believes in them, child! God believes in them."

"So we can be sure that wee Alex is with God now, Da, and not just at the bottom of this cold, wretched sea?" She looked up at him, with tear filled eyes that now held a spark of hope.

"Oh yes, my darlin', from our first breath to our last, He is with us all in our hearts tellin' us right from wrong. So it matters not, how old or young we are when we die, and it matters not where our bodies go once we are gone from them. Our souls are with Him in heaven together with all our beloved family."

Katy smiled up at him, her tears drying up. "Thank you, Da. I was sa sad before, thinkin' of wee Alex. But, now I can try to think of him in heaven. He can be with his Ma and Da again now too, can't he?"

James felt his guts twist as her youthfully honest words caught him off guard and he began to cry again despite himself, hoping with all of his heart that it was true.

"Da, what is it?" Katy asked fearfully.

James pulled her close for a hug. "Oh Katy, my girl, ya ha' no idea how much you ha' helped me yourself with those words! I ha' been so busy I hadna let myself think on it, as there's been too much ta do." He wiped his sleeve across his eyes, feeling her sweet words spread like balm across his guilty soul. "Yes, my dearest angel! Alex is with his Ma and his Da now and they are all together up in heaven."

He glanced over her shoulder at his nephew, William, the surviving twin. He would now never be called wee William again, since his Da was gone. No longer would he have a twin; they would never again be Alex and William. He would always just be William now. James vowed he would do his very best to see that this babe was made into a fine man, no matter what it cost him. All of his bairns, he thought ferociously. Little Lizzie was recovering and the rest of them were right as rain. He dared to believe now that the rest of his bairns would still have a chance to live to see adulthood. He silently promised God that he would do his best to see it done and give his life if necessary, as he held his eldest daughter, with a love that was all consuming. He hoped and prayed that as many of all the ill little ones as possible would live to see their own adulthood too.

Hope had returned, like a flickering candle, to keep the darkness of fear at bay. A taste of salvation seemed to have come to them, in the unexpected form of Miss Jane Forbes. At least some comfort that they didn't have before, could now be brought to the sick or dying. He said a quick prayer of thanks for this border woman and another prayer that Captain Spiers would never discover that she was tending the ill more than she was teaching. He realized the risk she took to help them and found that he did not like to think of the young woman being the victim of the captain's wrath.

He did not want to leave Katy alone, but he was feeling restless with his thoughts. His eyes wandered over the crowd of passengers nearby. They stopped on Elspeth McLeod's curly red head. Maggie was clutching her goats and talking to them erratically, still lost to her grief. Her man, Davy, sat next to her, his head hanging morosely. Old Hugh was tending the sick also; as was Elspeth's mother, Janet, who was with Jane and Mary and the other sick children, including Elspeth's little brother Finlay. Her older brother Willie was still with Sgian and the McKenzie boys. Poor Elspeth looked as lost and forlorn as his Katy had, so he waved to get her attention. She glanced behind herself first, to make sure he wasn't beckoning to someone else, and seeing no one else looking, she put her own small hand on her chest, a question in her large blue eyes.

James nodded, and she hastily rose and dusted off the back of her little skirt, unknowingly scattering dust toward an annoyed looking older woman. The woman hastily began waving away the dust in the air with her shawl, as Elspeth climbed over to the McDonalds. Katy giggled a little behind her hand, at the expression on the older woman's face. James leaned in close to Katy and said quietly, "She looked like she was aboot ta bite the lass in the arse, did she no?" They both laughed as the solemn mood was broken. When Elspeth reached them, James started to make introductions between her and the rather shy Katy, but Elspeth began first.

Elspeth was so delighted to have someone near her own age to talk to, that she introduced herself and flopped right down by the babies' baskets next to Katy to talk and ask rapid questions. James hoped this bright, talkative little girl would be just what his Katy needed to lift her spirits right now. He excused himself, as a somewhat overwhelmed Katy stared after him for a moment, and then turned her attention back to Elspeth, trying to pick up the threads of her excited chatter. She was used to talkers, from her little sister Lizzie, so she quickly caught up to her pace and then began patiently answering Elspeth's incessant questions one by one.

James wound his way toward the nearby hold and climbed up the ladder for a few minutes of much needed solitude on deck. Ian, who had been talking to another man nearby, saw him go up. He waited a few minutes, sensing that James needed to gather his thoughts and then he followed. His brother-in-law had been through much in the last few days and he felt he might have need of his friendship.

James smiled back at Ian when he tapped him on the shoulder. He had to catch him a little as his weight shifted on the icy deck around them. But then James eyes slid away from Ian's to search the empty seas surrounding them, as if seeking answers out among the lumbering swells of the sea.

Ian sensed that he did not want to talk yet, but he stayed by his side. The boat skimmed effortlessly up and down the huge rollers as the wind blew its frostbitten North Atlantic breath into their faces. It was frigid up on deck and Ian could feel his breath freezing in his nostrils already. It was slippery and frightening out here with the icy decks and the waves. He glanced back at the hold. To him, it looked like a large open mouth; the way it was trimmed with red paint. Even though he was cold, it was better and cleaner out here and somehow less frightening to him. Anything seemed better than going back through that mouth and into the stinking body cavity of the ship's guts that waited for them below. Ian stared back out to sea, letting its vastness swallow his harsh visions.

James cleared his throat finally, and asked the real question that was on his mind. "Do you think it will all be worth it, Ian? I mean all this death and suffering, just for a new start and some land? Better still, do ya think my brother William would ha' agreed with what we ha' done?"

"Yes, James, I do or I wouldna ha' brought the offer ta ya! Ta owns our very ain land? Beggin' your pardon, but are ya daft, mo brathair? And as for William.... well, I think that he, Ann and the bairns would have been here with us too, if they'd ha' lived! What this is really aboot, is the same thing tha' struggle is always aboot. Its aboot freedom and makin' a place to call your own and do as ya please with and all the risk that tha' implies."

James stood there a moment longer and then turned to Ian. "You are right, Ian. I had lost sight of that with all this," He said, waving weakly toward the hold's now hated opening. "This voyage will take some of us, but not all of us. And we tha' remain will make it work. Because there is no goin' back now, lad. There is no goin' back." He finished, with a sweep of his hands around them, with nothing but the vast ocean to be seen. They both stared at the sea as it swept by in icy swells under them. There was nothing else to say, but still way too much to do. So, James walked back over to the hold. "After you," He motioned to Ian.

"Weel, er.... Have ya e'er noticed tha' this looks like a... well like a mouth, brother James?" Ian stammered.

James glanced at it and smiled ironically. "Not until now, I didna, thank ya kindly," he said with a sigh. "Fine, I wull go down first and get eaten by the great beastie," James teased.

Ian said nothing but grinned at the small joke between them and then followed, but not before he saw Tom Mandler glaring at him from down the way. He had a deranged gleam in his eyes, like he had too much grog, and smiled cunningly at Ian as he leaned against the mainmast. Ian pretended to ignore him as he descended, but felt all the hairs standing up on the back of his neck as he climbed down the ladder. He knew that Tom was after him on this trip, and that eventually it would come to a head. He just hoped he could continue to avoid him until they were closer to Pictou. They did not need any further trouble than they had just now. He smiled at Tom Mandler as he ground his teeth, wishing for the time when they would reach port and he might be free to smash that ugly sneer off Tom Mandler's scheming face.

Chapter Fourteen

Unexpected Hope

Mary and Janet had been given a quick lesson in advanced herbal remedies from Jane. It was decided to take the very sickest children and brew them a tea out of thyme, chamomile, valerian root, juniper and a few drops of the opium. Jane said this would be soothing and also might help them beat the illness, by giving them much needed sleep and some relief from their discomforts. Both Mary and Janet agreed readily, eager to do anything could ease the misery of the children.

Secondly, they took some of the oatcakes from the leftover meals and ground them up with some comfrey, thinned it with Abby and Ana's rich goat's milk and several drops of lavender oil to make a creamy, if somewhat lumpy mixture. This they began to pass around for each parent to smear on their children, to help relieve the itching skin sores of the pox. They found this had to be supervised by them, after one woman started trying to feed it to her children in the worried confusion.

Thirdly, they instructed the women to sew the sleeves of their sick children's clothes shut, to prevent too much scarring from their itching.

All three women sat back, exhausted from their efforts, to observe the effects of their concoctions at work. Nearly all itching and squirming had stopped within a few minutes of the application of the oatmeal mixture; even though the children all looked quite hideous with the grayish mess drying on their already bumpy skin. The ones that had been given the tea were getting noticeably sleepy a little while after they had drunk it all. Some of the littlest ones could not be persuaded to drink more than a few sips, and Jane hoped that it would be enough to help. They were already in serious need, their little lips cracked and dry and their small faces pinched in misery. Most of these sickest little ones were listless and the babes were not nursing well.

Jane whispered quietly to the other two women that if these bairns did not drink today, they would likely not last and to be prepared for several grieving mothers in the morning. There were a half dozen of these youngest children that were not doing well at all. The fear that showed in their mother's and father's faces was obvious to everyone. It made them more than willing to try any remedy that was offered. Desperate mothers were dipping their fingers into the tea, trying to get the babes to suck it off little by little. Gradually the room grew very quiet, quieter than it had been since the epidemic had begun.

Mary excused herself to go and nurse her babes and Janet sat with Jane for a while longer in the silence. Janet finally whispered the question that had burned in the back of her mind for several hours. "Are ya a witch, lassie? Is tha' why ya know sa much aboot the healin' Airts?"

Jane smiled. "Nay, I am no witch. I am a Christian, same as you. I just have the benefit of coming from a family of healers, on my mother's side. She is full Scots you see. Lowland Scot," She said, with a girlish grin, "not a Highlander, such as yourselves, but a Scot just the same. Her maiden name is Danforth." There was a pregnant pause and then she said, "But not my father. He was as English as an Englishman can be and so I am the product of both. He never approved of my Mother's healing either; he called it her Scottish witchcraft," she paused, with a small rueful smile on her lips, her eyes seeing only the past. "But she taught me in spite of him; all the family remedies and crafts she could remember, and a few of her own devising when he was not around. It was easy, since he was not around very often." Her eyes darkened at the remembered pain of those last years.

"Where is he now, lass?" Janet asked carefully.

"He is dead. My mother and I are alone in the world now." Jane said, dry eyed.

"Surely, he left you with a hame and some means, this Englishman?"

"No, he didn't. When my mother and he were wed, it was apparently arranged so that upon my father's death the estate would return to his next of kin who ended up being his awful sister, Lavinia and her husband. My mother knew nothing of these plans, assuming a solicitor would be appointed for us until... until it was too late and then we were informed that we must turn our home and all of its furnishings over to Lavinia. She graciously said we could stay for a while," she finished bitterly. "I do not think that either my mother or I could have borne that situation for very long. Duncan Senior, my grandfather, hated the Scots so much that he wanted no Scot to ever own his English estates. Not even his own son's wife and child," she finished angrily.

"So, how goes it with you now, then? Surely you don' intend ta farm, or fish in the New World?" Janet asked.

"My mother and I were left with a small sum and a good family name and that is all. Her brother is a factor and he found an old friend of the family that wishes his son to wed in the New World. He is willing to take in my mother as well, and so I have agreed." She shrugged her shoulders. "It was the best offer to be had at the time and he is from a very well respected family of merchants. They are expanding their business to the Americas."

"That's well then, lassie!" Janet replied. "I know I am sa grateful that my own Da decided to come wit' us," she said with a nod toward Rob Innes who was holding little Finlay. "Why then even if your man looks like a wee toady, you can at least live in style and security and ha' your ma with you too."

Jane laughed out loud, delighted with Janet. "He does not look like a toady, I can assure you! I have a portrait of him and he is quite handsome!" She rummaged through a pocket in her skirt and to Janet's private amusement she pulled out three marbles, two pieces of hard candy, and a piece of string, a button and finally a small portrait. The rest of her boyish booty she put back in her pocket and the portrait she handed over proudly to Janet.

Janet took a look at her betrothed's portrait and said, "weel all the better then! You willna have ta put a feed bag ower his head to bed him!" Both women burst out laughing at Janet's wisecrack, earning them some glares from the surrounding women with sleeping children. They managed to stifle themselves and they shook from the effort of holding back the giggles that threatened to rise at the mental image Janet had shaped with her joke.

When they had calmed down a little, Janet handed the portrait back and whispered, "My, oh my! It seems years since I ha' laughed or e'en felt like doing so! And in the midst of all this terror too! If ye are a witch, then you're most certainly a fine one and most welcome."

"Well, you have asked your questions, so may I ask a few of my own? Which man is your husband?" Jane asked. Janet's face fell and as soon as Jane saw it she was sorry she had asked.

"My husband, Young Hugh, went down with his boat and his partners while they were out fishing the Minch. That is where the sea meets Loch Broom at Ullapool. They were coming into port, loaded down wit' herring and racing an incoming storm. His brother, Davy, and his crew were ahead of them rowing in and they barely made it safe ta harbor. My Hugh's boat disappeared beneath the waves before they could do the same. We never found his body or his boat." She bent her head to wipe her eyes. "His Da, Old Hugh, has since moved in with us ta help out where he can and to no be alone, since he lost his wife, Flora, many years ago. My son, Willie, he is in his twelfth summer now and he is a big help ta me. Then I have my Elspeth, who is nearly ten-years-old ta help me with wee Finlay there." She cast a gentle loving gaze across to the nearby Finlay in her father's arms. "They are all red-heided, like me, where their father was dark. But both the boys ha' their father's face, sa I feel I still ha' a part of him with me."

"I am so sorry for your loss. I wish I hadn't asked now; we were both laughing a short while ago," Jane said, tears glistening in her eyes.

"Aye, weel, laughter and tears are both a part of life, are they no? I count myself lucky ta still be among the livin' and able ta do both. More so on this awful day." Janet shook her head sadly, thinking of the lost children. "I am truly grateful for your gift ta me of the laughter, lass. So, don' you go regrettin' a thing! I feel more alive the noo than I have in a long while. I feel hope for these little ones too for the first time in many days. I do believe the worst is over for my Finlay and Miss Lizzie here. I am thankful because tha' is more than many people have ta be thankful for right now."

Her memory prompting her, Janet asked, "If you don't mind Jane, while most are sleeping, I need ta go and check on my good-sister, Maggie. She lost her only bairn yesterday, and I mun check on my ain bairns too. Why don' you go and rest and come back with your simples tomorrow. If ya can," she added, looking at Jane Forbes hopefully.

"I will leave the care of my books and the basket to you, in case more is needed this night, but I will be back in the morning after first light," Jane answered, determinedly. "I will see what can be done about getting more light down here, since it discourages the rats somewhat. Surely, there are more lanterns aboard, and if there are, I will bring them with me when I return." She began mixing some items in a small bottle, showing Jane how to duplicate it. "In the meantime, mix an equal amount of the chamomile tea with some of this bottle labeled tonic, and then add just a few drops of the opium. Just a few mind you, or they may not wake - I cannot stress that enough! The mixture is for Mary and Maggie. It should help calm them and strengthen them against their grief," she added, handing the bottle to Janet.

"Thank you, lass," Janet said, nodding in understanding as to the poisonous nature of too much opium. "Come! I will walk you ta the ladder, as tha' is the least I can do for all you ha' done for us," Janet said as she stood up. Janet leaned over and gave strict orders to Lizzie to go ahead and scream loudly, should anyone or anything try to get into the basket. George was nearby and could not help but overhear her, so he gallantly offered to help guard it.

The two women left the quiet sickroom behind, only to enter the equally smelly and more crowded main hold. They climbed over and around resting people until they reached the ladder. The sky was reddish on the sails above, already displaying the coming sunset. It would be time for their makeshift funerals very soon.

Mary spotted them and quickly rose to meet them at the ladder's bottom. "Goodnight, Jane. And thank you for everything! You are truly the miracle we ha' all been praying for! I hope ya will return?"

"Of course I will! I only wish I had known about your suffering before now. As I told Janet here, I will be back tomorrow. Until then, my things are in her care, in case they are needed." Both women nodded and hugged her gratefully. Janet and Mary continued to thank her profusely as she left them for the upper deck.

Jane climbed up the ladder with the nimbleness of a girl, but the dignity of a lady, as she held her skirts back out of the way. She stood in silhouette for a moment, with the reddish glow behind her then she disappeared into her own world above.

"Finlay and Hector are sleeping already, so I am going ta check on our Maggie and try ta give her this tonic," Janet informed the weak and peaked looking Mary. "Drink a swallow or two of this, before you go back ta Lizzie and Hector, and maybe you can get some rest with the bairns while you can. I will be back ta help wit the funeral services." Mary sniffed the bottle and obediently drank a swallow, smiled weakly at Janet and then returned to her family. After a brief conversation with each of them and a hug for Katy and Sgian, she went back to the sickroom to lie with the sick bairns. She lay down next to Lizzie and gathered her into her arms.

Elspeth, seeing her own mother heading for their family, rose and said a quick goodbye to Katy and her family and followed her mother. She had been terribly worried for her little brother, Finlay for days now. Especially, when her Aunt Maggie had come back from the sickroom so obviously grieving. She did not need to be told that poor wee Alex was gone to heaven. She knew from her Grandda's creased and somber expression and the look of her Uncle Davy when he came back too, that more were dying. They were changed men and frightened. She had never seen them scared of anything in her whole life and that made her even more afraid. Her mother had been so busy that she had not spoken half a dozen words to Elspeth and she felt younger and smaller inside from the lack of her affection and company.

Her mother reached the family first, going immediately to Maggie. She whispered something to Davy and then knelt by Maggie's side, convincing her to drink a few swallows of something that she was carrying. Maggie responded to her, but Elspeth felt that there was something scary about how she looked, like a doll that could move rather than a real person. Elspeth heard her mother whisper some words to her aunt, but she could not make them out. Maggie nodded as if she was a puppet and her head was being pushed up and down by someone else. Elspeth approached quietly and grabbed hold of Janet's free hand. Janet pulled her gaze away from Maggie and looked down at Elspeth. Her frown immediately turned into a smile, but she placed her finger in front of her lips to keep Elspeth from speaking for now. Janet held fast to her hand and led her a short ways away so they could talk in relative privacy.

First, Janet just hugged her little girl fiercely to her, thanking God for sparing her and her other children. They were all she had left of Young Hugh and the thought of losing any of them terrified her. She tried to gather her thoughts, feeling her emotions spinning out of control, as she gradually faced Elspeth and they locked eyes for a silent moment. "First, I want to thank ya for bein' sa patient with my being busy with Finlay and the other sick bairns."

"Of course, Mama," Elspeth answered her, "I ken you're needed. But please," she said as she grabbed her mother's hand firmer, "tell me the truth aboot Finlay. Is he dyin' too?" She looked so old for her years and she began to cry as soon as she said the awful words out loud.

"Oh, my poor lass," Janet cried, her heart squeezing sympathetically. "You ha' been left out here a'wonderin' and I didna even think of it. He is coming oot the other side and is gettin' better every day. So much better, that tomorrow if he still seems better, I will bring him oot here for you ta see for yourself. The wee devil is raising a ruckus when he is awake in there the noo."

Elspeth cried even harder, all of her relief and bottled up fear bubbling over beyond her control as she was held in her mother's arms. "Whist, now, whist, child. Hush yourself! It wull all be fine for our wee Finlay. And now we have a wee bit of help tha' seems heaven sent and maybe we can save a few more." Then Janet cried with her, finally able to believe it herself, that her child would indeed live. The two loosened their hold on each other long enough to look into each other's faces, and the first trembling smiles came from both of them.

"Oh Mama, I was sa scared with all the crying and everyone running around again. I kent that more had died, but I didna ken who. And I kept thinkin' aboot how I was mad at Finlay the night he got sick and slapped his hand away when he was pluckin' at me and botherin' me. Since then all I could think aboot was how nice I would be to him even when he is makin' me angry, if he would only get better."

"Elspeth, my dearest, I am sa sorry that I wasna here for you ta talk to! None of this is your fault, and even had we lost our Finlay, he knows how much we all loved him. He would bear you no grudge, nor would I! Little brothers can be a pain and I should ken that, having had several of the wee heathens my own self. I have seen how ya are with him and oft thought that ya had more patience than I do, when he gets himself into mischief. Doona carry this burden anymore!"

Elspeth sobbed with relief in her mother's arms as she listened to her comforting words. "You are a good sister to both your older and your younger brother and more help to me than you will ever understand until you have wee ones of your own. And whether I am with you or not, always know this.... I am sa very, very proud of you, lassie! I love you with all my heart, no matter whether I am angry with ya or no. No matter where you go, or what you do in life, you wull always be loved by me. You are my precious girl and the light of me life! You and your brothers are all that is left of the love tha' your father and I shared. My love for you canna ever die, even when I do. Remember that always. Can you promise me that?"

Tears of happiness and relief shining in her eyes, Elspeth nodded. Then she grabbed her mother around the waist again, holding on desperately. "I promise, Mama! I love you too, Mama, always and forever!"

They let go of each other again and then sobered, Janet whispered to her, "There is something else I need you ta do, Elspeth. The boys will likely be busy along with your grandfather helping with the burials of the poor mites that died this day. I need you ta help with the goats and the milking. We are going ta start passing out what we can spare ta the people with busy mither's and some of those tha' have babes that are nursing poorly. Ta get the most out of them, we need to collect any leftover food scraps or anything else you can find tha' the goats may eat. Then milk them three times a day, ta really gets their milk going. Do you understand, lass?"

"Aye, I can do that, Mama," Elspeth answered, nodding enthusiastically, and grateful for something to do.

"The second thing I need is for you ta do is ta watch over your Uncle Davy and Auntie Maggie. I just gave Maggie a tonic that should calm her down and get her ta sleep for a while, but let me or your grandfather know right away, about any unusual talk or strange actions by either of them. Right away, mind! This is very important and you mun understand. Can ya do tha' for me?"

"Aye," she answered a little more slowly. "What are ya thinkin' they may do, Mama?"

"Well, they ha' had much ta grieve aboot in the last few days and only time can heal wha' has happened ta poor Alex. But people oft times get confused in their minds after somethin' sa awful and start goin' a bit daft. It can be a verra dangerous thing. I want ta know right away aboot it, as I may be able to help it. Do you see?"

"Aye, Mama, I do. She has been talkin' to the goats more, but I ken how sad and lonely she must feel. That isna so bad, is it?"

"Well, tha' depends on how long she does it and if it gets worse, Elspeth. If anything feels wrong at all, just tell us right away. Now I hate sa much ta leave ya again sa soon, but there are three more ta have prayers for today, and many more yet ta try ta help through this night." She glanced at the deepening red of twilight behind them through the hold and knew that time was short. Blood in the gloaming, she thought to herself. Ill luck and death have visited this day. Janet shook off the superstitious thought and tried to smile for her daughter. "Sa I must leave you again for the night, but I promise to bring Finlay to ya tomorrow if'n he is better. Then I can mebbe catch a wink myself whilst ya play with him."

"All right Mama. Oh, I can't wait ta see him!" Elspeth exclaimed, excitedly.

They both went in opposite directions, but they were feeling the renewed connection of mother and daughter again. The older woman went back to care for the sick and the little girl had tasks almost as difficult, for one so young. Anyone looking at them could tell they were mother and daughter, not only by their red locks, but also by the determined set to their square jaws. They bravely faced all that needed yet to be done with head up and eyes forward.

All the words that could be said for today's dead had been said. Hugh finished with a final plea to God to spare the rest of the children if He could. He also added his own silent thanks for the addition of Jane Forbes and her welcome medicinal relief. He felt his heart breaking as he looked over at Molly McKenzie and her John as they held their children's wrapped bodies in their final hugs and goodbyes. Elspa's, he knew was the smaller one, while her brother Colin's was the larger bundle. Their remaining children, William and Angus, who were fourteen and twelve respectively, touched their sibling's wrapped little bodies, letting their tears fall on the wrapping shrouds like soft rain.

Next to them were the Murrays, Abigail and Christopher, and their two boys Adam and Walter, who were much younger, nine and seven-years-old respectively, crying over their own tiny sad bundle in a similar fashion. The dead baby, Margaret, was wrapped in a colorful piece of the Murray's red, blue and green family tartan. All knew what had to happen next, but no one said anything, not wishing to hurry the inevitable separation along.

Old Hugh stood watching, thinking about how he had seen the McKenzie children laughing and playing back home, every time he passed downhill from visiting his Flora. Molly and John were good people who did not deserve such harsh tragedy. And the Murray's.... well he himself had seen young Adam rushing by the widow Murray's to fetch the little midwife to aid his mother on the day this doomed little girl child had been born. He had walked by their house and heard Abigail's birthing moans and the screams that had brought this very babe into the world. He sighed feeling very old. Morosely, he gathered the fathers and the other men necessary to him, to conduct the quiet burials at sea. In the meantime, he had sent both Willie and Sgian to make sure Nate was aware and had taken the precautions needed above, as he had the previous night. They crept back down to the hold after finding Nate and told Hugh and James that the deck was clear of spying eyes.

Seeing the messages being given to Hugh and James, John McKenzie took his son Colin in his arms for the last time and bravely stood up to make ready. When James took Elspa from Molly's arms she did not resist him. So deep was her sorrow, her hands merely fell limp in her lap and she just stayed on the floor, weeping in despair. Christopher Murray attempted to take his infant daughter's small body from his wife, Abigail, and she began to wail and held on even tighter. He sat back down next to her, and began talking soothingly to her, while stroking the smooth velvet finish of her tear streaked face with soft caresses. She held their bairn tighter than ever, closing her eyes in desperate denial. After a few moments, she softly kissed the babe's swaddled head and slowly released little Margaret to her father's care. Her boys dropped to her side and began crying harder as the three clung to each other lost in sorrow.

Old Hugh and Ian made ready to go with them to keep watch and assist as they could. George would keep watch at the bottom of the ladder this time, where he could check on his Hector from time to time. Now that he was feeling better, Little Hector was being naughty, like any three-year-old that's kept cooped up too long. George was especially watchful over him now after coming so close to losing him to this awful pox and had been hard pressed to even discipline him too harshly.

The secret sea burials went off without a hitch and the men scrambled back down the ladder, once again empty handed and grim faced. Before the men could disperse, Alex Ross approached them and introduced himself, rocking back and forth importantly on his heels and preening his clothing like a dandy. "I would like to know if the captain has been notified about the deaths of these children, since you are obviously conducting unlawful burials." He paused when no one answered, mistaking their deadly silence for intimidation. "My brother, who is the agent of this journey, said that anything amiss should be reported directly to the captain. I feel it is my responsibility to do so." He stopped and examined his fingernails a moment, frowned and then polished them unnecessarily on his smudged lapel, before glancing back up at the men.

James and Hugh were the first to step forward and they quickly pushed him back into the smallpox room, so that no sailor would overhear them. Some of the rest of the men quickly dispersed back to their own family groups, but several stayed nearby, curious to see what they would do to this pompous little man and ready to help restrain him, if needed. "I think we need ta have a wee chat, laddie," Hugh growled, as he and James pushed the surprised Alex Ross hastily into the sick room.

"Take your hands off me, sirs, or I shall go report you this very minute!" Alex sputtered.

"Oh, I doona think there will be any reportin' goin' on here. Not if you value your life, that is?" James said, in a menacing growl that was all the more frightening because of how softly and calmly he spoke the threat. They kept pushing him until they were far into the shadows of the ship's stern and away from the resting children. "Take a good look behind us at the sick children here. Tell me, what does it look like to you?" A frightened Alex peered into the candlelit gloom and saw the deadly red spots on young pale skin everywhere. Miserable youngsters of all ages lay or stood in various stages of illness, their mothers and kin trying to nurse them the best they could, or they slept miserably, sitting up.

"It looks like the bloody pox to me! And all the more reason it should be reported!" Alex answered angrily. "Maybe there are steps that could be taken to keep the rest of us from getting it!" He exclaimed, placing his handkerchief protectively over his mouth in rising terror. He made to run and Hugh pulled him back, slamming him roughly against the bulkhead with more strength than either expected from the older man.

"And just wha' do ya think those steps would be, laddie?" Hugh growled. "Do ya wish ta see all these sick children thrown into the churning sea, alive and screaming? Is tha' what you want?" Hugh hissed into Mr. Ross' ear.

"The good captain would never do that!" Alex Ross exclaimed in horror.

"Would he no? That is the standard method of dealing with the pox at sea, you ignorant wee rascal! And I will kill you myself, afore I see that done to any of these folk!" He whispered his normally kind face screwed up in barely suppressed rage. "I am an old man; I care not what the punishment might be, so doona test me!"

"How dare you threaten my person?" Alex retorted. "I will do as I please!"

This time James grabbed him by his lapels and shook him until his teeth rattled in his head. "You just don' see it, do you, man? How's aboot we take a trip ower ta visit your family, so's ya can say your goodbyes before we throw ya owerboard, ya lousy lang nebbit, hmmm?" Both men were past all patience with this man. It had been a horrid few days and poor Alex Ross had no idea how close to breaking they both were. Old Hugh grabbed his other arm and they marched him quickly out to the main hold and shook him until he pointed his family out in the crowd.

His wife stood as they approached, nervous when she saw the fear in her husband's eyes and the men that flanked him, restraining him. She was holding a child of about four on her hip; who was listlessly leaning on her, his nose running freely, and showing the beginning spotty signs of the pox on his face.

"Weel, weel," James said, looking pointedly at Alex Ross. "Mistress?" he said politely to Marion, as both he and Old Hugh bowed slightly. "Mr. Ross, perhaps you would like ta explain ta your wife what you were just suggesting should be done aboot the pox patients? Especially in light of your own son being one of the ill now. Would ya risk your own ta be thrown owerboard, or just ours?"

Shaken, Alex reached out a tentative hand to his wife, the question in his eyes. "Yes Alex, our wee Donny has come down sick. I was just about to take him to the women in the sickroom to see if aught can be done for him." Her eyes filled with tears. "What do you want to do about the sick? What are these men saying?" Her eyes searched his fearfully.

"Oh, Marion, I am being a fool that is all. I wanted to report these illnesses and deaths before it could touch us, but it will touch us after all. Oh, our poor little Donny!" Alex began to weep and he fell to his knees in defeat, as Hugh and James let go of him. "You men are right, I canna risk my own, so I have no right to risk anyone else's child, either. I am so sorry! Please take my wife and son back with you to the sickroom to see what help might be found there. I will stay with our other two children and keep watch for more signs of this dreadful illness."

"And you promise ta say nothing? It puts a great many that can and will recover at risk of certain death, for you ta tell the captain or crew. We will throw you owerboard if ya try it and be damned with the consequences! Do ya understand?" A still shaken James stood over the man trembling, meaning to put an end to this threat, one way or the other.

"Aye, I most certainly do," answered Alex, as he stared into James' fury filled eyes. "I promise, I shall say nothing. You have my word on it."

"Verra well, then." James left him to sit on the floor and he put his head in his hands as he sat near his two remaining children. James was still shaking with his own anger, but he could see that the fight had gone out of the other man.

"Mrs. Ross? Come back with me and I will introduce you ta my wife, Mary McDonald. She and the other women will see what help they can give ta your wee Donny."

Marion started to cry harder and put a hand on her husband's shoulder in farewell. By her expression, she apparently did not expect that either she or the child would live through the pox to return to him.

James saw her defeat, as well, and his anger melted away. "Doona despair, Missus! Many have come through this and not died, thanks ta the women. Your Donny has as good a chance as any of them," James said softly to her. "Follow me noo."

Meekly and with terror in her heart, she followed him into the unknown of the sickroom, praying that she and her child would both return whole to her family. She was weak with fright, stumbled and nearly fell.

James held her arm and bore her up across the rolling hold, meanwhile promising himself that she would never hear from him the selfishly spoken, harsh words her husband had uttered. Old Hugh trudged behind them, his face grim and unreadable.

Chapter Fifteen

The Storm

In the wee hours of the morning, the storm hit them hard from the northwest. All hands were called up to go scrambling and sliding around on deck to pull in sail and secure flapping lines and loose cargo. Nate was no exception. He was being yelled at to help from every direction it seemed. He had been swept off his feet by crashing waves three times in as many minutes.

Nate had been the one ordered to shut the hold door and bolt it to prevent water from rushing in. Everyone knew there was no other way out of the ship's hold. They all also knew that if the storm won, they would all be doomed, whether above or below. It just seemed so much worse to Nate to be trapped below. He had looked into the eyes of Old Hugh and James, with Sgian and Willie behind them, before he had closed the big door and seen the fear in their eyes.

"God be with you, laddie," James yelled up to him, at the last moment.

"If any barrels or anything comes loose, strap them down!" Nate yelled above the storm's rising wail. He looked around, searching frantically for anything that would help them below and quickly tossed down a heavy coil of nearby rope. He muttered a silent prayer and crossed himself and James nodded to him in grave acceptance, as Nate reluctantly shut the door and bolted it over them. They were in the captain's, the crew's and God's hands now. If they failed, none of them had any chance of survival in the open sea. Nate felt the weight of it fall on his heart, echoing the final bang of the main latch on the hold. Even being left in the dark and not knowing how it went above, he would rather be below with his friends, instead of on deck in this nightmare.

All sail now in, several of the larger men took to the huge wheel to try to hold the Hector steady to the captain's orders and steer her into the waves as they broke over the bow in ever increasing fury. The rest cowered down in their positions watching for anything to come loose and holding on as tightly as they could. The big ship tilted and swayed as huge, bitterly cold waves swept the decks and sometimes the crew members from side to side. Having been as helpful as he could to his shipmates, Nate stood in the hallway to the rear cabins trying to catch his breath, as his small body was bashed from one wall to the other. He kept to his feet and finally managed to knock on the Forbes women's door.

It opened just as the ship tilted on a cresting wave and he tumbled into the room headfirst. He banged into the opposite wall before Jane or her mother could catch him. He hit the opposite wall with shocking force on his forehead and right shoulder. Nate immediately slid down the wall, knocked unconscious by the blow. Jane quickly closed the door, before he slid right back out, as they fell down the other side of the huge wave. She caught him as he slid limply back against the closed door and knelt by his side.

Nate opened his eyes after a few minutes and winced, obviously in pain. Still he asked through gritted teeth, "Are ya both all right, Miss?"

"We are fine so far, young man, whilst you seem a bit worse for wear." Mrs. Forbes said from her seat on her trunk, where she was holding onto a shawl tied to the bunk. She slid slightly as they dipped and slid on the massive waves, but was staying surprisingly steady. Their makeshift anchor was working well.

Jane grabbed him and slid back toward her mother and the hull with the help of the next swell. Her Mother grabbed hold of her daughter by her arm and shoved another shawl tied to the other bunk into her free hand. Jane struggled and finally pulled her and Nate up to a sitting position again and secured them as best she could. Jane tried to check his shoulder for ease of movement. He groaned and she immediately began searching along the lines of his bones with her sensitive fingers. There! She could feel a break in his collarbone. And here was another in the long line of his forearm bone. Luckily, they felt like clean breaks and did not feel shattered, nor had any broken through his pale skin.

Jane removed the scarf from her head and quickly fashioned a sling which she slipped over his head. She held onto him with a rotation of hands to hold the shawl with one hand and Nate with the other. This kept them both from sliding too far back and forth again, the whole while smoothly performing the slinging task. With his arm snugly in the sling, the pain wasn't as great and he smiled wondrously at her, as if she had just performed some mystical dance.

His head spun and he felt himself slip into unconsciousness for a few moments only to be roused by Jane's lips next to his ear, yelling at him to stay awake. She grabbed some wet garment off the floor as it floated past during the next swell and applied it to his bruised forehead. It was cold and wet, but it felt soothing on his throbbing head. He allowed himself to be held by her as they slid back and forth and was again reminded of his own mother. He yielded to the comfort she offered, as he was in no shape to help them. As he guiltily slipped in and out of consciousness Nate felt powerless to help even himself.

Jane looked down at him with pity on her face and then up to her mother's eyes. Mary Jane smiled in a way that Jane knew she understood how much affection she felt for this poor cabin boy, who had been so good to them on this horrible voyage, even though his own lot in life seemed so great to bear.

"I find it is much like riding a horse, my dear, just hang on!" Mary Jane told her firmly over the storm's keening.

Jane smiled at her mother's attempt to lighten the mood. They would take care of him here until after the storm then Jane planned on talking to a few of the men below about a plan that had been forming in her mind involving this young boy. She would then be ready to speak to their captain again.

Jane refused to acknowledge that they might not make it through the storm, as she held Nate tight. She merely hung on to him and occasionally grabbed her mother unconsciously, as she thought hard through the long, bruising hours of the tempest. She was thinking about her growing plan and who would be best to approach first with her idea.

Her mother could see her frowning face every few seconds, during each lightning burst. She knew her well enough to know that it was not the merely the storm making her frown so. There was something even more important to her than this storm that was making her think so hard.

Many of the women and children below were screaming while they pitched back and forth helplessly, as the ship first struck and then rode over each monstrous wave. The mere numbers of people kept anyone seated from sliding too far, but walking was nearly impossible. There were a few inches of cold seawater floating now at the bottom of the hold. Many were squashing themselves upward, clinging to the convex sides to escape the cold, filthy sea water down the center. People crawled if they needed to move about, but most just clung to their children and tried to secure these, their most precious possessions.

In the McLeod family circle, Elspeth, Maggie, Davy, and Janet's father Rob clung to each other and to the goats. The goats were bleating with fear and they kept trying to get them to lie down, but they were just too frightened and skittish. Finally, they had to be restrained physically by laying across them to weigh them down. Their pitiful cries mingled with the din all around them.

It was just as difficult in the McDonald's family group as it took all of James' and Ian's strength to hold onto the children. Katy held on tight to her brother, Sgian, and they pinned themselves next to Jane Gibson and her brother, up against the hull to avoid sliding. There was no way to avoid the occasional rap to the head by an overhead beam, when the ship hit the trough of a large wave and their seats were lifted off the planks, but at least they were no longer sliding into the cold murky waters sloshing about in the bottom of the ship.

In the sickroom, things were even worse. Mary, Janet, and some of the other mothers, had tried to secure themselves and the children to the huge casks that were tied along the ship's bulkhead at the ship's rear. Even the bereaved Molly McKenzie had returned to help them, finding the outer hold just a cold reminder of all that she had lost. Everyone had a grip on a child and another grip on one of the ropes, which bound the huge barrels. Most of the children were crying or vomiting or both. There were not enough basins to go around and no way to empty them even if there had been. The slurry of dirty seawater became increasingly fouled, between the chamber pots beyond the partition and the vomiting within the sickroom, as it swept back and forth between the two. Panicked rats ran across the women and children, seeking sanctuary from the rising waters.

Janet had given up hope of dispensing any herbal remedies, for fear of spoiling the rest of the medicinal goods, so she had tied the baskets securely to the overhead beams. She and Mary eyed them longingly as they swayed above and then looked at each other and shrugged. There was nothing they could do about it now, but hang on and hope to survive.

Thirteen-year-old Charlie Mathewson was trying his best to hang on, but in his weakened state he would occasionally let go and slide away into the bilge water, only to be brought back to them again by the next set of waves. At least they had one overhead lantern in here. The main hold was very dark. Molly McKenzie caught Charlie Mathewson after several missed grabs and pulled him into her ample arms and out of the water. He was gray and shivering, so she quickly wrapped her large body and cloak around him to warm him up. His parents were out in the hold and he had refused to have them near him, lest they get sick as well, so he was there all alone. He and Molly clung to each other, like so much flotsam above the water line.

Janet hung on to Finlay as hard as she could whenever she could feel a wave coming and only relaxed between them. She looked around often and tried to assess how her neighbors were faring. Old Hugh was between her and Mary and he was trying to help both women and hang on. Mary's Lizzie was hanging on just as tightly to her mother, as her mother was to her. She was one of the few children not crying or vomiting, but fear made her dark eyes look larger than ever in the gloom. George sat next to Janet on her other side and grimly held on to Hector, off and on checking the ropes on the barrels nervously to make sure they were not loosening. He also eyed the quivering bulkhead nervously, now and then. As a carpenter, he understood the fragility of old wood. He was trying not to think about how easily the rotten old planks could be smashed in by this continual assault of wind and pounding ocean waves.

Hector and Finlay were crying off and on, but faring a lot better than some of the nearby little ones who were still dangerously ill. George strained to see a woman several feet away whom he thought was holding a dead child. Its limbs flopped back and forth like a sad little rag doll with each wave. A bundle of rags floated by in the filth followed closely by a curious rat and he chanced to let go and grab for it between waves. It was a dead infant that had been face down in the water. He and Janet rubbed it frantically for a few minutes, but all life was gone from the small body, no more than a few months old. Tears ran down their faces in unbridled horror.

Janet looked around the corner of the barrels when she dared and saw a young woman of about sixteen, slumped down and staring straight ahead, obviously dead. The only thing holding her up near them and not letting her slide down into the water was the group below her and one white arm slung through the barrel ropes at the elbow. It was chafed so deeply, that blood had run like a small river down her body staining her dress and the barrels along the path it had run. The poor woman had likely bled to death trying to hold onto the casks and her baby.

Janet turned back to tell George, only to find him tearfully trying to secure the baby to the ropes, with one hand. She reached over and pulled on the hanging end to finish the knot and then quickly grabbed for the rope behind her again. George smiled at her through his tears and she found her heart pounding with warm feelings, even while enduring what they were. She had not felt this fluttery feeling in her breast for several years now and she actually felt herself blush, as she smiled back. She started to tell him about the babe's mother, but he could not hear her above the roar of the storm, so she just shook her head to show that she would speak to him later.

She looked away from him feeling confused and yet highly aware of his body next to hers. She examined her feelings and found that she felt very grateful and safe in his presence. She was glad they could not talk above the screech of the storm, as she suddenly felt awkward and naked with her feelings. Her father-in-law, Old Hugh, was also eying the riggings of the casks, when she chanced a look his way to see how he was faring.

Another huge swell hit the ship from the starboard side and there was no more time to think as everyone gasped and hung on during the ship's slow lumber over onto one side. In moments that felt like hours she lay over on her side, then the Hector abruptly righted herself. They were just as quickly hit by another swell and again, tipped sharply sideways. The old ship creaked and groaned, but she once again righted herself.

George glanced up and around and saw that what he had feared all along was happening. The now wet ropes were stretching and the barrels were beginning to sag from their fastenings. "James!" George bellowed through the tumultuous racket. He abruptly shoved Hector next to Finlay and pointed the situation out to the quick-witted Janet, who saw what the problem was immediately. Another brief, grateful smile passed momentarily between them as she took Hector from him. Then he was gone, climbing up on the barrels, undoing knots and trying to pull them taut. Old Hugh, amazingly limber for his age, climbed quickly up beside him to help. James had heard George yell from the hold, despite the din of the storm and was soon by his side in, after forcibly enlisting Charles Fraser, to help Ian with the bairns.

James stood in the swaying slurry of water and pulled on the bottom lines from below, trying to take up the slack as George did the same on the stack from above. Both men were tossed around roughly against the barrels, slipping and sliding on the wet wood, but managed to mostly keep their footing and their hold onto the ropes. Their faces and bodies strained with the effort to keep the barrels in place on each slide over of the ship. They scrambled with the slack on each tip back up, struggling to tie off the loose lines in between before the next set of waves came upon them.

Suddenly, a few of the biggest barrels on the top slid with the ship's rocking and began to tip over. Several ropes snapped with a loud twang, causing more screaming from the women and children. "Make for the hold, get out of the way!" James bellowed. The big barrels tipped slowly over then instantly rolled down the stack, hitting and smashing everything in their path. Most people got out of the way fast enough, but some unlucky few were caught under the rolling barrels. Several other men bravely came running in from the hold, heedless of the sickness in the chaos, to try to help secure the remaining barrels.

Janet and Mary slid around trying to keep the rest of the children up out of the way and to see what could be done for the injured on the floor. Three dead bodies were dragged out from the splintered mess in the bottom of the boat, two boys and a girl. To their amazement, one older girl was still alive, but she had an obviously broken left leg. They haphazardly pulled the battered children up near the group, sometimes sliding back into the water that was filling the bottom before making it back to the higher ground. In most cases, their mothers were right there to grab them and their grieving wails could be heard even above the screaming of the wind.

The girl with the broken leg, however, was not greeted by anyone. Mary leaned close to her ear after she had been dragged from the wreckage and placed near her own family. "What is your name, lass? Where are your people?"

"McKay. Margaret McKay," she managed to get out through her gritted teeth. "I ha' kin on the ship, but my Mither and Father are both dead. I am here wit' my relatives, but I didna wish ta risk the pox for their bairns. Besides," she yelled, above the storm, "I be no bairn! I be old enough ta take care of my own self," she finished with a stubborn set to her jaw and a fierce grimace from the effort it had taken to speak.

Mary nodded in understanding and held Margaret fast the only way she could, by wrapping her own two legs around her. She could tell from the fierce look in Margaret's eyes that this was the kind of girl who dared you not to take her at face value. She had always admired that kind of strength and Margaret nodded at her in reluctant acceptance of her help. Hopefully, they could attend to her as soon as the storm calmed down. It had been so long already, and Mary wondered if it would ever stop, or if it were morning by now.

Janet leaned towards them, yelling as best as she could over the storm, that she could help the girl. She instructed her to just lie as still as she could for now. The girl nodded grimly, seeming to understand what was said and why.

People began to calm a little as the swells were still high and long, but the ship was no longer being hit quite so hard that she was lying over. Some people watched wide-eyed, many were crying, other's mouths moved in silent prayer. The old ship groaned over the lessening waves, as if complaining about her prolonged effort to stay together. The wind continued to screech like a banshee, but gradually it chased the storm into the distance as the thunder and lightning followed.

Up on deck, the crew had one especially bad moment when lightning hit very near the spar of the mainmast. If it had taken out the mainmast itself, the ship would have been doomed to flounder about at sea, like a gull with a broken wing if the weight of its fall had not taken them straight to the bottom first. All who saw it swore later that it had looked like the sky itself had opened up and let loose a fury upon them, throwing a rolling ball of blue fire rolling right down the mast. It had spun wildly across the deck and then over the port bow to douse its unearthly light in the sea with a hiss.

A storm was always frightening to the sailors, but they were used to the ocean's temper, especially the moody North Atlantic. All of them were seasoned sailors and many had been on dozens of Captain Spiers voyages. Tales had been told for centuries of the blue fireballs from the sky. None of the Hector crew, however, had ever witnessed such terrifying lightning first hand. For hours, the sky was alive with light and color followed by ear-splitting booms of thunder. The crew was unusually quiet afterward, lost in their thoughts about the strange phenomenon and thankful to be alive.

The captain hardly ever took on young sailors for his voyages and felt no regret turning them down. He had no time for training if he wanted to get in two crossings each season. His men had to understand what could and could not be survived and be willing to risk it, despite the odds. On his ship, the sea had to be their only wife, their only true love. They had to be men like him, who cared not so much about death as they did about making their living on the sea that they loved in spite of her treachery.

His exception had, of course, been Nate and he had regretted that even before he had left port. Whatever had possessed him to bring him along when he was such a liability, he did not even understand, other than some vague notion of his worth as his cabin boy and some queer sense of obligation. The boy had been a disappointment right from the start. Many good men, who had more important work elsewhere, had risked themselves to keep him onboard as he often floundered about during the ocean's frequent gales. Nate did not seem to be made for the sea. These last few voyages had proved that to the captain, as far as he was concerned. He wanted to be rid of him. But he did feel that he had a right to profit from the boy somehow.

Captain Spiers looked around suddenly, as his mind cleared along with the abatement of the storm. Weak sunset pinked light filtered through the clouds at the horizon and hopeful patches of blue sky could be seen in the northwest sky. The waves were still hitting them hard, but the storm was definitely ending with the daylight. His fierce eyes scanned the deck for signs of the boy. Maybe he had been washed overboard, as he had seen no one catch him this time. But his eyes had been set firmly on the next wave all through the day and he hadn't thought to look for him. He examined his feelings and found them lacking of any sorrow, if that were indeed found to be the case.

He barely knew the boy, after all, and what he did know of him led him to believe that he was soft and stupid. He annoyed him incessantly with his questions and his snooping and his gangly slip sliding around. Not to mention the unspoken accusations he constantly saw reflected back at him that he had no wish to acknowledge, even to himself. He dismissed thoughts of Nate and looked back to the west. He could see clear skies at the edge of the horizon and beyond the large swells to the north and west. A fierce wind was still blowing out of the northwest, but the storm's wrath had passed them by.

Dewey, his first mate began the cheer. "Three cheers for Captain Spiers, mates! He done brought us through anither one!"

All on deck chimed in, "Hip, hip, hoorah! Hip, hip, hoorah! Hip, hip, hoorah!"

✦ ✦ ✦

Everyone below heard the cheer as well and there was sudden chatter and many expressions of relief in the main hold. Many were bruised and sore, but most had survived the ordeal mainly intact. In the sick room, the men were busy picking up pieces of broken barrels and wet cargo, trying to secure them in a less haphazard fashion. There was whispered conversation about the several water casks that had ruptured, along with a few barrels of raw oats and dried beef.

A few of the women and Old Hugh were busy trying to salvage what was not yet soiled of the spilled oats and the beef. And many kept glancing, shaking their heads sadly at all the spoiled food and water down in the bottom of the Hector. It was now mixed into the slurry of vomit and blood and oats and none would touch any of that; there was nothing worth saving. James and Hugh spoke up and told everyone that it would be bucketed out when the hold was opened.

Janet and Mary quickly brought Lizzie and Finlay out to their siblings, as promised, and watched for a few satisfying moments the great joy and relief that it brought to their families. Elspeth was hugging Finlay so hard that he was struggling to get away, as tears of gratitude poured down her young cheeks.

Katy and Lizzie were done hugging already and Lizzie was off hopping about and talking in her usual quick witted and wondrous way. She seemed to remember every detail of her illness even better than her mother did and was happy to regale everyone present with every moment of it. Janet motioned to Mary. They could not stay long, as there were others in a bad way and so much yet to try to do for them.

Their first urgent task was the girl, Margaret McKay, with the smashed left leg. Some of the other women were holding on to her in Mary's absence. She was sitting up, but gray with the effort and shivering. Janet sat next to her and felt along her leg. The bone was broken several inches above the ankle and already swelling monstrously. Janet did not think it was as bad as it had first seemed. There was still solid bone to work with on each side of the break. The bones still lay straight and none protruded out of the skin, so she believed it would heal straight and cleanly once splinted.

She addressed the swelling first, by dipping a rag in some cold clean water in what was left in a barrel and setting that aside. She made a poultice of Thyme, Comfrey and a little water, grinding it to a pulp with the mortar and pestle, which Jane had left in her basket of herbs. She applied the poultice and wrapped the cold, wet rag around it, careful not to wrap it too tight and tucked in the edges neatly top and bottom. Next

Mary gave her a few drops of the precious Opium for the pain. Within a few minutes, Margaret began nodding off, and they placed her over in the corner with her leg up on a small ledge, so that no one would carelessly bump her leg in this cramped space. They would splint it when some of the swelling had reduced and before she awoke. Mary put one of her own quilts over the girl who shivered even in sleep.

"She should heal just fine, if we can keep her off tha' leg for a fortnight or two." Janet said, as she straightened up as far as the low ceilings allowed.

"Good, bloody luck!" Mary said, louder than she had meant to. Blushing from her outburst, she wiped at her sweating face. "What I meant was, that I was wit' her when she was pulled oot and she didna strike me as the kind ta take orders from anyone."

"No am I stupid, Mistress," said Margaret, surprising them by suddenly opening her large brown eyes and looking straight at them. "I've seen the healin' ya both ken, and if ya wish for me no ta move, than I willna." Her willful eyes flashed with temper, then fluttered closed as she fell into a deeper sleep.

"I see what ya mean," Janet said to Mary, with a knowing smile. "The strength of her will is a powerful help in the healin'. I doona think we ha' mun ta worrit aboot wit' this one." They left Margaret to her opium dreams, confident that she would follow their instructions.

The good news was that those afflicted with the pox seemed better this evening, than in many days, despite the storm; all of them except little Donny Ross. His mother Marion was white with fright and exhausted from the ordeal, but she had held onto little Donny. Now Janet and Mary could continue Miss Forbes work. They treated little Donny with the oatmeal mixture spreading it gently over his mottled skin. Marion sewed his sleeves shut to prevent scratching and administered the tonic that they mixed according to Jane's directions. Janet offered to take Donny for a little while, so Marion could rest, but she adamantly refused. She sat near a big beam down the bulkhead and held little Donny, crooning to him and sometimes praying out loud for him. Janet and Mary shrugged at each other, helplessly and moved on to the next child, hoping for the best.

They quickly made the rounds of those that needed attention, making a few slings here, and some more poultices there. Several people had rat bites that needed tending. The rodents had come out of their hiding places with the rising water and had been frantic to find higher ground. They dispensed more nerve tonics mixed into cold teas for people to drink, along with the pox remedies that still needed to be applied to the sick. After doing all they could, the passengers settled in for an uneasy night's rest.

In the morning, the women resumed their care of the sick and injured. The adults with the pox had made faster recoveries and Janet and Mary knew that it was the infants and younger children that were still most vulnerable and needed the most urgent care. Janet hoped out loud that Miss Forbes would be able to come down. They could certainly use her help with some of the more unfamiliar problems and injuries from the storm that they had little experience with.

"I miss her smiling face too," Janet admitted. "We need tha' as much as aught else the noo," she sighed, looking around the hold. Tear streaked, exhausted eyes shone everywhere in the gloom and Janet had no idea how to ease that, with anything from Jane's basket. She turned to go back to the sickroom, just as the bolt was pulled back from the hold. She quickly handed Mary the large basket and rushed expectantly to the ladder bottom, literally crashing into George Morrison as she did so. He was breathing very rapidly and his face was ashen, so she reached for him. As the first rays of sunlight hit the hold, George collapsed back into her arms and they both fell away from the ladder into a heap.

Now that the storm was over and they had rested overnight, Jane made ready to go out on deck. Nate and her mother were still sleeping. She had helped her mother climb into her bunk a half hour ago, after she had placed Nate into her own upper berth. Jane quickly changed her plain stomacher out for a blue embroidered one and re-tied the lacing over her bosom. Then she replaced her plain brown skirt with the matching blue one and fluffed the hip pads.

Her mother still enjoyed wearing the panniers, but Jane could not bear the cumbersome hoop skirts. She now preferred the neat little hip pads that had recently come into fashion. She rapidly brushed out the tangles of her hair and swept its coils up high atop her head, deftly pinning it here and there with her stylish pearl studded pins. Jane snatched her hooded cloak off its nail and crept quietly out the cabin door.

As she came out on the upper deck, Jane was surprised to see the morning sky had cleared into a stunningly beautiful blue. No trace of the storm remained other than some low clouds on the eastern horizon. The skies above looked more promising than they had for many weeks. She finished buttoning her cloak against the chilly wind, but left her hood down to enjoy the sun's warmth on her face. The captain was only a little ways away, yelling orders to the crew to run up the sails and take full advantage of the stronger winds. Jane just watched him for a while, as he checked his instruments and compass and made adjustments to the large wheel correcting their course.

When he seemed to pause, she grasped her chance and hurriedly approached him to tell him about Nate. She watched him carefully for any emotional reaction to Nate's injuries as she described them and saw none. It only served to reinforce her plan in her mind.

"I was thinking about going below to see to the children later and I was wondering if Nate might not be better off below with the passengers for now." Seeing his scowl, she quickly pinned a bright smile on and added, "Certainly you are much too busy a man to care for him yourself and the crew are needed here on deck, as well. I just thought that one of the mothers I met during my teachings would be happy to care for him until he heals. Surely, he is no good to you with a broken arm and shoulder."

"Well, I don't know, Miss. It was most kind of you to mend him up and take care of him during the storm, so I certainly don't want to impose him on you any longer...." Captain Spiers waffled.

She pounced as she felt him wavering her way. "I know a mother who would appreciate another hand with her bairns, even if he only has one arm to help with right now. He could help me with the children down there, as well, while I teach and I won't feel so very alone. A woman unescorted is so improper, after all," she added with a pretty flutter of eyelashes and a girlish pout. Jane hoped she had calculated his response correctly.

The captain stared at her thoughtfully for a moment and then said, "Agreed, on one condition."

"And what is that, kind sir?" She asked, coyly.

"That you have dinner with me this night in my cabin, so I won't be lonely."

Without missing a beat, she pretended naiveté by answering, "Oh my Mother and I would be delighted to join you for dinner! That is so very gracious of you! We have grown so very bored with only each other for company these many days. What time shall we dine?" She asked with the pretended ecstatic excitement that only a great actor could muster.

"Er, just after sunset, will be fine," he stammered, feeling that he had lost the upper hand. He had hoped to dine with the girl alone, but now there was no graceful way to back out.

"Oh! How wonderful! I shall go and tell Mother straight away. She will be so pleased! Maybe she can accompany me to the hold later today and show the girls how to embroider roses. We will make haste to be sure to be on time for your generous invitation!" She giggled like a foolish schoolgirl, and rushed back toward her cabin seemingly enthralled.

As soon as she reached the darkness of the hall before her cabin door, the schoolgirl smile was quickly replaced with a moue of distaste. Fine, she could play at his transparent intrigues too. Jane thought to herself. She had gotten what she wanted again, with only a small price to pay. She just hoped that she would not be asked to sing for her supper, as well.

She took a few more deep breaths of the clean salty air and then went back into the cabin, to change back to her everyday clothing and get ready for a new day of schooling below. She could imagine the injuries that needed tending below all too well, after such a rough night at sea in crowded quarters.

Captain Spiers had actually been more than happy to be rid of Nate for a while and had readily agreed to Jane's proposition of bringing him below. But, Jane wisely brought Nate down to the hold as quickly as possible, before the captain had a chance to change his mind.

"Mr. McDonald? Mr. McLeod?" Jane's voice came from the top of the newly opened hold. She knelt down at the edge, squinting to see into the murky depths below.

James' face appeared in the gloom, with his brother-in-law, Ian, standing right next to him. They both looked up at her, like moles peeping out of their holes, half-blinded by the bright daylight from above.

"Nate is coming down and he has injured his right arm and his head. Could you help him down please?" The men caught Nate as he slipped and slid down the ladder, woozy and one arm bound in a sling. "Now here comes my mother too!" She called. Janet helped pull George out of the way, as he came to and pushed himself weakly away from the ladder. He came to his senses just in time to watch a swish of skirts go by, belonging to Jane, who was carefully following her mother down the ladder.

"Thank you Clancy!" Jane said to the sailor left up top. "We are fine now."

"Aye, Miss, you watch out for our Nate now then," Clancy said, smiling down at her gratefully. He liked this spirited young lady and he was grateful for her help with Nate. He had come to like the boy and felt sorry for his rough treatment from the captain.

"Yes, we will doona worrit!" James' assured him.

"If'n you need anything, you let me know." Clancy said, and then walked away from the hold, feeling less worried about the boy than he had in many months. It was well known on the ship, despite the captain's efforts at secrecy, that the boy was mistreated by the captain. Anything that kept him away from the captain's harsh anger seemed like a blessing to Clancy, despite how it happened.

Jane quickly explained about Nate's injuries to the group at the bottom of the ladder, and told them that Captain Spiers had agreed to let him stay below with them for now, since he could not perform his duties. Then she made quick introductions to everyone for her mother. She had to elbow her sharply, to get her to close her shocked and wide open mouth. Mary Jane came to her senses and shook off her initial shock at the deteriorated conditions in the hold, snapping her mouth closed and abruptly pasting on a smile. "My Mother, Mary Jane, will be helping me today, by helping some of the children start on some needlework, and reading. I could also use her advice in some of the more difficult matters," she said in an aside to Janet. "What is wrong with Mr. Morrison?" Jane asked her, peering down at his waxy face.

His gray face suddenly bloomed red as he realized he had fallen and his head was still in Janet's lap. He sat up too quickly, looking even more ashen than before. "Excuse me, Mrs. McLeod. I just need a breath of fresh air is all," he replied. "Excuse me please!" He said loudly, as he rushed to the ladder. James motioned with a dash of his head for Ian to follow him. They watched as he climbed shakily out of the hold and up on deck with Ian behind him for support.

By now, Sgian and Willie were at Nate's side, asking all kinds of questions and clearing a spot on the floor for him to sit with them. They were eager to hear tell of what had happened above, during the storm. Jane had given him more of the opium before they came down, not much because of his head injury, but enough that he was starting to get sleepy.

Nate began sleepily describing the storm and sliding around the wet deck. He told them about the huge waves and the monstrous wind that had forced them to pull in all the sails. He watched the two boys mouths go round with wonder, as he described the blue ball of lightning that had danced down the main mast and across the deck. Then he told them about falling into the Forbes cabin and smashing against the hull. The opium made him embellish the glorious medical ballet that Jane had then performed as she had anchored them with the shawl tied to the bunks. He told them about how both women had so intelligently sat on their heavy trunks to avoid sliding too much as the waves pitched the Hector around. He also dreamily described how Jane had held him through the long hours of the violent storm.

Sgian and Willie both sighed, picturing it all in vivid detail. They were also thoroughly charmed at the thought of pretty Jane Forbes holding him in her arms all through the storm.

"What a lucky gowk ya are!" Willie exclaimed, with a big grin, and a boyish push at Nate's chest.

"Aye," Sgian added, glancing at Jane Forbes talking animatedly with his parents. "I would ha' traded places with ya at any time, man, broken arm or no!"

Nate smiled back sleepily. "Aye, a sweet night it was too, even with the arm and the bash on the head and all. I am happy to be down here with you too, lads. Very happy..." he trailed off, as he fell asleep.

Sgian motioned to Willie with a sideways nod and they picked Nate up gently, Sgian at his back and Willie at his feet. Careful not to hurt his arm or head, they moved him over to the McDonald's family place. Sgian picked up his own blanket and covered the now soundly sleeping Nate. He mumbled something that neither boy could make out and smiled in his sleep. They looked at each other and shrugged, then set about telling their families what had happened to Nate, between listening to the men and women talk.

Jane brought her mother, Mary Jane, to Mary McDonald and began making their introductions. Mary gathered several willing mothers and their children and they set up a makeshift school area by bringing piles of bedding over to a dry spot, so that Mary Jane could sit comfortably on the decking as she taught. As she settled herself, she tried not to let it show on her face, how appalling she found the hold, with its sea slime and smells. She knew these people could not help it and she had no wish for them to feel embarrassed. Mary Jane smiled brightly at the dirty little faces gathering around her, looking past the filth to the bright children underneath.

She was here to teach needlework, reading, and spelling first, hoping to see where each student stood in abilities. William McKenzie, who was a teacher himself, came over to her school group immediately. After introducing himself, he graciously offered his own teaching skills, as well. He had all of his tutorials with him, since he planned to teach in the New World and could teach the more advanced students better than Mary Jane could. He had grown so restless, that he welcomed this opportunity to use his own skills for some good.

Mary Jane gratefully accepted his help, knowing it would allow Jane more time to help with the pox victims and maintain the ruse they had begun. She handed out knitting needles and homespun yarn to half the children. The rest she would work with on oral spelling exams, then the groups could switch subjects later. Many of the mothers stayed with their children to help them and unobtrusively to learn something for themselves. To the women that were interested, she showed a beautiful vine pattern with pink and red roses on it. It was an embroidery sampler of her own design. She let them get their own linens, or if they had none, she gave them white handkerchiefs to practice on and colorful flosses for their eager restless hands to work into something beautiful.

The knitting group was instructed to begin to knit a sock. Both Scottish boys and girls were normally taught this helpful task at a young age, as it was a perfectly acceptable activity for both sexes to learn to clicket. It was useful not only to fill the sometimes long hours of the evening, but it also served to keep their active families in stockings for the colder months. She wanted to see which children could neatly turn a heel and work quickly. These she knew would be ready for larger projects like sweaters, patterned shawls, or coverlets.

With her spelling group, she asked them all their names in turn, having them stand and also spell their name. Nods and frowns from the mothers listening, or her own common sense usually told her if they were right or wrong. Then she started with three to five letter words, working her way up to the largest words, until she had a good idea of each child's abilities and needs. She rearranged their seating accordingly, with the more advanced students toward the back of the group to work with Mr. McKenzie on History, Literature, or Ciphering.

Once the first group was settled, she classed the second group the same way, pausing occasionally to instruct a child or mother with an intricate stitch that she was questioned about. When all were settled, she helped the littlest finish up their socks and passed around her primers for reading paragraphs out loud, gently correcting any mistakes or omissions.

She realized after a few hours, that she was thoroughly enjoying herself, having not once thought of the surging of the sea around them.

She was in her element and could clearly see beyond the dirt and smells now, to the lively people and the bright children beneath. They were not so different than she and she felt a kinship with them just for being onboard during this terrible passage, and also for their common native land, dear Scotland. They had all now forsaken her in all but their hearts. Most would likely never see her green and beautifully rugged shores again. She blinked away the tears that threatened to overtake her. There was little use for looking back now. She took a deep shuddering breath and pulled the closest little one onto her lap, as much to comfort the little boy as to comfort herself.

Across the hold, the buckets had begun their trip from one hanky masked man to the next. They scooped the foul water out of the sickening slurry in the bottom of the ship's keel, passed it from hand to hand and then up and out of the hold to be cast overboard. It was a slimy, smelly and nauseating business that made an occasional man leave the line to go running up the ladder to add the contents of his stomach to that which was going overboard.

At first, it seemed like the dozen or so men were making no leeway, but then the slime began to recede ever so slowly. Buckets of clean seawater were used to wash down the remaining sludge from the upper portions of decking and into the keel well, adding to the bucket brigade's burden, but opening up much needed floor space that was wet, but at least clean. Those huddled miserably up near the overhead beams, began to creep back down into their original family spots again, drying the planks industriously with rags, as the mess was cleared up.

People were also taking turns going topside between the buckets of slop to breathe the fresh, rain washed air. George finally returned to the hold himself, having overcome his fear of being confined again, and also having emptied his stomach completely. The storm had been especially bad for him with its forced confinement. All he had been able to do was to hold onto Hector, waiting and praying for it to be over soon, so he could get out of the crowded hold for a while before he went screaming mad.

When the barrels had fallen in the sick room, he had helped James temporarily secure them. Now he used his carpentry skills to re-build a firm rack for them out of the broken bits of wood. The worsened scene in there had sickened his soul. He knew that many were hurt and was grateful that Janet had help tending to them all.

When the hatch had been opened, he had scrambled for the much needed fresh air and ended up in Janet McLeod's lap instead. Now he went to find Janet and offer his help with the remaining ill and the newly injured. He also wanted to apologize for any insult he might have done to her, when he had collapsed into her and then woken in her lap. He felt his face grow warm again, at the thought.

When he was near Janet he was also feeling the stirring of something he had not felt for a woman, since his wife's death. He had noticed it just brushing up against her, even in the midst of the worst of the pox - the thrill that ran through him even at an accidental touch. George had been even more certain of that, when he had awakened with his head in her lap. He wanted to be near her and examine those feelings a little closer, to make sure of what he felt. He also wanted to watch her more closely and see if she seemed to return any affection for him. He was surprised to realize that he hoped she might.

That night, came the sorrowful, secret burials of more young victims. The pipers' laments had been playing softly at night for days and had everyone in a sober mood. Even the families that had escaped any deaths felt badly for their many neighbors and friends around them who had lost so much. Their relief was palpable as they felt fortunate to have been passed over during the ordeal. Everyone held their children a little tighter, showing more affection and appreciation for those who had not been lost.

The captain and crew were found to be in a sour mood after the storm, especially after James and Old Hugh had gone to report the broken barrels and wet packages below. The men had suspected that much of what had been spoiled was water and food rations for the rest of the voyage. They were correct. Some water could be collected with the sails when it rained, if it rained again, but the loss of the food rations was a serious matter.

What the passengers below did not know, and the crew only suspected, was that the storm had pushed them seriously off course. They were now well south of their intended course and would have to sail many miles north to get to Pictou. This would lengthen the voyage by as much as two weeks, depending on the prevailing winds. An additional two weeks could make the difference between life and death to many on board and the sailors knew it all too well. Smiles and laughter had now become an even scarcer commodity amongst the crew of the Hector, as fear began to undermine their usually unflappable fortitude.

Chapter Sixteen

New Loves

Finally the pox seemed to clear, as no more new illnesses were occurring and the rest of the sick were recovering steadily. Even little Donny Ross, the last one to fall ill, seemed better than he had in days. The survivors of the illness were now bound together, like an extended family. All of the passengers in the hold showed the greatest respect not only to Jane Forbes and her mother, but especially to Janet and Hugh McLeod, James and Mary McDonald, and all of their respective kin. The Hector's stricken passengers had survived the cruel loss and heart wrenching deaths of eighteen youngsters, ranging from three-months-old to sixteen-years-old, from the pox, the flux and then the storm's viciousness. Their reduced numbers were sadly lamented, as nearly every family had been touched by tragedy.

The women concentrated their efforts on those who had not recovered well. Maggie McLeod, Abigail Murray, and Jean Fraser were all mothers who had lost their bairns and were even more depressed than was usual. Their kin, and the women, were closely watching Maggie and Abigail. Neither had spoken sanely, since the deaths of their infants. Jean Fraser was also still seen crying alone too often, and would not yet speak to anyone about losing her daughter; not even her husband or her son. But when spoken to, she at least answered clearly, where Maggie and Abigail had not. Everyone had tried to be as helpful and gentle as possible with the three young mothers, but only time would tell if they would return from their depression, or not.

Jane and Janet still mixed up the nerve tonics with Chamomile and other sedatives for the three women every day, with only a half dose for Jean Fraser. They tried their best to bring them out of their shell by talking to them as if everything were normal. Maggie would rarely be separated from her goats, and only really spoke to them. They had at least noted some improvement when they were able to get her to help with their milking. Her husband Davy was also taking it very hard but he stayed protectively near his wife. His son was dead and his wife was in a world of her own. He often looked nearly as lost as she did.

Some of the recovering infants were still getting supplemental feedings of goat's milk, as well as the pregnant woman, Jane Gibson, and Mary McDonald and the other mothers who were still nursing bairns. Davy remained faithfully by Maggie's side, night and day, as did Old Hugh when he was not busy squirreling food away, both trying to gently engage her in conversation.

Abigail was now beginning to at least acknowledge her surroundings through the unwavering love and support of her husband and her remaining children; but it had been a near thing. She had been discovered just as she was about to climb over the rail a few days before, by Clancy. She had not put up a fight when he escorted her back below; she just seemed confused about following her child into the sea. The usually tough Clancy had been visibly upset when he had returned her to the hold. Now everyone was keeping close watch, in case she should try to suicide again. Her husband had not left her side since the incident and he had aged overnight from the strain of his worry for her.

Mary Jane had a long talk with her and she had exacted her promise not to leave her children and her husband to fend for themselves, convincing her finally that her daughter was gone. She had tearfully agreed, but she was still not functioning as the mother of the family. Her husband still relied a great deal on Jane's, Mary's and Janet's help. The schooling that Mary Jane had started at least kept their other children busy, so he could give all of his attention to his recovering wife.

Jean Fraser was at least functioning as wife and mother to her husband and son, but she did it as if she was a puppet and she immediately retreated to her shell of grief when the tasks were complete. Mainly, the three women concentrated on talking with her and relied less and less on the nerve tonic they had concocted. They also got her and her son Willie to come and join the school group, even though she often just spent the time silently crying as she struggled to finish piecing a baby quilt that she had begun after they had boarded the Hector. The women had tried without success to get her to begin a different project.

Molly McKenzie had mostly recovered from her depression, even after losing her two youngest children. Mary Jane said it was mainly because she had been too busy trying to help the women nurse the other survivors to spend much time alone thinking. Molly just insisted that she was grateful for what they had tried to do for her own children and wished to repay their kindness. Her doing so seemed to help her recover faster than some of the others from their disabling grief. "I am a lucky woman to still ha' a loving husband and two older sons ta comfort me," she told Janet firmly, when she was asked about her ability to help. "I canna sit by and just watch ya struggle alone. If I mun just sit here doin' nothing, I shall go mad."

Mary McDonald was also feeling the crushing weight of her grief over losing her Alex, but she was kept busy trying to nurse the two remaining babes, take care of her large family and still help out Jane and Janet with the ill. Time and activity had already begun to work their magic of healing the wound. Her determination to see the rest of her children make it through this voyage along with her husband James support, and her unexpected friendships with Janet McLeod and Jane Forbes had given her the extra strength she needed to make it through each long and terrible day.

Now that things were returning to normal on board, Mary felt great pride in what they had been able to accomplish so far, and great thankfulness to her new friends Janet and Jane Forbes and now Jane's mother, Mary Jane too, for their unexpected help. Her children were also getting a valuable education with Mary Jane and William McKenzie and this freed up some of her time as well. She used it to learn as much as she could of healing from Janet and Mary Jane, squirreling the knowledge away for later use on the rest of her own large family.

Now that the men were no longer doing the secret burials at sea, and had also moved and dried as much as possible of the undamaged cargo, they often sat together talking about their hopes and plans once they reached Pictou. Those that still had pipe tobacco shared what they could when they occasionally smoked, passing their pipes around the circle.

Many friendships had been forged through the horror of the epidemic and the storm, and now many wished to be neighbors and friends with those who had endured the hardship with them. It made them anxious to get to know one another. Family groups were now much larger than they had been at the beginning of their journey.

A strong alliance had now been forged through circumstances, between the McDonalds and the McLeods and many others wished to be a part of their circle of trusted friends. They had proven themselves to be caring leaders and trustworthy in a crisis, and it had not gone unnoticed by the others on board.

Ian had had not one, but two fathers offer their daughter's hand in marriage in their efforts to connect their families. Ian had politely declined, saying he was needed by his own family right now, but he was also careful not to insult either man. He was shrewd enough to know that their continued friendship could only benefit them all, once they were in their new land and he did not want to damage those friendships.

He was also busy trying to sort out why he was spending such a great deal of time with young Margaret McKay, since Mary had taken on the nursing of her broken leg. She was bright, pretty and very quick witted. Even though she was just sixteen, he felt an unusual attraction to her, finding himself often at her side before he realized it. He did not know if his affections were returned, but he found he was hoping more and more that they would be. He was nearly ten years her senior, but he hoped that she did not feel this difference too greatly, or that she had not already given her affection to another. She was always friendly to him, yet he could not discern if she was attracted to him or not.

Ian gradually began to get to know her family as they came over daily to see her and he took every opportunity to talk with all of them. He liked them and found them to be agreeable company. Although Margaret had the biggest stubborn streak of them all, he was amused by it, being used to his own MacGregor clan. His sister, Mary, was just that stubborn, if not more so. When Margaret was obstinately arguing with Mary that she could walk on her braced leg, Ian had been the only one who could talk her into staying off of it just a little longer.

He sat down next to her and said, "now Margaret, I ken how hard it be for ya to sit aboot doin' aught. But if my sister says ya should, then ya should if you want your leg ta mend straight! Now a pretty lass like yourself surely doesna want a limp, now do ya?"

She stopped arguing and looked straight at him with her bold blue-green eyes and he felt his heart stop beating for a few moments and then it raced ahead again in an attempt to catch up, like a frightened rabbit. "I meant no offense, Miss," he added, thinking he had angered her.

Ian could not have been more wrong. It was his saying that she was pretty that had caught her attention and made her take a look at him as a woman would; sizing him up as a handsome man and searching his eyes for the honesty and integrity to back his pretty words. He was obviously older than she, but she found a certain comfort in that and also knew him to be a trustworthy and helpful man during the trials of the pox and the storm. He had always been there to help, even putting himself at risk to help bring all the poor dead bairns to the sea for burial. Margaret had grown to like his family very much and felt comfortable with them, as they were much like her own. She decided that she would listen to Mary after all and stay off the leg until it was healed. She did not want to admit it to anyone but herself yet, but being near Ian a while longer was her biggest motivation to stay off her leg. Even the thought of crippling herself did not mean as much to her as his nearness now did.

In the meantime, she planned on watching Mr. Ian MacGregor for more signs of his caring and interest. She had not dreamed that an older and admittedly handsome man like Ian might be interested in her, so she thought she might still be mistaken. But if she were not, Ian MacGregor had no idea what he had gotten himself into. She would play no games nor be coy, like some lasses, once she was sure he felt similarly. She would let him know, in no uncertain terms, that the affection was returned.

James came to get Ian to join a conversation and Mary caught the speculative smile on Margaret's lips as she watched him go. Without realizing it, she began to comb through her long dirty blonde hair with her fingers, preening unconsciously as she untangled it. Mary smiled to herself. She knew very well what that look meant and she liked the match. This girl was strong and stubborn and Mary could see that under the layer of grime, lay the exact mix of beauty and temperament that could likely tame her beloved brother, Ian.

She rummaged through her packs and found the ivory backed hairbrush that had belonged to her mother. Mary sat down behind Margaret without a word of preamble and began combing the tangles out of her hair, revealing its deep golden shine with the gentle coaxing of her brushstrokes. Gently she plaited it and then carefully wound the long braid up onto Margaret's head and pinned it in strategic places to hold it fast. Then she took a rag and wet it a little from a nearby bucket of seawater and wiped at the girl's dirty face. The skin revealed beneath, matched the glow of ivory on her brush. Margaret sat completely still through it all, almost ignoring Mary's ministrations, watching Ian across the hold talking with some other men.

Mary was woman enough to understand the secret smile on her face. She was studying Ian as a love interest and she seemed to like what she saw.

Mary turned Margaret's face toward her own, to assess her work and was astounded at the transformation. Margaret was very beautiful with her high cheekbones and arched brows, despite the stubborn set of her strong jaw. Her shining skin and hair glowed as if lit from within, and her blue-green eyes looked like the ocean did when it lay quietly in the shallows near the shore. With her hair up, she looked years older and was truly a sight to behold. Unconsciously, she looked back at Ian again.

Mary interrupted her staring at Ian, gently turning her face her way again and said, "I ken ya be interested in Ian, then?"

Startled to have been so accurately read without having said a word, Margaret was at first speechless, then her eyes flitted back and forth searching for escape and finding none, they fell to her lap in embarrassment. "I.... I....was just thinkin'." She stammered.

"Aye, I can see tha'," Mary said with a satisfied grin. "I can almost see wha' ya are thinkin' aboot too!"

Embarrassed even further, Margaret's ivory skin suddenly flamed pink.

"Oh, doona feel ashamed, lass! I have no wish ta embarrass ya. I ha' seen him talking wit' ya and thought it a good match, but hadna seen the affection returned by ya! Until today tha' is. Today I saw wha' could become of it, if ya both feel the same."

Margaret looked up at her and smiled. "So ya approve of the match, do ya? Well and I canna say tha' displeases me. But I would have it be Ian's choice more than anyone else's," Margaret said meaningfully. "I have already made my choice, should he wish ta ask ta court me. I shall stay here wit' your family and help however I may. I willna try ta walk aboot, for as long as ya think 'tis necessary." Margaret smiled at Mary with girlish charm and raised one eyebrow in question, conspiratorially.

Mary laughed and the two women smiled at each other in complete understanding and with renewed respect for each other. "Fair enough," Mary said decisively.

"Now, aboot tha' dress," Mary said, frowning at the stained rag it had become. I think I have a dress tha' might fit. "'Tis nothing fancy, mind, but 'tis pretty and unstained. Would you care ta try it on?"

"I think tha' is verra kind of ya," Margaret answered, "and most appreciated too." She looked down at her ruined and outgrown dress, plucking uncomfortably at the torn, stained and thoroughly unsatisfactory fabric.

Mary quickly checked on the infants who were both sleeping peacefully for once. Then she glanced over at the school group to see that her children were all securely occupied there and also at the men, James and Ian. They seemed to be engaged with Old Hugh and Davy and four others about some matter. She knew from their expressions that they would be talking for some time. The women had some precious time to themselves.

She reached for her bundle and brought out a carefully folded chemise and petticoats, an embroidered stomacher and a homespun skirt. "Come on, lass; give me tha' blanket ta shield ya with, whilst ya try this on. Mind the leg now! Ye canna stand on it yet, so ya will ha' ta try ta manage it seated."

She handed the garments to young Margaret and stood making a curved wall around her, so that no one could see her as she struggled to change garments from a seated position. With a bit of direction and a tug here and there from Mary, Margaret managed it and then rocked from side to side until she had the skirt settled under and over herself, hiding the broken leg and its crude brace.

Mary removed the blanket and stood back to look at her. The effect of a clean, pretty dress was magically transforming. True it was mere homespun, but Mary had given it her pretty sewing details; a fitted waist with a full flared skirt, its edge embroidered with green vines and green laces on the stomacher to match. She smiled to herself with satisfaction about how the green embroidery brought out the green in Margaret's eyes. "Gi' me your old gown, lass, perhaps, I can make a wee skirt out of it for Katy or Lizzie," Mary added, always of a mind not to waste.

Margaret happily relinquished her old dress and looked down at herself with a girlish smile, thrilled that the gown was comfortable and that it fit her. She could also see that it was a much more grown up woman's dress, emphasizing her figure more than any she had yet owned. She felt great gratitude toward her new friend. "This is more than I can possibly repay ya for the noo, but I willna forget the kindness and the generosity tha' ya ha' shown me. When I am whole again, I wull make a grand dress for ya in repayment of the debt, ya ha' my word on it," she added as she looked back up at Mary with eyes that reflected her genuine thankfulness in their sparkling tears.

"Lass, the only repayment I need from ya is for ya ta love my brother Ian as greatly as he deserves. Because when he sees ya like this, there wull be no hope for him. He will be lost ta ya forever!"

"Do you really think so?" Margaret asked, smiling hopefully.

"I most certainly do!" Mary said, laughing, "or I shall personally wash his eyes oot for him because he would have ta be a right blind auld mumper ta no see your beauty the noo!"

They both began giggling like young girls and Mary sat down next to her, eager to talk girl talk about Ian, life and love in general. She was very interested in getting to know this girl she now believed might someday be kin.

Janet and Jane were getting increasingly worried over the state of Maggie and Abigail and still to some extent Jean, although they were not as worried about her mind, as they were Maggie's and Abigail's. They had been trying along with the rest of Maggie's family to engage her in conversation, but nothing seemed to hold any interest for her, other than her goats. She talked to them and no one else, but would quietly do as she was asked. Davy, her husband, was distraught about not getting Maggie to even acknowledge him when he talked to her.

Old Hugh tried to give him some solace. Seeing his lad suffer so, he had taken to talking to him a great deal more. Not having his wife to grieve with, made the grieving process that much worse for him. The whole family was hurting over the loss of wee Alex and it made it so much worse to see the normally cheerful and resourceful Maggie, in the doll-like state that she now lived in, seemingly dead to them all except Ana and Abby, her goats.

The women slowly weaned her and the other two women off of the tonics, thinking that might bring them back to the present, but so far all it had done was make them sleep restlessly. Maggie was still unresponsive, and Abigail just cried more often, as did Jean. Janet and Jane were in agreement, however, that Maggie's inability to cry was far more serious than the other's crying so often. They expected a breakdown of some sort after taking her off the nerve tonic and had been prepared for that, but her continued unresponsiveness worried them even more.

After much discussion, Jane went to speak with her mother about it, and she agreed to come and take a look at her. The adults looked on as Mary Jane touched her gently all over, speaking to her in soft Gaelic all the while, almost as one would handle a timid horse. She whispered a few questions and got whispered answers back. Just her response to Mary Jane seemed like a very good sign to the others. Mary Jane felt back and forth across her lower stomach area, whispered something to Maggie softly and then she slowly stood, reaching her hand out indicating Maggie should join her.

Maggie stared up at Mary Jane, for a few frozen moments, her mouth open wide with shock, and then she rose and stood next to her. She abruptly reached for Mary Jane's outstretched hand and asked her plainly, "truly?"

Mary nodded with a smile and answered, "yes, truly! So you have reason to wake from this tragedy and rejoin your life again. Something wonderful was lost, but there is still much to hold onto now, isn't there?"

Maggie nodded to her and then shook her head as if waking, the memory of the golden evening of her and David's lovemaking last spring coming immediately to mind. She had apparently conceived on that magical night! "Aye, aye there is!" She looked over at her husband, Davy and rushed into his arms. "I thought all was lost with our Alex. Please forgive me my love. We are ta have another bairn, another chance!" She broke down crying for the first time since losing Alex. She clung to him in mingled grief and joy, as the world finally broke through and into her dark dreaming.

Davy looked over her shoulder at Mary Jane, the question clear, in his tear-filled eyes.

"Yes, Davy, your wife is about three or possibly four months with child. It is hard to say for certain. The babe must have been conceived in Scotland and about the time your wife would have normally noticed the loss of her monthly cycle, you were readying to leave Scotland. Then when the pox struck, her mind was likely only on poor wee Alex. She is right; you have another chance with another babe." Her voice broke on the last word, as she too began to cry along with the others at the sad, yet hopeful thought.

It had been such an awful thing for them to lose their first and only child. No child could replace the lost one, but there would be renewed hope with this new and unexpected addition to the McLeod family. It was the miracle they had needed to mend Maggie's heart and mind. The family was overcome with emotion by this joyous turn of events. They took turns sobbing and hugging Maggie, welcoming her back from the waking hell she had been occupying since Alex's tragic death.

Old Hugh extended his big hands to cover Mary Jane's small ones in a heartfelt and teary gratitude to her that needed no spoken words.

After a whispered discussion, Jane and her mother moved on to the Murray clan, to see what could be done for poor Abigail. She had other children and could maybe be encouraged to rejoin life because of them, like Maggie had for her pregnancy. Mary Jane spoke with her and touched her as she had Maggie, but Abigail simply withdrew from her and would not speak. They reminded her of her two boys, Adam and Walter, who were still living, and her husband who remained by her side; but she remained catatonic and would not speak nor even look them in the eye.

They tried for about an hour and then spoke with her husband, Christopher, privately and encouraged him to keep doing the same for her and not to give up hope. He nodded in understanding, but he struggled to withhold the tears as they fell despite his efforts. The women felt awful for him, his wife and their sons. "It's just tha' she wanted a lass for sa long now, aye?" He wiped his face with both hands and then tiredly shrugged in despair. There was nothing anyone could think of to do for them, but pray that she would somehow heal.

John Sutherland had been suffering from a tooth abscess and his wife had requested that the women treat him, if they could. Mary Jane prodded the swollen area of John's face, inside and outside with gentle fingers. After asking John a few questions, she advised Janet to give him saltwater to rinse his mouth with, three times each day. In addition to that she told her to make a small poultice of whole cloves soaked in peppermint oil to be applied directly onto the swollen area of his gums near the affected tooth. She also told him that the tooth would need to be removed by any means necessary, should it not improve after a month. He nodded in mute acceptance of her assessment, letting his wife thank them while he held his hand to his face.

After that, they went to see the last little victim of the pox and make sure he was still recovering. Little Donny Ross's spots still showed, but they were no longer pus filled and were scabbing over nicely. The boy himself was back to his four-year-old rambunctious self and they could barely get him to sit still for the examination, so they took that as the final sign that he would be just fine. He was the last sick child in the squalid little back room that had been hastily made to care for the sick. Confident that the worst was now over, they told Marion that she could return to her family now with little Donny. The danger had passed.

Marion started to cry, the relief of the strain she had been under finally taking its toll. "Thank you so much, you and all your friends, for what you have done to help save my Donny! I can never repay you for your care!" Marion got out between sobs.

"It is all right, my dear," Mary Jane quickly said, shushing her. "Everything will be all right. Now wipe your tears and put a smile back on your face to go and greet your husband and your family with the wonderful news."

Marion smiled back at them through her tears and nodded. She wiped her face with a corner of her apron and then followed them out of the wretched sick room that they had been in for so many days now. When she reached the main hold, she made a beeline for her husband Alex, who was already standing, having seen her emerge from the sickroom with Donny. Marion dove into the safety of his arms with Donny wiggling and protesting between their relieved embrace.

Mary Jane and Jane glanced at the hatch door to the hold and saw the orange glow of the coming sunset. Jane nodded ever so slightly in grim acknowledgement of it. It was time for them to go and get ready for their promised dinner with the captain. Neither of them were looking forward to it, but it was imperative that they keep their promise to him, lest their below decks privileges be taken away. Jane found it ironic that they needed permission to be down here in the bowels of the ship, while these people here below decks must beg permission to even be up on deck for a breath of fresh air. Mary Jane went to tell the children and their mothers goodnight, while Jane went and said her farewell's to Janet and the McLeods, and then to Mary and the growing McDonald clan.

Jane was taken aback by Mary's transformation of young Margaret and complimented her on her attire. Mary winked at her and Jane knew that she would be told the reason for all of it at a more appropriate time. She checked on Nate and left some opium for Mary to give to him if he woke in the night, but he was sleeping peacefully. She told them all good night and they thanked her again for her and her mother's help, which she accepted gracefully.

Mary Jane came back and also said her goodnights and they both ascended the ladder with a gallant helping hand from James. He felt bad for having doubted the girl, when she had been so helpful to his family and friends. He couldn't help but wonder a little at their seeming reluctance to leave, since he assumed their accommodations to be very comfortable in comparison to theirs. He sensed there was more to it and asked his wife about it.

"Weel, I am sure they are none too pleased ta be obliged ta dine wit' the captain tonight is all. Who would wish ta dine with such a man?" Mary asked, with a shiver of repulsion.

"And why are they obliged, then?" James asked, puzzled.

"Jane told me tha' were the deal she struck with him, in order ta get his permission ta bring Nate down here ta heal."

"I see," James answered, frowning as his mind turned the facts over. "And what other deal has she had ta make on our behalf, I wonder?"

"Now, James! Don't you dare be thinkin' that girl improper! She keeps her mother close ta her side. That Jane's a smart enough lass no ta be caught alone with tha' villain, aye?"

"I know that, my dearest! I was thinkin' more aboot the ideas he may be forming in his own wee hied, is all. We may end up interceding for her, should things get ugly between them, and tha' could be verra dangerous; verra dangerous indeed," he added looking at the hatch thoughtfully.

Mary said nothing for a while, as she thought about a possible quarrel with the captain and the ensuing chaos that would bring about. She knew that must not happen. At least not out to sea as they were now, where the captain's word was law. She crossed herself and said a silent prayer that their captain would behave like a gentleman and that they were worrying for nothing.

Mary Jane and Jane had returned to their cabin and taken turns washing and helped each other change into their better, but not their best gowns. Jane had been sure to choose the long-sleeved, one-piece black wool that hid the most skin possible, in order to avoid any misconceptions about her that Captain Spiers may have been forming. It had a frilly white lace collar that buttoned right up her neck and its hip pads covered much of her slim hips and buttocks. She felt every bit the frump and was, for once, quite content with it.

Her mother chose moss-green wool of a similar style, but wide enough to accommodate her beloved hoops. They donned the family jewels, and primped and pinned each other's hair to great heights in order to dress themselves more formally for the occasion so that it would not be evident that they were dressing down for the captain. Lastly, they applied some of the rice powder that made their skin look fashionably pale and fragile, as if they were attending a ball. Hopefully, they would achieve the intended effect of great propriety and receive the respect due them in return from Captain Spiers.

They left their cabin, stood in the cramped corridor and rapped smartly on Captain Spiers' door. His First Mate, Dewey, opened it immediately for them and the captain rose from his seat at the beautifully set table to greet them politely.

"Good evening, ladies! Welcome to my humble table." He gestured for them each to sit on either side of him and they did so, as they curtsied to him in return. He was dressed impeccably from head to toe, even donning a fancy curled and powdered wig. He wore more frills at his neck than both of theirs put together and even had a large feathered hat lying nearby. His formality made him seem less of a rogue and more a gentleman than when he wore his everyday captain's attire.

The table was set with a bowl of fresh fruit as an alluring centerpiece, atop a red silk tablecloth. His dishes were fine imported china decorated with exotic green and red dragons around the edges of the gold-rimmed plates and cups. It was a surprise to Jane to see such exotic splendor out here on the ocean and it was in sharp contrast to what they had seen below, as he had known it would be.

Jane felt his eyes upon her, expecting her compliments and moved to oblige him. "What lovely china! Why it must have come directly from China!" Jane flattered him, witlessly.

"As a matter of fact, it does come from China," he said, as he leaned toward her to kiss her hand, lingering over it inappropriately for a casual dinner. "The source of some, but not all such beauty," he said, lifting her hand and smoothly complementing her. "I used to make the runs to the West Indies in my younger days and I acquired it there. I thought it most unusual and beautiful. So we share the same tastes then?" He asked, with one eyebrow raised, every bit the rogue again.

Jane smiled in what she hoped was a dim-looking smile and removed her hand from his grasp. She would not be baited with his false flattery and found a blush rising honestly to her cheeks. It was not from being pleased, but more from being embarrassed by his behavior in the presence of her mother. She had hoped that her presence would deter his advances somewhat.

"Well, I am sure that you will both like the wine I have procured to complement our meal tonight. It is a French Bordeaux that I find very pleasing to the palate. But here, you must taste it for yourself!" He indicated that Dewey should pour their wine from the previously opened bottle and then shooed him back into the shadows.

"I propose a toast, to both of the lovely ladies gracing my table with your winsome beauty this night!"

A skilled man with the ladies, it seems, Mary Jane thought to herself, her protective motherly instincts growing more heightened with each passing moment. They all took sips from the wine after enjoying its cloying bouquet that nearly disguised its strong alcohol content. Yes, a very dangerous man indeed. We must be careful with this one. She thought, eyeing him like a dangerous snake. She placed her glass down after a polite sip, eyeing Jane to do the same.

"Yes, it is very good. Rather fruity and flowery." Jane said. "But then I am no wine connoisseur." She set her glass down nearly untouched and smiled at him innocently. She jumped and nearly overturned her glass when Dewey stomped loudly on an unfortunate rat.

Captain Speirs frowned a little as he watched her put the glass down nearly untouched, but then quickly recovered his smile and his false charm and indicated that they be served the first course, some remarkably fresh pears with a pat of soft cheese on the side, atop tiny dragon encircled plates.

Jane had decided that she would not be seduced or made drunk on wine with him, but she would certainly enjoy the wonderful food as long as it lasted. It took all of her lady-like training not to devour the pear in one bite. It was delicious, but she ate it slowly with bits of the cheese and restrained herself from licking her plate like she was sorely tempted to do. Pears were one of her favorite fruits and despite their over-ripeness, she relished the treat. She could not remember the last time she had had such a delicious treat.

Mary Jane made small talk about the ship and the weather and with pretended innocence got the captain talking about the voyage and how much longer it would be, as he indulged himself with more and more of his own wine.

By the main course of dried beef and gravy over potatoes, Captain Spiers was obviously drunk. Both the women had been careful only to take tiny sips of the exceptionally strong wine and they were still working carefully on their first glass, despite them being topped off often by Dewey, as the captain indicated.

Jane joined in the small talk more, now that her appetite had been thoroughly satiated. She had also noticed that the captain was beginning to talk foolishly and thought they might be able to get him to talk loosely and discover more about the mystery of their young friend, Nate.

"Other than that awful storm, and the beginning when Mother was so ill, it has been a rather pleasant voyage, so far. It is too bad your boy, Nate, was injured though. Just terrible...." Jane trailed off.

The captain's icy blue eyes instantly flashed at her. "How'd you know he's my boy?" He asked sharply, before thinking.

"Nate's your boy? You mean your son? Oh, I am so sorry! I hadn't meant to.... oh my! I simply thought he was your cabin boy!" Jane acted flustered and embarrassed, which was easy under the circumstances.

Mary Jane quickly pounced. "I apologize for any insult. I can assure you that we had no idea that Nate was actually your son."

Angered by their discovery of his tightly held secret, he glanced threateningly at Dewey, who took his meaning and stepped back into the shadows discreetly. Captain Spiers took another large swallow of wine and then clamped his mouth shut. He had no intention of revealing anything else to these women. They were either very clever or very stupid and he could not decide in his state which one it was. He found neither thought was very appealing.

"Oh! Let us talk about something else! I am so sorry to have brought it up. Isn't the weather lovely now, sunny and warm, with such a lively wind?" Jane gushed, like a simpleton. "Surely we will be to the New World ahead of schedule?"

"Oh, I should think so, my dear," her mother said, picking up the thread of the unraveling conversation.

Dessert was served by a now smugly grinning Dewey. It was a surprising treat that consisted of Dutch chocolates and a wonderful cognac.

As they sampled the chocolate and took just a tiny sip of cognac, their eyes locked in unspoken agreement. The captain had not spoken in some time, had downed two glasses of cognac on top of the wine and seemed almost ready to pass out in his chair, the way he was tilting with the sea swells.

"So, what do you think, Captain Spiers? Will we arrive ahead of schedule?" Jane pressed him.

His eyes blazed open and he slammed his fist down on the table, knocking over his own glass. "By God, no! We will be lucky to arrive on time at this point. And as for our lively wind, young lady; in case you haven't noticed, we are in the Doldrums. We could rot here forever for lack of a lively wind! Lively wind, indeed, pah!" the captain spat, as he teetered drunkenly in his chair.

"I am sorry, but we must take our leave, Captain Spiers. It seems that we have upset you and that was not our intention." Mary Jane timed it perfectly with his rudeness and rose to go and Jane obediently rose with her.

"Wait!" He cried drunkenly. "You do not have my leave!"

"Well, never-the-less, I think that is best," Mary Jane said in her best motherly and disapproving tone. "Come along, Jane. Thank you for your hospitality and the lovely dinner, Captain Spiers, but we must bid you goodnight."

The First Mate, Dewey, opened the door for them and was now grinning ear to ear. He realized what they had done and was thoroughly charmed by their womanly shrewdness and the way they had handled his difficult captain. They nodded politely at him as they left and walked quickly out on deck and up toward the bow. When they were alone and as far as they could get from the captain, they hugged each other giggling and chattering, like small birds released from their cage.

"So much for his seduction plans," Mary Jane said with a sly smile.

"Yes, I think his tricks worked better on himself than they did upon us. Why, we got the answers to two of our questions out of the man and we were hardly even trying! Ha!" Jane cried in triumph.

"Shhh, yes, we did," Mary Jane said, peering around in the darkness for sign of anyone nearby. "But the answer was not what I had hoped in either case." A sailor began coming toward them. "We will talk more tomorrow and let those below know what we have found out. Let's turn in for the night." They both smiled and nodded politely at the sailor as he passed, but he did not return the smile as they made their way back to their tiny cabin.

Tom Mandler scowled as he watched the backsides of the retreating women as they went aft. They were up to something; he was sure of it. Just as he was sure that that rat, Ian, and his kin were also up to something. All of them quit talking as soon as he was within hearing range, but he would catch one of them sooner or later. He vowed to continue to bide his time and watch them all, until someone slipped up and one of their secrets was revealed.

He smiled a wicked grin, hoping as always, that Ian was at the heart of it. How he would enjoy seeing him flogged or taken off the ship in chains. Tom continued on his way to the forward mast position, thinking about how much he would enjoy watching the captain taking the Cat'o-nine-tails to Ian. He could almost hear the crack of the Cat and the rip of flesh, if he thought about it hard enough, and he was the type of man to truly relish the idea.

✛ ✛ ✛

George was helping Janet with her rounds to the injured and the grieving mothers now that everyone else had left her for their own families for the evening. Hector was with Lizzie, so he had been doing the lifting and helping with braces and wrappings that needed replacing or salves that needed to be applied. He quietly watched Janet as she worked, always smartly and efficiently, but also with a loving touch that he found healing to his own heart as he saw her caring for others.

He had no idea that she was also assessing him, in her own quiet way. She appreciated his helpful attitude and calm demeanor. It was what her Hugh had been like and what had made being in his company so very soothing. His quiet strength had always made her feel safe. George made her feel the same way. As they talked to others and worked around the hold as a team, many other eyes watched them and mused about what a nice couple they made. After they had moved on to the next needy family, there was a great deal of whispering and speculation about them.

Old Hugh had taken a special interest in the pair, since he was responsible for Janet. He had liked George Morrison from the first and he had proven himself to be a trustworthy and resourceful man in a pinch. He was always gentle with the children even though he was a large scarecrow of a man and he seemed to be a good father to his Hector. Hugh had also taken note that James McDonald trusted him implicitly and Hugh trusted James' judgment as he did no one other than his own kin. Old Hugh knew that George had come on board the Hector with the few passengers that boarded at Greenock, the McDonald clan, the pregnant lass and her brother, and the fair Forbes women. He also knew the man had a trade and was a resourceful carpenter. He had fashioned a new rack out of broken barrels and scrap wood that would likely not break again until the rotting boards of the Hector herself tore loose from her frame.

He watched them move around the room and took careful note of how quiet and gentle George was with his daughter-in-law and also how she seemed to favor him with the loveliest smile. He had not seen anything like it from her, since Young Hugh had been lost at sea. Old Hugh had thought that Janet would never re-marry, having seen the great love between her and his eldest son. He still felt surprisingly sharp pain when her thought about the loss, but would never be one to deny Janet a chance for new love.

He was very surprised the first time he saw George favor Janet with a smile, as it changed his somber somewhat homely face into a kind, handsome and wondrous thing to behold. They made a fine match to be sure, two widowers who were both lonely and both trying to care for their bairns alone. But he had to be sure, before it went any further. He grabbed his ragged jacket and made a beeline for James McDonald, who was talking to Ian earnestly over by the old sickroom.

"I ken she be young, James, but I canna see how tha' matters! Why Mary was barely sixteen summers when ya wed! How is this sa different, then?" Ian lifted one dark brow and crossed his arms across his chest stubbornly, as he waited for James' answer. He had the light of battle in his eyes and he was ready and waiting.

James was no fool and could see that Ian was spoiling for a fight on the subject. He had seen that light in both Ian's eyes and those of his wife's before and recognized that he had started something that he could likely not win. "I... it... isna... oh, bloody hell!" James stammered his mouth opening and closing like a fish out of water.

Amused, Old Hugh took this opportune moment to interrupt the lively argument by clearing his throat loudly, as he approached. "Ah, there ya are then, friend James. I've been meanin' ta talk ta ya aboot a certain matter. But doona let me interrupt!" He smiled innocently at both of them, as if he hadn't heard a word.

"Your no interrupting, Hugh, I was done talkin' ta this clot-heid," Ian said, and with a final glare at James he stalked away in irritation.

"I didna mean ta interrupt. If ya would rather finish wit' him....?" Hugh began, his innocence belied by a knowing grin.

"Acch, nay we are finished the noo," James exclaimed in obvious disgust. "I canna talk any sense into him any more than I can my own Mary. I'd as soon jump ship as try ta continue with it," he huffed.

"Is it anything I can assist with, friend James, since I am looking for a bit of chat myself?" Hugh asked, smiling his encouragement.

"Not unless you know a cure for madness, ya canna," James said, obviously frustrated. "All my kin have gone right daft ower this girl, Margaret McKay that my wife's been caring for. Ian seems ta fancy her ower all the other lasses that their folk be nearly throwing at him!" He gestured widely to the hold in general. "And many of them would be a right suitable match. But never mind all tha' since my opinion matters naught ta Ian, as he says he loves the lass."

"Let's step up on deck ta catch some air, as I have a matter of a similar nature ta discuss wit' ya," Hugh said with a grin, clapping James on the back with his gnarled, but still powerful hand. He leaned on his cane and turned toward the ladder.

"Aye," James answered. "I could use a bit of air the noo," James answered loudly, for Ian's benefit, as they made their way to the ladder passing the still fuming and glaring Ian.

"Achh!" Ian declared with dismissive disgust as he passed.

Old Hugh risked a wink at Ian as they ascended and Ian quit glaring and cocked his head, following their progress curiously.

Once on deck, both Old Hugh and James took great refreshing gulps of sea air and leaned against the starboard rail looking toward the horizon. The sun was setting on the port side behind them, so they seemed to be pointing more or less northerly, although at the moment there was little wind to move them much at all. Old Hugh's sea knowledge and sense of direction were still acute; he knew they were sailing straight north and he mentioned it to James.

"Aye, that seems so. Why would that be, I wonder?" James answered.

"Weel, I expect tha' the storm drove us off course and we are backtracking a bit," Hugh guessed as he looked behind them at the red-gold path on the calm water stretching from them across the sea toward the quickly disappearing sun. Old Hugh did not want to think about what that would mean, now that they were on restricted rations already. Hugh pushed the thought aside and opened his thoughts to James about the seeming love affair blooming between George Morrison and his daughter-in-law, Janet.

"So lad, I need your honest opinion of the man, so's I can see it more clearly. I am feelin' protective of the lass and had planned on carin' for her until the Good Lord takes me hame. But if her heart is set on him and he is a good man, I wouldna want ta stand in their way."

James smiled, ruefully. "You are right; you surely have a related matter! But in your case, I know a good deal about George Morrison, as he has become a trusted friend. If your Janet and he love each other as you say, I would be a happy man in your place. I canna think of anyone more kind and gentle than he. He is also a strong man and possesses a good trade that he could care for her and the bairns with, mind you! I would be happy for George as well, as he is a very lonely man and hasna been himself he says, since losing his wife."

"And how did his wife die?" Hugh asked James frankly, turning to look him in the eye.

"Childbirth, but if ya want the details ya mun talk to the man himself, as he told me in confidence on a particularly hard day," James answered carefully.

"Well and mebbe ya can tell me why it is tha' he flees for topside sa often? Why, he knocked Janet down tryin' ta get oot after the storm!" Hugh exclaimed.

"Well, he seems to have a great fear of small places that he has been battling all the way across the Atlantic. I myself was surprised he did as well as he did do wi' it, when they locked us down before the storm. I canna think tha' would make him a weakling though, if tha' is what you are a'thinkin'. He will likely never leave shore again, but then I should think tha' your Janet would like to settle near her kin and have her husband stay put on land, if ya don' mind me sayin' so. Losing one man ta the sea is enough ta break any woman. You had a chance ta see how helpful he was too, during the pox and the flux and then during the storm when those damnable barrels let go!" James added, trying his best to convince Hugh of George's good character.

Old Hugh smiled. "Aye, you make a pretty good case for your friend and that leaves me feelin' much better aboot the whole thing, as I ha' grown ta trust your opinion, my friend. I just had ta ken if what I believed about the man, was in line with what he really is. And a carpenter.... aye, he could build them a fine house I'm thinkin'. I can always move in with my son Davy, and that seems where I am most needed the noo." His face darkened with pain as he thought of his dear little grandson, Alex, who now lay somewhere behind them, forever a part of the sea.

James saw the shadow of pain in the old man's eyes and knowing the reason for it, he quickly changed the subject. "So, I ken ya heard me and Ian arguing' and I would like ta talk ta ya aboot that a bit, my own self."

"Oh, aye, and what were you and Ian on aboot, then?" Old Hugh asked.

"Well, Mary has been carin' for the lass that had her leg smashed in the storm, Margaret McKay?"

"Aye," Hugh answered, beginning to understand.

"Weel now Ian has gone daft ower her and wishes to wed," James finished abruptly, his hands flying up and slapping back down on the ship's rail in frustration. "I fear the lass be too young and carving oot a new life in the wilderness will be hard enough as it is, without losing Ian's help too!"

"Achh, I see!" Old Hugh said knowingly. They stood in silence for a while, waiting for a breeze that didn't come. The almost non-existent waves slapped listlessly against the ship as they bobbed all alone in the vast ocean. Not even a seabird was to be seen. "I think we are both suffering from the same ailment, my friend."

"And what is tha'?" James asked.

"Oh, I think it be selfishness; pure stubborn, selfishness. Who are we to put limits on how or when others love, aye? I'd venture a guess that nether of us would ha' stood for it ourselves when we were wishing' ta court; in fact I'd wager on it," Hugh added with a grin, as he turned to face James.

James snapped closed his mouth, as he was about to argue, when he realized Old Hugh was right, dead right. If Ian had been the older one and suggested that he and Mary had been too young to wed when they first fell in love, he would have given him a thrashing to remember it by.

"And besides," Old Hugh said, "whose ta say we are not gaining help right here on board already with our friendship? We will help your family, if yours helps mine, when there is work ta be done, aye? Havena we already proved that ta each other whilst on this awful crossing?"

"Aye," James answered with a wide smile of agreement. "It's a bargain," he said spitting on his right hand and then offering it to Hugh.

"Aye a bargain," Old Hugh said in the deepening twilight. He spit on his own right hand and clapped it together with James' in an age old gesture to seal the deal. The families would settle next to each other when they reached Pictou and help each other start over. The matter of the new loves in both their families need no longer make them uneasy. In fact, the more able-bodied people they could rely on, the easier it could be for them all.

"Thank you for settin' me straight aboot Ian and his lass. It was turnin' into a regular war as it was, and I was not thinkin' rightly aboot it. I owe him an apology and mun make amends. Damn, I do hate ta eat crow!" He said and then burst out laughing at himself.

"Aye, but when you are an old man like me, ya will find it goes down a wee bit easier each time ya have ta do it!" Hugh said, laughing right out loud.

Both men started whooping with laughter and were nearly holding each other up when a sailor came up to them. "What're ya doin' out here?" He barked.

James stopped laughing when he saw which sailor it was. Tom Mandler, the one who had it in for Ian. James wondered how much he had heard of the conversation, as he faced Tom's sly grin and angry demeanor.

Hugh turned to face the sailor, who to him was just a pup, but he could tell he was the kind of pup that bit. "We were just catchin' some air is all and planned ta return ta the hold shortly." He then purposely turned his back on Tom Mandler, as if he were of no consequence. That was a mistake.

Tom grabbed him roughly by the shoulder and pulled him back around. "You will go below now, as I tell you to, old man!" He added rudely.

Old Hugh seethed, wishing to smash in Tom's sneering face, but swallowed his pride for his family's sake. Old Hugh said between his teeth, "verra well. We will go down." He let a glaring James go down first and then he followed slowly and insolently. He stopped before lowering his foot to the rungs and leaned toward Tom Mandler, who was following them much too closely. "Though next time, laddie, you had better bring yer friends wit' ya, or the captain himself. If you approach me so disrespectfully again alone, I'll toss yer worthless bum owerboard. I've a feeling there are few who would miss ya." He paused, standing tall to give full effect to his threat. He was still an imposing man, despite his age. "Good night to ya then!" He finished, with sudden sarcastic cheerfulness and began descending the ladder in no particular hurry, his eyes never leaving Tom's until he was well below.

Chapter Seventeen

Ennui and the Doldrums

"But why, Mama?" Little Lizzie groaned.

"Because I said so, is why!" Mary answered her sternly.

"But I want ta go up on deck the noo!" She said, determined to get her way. She was hot, bored and crabby, but then so was everyone else.

"I told ya tha' only a few people are allowed up at a time and it isna our turn yet. Now quit complaining and finish tha' sampler, it will take your mind off bein' sa hot."

"Fine!" Lizzie cried as she plumped to the decking in a puff of anger and skirts. "Sampler, pampler, dampler... stupid sampler!" She grumbled, picking up her sampler and the dangling needle and limp thread.

Mary sighed. She too was hot and crabby, but she knew they had to take turns or the captain would stop even those few precious minutes on deck every day. The weather had been warm and there had been no wind now for seven days. Not even a breath of a breeze blew up on deck to move the sails and the air was heavy and oppressive. Here below decks, with all the humidity and the lack of fresh moving air, it was like living underwater. Mary pulled her sticky bodice away from her body to let a bit of air between the layers of gown and bodice.

Dear God, how much more could they take? Mary wondered. One week it was cold, the next it was so hot that you could barely breathe.

Sweat ran down all their faces. Most of the women and girls had put their hair into two braids to avoid the heat of a mob cap or wearing it pinned up on their heads. They had also taken off all woolens, loosened bodices and were down to chemises and skirts to reduce their body heat. The littlest children just ran around naked. The men and boys too, had mostly taken off their beloved kilts and were wearing their sarks, but well knotted between their knees in the traditional fashion they had worn them back in Scotland on the rare day that it was hot outside. Everyone lived for their short quarter hours on deck, where it was at least not as humid and crowded with warm bodies as it was in the hold.

The McDonalds were slotted for later in the afternoon to take their turn up on deck and had to wait along with the rest. Clancy would come and fetch the next group, after the previous group had come back to the hold. No one was in any big hurry to go back below, so they stalled to come back until they were physically escorted.

Nate was feeling more himself again, even though he still needed to mend, his pain had decreased to a tolerable level. The heat though was making him just as miserable as everyone else and he longed for time to move faster so that he could go up on deck with the McDonald group. He leaned toward the frustrated Lizzie. "Don' worry, wee lassie! We'll be up in the fresh air before ya know it and then ya will feel better. Why, we are lucky ta have the later time that we do, as it is more likely that we'll catch us a breeze later, than these others that are a' goin' now!" He finished, trying his best to make her smile.

It worked. Not only did Lizzie reward him with a big sunny smile, but so did Mary, Katy, and Margaret McKay. Just the thought of a breeze at this point made them all smile. Everyone was getting the idea now about just what kind of crisis they were in. They were low on supplies and water rations thanks to the storm and now they were not making any forward progress toward port at all. This could not last much longer, or they would die of thirst in the middle of the ocean.

Everyone on board was talking about the dwindling rations now and many were regretting their decision to come on the voyage at all. They had known the risks and bet everything, so they were well aware of the possibility of losing everything as well. It had seemed a safer bet while on land, then when they were far out on the Atlantic and committed. There had been no break in worries between the smallpox and flux epidemic, the storm, and now this Doldrums as the frightened sailors called it. Their obvious concern had everyone worried. When asked about the phenomenon, none of the sailors had given a good answer, being too superstitious to even talk about it, except for Nate.

"The Doldrums is when you've no wind for yer sails and naught ya can do, but pray for some ta come yer way." He did add though, that they should be in the North Atlantic current and at least floating the right direction, little by little. It was still a sobering thought for everyone. Now the heat and mugginess was adding to the already high irritation level of those below. The pipers had even been silenced by the passengers for now, as it was too hot for dancing music, and they were too irritable and heartsick for any more laments.

The only people on board who seemed to not mind the conditions were the two pairs of lovebirds who spent most of their time talking and planning happily for the future, blessedly blind to their current situation. George spent his nights near the McDonald clan, as he had for the entire voyage. But now he spent his days helping Janet McLeod on her rounds to the sick, or sitting and talking with her and her family. He mostly took Hector with him now too, so that he could get to know the family he hoped to marry into a little better. Hector and little Finlay played happily with Elspeth, but more often the McLeod and the McDonald children all played together now. Willie was good friends with Sgian and Nate, Elspeth had made a new friend in Katy, and now Finlay had a new friend and idol in the slightly older Hector. No one spoke about either of the missing Alex's, as the wounds were still too fresh.

There was still hope in Mary's and Janet's minds for a playmate for Mary's two babes, Alasdair and William, when Maggie was delivered of her coming babe. Maggie seemed more and more like her old self as the days passed and she embraced the thought of a new bairn. She was keeping busy by knitting a warm blanket for the babe and was often seen smiling to herself, her thoughts turned inward to the renewed hope now held in her womb. Janet kept a close watch on her day and night and was pleased by her progress.

"It is so nice to see Maggie smile," George mentioned, noticing Janet watching her one day not long after he had proposed marriage.

"Aye, it is," Janet answered, surprised, but pleased that he had read her so accurately. "Tis mainly due ta that good lady right ower there," Janet indicated, with a nod of her head toward the school group and Mary and Jane Forbes. "It hadna even crossed my mind tha' Maggie might be with child, although I suppose tha' is silly of me, when she is marrit." Janet trailed off, suddenly embarrassed by where she was leading the conversation. She could feel her face getting hot and knew she must be blushing brightly, so she pretended interest in a loose thread on her sleeve for a moment.

George touched her fingers and then picked up her hand lightly in his own. His other large hand he used to gently turn her face up toward him. "Janet, you have no need ta hide your blush from me! We are both grown adults with children and marriages that came long before we met. You need not be embarrassed with me about these matters. We will be wed in Pictou and then we will both become one. Bedding and bairns are a part of marriage, are they no? Or do you have a dislike for the bedding part?" He stared honestly and openly into her eyes.

"No! I mean ... Oh, I doona ken what I mean when ya look at me like tha'!" She looked at her hand in his, feeling the lightning flicker there between them, and felt a nervousness that she was unaccustomed to. "But no, I doona dislike the marriage bed." She finally finished, looking up at him boldly, but still blushing. "I just get nervous talking aboot it is all."

George pulled her to him in a hug and began whispering, "I am no tryin' ta embarrass you, dearest. I ken that when the time comes that we are wed, that I willna be disappointed. As a matter of fact, I feel we shall be quite the opposite and have ta take care that we have no more bairns than I can build a home ta hold!"

Janet giggled like a girl, but drawing a disapproving glance from her somber father, she quieted herself and put a small distance between her and George, as was more proper. They took pleasure in each other still, despite any distance, simply by staring at each other and imagining the pleasures that lay in the unknown future of new love.

Janet knew that she loved him and was grateful for another chance at love; a chance that she had never dreamed would come again. She had nearly given up when Young Hugh died and had since resigned to having Old Hugh as her housemate instead. Not that she minded the old man. He was helpful and funny and she and the grandchildren adored him. But it was not the same as a husband and it never would be. She found herself looking to Pictou with renewed hope and found their lack of forward progress that much more frustrating.

✦ ✦ ✦

The other young lovers, Ian MacGregor and Margaret McKay, were sitting close together talking and laughing. He had given up more and more time with the men lately, to make time to talk with her. His sister, Mary, had been correct that he had been stunned and then smitten immediately, to see her dressed more like a woman than a girl with her long golden blonde hair braided and wrapped up into a crown-like fashion. He had admired and respected her spirit and attitude before her transformation, but his male eyes recognized the new Margaret as a true beauty and he jealously wanted no one else by her side now except for him. He felt like he was the luckiest man in the world to have had fate throw this lovely young woman into his path, so that he would be sure not to miss her.

That a broken leg started their relationship, Margaret herself found extremely amusing, but very lucky too. Her family had always teased her for being somewhat clumsy and said that if it were it not for bad luck, she would have no luck at all. But now she felt like the luckiest lass ever, thanks to that broken leg, since it had brought her to the McDonalds and Ian MacGregor. "My Mama always said my fate would be decided by one of my many accidents," Margaret laughed.

"Well, how many accidents ha' you had tha' she should say tha'?" Ian teased, with a grin.

"Well, let's see.... I broke some of me toes - some of them more than once from stumping them on one thing or ta other, I fell into the well when I were a lass of aboot nine summers, I broke this little finger," she said as she showed him, "when I got in a fight with Keegan McKine at aboot twelve summers. And let me see… I was no bein' careful when I was milking our cow one day and got kicked in the heid and was knocked out cold for three days, I got ran ower by the pony cart when I was tryin' ta catch my rotten cousin Rupert and I remember another time...."

"Enough!" Ian broke in, laughing and holding his stomach. "I get the idea! I ken ya ha' a knack for bein' in the wrong place at the wrong time. But, no this time." He said, his smile changing, as he stared meaningfully into her eyes.

"Nay, not this time, I think my luck has finally turned for the better," Margaret answered, her blue-green eyes piercing his dark brown ones.

"I wish to speak alone with you when we get our turn 'round the deck today. Does that sound agreeable to you?" Ian asked, suddenly serious.

"Yes, that would be nice, could I walk, ya gowk!" She laughed, teasing him.

"I wull carry ya oot on deck and find a place ta sit alone." Ian persisted. "I ha' asked your clan's permission, so it will no be improper."

"Have ya now?" She said thoughtfully. "All right, Ian. I could do with some fresh air, sa thank you, I wull." she answered, looking away to keep her heart in place, in case she should be wrong about what she thought was likely he would ask her. She plucked at the chemise sticking to her sweaty chest having unbuttoned her new wool dress as far as was decent, in an effort to cool off.

Ian had to pull his gaze away from the glimpses of shining skin that were revealed during her plucking at her dress, and found he was fighting for control of the rush of emotion he was feeling. "I... well ... I am goin' ta talk ta James for a short while, but I will come back for ya before our turn oot on deck comes." He gave her a brief kiss on her forehead, chaste, but lovely in its tenderness. Then he walked quickly over to James and a small circle of gathered men.

Margaret watched him walk away, straight backed despite the ceiling height causing him to bend slightly at the hip. His long, lean limbs were strong lined and the clean curves of muscles on his back were visible through his thin shirt. She was lucky all right. And she also suspected she would be engaged before the night was through and could not be happier that he had chosen her. She knew that a few other fathers with more means had offered their daughters to him and he had declined. The ship's hold was much too small to keep any secrets for long. She rearranged her leg to get more comfortable and caught Mary's smiling eyes upon her.

"And so, what did I tell ya? Sometimes men are blind until you give them a more womanly glimpse of yourself. He liked you as a lass but he is lost in love with you as a woman." Mary smiled at Margaret, pleased with herself and with the match.

"Aye, I see that ya ken your brother well. Tell me more aboot him." Margaret asked her eagerly.

"Weel, he is no the kind of man ta turn his head at every pretty lass and he has never, to my knowledge mind, been sa serious as he is with you."

"Truly?" Margaret asked, with a streak of pretty pink blush, washing lightly down each of her ivory cheeks.

"Yes, truly, my dear," Mary answered, "now, let me tell ya sommat else. Ian can be a hard man, especially when it comes ta injustice and willna back down easily from a fight, but that improves with age, mind you. And he is as stubborn as a big auld rock in the fields, but tha' is no his fault. It be a MacGregor family trait, as you will soon see," she added wryly. "Sometimes it serves us well and other times... weel, it makes things more difficult, aye? 'Tis something tha' a good mate can help ya wit', which is where you come in. When he is bein' stubborn, try no ta be angry in return, but be soothing and caring and let him rant it oot 'til he calms down ta please ya. He wull always try ta please ya. Why, my James can calm me oot of a swivet like no other! And I ha' learned ta do it less and less ower the years, just ta please him," she said with an ironic grin. "There is nothing like the love of someone ya respect, ta tame the wildness and stubbornness oot of a lad, or a lass," Mary said, looking pointedly at Margaret herself.

"Aye, I can see how tha' works," Margaret answered, obviously listening and taking note.

"If ya remain steadfast at his side, he will be a verra good husband and do his best always, ta make a better life for ya both. I ken you are no a foolish lass, and would no try ta string him along, nor play him false and tha' is why I ha' been tryin' sa hard ta put ya together! I want you ta ken how much I care for you and will be a good sister ta ya. Our blood wull mingle with your marriage, yours and mine; from thereafter, we wull stand together as the women of our clan have always done."

"I appreciate your help wit' me leg and your kind words and look forward ta being your good-sister, if tha' is what Ian is planning and if your husband does not stop him," Margaret kept her keen eyes on Mary as she waited for her response, watching anxiously for any negative reaction. She knew that James was upset about Ian wanting to spend so much time with her, so she still felt uncertain of her welcome to the family should Ian propose marriage as she suspected he planned to.

Mary grinned broadly and inclined her head toward the group of men, so that Margaret would look. She could see James and Ian were hugging each other and then they let go to shake hands and clap each other on the back in male exuberance. "Don' ya go worrying your pretty heid aboot it. As if James could stop Ian from doin' anything he really wanted to do anyway! Achh, tha' canna be!" She laughed thinking how unlikely that was, given her brother's temperament, and how she had told James that very thing just that morning.

Margaret smiled and then started laughing with Mary. Both Alasdair and William woke up from their naps and began to fuss in the heat. Margaret reached over and picked up William at the same exact time that Mary picked up Alasdair. Both women smiled at each other and then Mary began to nurse Alasdair on her right and Margaret carefully handed her William whom she placed on her left so that both could be satisfied at the same time.

The babes were feeding more often in the heat, but less in amount, so she had adopted this temporary solution and held both babes in her two small arms with her legs crossed beneath her for extra support. Margaret draped her with her shawl for modesty, as she knew it bothered Mary to nurse out in the open in the crowded hold. Many men stared rudely at the nursing women, most without any seeming conscience about it and Mary, not being accustomed to it, had grown to dislike it intensely.

Margaret turned to the girls who were close to them and listening intently to the grown women's wisdom. "We will be goin' up for our time on deck very soon now, Katy, and my impatient wee Lizzie!"

"What does impatient mean?" Lizzie asked her, scooting closer to her, her curious little freckled nose wrinkling as her eyes looked up questioningly.

"Weel, it means that ya canna wait for something," Margaret answered.

"Tha' is true then. I canna wait ta go oot and see the sea," Lizzie exclaimed. "See the sea, see the sea, see the sea!" She chanted. "I made a rhyme, Katy!"

The much quieter Katy smiled at her precocious little sister. Her dark ringlets were spilling out of her braids and stuck to her perspiring face and neck, despite Mary's deft handiwork on them. "Yes, you did! Clever girl! Now then, can ya spell them both for me?" Katy asked.

"S-e-e and s-e-e!" She replied smiling brightly.

"Nay, lass, ta see something is spelled s-e-e, but the ocean type of sea is spelled s-e-a," replied Katy.

"Is tha' true?" Lizzie asked Margaret, frowning doubtfully, "They sound the same."

"Aye, your big sister is exactly right." Margaret answered, nodding firmly.

"Oh. Well, it still rhymes, don't it?" Lizzie asked.

"Doesn't it. It still rhymes doesn't it?" Mary corrected her.

"Doesn't it?" Lizzie corrected herself, looking somewhat confused.

"Aye, it does rhyme sweetling!" Margaret confirmed, laughing. "What an adorable wee lass ya are," she cried as she pulled her into a hug while they all laughed.

Lizzie looked around at the women and her sister and decided to join in the laughing. It didn't seem that it was mean or teasing, like her brother occasionally was, just funny. "See the sea, see the sea, see the sea....," she chanted again, gleefully enjoying being the center of attention.

The women laughed some more as the men approached the group, with Sgian in tow. "What is sa humorous, then?" Ian asked.

"Oh, just one of Lizzie's precious rhymes," Mary answered, still laughing.

"And wha' is tha'?" James asked picking Lizzie up as she squealed happily.

"See the sea, see the sea, see the sea!" Lizzie repeated joyfully.

"Well, lassies, 'tis what we are a goin' ta do, and right noo!"

"Hooray!" They all exclaimed and immediately stood and made ready to venture out on deck. James and Sgian helped Mary, Katy, the babes, and an excited Lizzie step up and out of the hold. Nate climbed out using his one good arm to steady himself and Clancy greeted him with a brief squeeze of his good arm at the top. Everyone breathed a sigh of relief just to be free of the dark, dank, hold, even if just for a short while. They quickly accomplished the necessary chore of emptying their chamber pots over the rail and then they all relaxed, finding space wherever they could stay out of the way of the crew and the Hector's massive ropes. Not that they had need to worry lately. With no wind, the ship was not moving and the crew lolled around the deck as well, with nothing to do but hope for a breeze to come their way and give them something to do. Clancy flopped down next to Nate and caught him up on the doings of the captain and crew. They also spoke in low tones about their growing desperation for the wind to pick up, as the daily rations were growing dangerously low.

Ian, true to his word, carried Margaret out of the hold and set her gently down where they could be alone, toward the bow of the Hector. Carefully, he sat down beside her, mindful of her splinted leg. He had the MacGregor ring in his pocket that had been handed down from their mother to his sister, Mary. She had given it to him, as soon as she was sure that he meant to propose to Margaret. James had given Mary his own McDonald clan ring when they were betrothed, so Mary felt that the MacGregor ring belonged to Ian.

The MacGregor ring was simple pewter, but carved skillfully with the lion's head of his family crest in the center and the family motto engraved on the inside. No one knew how old the ring really was. Ian had polished it until it shone and placed it carefully in his pocket, after making sure there were no holes it could be lost through. Now he sat beside Margaret, staring at her golden and ivory beauty and found he had no words. Royal is my race the inscription inside the ring read, but he felt more like a pauper than royalty at the moment, with his lack of a proper home to offer Margaret. He was counting on her faith in him and her love to get her to agree to the marriage, but staring at her made him wonder if he was mad to ask her before he had more to offer.

"Dearest?" Margaret asked, in her direct way, "You said ya had something ta ask me, what is it?"

He smiled at her boldness. It was one of the many myriad things he loved about her. Suddenly, he found he had the words, just from her encouragement. "Margaret Ann McKay, will ya have me as your husband as soon as we reach Pictou and a minister?"

He said it very fast and she could not help but giggle at his nervousness, since he was usually bold, like she was. But as the first giggle escaped, she saw his face fall in disappointment, so she quickly reached for his hand saying, "Yes, Ian MacGregor! I wull marry ya, and gladly so!"

She leaned toward him and he felt his boldness return with her affirmative answer. He grabbed her and kissed her full on the mouth for the first time. The strong feeling between them made them both feel shy again. As they pulled away from each other's lips they both looked down shyly. Ian pulled the small ring out of his pocket. Serious now, he took her left hand gently in his own and put the ring in her palm. She inhaled sharply, having never seen anything so lovely and she carefully picked it up and examined the engravings. "It's beautiful, Ian. What do the words say?" She squinted, trying to make out the well worn inscription.

"It says S'Rioghal mo Dhream, which means Royal is my Race - 'tis the MacGregor clan motto. The crowned lion is our crest and our badge is the pine. I feel, for the first time in my life, that we truly are descended from kings when I see your queenly face and know that ya truly wish ta be mine." He stopped to wrap a piece of his family's tartan around her hand as well. Its bold red blocks with the large green and the tiny white stripe through it was symbolic of the promise of family bond and lovely in its simplicity. It made her think of Ian and the blood that flowed through his veins along with the green and white of the land he so loved.

"You wull be my queen, my love, and my partner. We wull ha' our struggles as everyone does, but I promise ya tha' I will ne'er let a day go by that'll make ya regret marryin' me. I couldna ha' given ya my name back in Scotland without gettin' hangit for it, but in the New World we may do as we wish. We make our own rules the noo. Will you be happy as Margaret MacGregor?"

"Aye, Ian, nothing would make me happier." Tears were streaming down both their faces now, from relief and their overwhelming joy. Margaret looked deeply into his brown eyes, seeing the very heart of the earth reflected there, and she smiled up at him her heart singing with pleasure. She placed the ring firmly on her right hand for now, until they could be married proper, but they both knew that only death would prevent their being together now. Their marriage would be a strong marriage filled with love, bairns and joy, she was sure of it. Her heart had spoken long before she had admitted it to herself. She snuggled into the crook of his arm to enjoy their brief breath of fresh air and a long awaited happy snuggle with each other.

They stared ahead to the horizon and both wished with all their might, for the wind to return to the sails and bring them to their union all the faster. But the sun sparkled on the water around them and Margaret felt a peace come over her that she had never felt before, except at kirk. She wrapped herself in it, realizing it was Ian's love, taking it all in along with deep breaths of the sea air mingled with the manly fragrance of his skin. She reminded herself to memorize and savor this moment for all time. They held hands and then stared into each other's eyes, finding a light there that was so much brighter than the afternoon sunlight on the water as they gazed into each other's eyes mesmerized and oblivious to their surroundings, they were drawn inevitably into another kiss.

A shadow fell over the two of them, startling them out of their bliss. "What the bloody hell is goin' on here? You, again, eh? Why, molesting some crippled girl now too? You whoring son-of-a-bitch!" Tom Mandler yelled as he grabbed Ian by the arm and yanked him up and rudely away from Margaret's embrace.

"He was no molesting me! He was proposing, you big ox!" Margaret yelled, struggling to get up on one leg.

Ian pulled out of Tom's hands and leveled himself to pop him in the jaw for his insults, but a strong hand suddenly restrained his cocked arm.

"Doona do it, man! Let the captain decide, as is proper," James said quickly, as he stared meaningfully into Tom's eyes, while he held Ian back.

"Here, here," Clancy barked as he strode towards them, "what is goin' on here?"

202 - *Toward the Horizon*

Tom quickly spoke up. "This here fellow was molesting this crippled lass, I saw it with me own two eyes!" He yelled, his eyes bulging with anger.

"This man is a filthy, dog-faced piece of filth and a liar!" Margaret yelled hotly.

"Aye and more," Ian added spitting at Tom's feet in disgust. With a great force of will, he kept his arms down at his side. "I was proposing ta the lass, in private like, and this great buffoon came along and interrupted! There were nothing a' all improper aboot it!"

By now, the family and some of the other sailors had gathered to see what was happening at the bow.

"So, just what sort of molesting are ya on aboot then, Tom?" Clancy asked.

"Why, they were all wrapped around each other they was, just as cozy as can be!" He set his mean jaw and glared all around.

"We were huggin' ya great idjut!" Margaret cried, finally on her feet with Mary's help. "Merely, as people do whilst accepting a marriage proposal. 'Course you'd ken that, if any lass on earth were ever ta agree ta marry ya, which I doubt, ya rabid, motherless, moth-eaten clot-heid!" She nodded her head in finality, glaring defiantly at Tom and satisfied with the insult.

James spoke up, addressing Clancy. "They were accompanied, I can assure you, as we were all nearby and knew wha' he planned, aye? And both of them are behavin' most proper, I can assure you, being tha' they ha' both of their family's blessings."

Clancy took off his hat and scratched his tousled red head. "I still have ta report this ta the captain or it would be my ain hide. But it needna ha' been such a brew-ha-ha as you ha' made it now, Tom," he said with a glare at the stubborn jawed and sneering Tom. He turned to James, Ian and the girl, speaking to them quietly, "go and get this girl's kin ta represent her and then come back ta the aft deck, 'cause the captain will expect ta hear the whole story. I take your leave, Madam, Miss," he said tipping his hat toward Mary and Margaret in turn and then politely to each of the girls.

He put his hat back on and retreated dragging along a gloating grinning Tom, to go and fetch Captain Spiers. His tough old Irish mother had taught him well, to treat all women with respect. And his mistress, the ocean, had taught him to appreciate their brief company as well. When they did cargo runs, they went for long months without even hearing a woman's voice and none aboard liked it. He had long disliked Tom Mandler and knew him to be a scoundrel and a bully. He would just as soon toss his lousy carcass overboard, so he hoped this would be a chance to have him embarrassed in front of everyone. For Ian's sake, he hoped that Tom was not on the right side of the matter.

He had seen enough of the McDonalds and their kin to believe their side of the story, but he was now obliged to report it. Tom had called so much attention to the situation that it would reach the captain's ears in no time. That truly would mean his hide, for he would be lashed severely for not reporting any shipboard incident immediately.

Tom struggled to taunt Ian over his shoulder and Clancy roughly jerked him back around. "There will be none o' tha' ya wee rascal, eyes front," Clancy ordered. "Captain Spiers will get ta the bottom o' all this here nonsense." He sighed, hoping that his stern captain would see the situation for what it was.

Chapter Eighteen

A Twist of Fate

James and Mary went below to bring the bairns back down and have the oldest two keep watch. Everyone was upset at the interruption of their much longed for time out in the fresh air and the children were restless and weepy. James, Ian and Margaret talked to the McKays, William and Margaret, her aunt and uncle, to obtain their help in assuring the captain of their propriety. They were Margaret's guardians, since her real mother and father were dead and had been for going on a year. She had come with them on this journey to the New World, having nothing left to stay in Scotland for any longer. She quickly explained the situation and her uncle rolled his eyes. "I take it ya werena bein' improper now, were ya lass?" He asked her gently.

"Of course, I wasna bein' improper, Uncle," Margaret replied, indignantly, "I was bein' proposed ta, as you well know!" She clung to Ian's neck as he still held her in his arms, partially to keep her leg safe and partially out of an instinctive fear of losing her.

"Aye and so I believe ya," William sighed. "And did ya accept his proposal, then?"

"Aye!" She answered, with a beaming smile and a quick glance at Ian.

"Weel, let's go clear up this nonsense the noo, then," he answered, buttoning his waistcoat and straightening his rumpled clothes.

"You should know, sir, this was only made into an issue thanks ta a sailor named Tom Mandler, who has a grudge for my brother-in-law. He was the one made such a stramash ower it," James said to William. "The reportin' sailor is a fellow by the name a Clancy that is a friend ta us, so look only ta him for support. With Tom Mandler, wull...'tis personal between him and Ian and he has been spoiling for a fight ever since we boarded."

"Aye," William said thoughtfully, "I see. Come along then Ian, Margaret, and you had better come too, wife," he said, calmly addressing Ian and his wife and niece.

Five minutes later, Captain Spiers had all the parties in front of him, as he stood on the raised deck at the aft deck rail looking down over the people assembled below him. He donned his hat and coat despite the heat, as he had been trained to do whilst overseeing matters at sea when he had been in His Majesty's Royal Navy. "Ahem! Will the reporting officer come forth please?"

Clancy, his hat in his hands, stepped forward and stood tall above the rest of the men gathered in the front of the group. "Sir, the way I saw it, these here two young people," He paused to pull Ian forward, still carrying Margaret protectively, "was gettin' properly engaged and just enjoying a hug and a kiss to seal the bargain. Then Tom comes along here and starts a' hollerin' as they were doin' something improper."

Tom stepped forward, eager at the mention of his own name. "Aye, well it was plenty improper to my eyes, Sir, and that's the truth of it! Why she is just a bairn compared to him!" He sneered.

"What is your name, sir?" Captain Spiers asked Ian.

"I am Ian Charles MacGregor and this is my betrothed, Margaret Ann McKay," he said politely, as he held Margaret more securely in his arms.

"And how old are you? You first, Mr. MacGregor, please." Captain Spiers asked.

"I am twenty and four winters, sir," Ian answered.

"And I am sixteen summers," Margaret said, immediately after him. "And my own mither married when she was fifteen summers old, sir," she added, with stubborn sauciness.

"And were you doing anything improper, Miss McKay?" Captain Spiers asked.

"Absolutely not, sir!" she said immediately. "And I take it as a personal insult ta be accused of such. We ha' my new family nearby and were in plain sight of them. This man insults both me and Ian with his false accusations," She added primly, but obviously seething with anger. Her green acidy glare bored holes through the sneering Tom and for the first time since the incident, the sneering smile disappeared from his face.

"And who might that be?" Captain Spiers asked.

James stepped forward with Mary immediately. "It is us sir, and I can assure you tha' there was nothing goin' on, o' the nature this man says. I will bear witness tha' this Tom Mandler has borne a grudge against my brother-in-law since we left port. I was there, when he made threats ta him involving bodily harm, and I believe his exact words were, 'your friends canna be near you all the time, so watch out!' I have another man who will swear he heard those same words from tha' man, should ya need more evidence. He has been waiting for any opportunity to harm my brother-in-law. Tha' is wha' is truly goin' on here," James said.

"And the parents of this girl, would you please step forward?"

William and Margaret McKay stepped forward as the group parted the way for them.

"If you please, what are your names and what have you to say on this matter?" The captain asked.

"Firstly, I am the girl's uncle and she is my wife's namesake. Her parents are unfortunately deceased, but I am her legal guardian. We were approached properly, several days ago, by Ian MacGregor aboot proposing marriage ta our young Margaret. Seeing how happy he has made her, we readily agreed. Ian's people helped heal our Margaret when the storm caused a water keg ta break loose and smash her leg. Why, if it hadna been for them, she would be a cripple, or dead! Why would any of them molest her now? This is a fine young man, sir," he added with a pat on Ian's back, "who should no be bein' accused of such nonsense! They are betrothed now and will be wed as soon as we reach port at Pictou. I fail ta see what all the fuss is aboot." William said, finishing his speech with a shrug. His wife nodded solemnly beside him, stolid in her support.

"I see. Well, I believe I see the easiest remedy to this problem I find before us. To settle all matter of propriety, I can only see one way to mend things. I will perform the marriage myself, right here and now, as is my right as captain of the Hector. Does that sound agreeable to all concerned?" He asked the stunned crowd. A shocked Ian and Margaret both nodded.

"What? Have you lost your wits, man? You canna marry them!" Tom burst out.

"Seaman Mandler, I assure you, that I can, and I will. I can also have you flogged for talking to me in such a disrespectful manner!" Captain Spiers responded coldly. The tide had turned and the captain's temper had now been loosed on Tom. He stared unblinking at Tom, eyes dark and deadly, like a shark about to strike its prey.

Tom stood very still, in wide-eyed fear of his captain. He had overstepped his bounds and was foolishly just realizing it.

Captain Spiers walked down the steps to the lower deck and stepped to within an inch of Tom's nose and bored into his eyes at close range. "No one questions my authority on this ship!" He roared.

Realizing he had lost his chance to get Ian, Tom scrambled to repair the way between him and the captain before he was flogged instead. "I meant no disrespect, sir! I assure you! I apologize for my rudeness." He got down on one knee and took his hat off, bowing low to show loyalty to his captain.

"Very well, but I would advise you that in the future, Mr. Mandler, you should stay away from these people and cease in your harassment of Mr. MacGregor and his family. They are my passengers and my cargo and none aboard will interfere with my cargo whilst I am Captain of the Hector, lest they wish to feel the sting of my Cat. Is that clearly understood?"

"Yes sir, o'course, sir," Tom muttered, bowing and retreating in an attempt to fade back into the group of crew watching. When he turned though, his eyes stayed fixed on Ian for a hatred filled moment. Ian knew this would not be the end of things between them, no matter what the captain said or did today. It had only delayed the inevitable.

"Well, let us proceed, since the main family members are present," Captain Spiers said. He turned to Margaret who was still in Ian's arms, her splinted leg sticking straight out awkwardly beneath her skirt. "Do you, Margaret McKay, take this man, Ian MacGregor, to be your lawful husband - to love, honor and obey, until death do you part?"

"I do!" A surprised but elated Margaret answered.

"Then do you, Ian MacGregor, take this woman, Margaret McKay, to be your lawfully wedded wife - promising to love, honor and cherish her until death do you part?"

"I do!" said Ian, now gazing deeply into Margaret's eyes.

"Is there a ring?" Captain Spiers asked them.

"Aye," Margaret answered. She quickly pulled the ring off her right hand, where she had just so recently put it and handed it to Ian with a bright smile.

"Then Ian, say after me: 'with this ring, I thee wed,' and place the ring on the third finger of her left hand."

"With this ring, I thee wed." Ian repeated, smiling as he slipped the family ring home, where it belonged.

"Then I now pronounce you man and wife! You may kiss your bride!

Here or anywhere else, eh mates?" He added to a now laughing, hooting and smiling crew. They were all giving a whoop and a holler for the newly married couple, all except Tom Mandler.

Ian pulled her close and kissed her full on the lips and then pulled away quickly, leaving her looking dreamy and woozy from the promises that that kiss held. She was glad she was being held by him, because she was sure she would faint if she were standing on her own. It had all gone by so fast. She was a married woman!

The relatives circled around them, congratulating them and hugging them, now beginning to weep with joy, as the reality of what had just happened settled in. "Welcome to our family, Mo' nighean bahn, Margaret," Mary said first, kissing her blushing cheek.

"Mo' brathair," We have a new MacGregor this day!" James whooped and slapped Ian on the back.

"Taing, taing!" Was all the weeping Margaret said to each well wisher, still in a stupor of surprise mingled with an overwhelming joy.

"We could not be happier for ya, dear," William said, kissing Margaret's cheek and clapping Ian on the back. "Although, tha' must be the shortest engagement in history, aye?" He added, with a wink at Ian. "You take good care of this lassie, Ian. She is all tha' is left of my dearly departed brother, God rest his soul," William added on a more serious note, crossing himself at the mention of the dead.

"I promise that I wull, sir!" Ian answered, bowing slightly and beginning to feel the full weight of being responsible for a wife both literally and figuratively.

"We must have a ceilidh tonight!" cried the older Margaret. "Don' you agree, William?"

"Aye, a ceilidh is most certainly in order!" cried William. "Where are my bagpipes?" He asked, pretending to look around in his pockets for them and laughing at his own joke.

"Ahem!" Captain Spiers interrupted. "Please do not continue too late, as I find the sound of bagpipes extremely unpleasant," he added in his more usual gruff tone.

William lifted one eyebrow at the captain's insult of his beloved pipes, but prudently said nothing.

"Oh, by all means celebrate the wedding!" Captain Spiers added with a flip of his hand as if it meant nothing. "Fools that marry should at least get a good party out of the bargain. Just don't keep me awake," He snarled and turned his back on the crowd, going back to his post near the wheel.

Not that it matters much, he thought to himself. If they got no wind soon, they would all be dead long before they reached port. But he knew the passengers would remain more biddable, as things grew worse, if he remained calm and in control, especially if he handled his crew wisely too. They were all just a bunch of old salts. He had known that the impromptu wedding would tickle their romantic fancies and it had. The McDonalds seemed to hold a lot of sway with the passengers below and he had no wish to displease them at this crucial time either.

Besides, he knew Tom Mandler to be a troublemaker, so he believed the couple's story. If Mandler continued with his game, he would put him in irons, or maybe even have him tossed overboard, depending on what he might try. He could not play it soft by allowing any disrespect of his orders. Not now, not ever, he thought to himself gritting his teeth. Order on the ship would be necessary if any of them were to survive.

A breath of wind came to him as if called up by magic. His keen nose caught it first and he instinctively turned toward the source, as a puff of a breeze came from the southwest. He looked up at the sails expectantly, knowing with his years of experience that the wind was coming before he felt it. The sails above them flapped and wailed as gradually the yards of canvas they had up in readiness began to fill. "Man the sails, mates! Our little shipboard wedding may have blessed us with Lady Luck's favor! We have our wind! Let's be about it! I am going to have to ask anyone that is not a member of my crew to please return to the hold." He barked in every direction as he strode for the wheel to set the Hector in front of the wind at a better angle.

Nate watched in awe from his spot on the deck near where his new friends had wed. His father had not only acted unexpectedly kind toward the couple, but he now looked like a great sailor of old. The feather in his cap ruffling in the rising breeze, his cragged face transformed when he smiled holding the big wheel, while turning the Hector into the wind. Nate finally felt he understood about him and his mother, and about the man and himself. His father's only true love was the sea and his ship and that was how it would always be. He neither loved, nor was loyal to anything or anyone else. He was incapable of anything more. Nate felt a small piece of relief come to him as he finally realized it wasn't his own fault that his father mistreated him. Captain Spiers had no idea how to love him and his frustration came out in a sick rage. It was seeing him act so much like he had long wished that he would, that made it all seem so clear and finally opened his young eyes to the truth.

He still knew what the man was really like, but he also saw behind all of that and understood him at last. He would likely never forgive him for how he had been treated up until now, but understanding seemed closer to his grasp than it had before he had seen this more likable side of his father. Nate felt the years of resentment loosen their grip on his soul.

He also realized what his father had been doing when he had so generously married Ian and Margaret. He had simply been playing it smart. In case of a later panic, he had been smoothing the way between himself and Ian MacGregor and James McDonald. Along with Old Hugh McLeod, they were the representative leadership of the large crowd below; he had told the captain that himself earlier in their voyage. They would be called to account when the rations ran out and those below turned to them. Captain Spiers needed them as allies, not enemies.

Nate had noticed the wind come up almost as soon as his father had, but no one aboard knew if the race to port could now be run before the rations ran out. Jane Forbes and her mother had come out on deck to hear the ceremony when the ruckus began with Tom Mandler. They both stood next to Nate now smiling at the newly weds and pulling their shawls tighter around themselves against the chilled, but welcome breeze.

Ian and Margaret looked up together, watching the billowing sails above them fill. It seemed like a good omen for them, a breath from heaven, and they were moving again! Their loved ones gathered together and they trailed the newlyweds back toward the hold, smiling and chattering. They had a ceilidh to look forward to and that would brighten everyone's evening, at least everyone except Captain Spiers. Though he was bound to be in a better mood just to be moving forward again, so they were not too concerned about his objections tonight and they were grateful for his unexpected, but very real wedding.

William McKay was at his best at weddings and this one was for his beloved niece Margaret, who had a run of bad luck the last few years that would have killed a weaker lass's spirit. Well deserved was the happiness that shone now on her smiling, if sweaty face. The hold rollicked and thumped with music and dancing feet as nearly half the people were up at any given time. Sweating and red in the face, he made his bagpipes sing in joyous celebration. Not to be outdone, the canty Colin MacGregor was playing right alongside him in duet, for his own MacGregor clansman's day, as well as dancing along with his music in a most amusing way.

The movement of the sea again after so many days of calm threw many dancers off balance and there were hilarious spills and twirls into other people, as they tried to keep up with the music and lean with the tilt of the waves at the same time. Mary and James had been caught by the onlookers and pushed back into the group of dancers several times, as had the bride and groom who could only twirl in each other's arms as Ian held Margaret close. He was very careful about the waves, so as not to fall and injure his new wife. He still marveled at the word wife and was still reeling from the abruptness of their wedding.

Old Hugh had stationed himself with his cane on the stern end of the group to catch any people that tumbled his way. He was especially saucy with the lasses as he picked them up and pretended to begin to brush off their skirts, or steal a kiss, as they pretended offense and then laughed and twirled away. The people nearest him were out of breath from laughing at his clowning and flirting. None were offended, as he never actually did anything forward to any of the women, he was just reveling in being a part of this joyous occasion.

On the bow side, the pipers would use an occasional well placed foot to stop people from sliding into them as the waves tossed the dancers about. Both of them were wearing full dress kilts as they jigged from one leg to the other to balance their shifts in weight, while they fielded falling people. It gradually combined into an original jig that was growing more and more hilarious as the ship shuddered and picked up speed. The children gathered around the pipers laughing and clapping in time to the music and dancing and stumbling along with the adult's fun.

The bride and groom would try to catch their breath, only to be whisked off again within minutes, by some relative or anyone who simply wished to dance with them. Margaret had been carried off many times as a worried Ian was whisked off by some lass. Sweaty, exhausted, but still exhilarated, they managed to find each other again and Ian plopped down with her in his arms next to James. James was holding both his bairns near the edge of the circle. Mary had been dancing for a long time, but now they could not see her among the crowd of dancers.

"Where is Mary then, brother, James?" Margaret asked, looking around.

"Oh! Weel, I canna say for sure, she was here a minute ago," he said, with a grin playing around his lips.

Ian narrowed his eyes at James. He had never known him to be a liar, but he was sure that he was holding something back now. He wondered what they could be up to. But before he could think on it anymore, he was pulled back into the line of dancers as they tried to hold three rings of dancers inside of each other, going in alternating directions on the bucking and uneven floor of the hold.

There was a great deal of jostling and hollered good natured jibes as they spun 'round and 'round, getting more and more dizzy as the duet picked up tempo. Margaret watched them twirl until she felt like she was in the middle of a snowstorm. They spun 'round so fast that everything was a blur of faces and stomping feet and swirling skirts. Just when she had caught sight of Ian again, the pipers squeezed out their last few notes. A large wave passing under the ship sent the dancers spinning into a spiraled heap onto the onlookers closest to them. They all laughed and stayed where they had fallen for a while, chatting and giggling with those they had fallen on, many making new friends as they lay there panting and catching their breath.

Nate was dancing and frolicking wildly about, obviously having the time of his life. He ignored the occasional bump he received on his still disabled arm, using the one that was not bound by the sling to grab anyone that would dance with him.

The groom had fallen into a tired heap again near his bride. James and Jane Gibson sat nearby. Jane was watching and laughing, but also protecting her large pregnant stomach from any bumping about. Her brother Charles, ever protective of her, used his arm to help shield her as well. He glowered at anyone who seemed ready to approach too closely. Ian and Margaret apologized for any jostling she may have received and then began chatting with them, asking how Jane was feeling and how the babe seemed.

Jane patted her round stomach and giggled as a tiny foot pushed outward and could be clearly identified by its shape as a tiny foot. "I think the babe like's the pipes, as I am being danced on from within." She readjusted her sitting position and put one hand behind herself and leaned back to brace the weight and remove some of the strain on her sore back.

"Are you quite sure you are all right, sister?" Charles asked kindly, but with a worry line forming between his eyes.

"Oh quite sure, mo' brathair, but thank you just the same. I'm just a bit sore in the back is all, probably from all this sitting these last few weeks."

"Pur' lass," Charles muttered, as he moved behind her to rub her aching back.

214 - *Toward the Horizon*

Ian's had been watching the two thoughtfully, when his attention was finally caught by Mary, who was over by the old sickroom at the back of the hold, beckoning to them. James now stood beside them smiling and handing over the care of their babes to Jane and Charles. "Grab your bride, lad, and come wit' me," James said grinning.

Ian picked up his new bride and they said their goodbyes to Jane Gibson and her brother, Charles. Then Ian carried her through the backslapping, well wishing crowd, to stand near Mary and James. Margaret quickly informed Mary of Jane's sore back, worried that it might mean the beginning of the birth pains, but Mary shushed her assuring her she would check on Jane in a few minutes. Meanwhile, they led the two newlyweds to the old sickroom, where a soft pallet of blankets and quilts had been laid near a candlelit lantern and a bowl with two bruised apples in it, and some biscuits, courtesy of Jane Forbes and her mother. It was a feast compared to the recent rations. Margaret blushed as she realized what Mary had done. She had made a bride's bed chamber for her and Ian's first night as man and wife. Ian's face broke into a wide grin as he realized it too.

"Why thank you, Mary, and James," he said, nodding to each in turn. "I had thought our marriage bed would have ta wait until we reached Pictou, but I see ya have thought of everything, as usual. Tha' is wha' ya were both up ta, aye?"

"Aye, er... taing," Margaret murmured, now shy and looking only at the decking, she grasped Ian a little tighter by the arm.

Mary broke the girl's sudden awkwardness by pulling them both into a hug, with her small, but strong arms. "Mo ghradh, we are now sisters. I will share something with you. If ya doona wish children the noo, I ken a way ta prevent it. If you do want bairns now, then I will leave ya to it." She stepped back a little and looked Margaret squarely in the eye to see what the effect of her words would be on her new sister-in-law.

Margaret just lay in Ian's protective arms with tears in her eyes for a moment and then she glanced up at Ian. He shrugged to her, indicating that it was her choice. She decided then and there looking into his eyes that she did want bairns, lots of them, but not quite yet. "It would be best ta wait, just 'til my leg heals in order ta bear the weight of the pregnancy, wouldn't it?"

"Aye, it would, but ya can do whatever ya choose, dear," Mary answered, still leaving the decision to her. She had discussed the use of the whiskey mixture and the sponges long before now, with the Forbes women and Janet. She and James couldn't handle any more bairns yet. Their load was too heavy already, so she planned on using the whiskey soaked sponge herself. Even though they had no privacy on board for it to matter much right now, she would take no chances once they landed.

"Well, then give me your potion and that will be that, but just for the noo," Margaret answered decisively.

Ian nodded in approval and Mary handed Margaret a small corked vial and a piece of sea sponge. "This is just whiskey and honey, aye? You put enough on the sponge to soak it and then push it up inside you as far as you can. Mary Jane says ya must leave it in place at least half a day after you and Ian, er… consummate the marriage. Rinse it when you are finished with it and dry it carefully for your next use. By then, God willing, we will be ashore and you can decide for yourself, how long ya wish ta continue. When ya stop using it, you will be able ta conceive again, so doona worrit. Mary Jane assured me of that personally," she added.

Margaret took the vial and uncorked it, smelling it curiously. Then she slipped both the sponge and the vial into her pocket, slightly self-conscious of the other three watching her. She looked up at Ian questioningly as soon as she did it.

He smiled approving and grabbed her hand to kiss the back of it. "Ya made a wise choice for now, Mo luaidh. We'll help our kin settle in first and then start our ain place and family." He looked at James and saw him smiling in approval, as well.

This is what James had hoped for from the beginning, for his brother-in-law to help him get a farm started up. Then he and his wife and children would take over, as they helped Ian build a home the following year. Ian had thought it would go like that all along. But James had been frightened, by Ian's love for Margaret, instead of seeing it for the blessing that it was - another pair of hands to help with the work of starting a new life in a new place. The four hugged each other for a few minutes and then Mary and James made to leave. James stopped at the blanket partition and said "I wish we could ha' had better ta offer ye as a marriage bed, but I will at least be sure the piper's keep up with the loudest tunes for ya!" He grinned and threw Ian a bawdy wink, before he and Mary slipped out of the newlyweds' little cove.

"James! You shall embarrass them," Mary said, poking him censoriously.

James stopped Mary outside the partition, before they returned to their children. "I ha' been thinkin' aboot somethin' of late and need your opinion, wife." He held her in his arms as they listened to the sound of the sea rushing by, just on the other side of the ship's wooden hull.

"Oh, my, I'm no sure I'm likin' the sound o' tha'!" Mary said with a sigh, but she was still smiling.

"Its aboot havin' more bairns...." James said slowly.

"Oh, now I'm verra sure I'm no likin' the sound o' tha'!" Mary said, pulling away from him and laughing as she put her hands on her small hips. "There wull be no more bairns until we are settled! We agreed on tha'!"

"Aye, my dear one, tha' is why I am tryin' ta explain myself here and doin' a right poor job of it too," James said, running his hands nervously through his hair.

Mary stopped to listen, but now her arms were folded across her chest, readying herself for a possible argument.

James cleared his throat nervously, seeing her eyes flash. "I wasna thinkin' on you havin' another bairn....," he fumbled clumsily.

"Oh, is tha' so? And just who do ya plan on havin' it then?" She broke in angrily before he could finish.

James put his arms around her, but she remained stiff. He started again. "Love, I am no sayin' this the way I mean, please gi' me a moment! What I meant was, I was thinkin' on further help with the building and such now with Margaret and Ian needin' a place o' their ain soon, and I was thinkin' how much help Nate could be, when he heals up," he got out quickly, before she interrupted again. "What do you think, my love?"

Mary stood with her mouth open for a moment, looking deep into James' dark reflective eyes, seeing all the love and pity for the boy and the want of another older lad for help. She had not thought of it before herself and was now trying to rapidly put the pieces together in her mind, along with all the implications such an idea held. She had to admit that she had been attracted to the lonely lad from the first. "How do ya ken we could just have him, just 'cause we want him, then?"

James smiled. He had seen all the questions flutter through her brown eyes as she had quickly considered his idea. He also saw the moment that she realized she wanted this too even though he had seen her struggle to keep the idea at arm's length, and he knew he was halfway home to getting the boy. James had heard many terrible stories about the captain's treatment of the boy and knew he could give him a better life. He had also seen Nate stare longingly after his Mary, as only a motherless boy would do. He was an older lad and would be no burden. James could see no issue with one more mouth at this point. But, he was two more hands and could be a great help to them. He and Sgian had already trusted their lives to him and found him to be of rock solid character. "You let me work on how ta get the boy, whilst you work on how ta keep him, aye?"

She dissolved into tears and hugged him around his waist, since she was not much taller than that. "Aye, I would be happy ta call Nate my own, if ya can get him oot of the grips of Captain Spiers. Oh, more than happy!"

He held her small face in his hands and looked down into her wet lashed, but joyful eyes and felt the renewed strength to do it. He would somehow get that boy away from the captain. Captain Spiers had his weak spots and Nate seemed to be one of them, so he would continue to keep his ears and eyes open for anything that might get the captain to give him the boy in Pictou. As a last resort, they could convince Nate to jump ship, if they had to. He knew the boy would gladly oblige. James' heart was set on him and now so was his beloved wife's, so he knew he must succeed somehow.

James set out across the hold, with a smile on his face and a gratified heart. He needed to keep his promise to Ian, so he marched off to have a word with the pipers. He wanted them both to play loudly and cheerfully for the newlyweds and get some more people up and dancing to make as much racket as possible, affording them what privacy there was to be had. It was the best he could do for the young couple this night.

Margaret looked up at Ian with her heart in her eyes. He was still holding her, looking into her sweet face as he set her gently down on the pallet that had been so thoughtfully laid for them. She felt very shy suddenly and turned away from him, glancing around aimlessly.

"Mo luaidh, look at me," Ian said gently. Margaret turned her gaze to him, both shy and loving at the same time. "You arena thinkin' aboot our hasty marriage and regrettin' it are ya?"

"Nay, I regret nothing! It just all happened sa fast that I'm a wee bit stunned, is all."

"Well, let's just talk a while and get past our shyness slowly, aye?" Ian offered gently. Even though he wished to take her in his embrace now, he could see that she was not ready. He wanted her to enjoy their lovemaking as much as he and was willing to wait until the time was right. He put his arm around her and pulled her close. "Sa tells me some more aboot where ya come from and your life before this voyage."

Margaret relaxed and leaned into him, grateful for his patience. "I was born on a farm near Morefield. Up on the river Broom, aye? My father and brothers used ta fish for herring ta eat and ta spread as fertilizer on our fields. I used to enjoy helping them spread the wee fishes out in the fresh air. Except in mid-summer, when the rotted fish smell was just aboot enough ta gag ya, even back up at the hoose." She relaxed in his arms as she remembered home and she opened up as he listened. She talked happily of her childhood until she got to more recent times and then her voice turned somber.

"I went oot one evenin' last summer that the stars were especially bright and I couldna sleep no matter what I tried ta think aboot. Sa I went up the hill overlooking the Broom." Her eyes began to mist over as she spoke more slowly now. "I musta fell asleep oot on the hill, because I awoke ta screams and flames below me at our hame. I ran as fast as I could down the hill, but I was too late." The tears began to overflow and course down her candle lit cheeks. "Some of the neighbor folk were there with buckets and had tried ta fight the flames. Monroe McKay, my cousin, told me that they quit fightin' when the roof fell in and the screams stopped. The men had already found the burnt bodies of my little sister Meghan, my brothers Seamus and Ian, and both my mither and my father." Margaret paused and blew her nose on Ian's kindly offered kerchief, trying to control the sorrow that still felt as raw as if it had been last week, instead of last year.

"I didna ken ya had a brother named Ian," Ian said to her gently.

"Aye, I did," Maggie answered as more tears ran down her face.

"My Uncle William took me in, sa I was no homeless, but I was as dead as they all were on my insides and didna speak for months. I felt it was my fault somehow and tha' I should ha' died too." She stopped to wipe at her eyes and fought to get back under control of the well of fresh emotions she felt. When she had steadied her voice, she continued again, "my Auntie Margaret finally convinced me tha' if I had been there, I would just be dead too."

"Then there was all the hubbub of the Hector's offer and plans ta be made and making ready ta leave. Everything happened sa fast! My uncle sold his place and ours too, since I couldna hold the wadset on it, being sa young and a woman. There was little to keep me there after tha'." She stopped talking and looked up at him to see his reaction to her tale, some of the shyness having been dispersed. "What are ya thinking, my love?"

He smiled down at her, moving an errant golden lock of hair off of her face. He kissed her softly where he had just touched her skin. "I ken tha' it was no your fault, but a stroke of luck for me tha' ya live! I am sa sorry tha' your closest kin died in such a horrible fashion. "Tis sad they couldna see how lovely ya were, as you were wed today. I ken tha' ya were saved from that fire, just for me. I could never want another, as much as I want you, Mrs. MacGregor." A single tear ran down his face in the lamplight as the pipers began to play a fast paced wedding tune beyond the thin curtains.

Margaret reached up and wiped the tear off of Ian's face and kissed him where it had left its mark. Then she kissed him full on the mouth, taking him into her arms with all her gratitude for his understanding and love, as he took her into his own embrace in answer. They covered each other's face with kisses and lay slowly back on the pallet.

Margaret felt the heat in her belly begin, but she smiled to herself, because she sensed that this time it would be quenched. The flames would finally be drowned out by her Ian, the man she had always dreamed she would find. His cool relief flowed down her body along with his hands and she found herself more than willing to surrender to him.

Ian reached over and turned down the lamp, as they ever so slowly undressed each other for the very first time.

Chapter Nineteen

New Chances

Captain Spiers stood in his cabin, silently listening to James' plea to adopt the injured Nate. He really did not want the boy and had planned to put him off somewhere soon and be rid of him. But he found he resented this man standing before him boldly asking for his son. Of course, there was no reason to believe that James knew that Nate was his son yet. He hadn't mentioned it, he thought to himself.

James was still listing all the things he thought would be good for Nate that they could provide for him and that was the last straw. The captain interrupted James rudely. "Mr. McDonald, I think I know what you are trying to say, but I do not know what answer I wish to give at this time. I will think about what you have said and let you know what I decide, when I decide."

James stared into the other man's eyes for a few silent moments, trying to read the thoughts in those cold, blue eyes. All he knew was that he had somehow angered the man and he would have to wait now for another opportunity. He knew when to back down and wait when a man had been pushed too far. "Weel, fine then, I wull wait on your reply and I thank ya kindly for your time, sir! Good day ta ya, then, Captain Spiers." James bowed politely to him and left the cabin.

He was startled to find Jane Forbes standing in the dark near the door, obviously listening. He pushed her ahead and out onto the deck quickly, before Captain Spiers followed them out and saw them together. "What are ya thinkin' eavesdroppin', lass? Are ya daft?" He finally hissed to her when no one else was nearby. He squinted at Jane, the morning sun in his eyes, trying to see her face.

"I was coming out of my cabin and I overheard you saying you wanted to adopt Nate and I.... well I guess I was just worried about the boy. Is it true? You wish to take Nate into your family?"

"Aye," James said, running his hand down his face in frustration. "I had hoped ta tell the lad himself today, sa I went early ta speak ta the captain, but the auld gommerel willna decide the noo," James said, with a flap of his hand in the general direction of the captain's cabin.

"He will not, will he?" Jane said, arching one slim eyebrow. "Well, we will just see about that, won't we?" She made to move back toward the cabins.

"Nay, lass! Tha' man is a viper and wull spit ya out like bad ale!" James said, grabbing her by the arm.

"No, he will not!" She said, with a confident angry gleam in her eye. "I am going to get my mother to accompany me and then we will have a talk with Captain Spiers. I will come below and tell you what has happened, as soon as we are finished with him."

She pulled free of him and he just stood there, amazed at her boldness as he watched her flounce away. He found that he actually believed in her ability to persuade the captain, but could not imagine how she would do it. He realized his mouth was hanging open when a passing sailor winked at him, after seeing the direction of his gaze. He snapped his mouth shut and pushed angrily past the snickering man to go back below. He would not tell Mary anything about it, until Jane tried whatever mad idea she was trying, just in case it worked. And also just in case it didn't.

He needn't have worried, Mary was far to busy to question him. He found the bairns being watched by their siblings while Mary attending to a frightened looking Jane Gibson nearby. She was obviously in labor and terrified that it was too early. She was crying to Mary and begging her to make it stop somehow, when he approached.

"Nay lass," Mary said. "Shhh! Whist now, whist! The calmer ya stay the better twill be. It may be a false labor, aye?"

"But 'tis too soon!" Jane Gibson cried clutching at Mary's arm. "It will be a weakling or a foundling comin' this soon. I wasna due for at least another moon! Can ya not stop it with one of your philtres or herbs?"

"Nay, lass, tha' I canna do, sa doona speak of it again! It would make the babe die in the womb or cause it ta be... unnatural. The babe wull come when 'tis ready and this one seems ready the noo! I thought from the first tha' ya looked further along than what ya said, sa maybe it was a ciphering error on your part?" Mary spoke sharply, but quietly. "Anyways, I canna stop this, but I will stay by your side through it all."

"No, this canna be," Jane moaned.

"Aye, it can and it is," Mary answered matter-of-factly. "Now just breathe and calm yourself, lass. Have faith in nature, aye?"

She turned to James and he kneeled to hear her whispers. "Go and fetch Janet for me and then ya will have ta wake the newlyweds. I'm sorry, but there is nay help for it. We mun move her back into the hold whilst we still can. Then go and fetch Jane and Mary Jane for me. I wull need their help wit' this one, aye?"

"Aye, I will be right back with Janet, but I saw Jane on deck and she will be down after a fashion," James answered, leaving immediately to seek out Janet, but not in time to see the curious look on Mary's face. She wondered to herself what was going on now, by the strangeness of James' manner, but Jane Gibson demanded all of her attention and brought her back to the present.

"Aye, yes, get the healers!" Jane called after the retreating James.

"Whist!" Mary hushed her right away. "You canna refer ta them out loud like tha', be sensible lass. Someone tha' we doona wish ta hear, might hear ya, now whist!" She looked around quickly to see who was nearby. No one seemed to be paying them any mind, or they were at least polite enough to pretend that they had heard nothing.

"Help is coming and I am no goin' anywhere, so quiet yourself." Mary moved up next to her and held her in her arms like a small child. "Just harken ta me and we'll make it through this together. You are young and strong, aye? There is nay reason ta worrit yourself. I ha' been at several births including my ain four bairns. Just rest your head, there's a lass!" She finished, as the sobbing Jane quieted a little and leaned into her for comfort.

"I'm sorry, Mary. You must think me an awful bairn myself, acting like this. I am just sa frightened! I was no ready for it ta be sa soon."

"There, there lassie, see here comes Janet ta help us. Just rest and save your strength now," Mary told her soothingly.

Janet approached them in a hurry, carrying the basket from Jane Forbes. "How close are the pains then?" She asked Mary right away.

"Not close enough yet to worrit," She answered. "It's still early. Jane is most worrit that the babe comes too early, as she says she has at least a month ta go. There is aught can be done, is there?"

"Well, there are abortificants, ta be sure," Janet whispered very quietly to Mary. "But, they are not for use ta keeps a bairn alive inside. It would surely die as might she."

Mary shook her head. "Tha' is no choice a'tall then. I have seen bairns fare well when they are a moon early and I think we mun let nature take her course."

Jane looked back and forth at the women as they spoke, beginning to get frightened again. "But, this bairn is more'n a moon early! Oh! Please don' let it die, or I canna live myself! It is all I have had ta keep me company on this wretched journey. It was my biggest hope ta have her with my husband beside me!" She glanced at her brother, Charles, and began to sob again.

Used to pregnant women and their foresights and worries, Janet smiled. "And how do ya ken the child is a lass and no a lad?"

Surprised, Jane Gibson just shook her small mobcap in confusion. "I doona ken why I say her, but I ken tha' it be a lassie, just the same!" A stronger birth spasm hit her and she curled into a ball around the source of her pain.

Janet counted out loud for the duration and then stopped when it was over. "Tha' was a long one, aye? There's a good lass. Everything is goin' fine," she said patting her in encouragement. She looked up at Mary. "We need ta get her in the sickroom sa I can examine her in private the noo."

Mary nodded and watched the curtain where the newlyweds had spent the night, until James came out with the sleepy eyed pair. "All right now, up we go!" Mary said encouraging Jane to get up as Janet pushed her from below.

Jane's brother, Charles Fraser, had been sitting nervously nearby twisting his hat into a disreputable lump. He rose to go with them.

"Nay!" James said to him as he tried to follow, staying him with a gentle hand on his chest to stop him. "You canna help the woman lad. She must do it on her ain! But, we wull keep ya company until 'tis over and the bairn arrives safely."

Jane smiled weakly at him and nodded, "It will be just fine, Charles. You stay with the men, now," then she steadied herself against Mary and Janet, as she got used to the wave motion. She made directly for the curtain, with Mary and Janet on each arm. She did not want to be struck with another birthing pain while she was walking, so she hurried as best she could.

Once beyond the partition, they lay her down on an old quilt on the decking, where the newlyweds had so recently lain. It was still warm from their bodies and the warmth soaked through to comfort Jane when she lay down. Being on a sharply angled deck lying down was something she had become accustomed to during the journey, so she was as comfortable as was possible.

As soon as she was settled in, Janet explained that she needed to examine her with her fingers internally to see how far along she was and where the babe's head was. Jane blushed hotly, but hiked up her skirts awkwardly and obliged them by spreading her legs. Janet slipped two fingers inside of Jane as gently as she could; feeling for the opening she knew lay within. She could feel the babe's head pressed against her fingers and felt the inner opening for width. She could count her two fingertips across nearly twice, so she knew that Jane was almost halfway open. Janet knew they had a little time, this being Jane Gibson's first child, before the pains would take over and her body must do the painful work of birthing. She slid her fingers out and wiped them on the edge of the quilt. Then she let Jane drink a dram or two of whiskey right from the bottle to help her relax.

"Everything feels just fine," She told little Jane as she swallowed the whiskey. "The babe's heid is down and you are opened nearly halfway, but your waters have not broken yet, aye?"

Jane confirmed with a nod as another pain took over. Janet again counted out loud until it was over. "See tha' was aboot the same as the last one, so you've a ways ta go ta the hard part. Just doona push yet, even if you feel you mun! You mun wait 'til all is ready and I tell you ta do it. Do ya ken wha' I'm tellin' ya?"

Jane nodded her face still red with the effort of fighting the pain.

"Breathe through the next one now, lass! Breathe! Doona hold your breath! And doona bear down! Breathe through the pain and let it wash ower ya like water and it loses some of its power ower ya," Mary told her.

Jane began taking in large gulps of air, after holding her breath during the last contraction. "How much worse will it get?" She panted, as the pains receded.

"Slowly, slowly breathe now, lass. It is over," Mary said. "Listen ta the sound of our voices and we will help you through this." She moved up to Jane's head, placed it in her lap, removed her mobcap and began stroking her hair soothingly. "Whist, now, it is all fine and normal sa far," She crooned to her, while Janet took position between her legs below them. Mary had the question in her eyes: was she really fine?

Janet nodded to confirm that it was not just said to comfort Jane. She really was doing well. The two women stared at each other for a moment. They knew what was coming and poor Jane did not. That was probably for the best. There was no reason to scare her now, when what would be, would be. There was no stopping this babe, it was coming.

✦ ✦ ✦

Jane and her mother Mary Jane sat before Captain Spiers again. Jane was just finishing up her eloquent plea for Nate's adoption by the McDonald's. "And so, you can surely see why the boy would be better off with a real family to raise him."

Captain Spiers sat for a moment then he smiled ironically. "You should have been a factor, had you not been a woman. I find I cannot argue with your logic, but the decision is still mine," he smiled at her, reminding her of a well-fed, but still hungry dragon. His precious china plates nearby, just reinforced the notion.

Jane took a deep breath. "I understand that sir. That is why I am asking you, as his father, to do right by him!"

"Who told you I was his father?" He bellowed at her.

She just sat quietly, pretending naïveté, as he glared at her. "Well, I cannot quite recall anyone telling me that, other than when you did so at dinner, sir. I have also heard you refer to him as such, during loud arguments in your quarters that we could not help but overhear." The truth was out on the line now and it balanced there precariously, as she prayed she had not pushed him too far.

"It is my business what I do in my own quarters, on my own ship!" He snarled.

"To be sure," she agreed, but pressed on. "I merely thought that a man of your caliber would want the best for his son. I meant no offense, sir!" She demurred.

"Achhhhh!" He yelled as he got to his feet and swiped a pile of papers and maps off his table in anger. "I am tired of bein' pestered about that lad! He is as useless as a flea and yet all of you fawn over him as if he were somethin' special. Well, I can assure you he is not! His mother was merely one of many whores, in many ports. Supporting her and that lad and his sister has nearly broken my back!"

"He has a mother and sister?" Jane asked. "Oh, my, well that is different then. But why isn't he still with them, if I may ask?"

"Why ask me for permission to speak? That is the first time since we left Greenock that you have asked my permission to ask me anything and yet you still do!" He paced back and forth, glowering at her.

"Well, I only meant that he would be better off with a mother too, but if he already has one....?"

"Oh, don't worry your pretty little head about it. Both his mother and sister are dead!" He threw the news at her as if it were a knife meant to cut, yet his hand gesture dismissed it as unimportant.

"I see," Jane answered slowly, trying to gauge the possible reaction to her next move. "Well then, it just furthers my point; does it not? He has no home other than this ship and that is no way for a boy to live, or to die." She added, as she sat up taller waiting for the yelling to begin again.

Captain Spiers stopped dead, no longer pacing, but boring into her eyes with his own bulging ones. So these ladies knew everything then, even touching on what was locked in the darkest recesses of his heart. Well, he did not want his crew to know, at the least. That was how ashamed he was. Not of his own actions, but of the boy himself. He had been wishing to be rid of him for months now and he had nearly killed him the last time he had angered him.

I don't need all this trouble, he thought to himself. And right then and there he stopped fighting it. Not for Nate's sake, but for his own. Rations were getting dangerously low and he needed to keep order. Used to making quick decisions, he snapped, "Fine, it is done."

Captain Spiers scribbled his name on a quick note stating he was making James McDonald Nate's legal guardian and handed it angrily to the surprised Jane. "When we get to harbor in Pictou, he can leave with the rest of you. I wash my hands of him. Now will you kindly leave me in peace?" He hissed, marching quickly over to his door and opening it in a rude invitation for her to leave immediately.

Not wanting to spoil what she had just to her amazement accomplished, Jane wisely stood and grabbed her mother by the arm to help her up. She stopped directly in front of Captain Spiers and looked him bravely in the eye. "Thank you, Captain Spiers, for doing the right thing."

He glared down at her, "Goodbye, Miss Forbes, Mrs. Forbes," He nodded angry, but still polite. "I trust this is the end of the matter, as I do not wish to hear of it again, lest I change my mind," Captain Spiers said through gritted teeth.

"Of course, good day to you then," Jane finished as she pulled her mother out of his cabin doorway, grabbing their skirts just in time before the door slammed shut on them. Both women hurried into their cabin and grabbed their supplies and rushed back out again, Jane holding the precious legal paper tightly to her breast. They walked briskly down the steps and up to the hold's opening, descending quickly into the waiting gloom.

They encountered James first, who was waiting for them anxiously at the foot of the ladder. Jane pressed the paper into his hands with her own shaking ones and then began to cry from the sudden release of her tightly held emotions. He read it quickly and then once again more slowly to be sure. "You did it, lass! You did it! I canna believe it!" he pulled both women into an emotional hug and when he pulled away there were tears on all of their faces.

"Oh, but there is nay time for this the noo," he said seriously. "Jane Gibson has gone into early labor and my Mary and Janet McLeod are with her in there." He nodded toward the curtain nearby. "They were askin' for ya ta come straight away." He grabbed Jane as she turned to go, "I can never repay ya for wha' you ha' done this day, lass!"

"Yes you can," Jane answered. "You can be the father that Nate deserves, not the one who signed this paper." She stated quietly, staring meaningfully into his eyes.

"Ya mean.... Captain Spiers? He is that boy's father?" He asked, shocked down to his shoes.

"Not any more, he isn't! I will send Mary out, so you can tell Nate yourselves. He has a special place in my heart and I consider him a friend, so I am happy to see him handed over to your good care. He was badly abused during this and who knows how many other crossings. From what we could hear across the hall, he could use a kind father about now." She patted his arm and she smiled shakily, before following her mother into the curtained-off room.

Jane whispered to Mary that James wanted to speak with her and when Mary rose she took her place at Jane Gibson's head. When little Jane looked startled and asked where Mary was going, Jane Forbes quieted her. "She will be back and I am here in her place until then. Just rest now." She smoothed her hand over Jane Gibson's sweaty brow and she slowly relaxed against her.

She chatted softly with little Jane, as her mother got a whispered update on her condition from Janet. By her mother's face, she knew that all was well for now. She settled herself for a long day and offered Jane a small sip of water from a nearby bucket. "Not too much, dear, or you will be sick. Just a small sip.... there that's good. So tell me where you are from Jane Gibson?" She wanted to keep the girl's mind occupied and off the pain for as long as possible and she was also curious about this quiet girl who shared her name and was about to become a mother.

"Well, I was born on a small farm outside Port Glasgow...." she began, but another pain was building inside her and she stopped talking mid-sentence.

"Stay with me, lass! What is your husband's name?"

Again Janet began the measured count out loud. "One, two, three...." while Mary Jane scrambled nearer to feel her lower belly as its powerful muscles contracted. She also felt for her well hidden hip bones, feeling of their size. When the contraction subsided and Jane's stomach had softened, she felt carefully around the babe to estimate its size and reassured herself that all seemed well and the small lass was wide enough of hip to deliver this rather large babe. "You say you think this babe is early, Jane?"

"Aye," Jane answered fearfully. "Is she too small ta live? Can ya tell?"

"It is as big a baby as any other I have delivered, not to worry!" Mary Jane answered, while she rolled up her sleeves on her gown and put on an apron from her basket. "Are you sure you did the calculations correctly? This feels like a ready-to-be-born babe to me!"

"Well, I counted backwards from my last cycle three months, just like my auntie told me ta do and I am not due for more than another moon."

Janet and Mary Jane looked at each other. It was not the right way to figure it, so it explained a lot. "Next time, try counting forward ten months from your last cycle and it will come closer to the birth time, sweetie," Mary Jane said to her. "Don't worry though," She said to the stricken looking girl, "this babe is plenty big, so you needn't fear for it or be concerned."

"But, I wanted my husband to see our babe on the day of its birth," she said beginning to cry. "I had it all planned out!"

Mary Jane smiled at her. "Well, plans don't often figure in well with bairns and births. They come when they are ready, whether you are ready or no." She answered her, in her matter-of-fact manner. "It will all be all right, you'll see. We are here to help you and your man will be in for a double surprise when you greet him, now won't he?"

Little Jane nodded. "I suppose he will!" She agreed starting to laugh through her tears. Suddenly, she remembered something and half sat up, face stricken with fear. "What aboot the pox! She looked fearfully around at the old sickroom. Will my babe get it when it is born?"

Startled, all three women looked at each other. Janet spoke up first. "I canna say for sure, but I think that bein' that you never got it, the babe willna either."

Mary Jane nodded in agreement. "Yes, that is what I think, as well."

Jane lay back again onto the other Jane's lap. "That is well then, that is well...." She grimaced as another pain hit her again and she fought through it, wrapped in her internal battle. When she relaxed back again she said just one word to Jane, "Angus."

"What?" Jane asked, confused.

"Tha' is my husband's name, Angus Gibson," she said as she lay resting.

"Oh!" Jane said, having forgotten their thread of conversation, what with the drama of the girl's pains breaking into it. "That is a nice name," she said, recovering her wits. "And so, what does your Angus do?"

"He is a cooper, you ken, and he makes barrels, so he can find work nearly anywhere," she said proudly. "That is why he went on ahead. Oh, I hope he is safe and has found work by now," she answered sleepily.

Jane looked up at her mother, a question in her blue eyes.

"Just let her sleep, darling. She will need to doze between pains to keep up her strength," Mary Jane said smiling at her reassuringly. "It is all as it should be."

Mary held James fiercely to her after he told her about Nate and showed her the paper. She had been too afraid to even hope before now. He quietly explained what Jane had told him. "Sa our beastly captain is worse than I ever imagined. Imagine a father treatin' his son that a' way! It makes me ill just ta think on it, the bully! It is one thing ta discipline your children, but quite another ta beat them regularly because of yer ain inner demons."

Mary shook her head sadly, her hand over her mouth in horror, thinking about all that Nate had endured, and after the painful deaths of his mother and sister too. "We will never lift a finger on the lad, promise me tha' James! He is such a good lad, I canna think why Captain Spiers could do such things and live with himself! But no one else kens, except Nate, that Captain Spiers is his father?"

"I was told no and he told Jane ta keep her mouth shut about the matter, sa as long as we are on board, tha' is what we mun do, as well. I canna wait ta be done with this ship, for more'n one reason the noo."

"Neither can I and I would as soon skin tha' man as look at him," Mary fumed.

"Well, my love, I feel the same way and maybe I shall punch him in the heid on our way off the ship, but no 'til then. We mun keep the boy with us and not risk the captain changing his mind, aye? Besides, he needs our love and guidance the noo, as much as he needs your healin' Airts."

"I feel terrible tha' I have no given him more affection, when I could tell he was cravin' it! I ha' held myself back, my husband. I was sa afraid that we would get attached and then.... ya ken what I am saying? He would be taken from us in the end, never to be seen again. But I have been such a fool!"

"Well, no more than I ha', mo mhurninn, no more'n I ha'. Let's nay look back and look only forward. We are nearing our destination, and God willing we'll soon be away. Let's go and speak to Nate and our family. There is a new McDonald this day! We should be rejoicing! He will be a great help to us in building our new hame."

Mary smiled at him and eagerly took him by the hand, leading the short way over to their family. Little Alasdair was hungry, so she picked him up, throwing a small blanket over one shoulder for privacy, and sat down in the midst of her children. Nate was off to one side with Sgian, his arm still in its sling, with the bruise still visible on his head from his injuries during the storm. James told them to gather closer, especially Nate, so all could hear him speak.

"Your mother and I have an announcement for the family." George was nearby with Hector and his head popped up to listen also. James did not mind, as he was such a close friend now as to nearly be family. "You all have a new brother this day! Nate, welcome to the McDonald clan, laddie!" James bent down to give him a big hug and Mary leaned over to kiss him on the cheek. All the children were staring at Nate now, wondering how this had come about. Nate just sat with his mouth gaping open in shock, saying nothing.

Sgian spoke up first. "Weel are ya deaf, man? You're a part of the family, mo' brathair! Have you naught ta say aboot it?" He gave him a good natured shove.

"I.... how.... is it true?" Nate stammered, not daring to believe it.

James unfolded the piece of paper he had carefully placed in his pocket and showed it to Nate. He could not read very well, but he recognized his own name on it, and that of James McDonald and then his father's signature at the bottom. It was true! He was so overwhelmed, having never thought such a thing was possible, that he began to cry. James and his beloved Mary were now his Ma and Da! It was too much for the lad, after quietly wishing to be a part of their lives for all these long days at sea and now it was suddenly true. "Are ya sure it is permanent-like, and he willna go back on it? Are ya sure ya want me then?" He said, sniffling and trying to manfully make the tears and the questions stop flooding out.

He looked up at both Mary and James, with such a look of hope and fear, that Mary could not help but take him in her arms. "Oh, we are very sure, son." It felt good and right to her as soon as she said it.

"Oh, aye, aye!" Everyone clamored all at once. "I ha' a new big brother! I ha' a new big brother!" Lizzie chanted, jumping up and down excitedly.

Sgian too was tearful and shocked, but tried to conceal it by patting Nate on the back and turning away now and then to slyly wipe at his eyes. His best friend was now his brother too! He could scarcely believe it and wondered just how his parents had managed it. Katy just smiled at him shyly. He had always been nice to her, so she certainly had no objections. The bairns were too little to say anything, but Mary and James knew there was no question that they would accept him, because they would grow up learning to love him. To them he would have always been their brother.

With a little nudge from Sgian, Nate stood up and went to give each of his new family members a hug and kiss. Trying to express with words all the joy that was in his heart was more than he could bear, so he was relieved to show them instead. By turns, he kissed the cheek of his new sisters, Katy and Lizzie, and then the babes, Alasdair and William. He hugged and kissed the rumpled looking newlyweds too, as his new Uncle Ian and Auntie Margaret also welcomed him into the family. When he came back around the group to Sgian, he plopped down by him.

"Don' ya go and try ta slobber me with any kisses!" Sgian warned, laughing.

Nate laughed too and just hugged him with his one good arm. "Doona' fash yourself, I wouldna kiss you, if ya paid me, ya wee toady!" They pushed and shoved at each other good naturedly, to cover their awkwardness as young boys often do.

"Oh! What about Willie?" Nate asked, suddenly. "Can we tell Willie?"

"Aye, ya can tell whomever ya wish!" James said. "But, first let us speak alone for a moment."

"Aye," Nate answered, rising obediently to follow James a short distance away.

When they were well away from everyone, James leaned in close and put one hand on Nate's good shoulder. "You may ken what I am going ta tell ya, but hear me oot anyway. We know all aboot your father, son, and a bit aboot how he has treated ya."

Nate looked down at his feet in shame, his face growing warm. He was embarrassed that anyone should know about the beatings, especially this man that he respected so very much.

James lifted his chin gently, to look into his eyes, reading the emotion in his eyes. "Doona ever be ashamed. It is nay your fault that Captain

Spiers is, what he is." James could not bring himself to call the man this boy's father. "It is his ain fault. Blood can mean everything, or it can mean nothing; you will learn this as you grow older, aye? Remember what my auld Grandda used to say: 'Keep your heart true and the love that you give, you get back times one-hundred and two.'"

Nate hugged James and his young heart expanded with joy as James' older one opened to him. "And one more thing that I wanted to say to you, son, is no ta talk of the captain being your real father ta anyone else on board including your sisters and brothers, the noo, just until we can get off this damnable ship," he added. "I doona wish ta risk losing you, by angering Captain Spiers. I am no factor, and I believe this piece of paper would stand up as a legal document, should he change his mind." James said patting his sporran, where he had just placed the paper. It was now kept hidden among his other valuables. "But, let's no press our luck, aye?"

"Aye, I understand, sir."

"Tha's a good laddie. I knew you would see where I was goin' with this matter. We needna speak o' it again until ya are ready either, aye? We willna press ya further and you need never speak of it, unless you wish it."

"Thank you, sir!" Nate said, sighing with relief. He was not sure that he would ever be able to tell them all of the things that Captain Spiers had done to him these last years. He could scarcely admit them to himself and he was not even sure he ever wanted to. "And thank you, sir, for wanting to be my Da. I am more grateful than you will ever know." His young voice cracked with strong feeling. "It is a debt I can never repay!"

"Sure ya can! Ya can start the noo and quit calling me 'sir' and call me James or Da, or whatever feels right ta ya," James said smiling.

"Thank you then..... James," Nate said out loud. Then he whispered, "thank you Da," and his throat closed over the words as he began to cry in earnest. He hugged his new father gratefully with his good arm and James wrapped both of his big arms around him holding him close. James promised himself that this boy would never suffer at his hands. He had suffered far too much already. If he gets into any boyish mischief, I can just punish him with extra work. I've never known that to ruin a lad, the way beatings and cruelty do. He thought to himself. Beating bairns just kills their young spirits and then they either turn into timid, frightened adults; or worse they grow up bullies and do it to their ain bairns. He wished neither fate on his new son and he was thankful that Nate's strong spirit still remained intact. James knew that children needed all the strength and encouragement they could muster, just to survive in this harsh world, not constant punishment.

They pulled away from each other and James held him at arms length to look lovingly into his eyes. "Now, wipe your eyes and be off with you then, laddie! Go and tell your friend, Willie, your good news."

"Yes, sir.... I mean James, I mean Da!" Nate said haltingly through his tears. He wiped his good arm across his eyes, took a shaky breath and with the quick recovery of youth on his side, scampered back to get Sgian. The two of them went loudly clambering over to the McLeod family, causing a great deal of objection to their clumsy ways as they excitedly made their way across the neighboring passengers.

James smiled as he watched him go. The lad was smiling ear to ear now, in a way that was heartening to see. He had never seen such a joyful look on his young face and he felt proud of him already. James went back over to the rest of his family and sat by Mary. She was just finishing with William, who had also demanded a feeding, and she was just placing his sleeping little body back into his basket near the sleeping Alasdair.

Mary hugged him close and then spoke, "weel, I mun get back ta the other room. A new Gibson is coming this day and they will need help with the birthin'."

Katy looked up at her mother as she stood. "Is all well with Jane and her bairn then?" She could not help herself from thinking about the sad trail of small bundles that the ship had already left in its wake, including her own sweet little cousin, Alex.

"Yes, dearest, I believe 'tis. But birthin' is a dangerous time in any woman's life, sa they will need all the help they can get, aye?"

"Come and tell me if ya need me to do aught, Mama," Katy said.

Mary smiled at her sweet eldest daughter. "Thank you Katy, I wull, but I need ya most ta help with your wee brothers and Lizzie, sa I can help little Jane. Come and fetch me, when they need the next feedin', aye?"

"Yes, Mama, I will." Katy smiled back at her mother, nodding confidently.

Mary gave each child a kiss, except the older boys who were across the way excitedly telling a rather confused looking Willie, that they were brothers now. Then she gave James a long kiss. "Thank you, my love. I will be back when I can."

"I will be here with our bairns a'waitin' for ya, so you go on."

Mary left them and headed back for the old sickroom that was now a birthing room after stopping to rummage in one of her packs. She grabbed a small blanket that the bairns had outgrown and a few tiny clouts. It would have to serve for the babe's first washing and wrapping, since she did not want to go rummaging into Jane's things. A worried looking Charles met her before she could part the curtain to the new birthing room.

"Mistress," Charles asked, politely restraining her, "could ya tell me how my sister is faring as soon as ya may? I am worrit sick over her going into the birthin' this early on."

Mary laid a reassuring hand on his forearm. "I don' believe the bairn is early a'tall, so you can cease your frettin'. I will be back out in a short while ta tell ya, and as often as I can after tha'. I can tell ya the babe will be coming this day or early into tomorrow. From what I ha' seen sa far, Jane is doing verra well. Try not to worrit, it won't help her. Mebbe ya can get out some of the bairn's clothes she has sewn and clicketed out of her things, as she will have need of them verra soon, aye?"

"Aye, I can do that!" Charles said, glad for something to actually do. "Please," he implored her, "take good care of her, Mistress McDonald! She is the only sister I have and I am responsible for her reaching her husband safely!"

Mary smiled at the earnest young man. "A charaid, ya are a good brother ta her." Mary pushed a stray lock off his creased young brow. "But, noo is the time for women's work, aye? Ya canna help her with this one thing. She is gettin' the best care, with several skilled midwives attending ta her, sa stop your frettin' and get busy gathering the babe's things."

"Aye, I understand," He said, passing a hand over his sweaty face, and sighing in frustration. "Please do let me know as soon as ya may," Charles muttered, as he began walking back towards their packs.

He nearly stumbled and Mary shook her head, smiling. Men were almost always more nervous than women when it came to birthing. It was the same with nearly every birth she had ever been involved with over the years. She failed to understand why the men were nervous, when it was the women who did all the work and faced all the danger.

Of course, she remembered her own James saying as how he was afraid because it was something he couldna help her with. The men must feel things slipping out of their control and that was what truly scared them, Mary thought with sudden insight. Jane's brother was no different than any of the other husbands or brothers she had dealt with over the years. She smiled to herself and then slipped past the blanket curtain.

It was brighter in here as another lamp had been brought in and things seemed to have speeded up since her absence. Mary Jane was between Jane Gibson's legs and doing another internal examination. Jane was just easing out of another contraction as Jane Forbes held her head and talked soothingly to her, wiping at her sweaty brow with a wet cloth as she relaxed back onto her.

"Weel, how are we doin', ladies?" Mary asked, rolling up her sleeves again and squatting near Mary Jane and Janet.

"Well, she is coming along nicely, and the babe is in position, but the waters have not broken yet and the contractions are not progressing much right now. She is nearly open on the inside, and during the contraction the passage opens more, but it slides right back to four fingers afterwards," Mary Jane told her, as she wiped her hands and poured a little whiskey over them. She then handed the whiskey flask up to Jane Forbes who let Jane Gibson take a few gulps to ease the pain.

Curious, Mary asked Mary Jane about the whiskey cleansing. "Well, just as we did with the pox, we are using it for washing. One whiff and you will know it would strip dirt off anything, wherever it is poured. I believe, as my own mother did, that whiskey is a great cleanser for all sorts of purposes."

"Aye," Mary nodded. "My own mother taught me likewise. Tis' good to know that others ken its medicinal uses."

"It can burn like hell itself, when it's applied to an open wound, though. So, I always take care with it," Mary Jane admonished them all.

"Aye," Mary agreed quickly, a wry smile on her face as she thought of a few of the strong reactions that she, herself, had witnessed over the years with its use. Her thoughts were quickly pulled back to the present when Janet tugged on her arm and another contraction began to make young Jane writhe with pain.

The contractions were beginning to speed up and Mary automatically stationed herself on one side of Jane and took her hand, as Jane Forbes followed her lead and did the same on Jane's other side.

"Doona push, lass! Just breathe that's it!" Mary Jane instructed from between Jane's bare legs, reverting to her native Scots when she was excited. The four women instinctively formed a comforting circle around her. They talked softly and soothingly to young Jane Gibson to bring her through the pain, while reminding her not to give in to the urge to push. She held on for another hour or more, the women encouraging her and speaking softly to her.

Small moans now began to escape with Jane's labored breathing, despite her best effort to stay quiet and be strong. The pain was now an aching fire that consumed her belly and her mind. There was a strange sense of intense pressure and then suddenly it released, when the birth fluid flowed freely out of her as her waters finally broke. The contraction strengthened instead of waning as the force of the water helped to shift the baby into the birth canal.

Mary Jane quickly confirmed with her experienced fingertips, that the way was open and it was time for the real labors to begin as this child made its way into the world. "Push, Jane! It is time to push now. Your bairn wishes to make haste! Pull your legs toward you, girl, and push with all that you have!"

Janet and Jane moved behind little Jane and helped support her as she rolled her upper body forward and pulled upward on her legs. Mary moved down below next to Mary Jane to help hold Jane's shaking legs and to be ready to help with the arriving bairn.

"Ugggghhhhhhhhh!" Jane groaned loudly, straining to push with her contracting belly muscles. It seemed to go on forever and her face purpled from her extraordinary efforts. When the contraction was finally over, Jane said, "oh, Mary! If I die, please take my child to Angus! Please!" She pleaded with them, as the contraction subsided and they lay her back for a few precious moments rest.

Jane Forbes looked at her mother, frightened by Jane's words. Her mother shook her head slightly, to reassure her daughter that the girl was not dying. She knew from experience, what her daughter could not know. All women think they are going to die during the final phase of birth. The pain seemed too unbearable to be possible to survive. Granted, some did die during childbirth, but this lass was strong, even though she was small and all was going quickly. There was no profuse bleeding so far, this birth was normal in every way.

Jane sighed, despite herself. Comforted by knowing that her mother seemed to think all of this was normal. She had never seen a birth before and it was all very frightening. Jane did not react well to being scared and would generally not allow herself to let those feelings hold sway. Now, she felt helpless with her fears and the knowledge that she could not fight to help this young girl, any more than she was already. It was her fight alone. They could only encourage and help. She swallowed hard and shuddered, thinking about how she would have to go through the same ordeal some day.

As yet another strong contraction began, having only let little Jane rest a few moments, Jane leaned against her back with Janet to support her efforts again as her moans became more anguished. Jane Forbes silently wondered if she could keep her new husband from wanting children for a while. She did not feel at all ready to endure what she was witnessing here.

Little Jane pushed until she was exhausted and out of breath, then she lay back again, exhausted, as the contraction finally receded. Mary Jane quickly slipped a finger into her, to check her bairn's progress. To her great surprise, the babe had moved into the birth canal and would be crowning within the next couple of pushes. Sure enough, Jane was not allowed any more time to rest as the next contraction moved in on her again with a purpose.

"It won't be long now lass, I can feel the bairns head," Mary Jane encouraged her. "Push with all you've got lass. Let the pain wash over you and push!"

With a great groaning growl from deep within her, Jane pushed with all her strength, willing the babe to be born, so that the pain would finally stop. She felt the ache in her groin as her body allowed the babe to move into final position and the movement could finally be felt. She didn't stop to even breathe, but kept pushing.

"That's it, lass! I can see it! Come on!"

With her face purpled and contorted in pain, Jane kept pushing and the head slid free. With a satisfied grunt and a gasped intake of air, she lay back, but only for a moment. The pain seized her again in its jaws and she could think of nothing but obeying her bodies urge. Tiredly, she let the women push her forward again and she strained again with all her might. "Agghhhhhh!" She felt her lungs say. Her bladder let go in a rush. "Oh, my," she said automatically. But it didn't really matter to her; she was beyond anything but the commands of her body now.

"Good, good, I've almost got it," Mary Jane encouraged. And with a final brutal effort from Jane, and a little gentle tugging from Mary Jane, the rest of the wet little body slid free into Mary Jane's waiting hands.

"It's a girl!" Mary Jane exclaimed, handing the slippery infant to the competent Mary McDonald. Mary Jane stayed with her patient and began to vigorously massage little Jane's abdomen, while Mary took over with the babe.

Jane moaned as more blood gushed forth and tried weakly to protest. "It hurts! Please stop!"

"It's sorry, I am, that I must do this to you, lass. But if I do not, the afterbirth may stay inside you and make you very ill. You must get your inner muscles to continue to push out everything that is left inside. Help me now, lassie, I ken you are tired, but it is almost finished!"

While Mary Jane dealt with Jane Forbes, Mary quickly held the infant upside down and used her fingers to clear the tiny mouth of fluids as they ran out and wiped carefully at the tiny eyes and nose with a clean clout dipped in water. The infant began to breathe and then, as Mary quickly finished cleaning her little body and expertly bundled her into a fresh clout and the small blanket she had brought, she began to cry lustily.

"Hurrah!" Came a loud cheer from the other passengers outside, echoed almost immediately by the sailors up above. Word passed quickly on a ship hungry for hope. Everyone had been expectantly waiting to hear that hoped for first cry of a safely delivered babe. "Huzza! Huzza!" Lively chatter began again as the tense spell of waiting was broken.

Mary leaned up to hand the child to its mother for the first time. Tears stood in little Jane Gibson's eyes as she took the small bundle from Mary and they were not from the pain. She was awestruck that it was over and this child was so suddenly there, alive and squirming in her arms. But, her joy was somewhat dampened by the inability to share the moment with her beloved Angus and by the increasingly annoying massaging, that both Mary and Mary Jane were taking turns performing on her sore belly. Suddenly, she remembered her brother Charles, and knew he must be half mad with worry. "Mary?" she asked.

Both women looked up and Jane smiled, apologetically. "I'm sorry, I mean Mary McDonald."

"That is all right, lass. Confusing it surely is, what with all the Mary's and Jane's in the room this day," Mary Jane consoled her with a chuckle.

"What is it Janey?" Mary McDonald asked.

"Could I trouble you to go and tell my brother, Charles, that we are both fine?"

"Of course, silly me! I was supposed ta do tha' straight away!" Mary muttered to herself, as her small form was already moving away.

"Wait!" Little Jane called to her.

Mary stopped at the curtain and came a few steps back to listen.

"Tell him, that she will be named Hope Charlene Maryjane Gibson. For she would not be here safe, were it not for all of you. Because of you, my hopes have been restored!"

Tears shone in Mary's eyes, as well as everyone else's in the room. "Tchaa! We helped ya do what God made ya ta do, is all. But I am honored. And I am sure Charles will be honored to have a namesake too." She bowed slightly and her weary smile flashed in the gloom, as she exited the birthing room.

Mary was still smiling to herself, when she ran right into the chest of the anxiously waiting Charles. She could see by the tears in his eyes and his euphoric grin; that he had been listening and heard what his sister had said.

Still, he asked, "So all is well then, for my sister, as well as for the new babe?"

"Yes," Mary answered. "She had a rough time at first, but then the babe was in some hurry to be born! She suffered only a short time for a first birth. They will be fine, just fine. I was asked ta tell ya tha' the babes name will be Hope Charlene Maryjane Gibson, for you and for me and the other womenfolk."

In an uncharacteristic show of emotion, Charles scooped Mary up into a big hug, and started dancing madly in a circle with her, her small feet not touching the deck. He whooped and hollered and then set her down again, kissing her square on the mouth, despite the imminent approach of her husband, James.

James smirked at Mary's shocked face and did not take issue with the obviously overjoyed Charles' momentary lack of manners. He could well remember his own relief after Mary was safely delivered of their bairns. "Sa it's an uncle ya are this day!" He said, while clapping him on the back enthusiastically. Ian and other well wishers gathered around the near giddy Charles and shook his hand or clapped him on the back in congratulations.

Still surprised by Charles' unexpected outburst, Mary backed away to check on her own bairns, blushing, but still shaking her head. Charles was positively transformed from his usually quiet demeanor and he climbed the ladder to address the crew, boasting and crowing loudly.

Mary saw Katy and Lizzie and the bairns sitting by their Uncle Ian and their new Auntie Margaret. The boys, she could not see anywhere, but they were likely with Willie somewhere and she was not concerned. They were eating the smaller than usual daily ration of food together and it broke her heart to see their pinched faces hunched over the meager meal.

She spied little Lizzie hungrily picked at the decking, trying not to waste a single crumb. It pained Mary to see her lively youngsters reduced in such a way. She put a bright smile on her face as she approached them as she silently prayed that they would sight land soon, very soon.

Chapter Twenty

Starvation and Hugh McLeod's Gold

Janet was getting very frightened. People were coming to her in desperation for some goat's milk, since their rations had been cut so drastically as to be nearly nonexistent. Even water was in very short supply and it was beginning to show in the parched lips and sallow skin of the passengers. Too many skinny children were getting too weak to even play. Despite their stepping up the goat's milk production, there would never be enough for all the hungry people in the hold. There might be enough for all the children to have a sip or two, but that was all.

When rations were given out, there was a near riot that was nearly as frightening as the hunger itself, as desperately hungry people pushed and shoved for a share of the meager offerings. Some of it was always spilled on the dirty floor of the hold in the chaos that ensued. Janet thought her heart would break, watching the children fight and scrabble with the rats under the legs of the adults for whatever crumbs fell or even to pitifully lick up some precious water that was spilled on the floor.

A few of the men had approached the McLeods one day, offering to pay in gold guineas for one of their goats for slaughter. When they were refused by an outraged Maggie and Davy; Hugh, George, and the McDonald men had been forced to step in and break up the mob that threatened to take one by force. They had barely been able to restrain the men, even after much explaining about the need for the goat's milk being more important than the meat. Force was the only thing that kept the mob from taking one and now they needed to be guarded at all times.

During the scuffle over the goats, one man had pounced hungrily on a rat that scampered by and to everyone's horror he promptly broke its neck and starting chewing on it. Seizing on his idea, other desperate people began hunting the rats as the only other available food. Order and decency were falling apart before their eyes and they felt more and more helpless to stop it.

"Oh George, how long can we hold on like this?" Janet cried against his shoulder one day as the last chicken on board was ripped out of an old woman's hands. Janet could not imagine what they would do in the end. Would they finally fall down from weakness and just never get up again? Or would a merciful storm claim their lives before the dying began again? "I canna bear another round of dying children again, I canna do it!" She sobbed.

George held her close feeling the intense frustration of being unable to aid the situation. He could make anything with his hands, but he could not give them the food they needed to survive. One thought had occurred to him lately as he stared at the ship's hull, but he refused to think more on it, unless things became truly hopeless. It seemed a more palatable choice to him than the rats were, but only marginally so. He clenched his teeth and said nothing as he smoothed the hair back from her face and tried to comfort her.

Mary's efforts to care for everyone, but herself, had finally caught up with her and she was doing very poorly. Janet McLeod and Jane Forbes had several conversations about her and they were both deeply concerned. They had been giving her some of the goat's milk and whatever Jane could scrounge above decks in an attempt to keep her strength and her breast milk flowing. Little Alasdair had taken well to supplemental feedings of goat's milk from a cup, but little William was totally dependent on Mary's milk to survive. Both of them looked wan and tired and Mary was suffering a great deal from the strain of worry.

The family was doing all they could to keep Mary from doing too much and helping with the care of the children. But her stubbornness had proved just as difficult to deal with, as she resented being so coddled when she could see that all were suffering. The family had to persuade her several times a day to stop trying to help everyone else and take some rest.

"Please, Mama," Katy begged her, her dark eyes pooling with tears, "you must rest, if no for yourself, then for the bairns." She held little William in her arms and rocked him as he fussed. Her milk had proved unsatisfying to him and he was complaining loudly.

This was too much for James. He had vowed he would raise William to adulthood and get them all through this. He put his foot down very firmly, something he had never done with his wife before. "You are killin' no just yourself, but all o' us. I willna have it! We canna do this without ya!" He yelled in frustration. People nearby, shrank away from him, fearing his unaccustomed rage.

The only thing that gave him the advantage in that particular argument was that Mary fainted during the first real argument of their voyage. As far as James was concerned, that was the last straw and she had to reluctantly agree. It was the first argument he had ever won with her, but he found no pleasure in the victory. James was scared to his very bones not only about his wife and bairns, but for everyone else on board. He was no fool and he could see control unraveling as real hunger set its sharp teeth upon them. They were all used to the suffering of illness and hunger pangs, but this was different. There was no land to even go and forage on. They were truly helpless. People that had looked to him for his leadership for the entire journey now began to turn their eyes away from him in helpless despair.

Trapped on the Hector and surrounded by temperamental seas they were all alone and away from their familiar hills and glens. The sailors too had already exhausted themselves trying to not only net enough fish to feed everyone, but man the ship on little sleep, rations or rest. They had been using their own hammocks to fish for anything they could net during their free time. When Clancy had come down to check on them and Nate, they were shocked at his appearance. He had lost a great deal of his massive bulk. The skin sagged around his face and under his tanned arms and he looked at least ten years older.

Some of the other sailors looked just as bad, if not worse, when they poked their heads in to worriedly check on the passengers. They felt responsible for the suffering that was going on below and were bravely trying to help out in any way that they could. Many of them had surreptitiously stopped by the hold dropping small packets of their own leftovers whispering that they "please be given to a hungry bairn." Sometimes an extra bucket of precious water would appear in the hands of a nervous sailor leaning into the hold. Clancy told James later, that the men had each given some of their own daily ration to fill that bucket.

Many passengers had been moved to tears by the generosity that so many of the sailors had shown in their small ways and the courage that it took to sneak away to present each gift of food. James was no exception. He knew better than most, the risk that they were taking. Their captain would punish them severely if they were caught.

James had been up on deck a few days before and personally witnessed a young man that had apparently fallen asleep on duty, be viciously flogged with a Cat o' nines. It was something he hoped to never see again as long as he lived. He could not keep the horror from his face when the young lad had finally slumped in his ropes and mercifully passed out from the agony of the shredded flesh on his back. He could not help but picture Nate in the place of that young sailor.

James glanced at the captain during the flogging and saw the gleam of sick pleasure ripple through his dark eyes, moments before the captain looked up and caught him watching. The smile left the captain's face and he abruptly turned on his heel to return to his usual position by the wheel. Later that day, orders had been given that no passengers were to be allowed on deck unless delivering messages, until further notice.

Now in the silence of the night, James knew that the captain's pretense of caring about the welfare of the passengers had gone by the wayside now, in favor of just saving the ship itself. They could expect no sympathy nor any more help from him. He lay in the dark cradling Mary and little William as they dozed fitfully and felt more helpless than he had ever felt in his life. His feet itched to be on land where he felt more confident about providing for his family.

Old Hugh McLeod also lay awake in the dark across the hold, but he was thinking about something else. He was thinking about his hidden treasure and how best to distribute the food scraps he had managed to save and the bag of damp and moldering oats from the storm. No one else knew about it. Hugh had kept it all hidden back in the sick room, ever since the big storm.

He had salvaged everything that he could over these last weeks, oats and moldy half-eaten biscuit mostly, but it might be enough to last them a few precious days. He knew it was now time to bring it out before anyone died, as his precious wife Flora had warned him in his dream. Thank you Flora, my dearest, your warning may save us all from the slow death, Hugh thanked her again silently and he prayed that it would prove to be enough to hold off death until the Hector could reach shore.

Hugh knew that he must soon reveal the hidden food, but he was frightened of doing so too soon. He was weary of seeing the pinched look of hunger on his people's faces. He knew that the half-spoiled offering that would have been refused by most a week ago, would now be more than welcomed by them all. He also worried about probable uproar his revelation might spark, after seeing the desperation in the eyes of the men that had tried to take their goats. Feeling fretful, and unsure of himself, he dozed off.

"Hugh," she whispered.

"Flora? Is it you, my love?" Hugh answered.

"Yes, 'tis I, mo' cridhe."

"Am I dreaming again then?" he asked.

"Aye and it is the last time that we shall meet until you die."

As if waking, he could suddenly see her lying beside him on the boards. She was as lovely as she had been on the night of their wedding, her red hair spilling out all around her fair face. Hugh pulled her tenderly into his embrace, as he had on that special night so very long ago. "Why the last time, love? Am I dying then?" he asked. In his heart he longed to be with her and a large part of him hoped it might be true.

"Nay, this is no your time ta die. There are tasks still needin' ta be done, but ya will have no more need of me soon. The food ya ha' saved will help get ya through."

"I care naught aboot myself, but what aboot our bairns and their ain bairns? Will they all live ta see this New World, our Alba Nuadh?" Hugh asked her, peering anxiously into her eyes.

She looked away from his frown, as if listening to some inner voice. "I canna say for sure," Flora finally said, "It will be a near thing. But ya ha' done your best ta save some food and that may be enough."

Hugh gently pulled her face toward him with his large craggy hand. "I wull always need ya Flora, that shall ne'er stop."

She smiled up at him, her eyes sparkling bright in the darkness. "And I, you, but our bairns still need ya and sa ya mun stay. There is more I need to tell you, husband," Flora said sadly, touching his rough face with her soft hands. "It wull be a very hard winter ta come in the New World. Prepare as best ya may or all wull be lost. Do what you mun, Hugh McLeod, ta see them through safe!"

Her anxious words frightened him. "What is it Flora, more illness?" Hugh asked, searching her eyes for an answer.

Her eyes revealed nothing but her love for him. "Nay, not illness, poor provisioning," she answered. "Just do what ya can my darlin' and remember what I ha' told ya."

Shame filled Hugh's heart as his tears began to fall. He had always hated to cry and especially in front of Flora. "Aye, I wull remember," he answered, choking on his words and unable to imagine how they would endure for much longer.

"Whist now man and hold me close one last time. You have done all ya can, and it wull be enough to restore hope. Hope is verra important the noo. Prepare as best ya may for the winter ta come and tha' is all anyone can do. There is nay more need of words between us now, just our love. I will be waitin' for ya when your time comes, so have no fear, mo' cridhe." Flora gently held his face between her hands and kissed him in slow, lingering, exploration just like she had in life.

Hugh's head spun with both grief and desire as their kiss ended. He held her close relishing her unique sweet scent of herbs and flowers as he laid small kisses on her upturned face and neck. He wrapped himself around her with his arms and legs, trying to get as close to her as possible, as he buried his face in her hair. "Flora, my ain, I love you so," he choked through his tears.

"And I love you, my own, forever and forever…."

Hugh opened his eyes to the bleak gloom of morning below deck. His bunched up tartan was all that lay where his Flora had been. He pulled it to his face to try to retrieve her scent, but it had vanished with her. The rumpled McLeod clan tartan was still damp from his tears. The sight of its yellow and black plaid with the tiny stripes of red usually cheered him, but not today. The usually sunny yellow was now dirty and reminded him more of sickness than of sunshine and the black and red reminded him of the death so near to them and of the blood of his family that had already been spilled.

The sounds of the old ship groaning through the waves towards land and life began to filter through his grief to his ears. He indulged himself in a few more moments alone, his face in the tartan, and then he resolutely wiped his face with it. He stared down at the rumpled plaid for a few moments, smoothing the fabric with his knobby fingers. Hugh stood slowly and began wrapping the McLeod colors firmly around his waist. Through all the blood and death over the years, the tartan had survived and so would his family. Hugh defiantly threw the end over one shoulder and tucked the end firmly at his waist.

It was still very early and very few eyes were open nearby. He looked around at his fellow shipmate's thin frames and the children's gaunt faces. They must find a way to survive this; they had all suffered so much already. He felt his strength returning with his resolve to save his own family and his fellow Scots on board. He woke his son, Davy, with a shake and he rose obediently without question. He could tell by his father's face that he was about some important business. Silently, he followed his father as they went to gather James and the other men together.

The men stood around the revealed crate with its cache of food in silent awe, as if it were a treasure of gold coins. James McDonald was the first to speak out loud. "It be a treasure! 'Tis Hugh McLeod's Gold! This may verra well save us all," he said softly, as he crossed himself and silently gave thanks.

"Aye," Davy whispered, still in awe of his father's resourcefulness.

"It isna enough for more than a day, maybe twa' with sa many people ta feed, but it wull gi' us some time," Hugh said eyeing the crate critically.

"It wull do more than tha', it wull give people hope," Ian said, laying an encouraging hand on the old man's arm.

"Aye, that it will," George said. He put his large hand into the oats and then let them slip back through his fingers into the sack. The sound of the swishing oats made him grin. His broadening smile took his sad face and altered it into a thing of beauty. Just seeing that warm grin made them all smile for the first time in many days.

"Let us be aboot it then, men! We can divvy it up and see how many portions we can make with wha' is here," Hugh said, grinning proudly. "We need ta get some food into everyone today to keep up our strength," he said, his smile fading with Flora's remembered words ringing in his ears; Nay, not illness, poor planning. He came back to himself with a shake and found the others peering at him curiously.

"What is it, Father?" Davy asked him, frowning worriedly as he put a comforting hand on Old Hugh's suddenly trembling shoulder. The old man was obviously shaken.

"Achh, doona worrit about this foolish old man," Hugh said, taking a shuddering breath. "Your mother told me in dreams that this was a'comin', is all. It is still sa fresh in my mind…. I am no quite myself."

"What did she tell ya, Da?" Davy asked gently.

James cleared his throat, "Ahem, would you like us to step out then, Hugh?"

"Nay, you are all a part of this too…. please sit," Hugh reassured him with a flap of his hand, as he lowered himself gingerly to the slanted decking, favoring his leg.

Looking puzzled, but too curious and respectful to question it, the other four men sat down around him. They patiently waited for Hugh to gather his thoughts and tell them what was on his mind.

"Wull, it started when I dreamed of her whilst I lay sick wit' the bloody flux. It was my Flora tha' came ta me then and again just before I woke this day. She was sa real in my arms that I thought I had died and gone to her in heaven." Hugh caught a ghost of a smile from his son and was encouraged to continue. "She warned me in that first dream ta start saving these food scraps, as we would be in need verra soon. As ya ken already, she was right."

The men nodded and murmured in agreement.

"This night past she came ta me again. She said I should use that food now, or more may die." Hugh choked on that last word and stopped speaking.

"Did she tell you anything else, Da?" Davy asked, as gently as he could.

"I ken wha' ya are askin', lad. She couldna tell me if we wull all survive or no, nor who may yet die, but I believe it will have much ta do with our actions on our ain behalf. She warned me tha' this coming winter would be verra hard because of 'poor planning.' I mun confess, I doona ken wha' she may mean by tha' and I wull likely be thought daft by the lot o' ya. But I believe we mun heed her advice because of the gift it has been ta us thus far. More than this, I doona ken."

Davy put his head down to hide the tell-tale shine of tears in his eyes. He could well remember his mother and her forward seeing ways. He needed no further explanation. What she said, would come to pass; he could feel the truth of it resonate through his soul.

The other men were silent, each lost in their own thoughts and fears.

Finally, Ian broke the silence. "Let us be up and doing then!" He stood up as far as the deck beams would allow. "I wull keep my vows ta my new wife and family and we willna starve. We didna starve in Scotland and we willna starve now!" He stated forcefully. "We mun do all we are able ta prevent this thing. We wull do it together, and we will fight for them until we canna fight any longer. What say you all?"

Ian's impromptu speech had the effect of a military leader on his men before battle. They stood up as a group and as one body firmly answered, "Aye!" Nothing further was said as the foodstuffs were unpacked from their secret crate and divided. There would be an answer to the hungry voices in everyone's stomachs, at least for today. When they had divided it as best they could, they called the women to help distribute it to all aboard, including the crew.

There was a flurry of activity that immediately caught the interest of the closest passengers. As closely packed as they all were, the news spread like fire in dry grass. Hope shone on the people's faces in the grey morning gloom as they surged forward to gratefully collect a precious share of a stale biscuit or a handful of damp oats to ease their hunger pangs. Janet was mixing drammach to be given to the bairns. This was merely the stale oats dampened with a little water, but it was ambrosia to the starving children. The hold was filled with the sounds of lip smacking and the licking of fingers. They shared out a portion to the crew as well, who could not have been more surprised at the gift.

Old Hugh stood modestly aside, with a strange look upon his face. Many approached him as word spread of his thrifty caching of this life-saving food. Several grateful passengers approached Hugh and offered what goods they had, or promised to repay him once they were settled in the New World. One young sailor even offered Hugh a piece of Spanish gold for good luck and a grinning Mary Jane Forbes even saucily offered herself in marriage. Hugh waved them all away, refusing all offered payment from the grateful passengers and thankful crew, but accepted all offers of help for his family once they landed. He laughed heartily, for the first time in days, at Mary Jane's spontaneous marriage proposal, knowing it to be a joke.

Hugh, himself, felt encouraged again for the first time in many days. He sat down near the ladder and watched the McDonald children as they laughed and joked nearby with his own grandchildren, having long ago accepted them as part of their own tightly knit group. He sighed enjoying the smiles on the people's faces, the renewed hope in their eyes, and the sight of the children eating again. That was all the repayment he would ever want.

Maggie seemed more her old self of late and was chatting animatedly with Margaret, Ian's new wife. The two had become fast friends and were often seen together now, helping with the other women's children. The children seemed to give her some comfort as she anticipated the arrival of a bairn of her own, once again. Davy sat down next to her and put his arm around her shoulders, a warm look passing fleetingly between them, before Maggie resumed her conversation with Margaret MacGregor.

Hugh's red-headed granddaughter, Elspeth, came to sit with him and he opened his arms to welcome her into his lap. She had a small book in her fair hands. He recognized it as her small, well worn Bible - her most precious possession. She smiled up at him, and a fierce pride shone in her blue eyes, making her look so like her grandmother Flora that his heart hitched painfully. Hugh watched, his throat tightening with his overflowing emotions, as Elspeth slowly opened her bible to the correct place without even looking down. Her small hand removed one of her dried pressed plants and she placed it gently upon his knobby kilted knee.

"Tis from Grandma Flora, I dreamt of her last night. She wanted me ta give this ta you," Elspeth said softly. Her now brimming eyes held his for a moment then a single tear spilled over to slide down her cheek and then ducked into the corner of her crooked smile to hide.

Old Hugh carefully picked up the posy to see it more clearly through his tears. It was a perfectly pressed purple thistle, thorns and all, its bloom spread wide into a perfect lavender fan. His heart was as full, as his stomach was empty, so food could wait.

He silently grasped Elspeth's small hand in his own. Unable to speak, but knowing it was unnecessary with this special granddaughter, he placed the bloom carefully on the sash of his tartan and pinned it into place with the McLeod family badge. He thought it the finest decoration he had ever worn. The badge with its bull's head encircled by the words "Hold Fast" holding down the purple thistle of his homeland seemed more appropriate than ever.

He pulled Elspeth into the warmth of his arms and pressed his silver head against her red one hugging her close. He knew, without question, that Flora had sent this message of hope to him through both his dreams and those of Elspeth's. The excited activity in the hold faded slowly around them toward a satiated silence, as their two hearts finished their wordless conversation.

George stood at the forward port rail with Clancy, watching the ship slice through the swells. He knew the captain wanted the passengers to stay below, but he was willing to risk his wrath for a short breath of freedom. George was worried about how little remained of Hugh

McLeod's rations, after most had been handed out among the passengers and crew. Ian was down in the hold with Hugh guarding what was left. They and the rest of the men would take turns guarding the remainder until tomorrow, possibly the next day, depending on the ship's progress.

"Sa Clancy, do you ken how many days oot we are?" George asked, squinting at the distant horizon.

Clancy shaded his bruise colored eyes and stared at the unchanging sea where it met the blue of the sky. His already rough features looked even more chiseled. He was as gaunt and hollow looking from their days of hunger as any of them, but looked more so with the sagging skin that showed that he had left Scotland a much larger man. "I canna say, man, wit' nay land in sight." Catching George's stricken look he began again. "My ain gut tells me we are steered rightly, but there isna a way ta ken how far east we still lay until we spy land or at least a wee rock of some kind, ya see." Clancy paused and then wanting to give George the truth he said, "Even when the lookout spots something we ken, it could be days ta a port of any kind."

George met his gaze and nodded in grim acceptance. Days, dear God! He knew in his heart that many people on board did not have many days left. He remembered all too well how weak Mary McDonald now seemed and how Janet had said that she and the youngest babe, William, were weakening at an alarming rate. The fierce look in her husband, James', eyes the last few days told him volumes more. His mind raced to come up with another answer, finding nothing but the dwindling population of rats as a possibility.

No schools of fish had been spotted for a long while and the last group they had come across had torn the sailor's make-shift hammock nets into tatters with their strange razor-like fins and noses. The sailors called them Sword-fish and George thought that a very appropriate name indeed, as they had sliced their fishing prospects to pieces. George had been on deck getting some air when the sailors had been fighting the huge fish that day, struggling valiantly to pull one of the massive fish onboard. He had never seen such monstrous fish such as these, with long saber-like snouts than sawed through all their lines as they thrashed to and fro, only to return to the dark depths below, simply refusing to be caught. Old Hugh and Davy were still lamenting their inability to catch one or two of the great beasts. George felt the same way, judging by their size that just a few of those huge fish could have fed the entire ship a much needed meal of meat.

Clancy nervously tapped a tattoo with his fingernails on the half-rotted rail. His mind was also turning in frightened circles, like a ship with a broken rudder. A movement near his right hand caught his attention and he drew his hand away in revulsion as something crawled near his finger. "Achhh!" He exclaimed, moving away from a large ship worm that crawled out of the wooden rail that he had been tapping on. "Bloody worms are going to eat this auld ship oot from under us afore we get ta shore!" Clancy moved to flick it into the sea and George quickly stayed his hand.

"Clancy, wait!"

"Achh! What fer? It's just a wee ship worm." He picked it up to let George see it.

"Aye," George answered slowly. "I ha' seen them before in the shipyards on the older ships. I have been thinking on it and it may well be the only meat for miles other than the damned rats," he said thoughtfully. He gingerly picked up the worm from Clancy's hand. Clancy had very large hands and this worm was nearly as long as his huge callused palm was. George examined it and discovered that it had strange curved, shell-like pincers on what seemed to be the worms head. "Is this what it tunnels in the wood with, then?" He asked Clancy.

"Aye, they can do quite a bit o' damage to the wood of a ship, they can. I ha' seen even larger ones than this wee beastie on our runs to the West Indies. I reckon the warmth encourages their growth."

"Aye, I suppose that it would," George answered thoughtfully, as he poked at the worm, which made it promptly curl up in self defense. "I have seen many of these worms in the wood of the ship's hull below. Ever heard of anyone eating them, Clancy?"

"Aye, I've seen slave ships where the poor souls were fed aught else," he answered, frowning with disgust. "I've heard tell that they are none sa bad to et. Tastes more like a clam than a worm I heard, but I never tried 'em me self," he said with a grimace.

"A clam, eh?" George quickly tore the head off and popped the shipworm in his mouth before he could think about it too much. The horrified look on Clancy's face nearly put him off, but he chewed it gingerly, grinding it between his teeth as he tried to tell himself it was just a shellfish. He swallowed it quickly and discovered that the after taste was indeed, more fishy than anything else.

Clancy peered at him with concern, as if he might fall over dead at any moment.

He saw James approaching them, bearing a similar expression that showed that he had arrived in time to see George eat the shipworm.

"George?" James and Clancy queried, in unison.

George leaned heavily on the railing and cleared his throat experimentally, raising one hand to signal that he needed a moment. He swallowed hard trying to concentrate on the image of a clam so that his rolling stomach would stay put. "I'm fine," he said, as his watering eyes made a liar out of him.

James put a comforting hand on his shoulder as George took a shuddering breath and let it out slowly.

"I am fine, truly," George said.

This time James felt he could really believe him. "What in the name of heaven are ya aboot, man, eatin' a wee worm?" James asked. "There is still oats to be had."

"It was a test, see? To see if the things could be eaten, aye?" George added, seeing James confusion and disgust.

"Aye, I ha' heard of the wee beasties making a meal for a man, my own self, and told George about it," Clancy offered. "George, here, just proved it, I'm thinkin'." He looked at George with wide-eyed respect, for confirmation.

"Aye, not the tastiest bit I've ever et, ta be sure, but edible none-the-less," George answered, patting his tummy as it growled in agreement. The three men laughed. "Do ya suppose that there are verra many of those wee worms on board, Clancy?"

"Weel, I canna say how many," Clancy said, stooping over to peer at the tunnel the worm had peeped out of. He noted several similar holes nearby containing the same odd shell-like lining within the tunnels. He pointed them out to James and George, "but it seems as if there may be more, that is sure."

As a hunter, James immediately recognized the possibility of a meat source. He was also painfully aware of the need for meat for some of the weaker folks on board the Hector, most notably, his wife, Mary. He had been hoping and praying for a miracle nearly non-stop, as her life force faded before his very eyes. James saw this for the gift that it was and moved quickly to act on it. "How did you get the worm out of the wood?" He asked Clancy, as he leaned close to one of the strange tunnels, closing one eye to get a better view into the dim interior. Most of the tunnels were a little smaller than his pinky finger, but he noted that some were finger size as he pried at them.

"I was just a standin' here and saw the wee thing a wriggling by my hand." Clancy said, with a helpless shrug. "Hang on," he said, scanning the riggings above them. "Ho there, above!" He bellowed. Three or four men glanced down at him. "You there, yes, you man. Seamus McSorlie!" He said pointing at a sailor with curly sand-colored hair and a grey on sand beard that was standing on a yardarm halfway up the mainmast.

"Scuttle on down here!" He ordered.

"Aye, sir," the man yelled back and he nimbly began his perilous climb down the riggings of the main sail with haste.

"Seamus there, he knows more aboot such things. That lad is Irish, like me," he said, proudly pointing his thumb at his own barrel chest. "An' he says he used to make regular runs between the Mediterranean and the Caribbean aboard the Eastern Ruby, then he did," he said to James and George. In an aside, he added, "those worms get turrible large down that a way."

Seamus reached the nets end on a platform above the waves and swung around it fearlessly, dropping onto the deck a moment later. "Aye, sir," Seamus said, after approaching respectfully and removing his hat to stand in front of Clancy and await his orders.

On closer inspection, it was difficult to ascertain whether he was a middle-aged man or a younger man that had seen many especially hard years. James could not be sure either way.

"You made the runs to the tropics for a time, didn't ya man?" Clancy asked.

"Aye, sir, that I ha'," Seamus answered, bobbing his head up and down and looking in the vicinity of the hat he held in his hands.

"Well step up, as we've a few questions for ye," Clancy indicated him to come closer and relax with a brusque wave of his big hand. Then Clancy nodded to James to continue his questions.

"You ken the worms that live in the wood of the ships, Seamus?" James asked.

"Aye, sir," he replied, his blue eyes sharp, but his face visibly relaxing. He was usually up in the riggings or doing his second favorite activity, sleeping, yet he knew this man to be one of the leaders among the Hectors passengers below and he gave him the respect he felt was his due.

"Well, Seamus, I wish ta hear anything you can tell me aboot them and how they can be taken from the ship's wood," James said.

Seamus' blue eyes crinkled as he smiled knowingly. "Thinkin' o' eatin' 'em, are ya? Aye, I ken what you're aboot without you having to spell it out for me. Been thinkin' on it me own self, I ha'," he answered, his hand shielding the words from nearby listeners confidentially. "I had ta resort ta that verra thing onecet, a particularly nasty run on the Ruby, that was," Seamus' eyes clouded with remembered fear and anxiety. "A French privateer, she fired on us! She meant ta take us as a prize, she did. One of her cannonballs nearly took us straight to the bottom o' the sea." He stopped for a moment his glazed eyes belying his sharp mind as it drifted back to the place where he saw it happening all over again.

James cleared his throat and Seamus startled back to the present in an instant. "Aye, the worms," He said, coughing to cover the nakedness of his shattered memories. "Well, Captain Goodson, he got the Ruby out of that privateer's range and headed her straight into an oncoming storm instead o' making for the outer islands. I thought that was wise, I did! She could ha' had her way wit' us all, had she caught us afore then. Trouble was, we took on so much water from that bloody cannonball tha' we barely came through tha' storm with our skins in one piece, let alone any dry rations."

Seamus stopped and began to cough and it soon turned into a near fit. Anxious to hear the rest of the tale himself, Clancy quickly handed him a dipperful of water from the nearby crew's cask. Seamus drank it quickly and thriftily didn't spill a single drop, even licking his lips afterward. "Thank ya kindly, sir," he said sincerely to Clancy. "I've no spoken this many words all of a piece since port," he said apologetically to the men.

"Well, as I was sayin', we were sommat short on edibles and darena go into any port until we were out of French waters. One old feller, he showed us that those shipworms could make do ta fill your empty gut. They's best cooked in a soup, but tha's just me own opinion, o' course." He stopped talking as suddenly as he had started and waited expectantly for them to respond.

Caught off guard, James stammered, "Er, of course. And how do ya go aboot catching them then?"

"Yes, man, how do you raise the wee beasties oot of the wood?" Clancy asked, somewhat impatiently. "Go on, tell us!"

Seamus smiled easily, taking years off of his face as his blue eyes danced. "Why, tha's the easy bit. You bait 'em, just like fishing, aye? 'Cept you bait 'em with one o' their ain. You dangle anither one over their hole and the other comes a wiggling oot to see what all the fuss is about and ya snatches it!" He laughed at his own joke and slapped his knee heartily for emphasis.

"How many do ya think could be caught on a ship like the Hector?" George asked, his appetite recovered from the shock and his interest now piqued.

"Weel, she did take a voyage to the Carolina's her last time across, did she no, Clancy?" Seamus asked thoughtfully.

Clancy nodded in agreement.

Seamus shrugged and said, "I canna say how many ya may catch, but you're sure to find some dandies. They get so much larger in that warmer water, you see. Old gal like this, she is sure to have several score of the big 'uns, mebbe more."

James mind was whirling along faster, renewed purpose rekindling his hopes and burning away the dread and fear. "Thank you Seamus. I am indebted ta you more than ya could know," James nodded and shook Seamus' hand politely, but then he quickly turned away. His eyes were frantically scanning the nearby wood for another worm with which to bait more of them.

Clancy dismissed Seamus, who quickly scurried back up into his familiar perch above the first spar. His smiling face betrayed his preference to the more familiar environment of the ship's riggings, rather than the ship's deck below.

"The man said soup tasted best," George said slowly to James, knowing he would be thinking first of his Mary. "I am going to run down and tell Janet to gather some goat's milk and mebbe some of the oats to start some broth wit'. The lads can help us catch more of the wee worms too. Mebbe 'tis a good time since it be the captain's luncheon?" His mind was racing ahead as well. It was a now well-known fact that Captain Spiers kept a strict schedule with not only the crew, but himself. It was a boon to the men, as that made it much simpler to evade his notice and his strict censure during certain times of the day.

James suddenly pounced on the decking near the railing, like a cat on a mouse, capturing one of the strange worms. "Gotcha, ya wee beast," he crowed with satisfaction. "Noo let's find your mither," He said with a predatory growl.

George and Clancy passed a knowing smile between each other. James was on the hunt and would not stop now to chat. Clancy inclined his head toward the hold and George nodded and left to gather the boys and speak to Janet. Clancy stayed nearby scanning the deck for the captain or any other possible intrusion, as he assisted James with more worm captures.

By the time George returned, the two of them had a half dozen or so worms carefully imprisoned in James' handkerchief and about the same number in Clancy's large cap. "Janet has sent Nate to tell the Forbes and they have a pot warming to start the soup for Mary and the others."

"Good, good man," James hastily replied. He placed the handkerchief full of the now precious worms he had already caught into George's hands, as if they were a bag of gold pieces. "Take these down ta them and have them behead them and put them in the pot. I wull be down directly ta feed some ta Mary, my ain self." Tears stood evident not only in his dark eyes, but in his quavering voice, yet he would not grant himself the luxury of shedding them just yet. He did not know why the tears were rising, but he suspected it was because he was finally able to provide some meat that might save his frail and failing wife. The hunter in him was extremely grateful for this unexpected gift.

Clancy gently took the handkerchief from George and opened it carefully. He tipped his hat upside down dumping the contents into the hanky then peered into his hat to double check its complete emptiness. He plucked out a lone straggler that he could continue to use as bait, as James had done. "Take these to them as well," he said gruffly, as he handed the hanky sack back to George. "I can catch more of 'em. Besides, these braw laddies here wull help us ta catch more," he smiled, as he shoved playfully at Sgian's shoulder.

Both Sgian and Willie stood quietly to the side, eyeing the large worms with the intense interest of curious boys. Nate came trotting over as they were speaking. "We'd best hurry, the captain will be finished with luncheon soon," he said, his nervousness evident in his way of shifting his weight from one foot to the other, like an excited pony that had been tied too long.

"Come then," James said smiling and indicating with a finger that the boys come closer. "Let us show you how this wee bit o' fishing is done then, lads." The men quickly explained the baiting method and within a short time, all of them had made their own successful captures. Not wanting to be caught, they took their bulging pockets and caps full of booty below before the captain came out on deck. They supposed that there would be plenty of worms in the wood below decks as well, which they quickly found to be true.

Clancy, for his part, passed the word to the crew members about the available "fishing" on board. Everyone on board would eat some much needed meat today. Not a single person turned their noses up at the idea. At this point, meat was meat. The starvation was too deep now for it to matter to anyone what kind of meat it really was.

Below decks, the smell of hot soup greeted the fishermen on their return. Willie sniffed audibly as they descended the steps to the hold. "Ahhh," he said in appreciation. "It smells like fish chowder, it does!"

"Aye, tha' it does," Nate agreed, stomach rumbling in pleased agreement.

James glanced at the whey-faced sleeping Mary and headed straight for the smell. A group had gathered around the bubbling pot, which was placed inside another much larger one filled with burning broken barrel wood. Both were placed in the center drainage area of the hold in the ever present sea water that gathered there. Steam rose from the damp area and made a warm and cozy spot where people gathered to warm themselves and smell the wondrous soup.

Janet and Jane presided over the soup pot with Old Hugh nearby tending the fire below. James did not even have to ask and Janet handed him two wooden quaichs, each half-full of the soup. He thanked her and smiled as he passed the hanky filled with more ship worms over to her in exchange for the second bowl. He turned to immediately bring the soup to his Mary and the children; carefully spacing his feet in order to balance himself in the rocking ship so as not to spill one precious drop.

James sat beside Mary as he carefully handed one quaich to Katy. He did not have to tell her to share with the waiting Lizzie and Alasdair. Katy let them drink before she herself took one sip. James winked at her in approval and carefully pulled Mary up into his arms and helped her to a sitting position against his chest. She roused as he placed the fragrant soup beneath her nose and he encouraged her to take a sip.

"Broth, wherever did ya get broth?" Mary asked, in confusion after the first sip.

"We had some luck fishing, love, now drink," James answered, as he placed the bowl gently to her lips again.

Mary nodded slightly and obediently drank more of the soup. "Aye, it tastes fishy," she agreed sleepily, "'tis good though."

"Whist now, my love, and finish it," James said gruffly, feeling the relief rise again as a lump in his throat.

Waking more, Mary's concern strayed, as always, to her children. "The bairns, James, give them the rest," she said, pushing the quaich gently away.

"Nay, love. Katy is sharing some with the others, this bit is for you alone," James scolded softly.

"Aye, 'tis good, Mama, drink it!" Little Lizzie said from behind them.

"Please drink, Mama, we ha' our ain," Katy echoed, gently. "Even Alasdair likes it," she added.

Mary turned to them and smiled weakly, confirming what they were saying. "All right, all right, I am oot numbered and too tired ta argue." She grasped the bowl with both hands and then stopped, looking over her shoulder and up at James who was holding her close. "What aboot you, mo' mhurninn?" she asked quietly.

"I ha' already eaten, A luaidh," James lied. It was the first lie he had ever told in their marriage, but he felt no guilt for it. "Now drink, my jo."

Satisfied that she took nothing from her loved ones, Mary gratefully obeyed him and made quick work of the rest of the soup. Her eyes began to close again even as she finished and James kissed her wet mouth as he gently lay her back down on their pallet of blankets. One side of her sweet mouth curled into a tiny smile as she drifted into a more normal sleep. James quietly turned to check on the girls and the bairns.

He left his family for a moment and got the quaich re-filled from the simmering pot. This soup was gone in a few minutes, shared between the children. They also began to look sleepy from the hot soup. James took a sleeping William out of Katy's arms and placed him in the crook of Mary's arm, hoping the soup would make her able to nurse him well when he woke. He whispered to Katy that she should lay down with the others and she obeyed, sleepily gathering the others to her and cuddling against their mother's back. He pulled the remaining blanket up over all of them. Feeling the full impact of his relief wash over him, he allowed himself to shed a few tears as he watched his little family sleep with full bellies for the first time in weeks.

Shaking his head to clear it, he hastily wiped his eyes as he saw the boys approaching. With a finger over his mouth he motioned for their silence and rose to meet them before they could come much closer. Feeling useful for the first time in a long time he had forgotten his own hunger, but now it surfaced, like one of the whales the boys often talked about. He led them back toward the wondrous smell of the soup. "Did you three ha' some of the soup yet?" He asked when they were away, looking from Sgian, to Nate, and then to Willie.

"Aye, Da," Both Sgian and Nate said, simultaneously. Then they smiled and shoved at each other with their brotherly private joke.

"Aye, it was verra good, Mr. McDonald," Willie answered on his own, scowling at the scuffling of the two new brothers. "Show some manners you two!" He said, censuring them as if he were an older sibling of theirs.

"Oh, Aye, Wee Willie," Sgian said, sarcastically saluting him.

"Don' calls me that again, Sgian, or I shall forget me ain manners and cuff ya a good one," Willie hissed back at him.

"Oooh!" both Nate and Sgian said, saucily taunting him.

Willie glowered at them both. "Ya both are lucky tha' your Da is here, or I'd..."

James interrupted with a firm hand on both Sgian and Willie's shoulders. "Tha' is aboot enough out'n ya both! Now someone please get me some a tha' broth afore I faint dead away," James ordered.

"I wull, Da, sorry," Nate offered, grasping one of the empty quaichs from James' hand and making haste toward Janet and the soup pot.

Both Sgian and Willie were wise enough to look down bashfully, under James' stare. They both knew without needing to be told that they were being rude to argue and play about with no thought to whether James was still hungry. Especially, when he had helped to provide the meal they had all just partaken of.

James cleared his throat. He had no wish to shame the boys, just keep them in hand. "Achh, I ken wha' it's like ta be a laddie, my ain self. 'Tis no shame in it, as long as ya keep a civil tongue in yer heid and mind yer manners," he added, in mild admonishment. Nate returned in time to hear the end and handed James some of the hot soup. James continued before partaking of the soup, "Now mind me, you mun never malign a man, even in jest. It wull do ya no good and may do great harm ta the other party, even if it doesna seem so at the time. Do ya understand wha' I'm tellin' ye?"

"Aye," the three boys answered as one.

"Good, now be off with ya then. See which one o' ya can fish the most worms out'n this old ship before sunset, aye?" James challenged them, knowing a little competition would be good not only for their attitudes, but for tomorrow's batch of soup, as well. He took a swig of the soup as they scuttled away, letting the heat of it trick his stomach into not thinking about what it was made of. He had eaten many things when he had been hungry during his lifetime, and he decided that this was no where near as unpleasant as boiled grass, for instance. After taking another healthy drink, he decided that it was actually rather tasty and polished it off, stifling a belch as he did so.

Old Hugh and Davy were chatting with George between the soup pot and the ladder to the deck. James tipped the quaich up to thriftily glean the last few drops from it and then walked back over to the family's place and tucked it into the bedroll. He checked his family, seeing to it that all were sleeping soundly then he walked back over to join the men, smiling brightly. The returned smiles on the men's faces told him what he wanted to know - everyone's spirits had been uplifted and renewed by the hot soup. Even though the ceiling prevented him from standing up to his full height, he felt he could walk proudly once again.

Chapter Twenty-one

Of Whales and Dolphins and Men

Jane lay listening to her mother's almost dainty snoring. That wasn't what was annoying her, it was really rather sweet and homey. What bothered her were the people she had come to care so much about who slept in the hold below. Many were so thin and wasted that they could barely stand. The children especially worried her, but also Mary McDonald who was better, thanks to the men's' resourcefulness with the ship worms, but she was still not producing much milk for the two babes and she was so very fatigued. The three of them were so very frail and fragile looking that it hurt her heart to see them each day. She knew that they could not continue in this manner for much longer and that frightened her. She felt helpless and she had rarely had to experience that feeling without some recourse at her disposal.

If only we were home, she thought to herself, I could get a honeycomb from one of the many hives at our home in Blantyre, or a good milk cow, or even a wet-nurse. Then she remembered that they would never see her childhood home again and the realization hit her like a thunderbolt. Tears rose, unbidden, to her eyes. A small frightened sob escaped her, before she could keep it inside. Her mother shifted restlessly in the berth below her. Jane covered her mouth with one hand before it could betray her again, but the tears flowed despite her efforts. What have I done? She thought, feeling panicky. We will never see Scotland again, and all for a marriage to a man I do not even know!

Her sensible nature struggled against her rising panic as she reminded herself that there were few other options available to her. They could never have stayed at the estate in Blantyre for long, not with Lavinia as the new lady of the house. Still, she felt such a sudden longing to return home that she felt the pain physically, enough so to make her stomach ache. In her mind's eye, she could picture the lovely flower and herb gardens lined with stone pathways that she and her mother had so carefully cultivated and tended over the years. Jane had taken them for granted when she could wander aimlessly through at will, picking an apple here, or a sprig of fresh mint there. Now, she realized how lucky she had really been and she longed for just a small bit of it back.

Sliding as quietly as she could off of her upper bunk she moved surely, even in the dark, to her nearby trunk. She blindly felt for the small box that she knew lay just inside, near the lock. When she found it she sat slowly down on the hard planking, placed the box in her lap, reached inside and pulled out the dried rose bud that she had tucked away inside of it. Gratefully, she put it to her nose inhaling its sweet scent.

It was too dark to see it, but she remembered the lovely shade of apricot that it had been when she had cut it, what seemed like ages ago. It had dried to a toasty orange lined with a softer pink. Jane could feel the scratchy stem head and petals, crispy in their dried state and was glad she had cut the thorny stem off completely. She cupped it gently between her hands, so as not to damage its fragile petals and cuddled it, stroking it as if it were a small bird. It was a treasured piece of the home that was now lost to them forever; a home she had known all of her life.

Gradually, the pain receded as the rose's fragrance returned to her the sweet memories of her childhood and washed away thoughts of the long weeks of hardship and the many miles of ocean and time that now separated them. She remembered the old willow that she had so loved to climb as a child, its vine covered trunk flying by beside her as she played on the swing that hung from its sturdiest bough. The old tree grew by the small pond at the end of the lower garden path and it had always been her secret retreat. She had often jumped off the swing to hide among the green vines that grew lush upon its trunk, peeking out at the worried servants, when they were dispatched to the garden to find her.

She smiled in the dark, remembering the secret solitude of that special hiding place. When her father had hung the swing in the old tree for her, she had laughed until she cried, as he struggled with the menial task himself, rather than allow a servant do it for him. The ropes had fallen many times and both he and she had taken many a tumble from it, before they got it set right.

Thinking of her father, Duncan Forbes, she began to cry again. Who would tend his grave in that same garden, now that they were gone? Jane wished that she had thought of that before they had departed and at least asked the gardener to take care of it. She and her mother had made daily visits to that grave to lay fresh flowers on it, or to talk to him in their times of need. Even though she felt that her father was no longer there, his spirit seemed nearer in that place that bore his name and the dates of his birth and his death, than in any other place. It made her very uncomfortable to think of his headstone growing moss-covered and dirty as time passed, and she frowned in the dark. Forgive me, father, she prayed silently. Even though he had been so often absent in her later years, her love for him had not ebbed. She prayed over the dried rose, sobbing quietly and holding it close to her heart.

Soon, she felt somehow comforted, as if he had laid his hand upon her head, like he had so many times when she was small. Her tears gradually dried up and her fears began to recede into the night. There were simply no more tears left to cry. Jane carefully placed the beloved rose back into her small treasure box and put it back into her trunk, its squeaky hinges giving her away at the last moment.

"Jane," Mary Jane asked sleepily from her berth, "Is that you, dear?"

"Yes, Mother, I am sorry to wake you."

"Nonsense," her mother answered immediately. "Are you all right?"

"Yes, I am fine mother," Jane answered, quickly crawling back up on her bunk before her mother got up, lit the lamp and discovered her tear stained face. "Please go back to sleep. I just wanted to get another blanket from my trunk, that's all. It's getting quite cold." Climbing back under the bedclothes, she felt no guilt for lying; she really was chilled and shaking now.

Her mother yawned sleepily and Jane felt her settle back into her own berth. "Yes, it is. You can feel autumn in the air these last few nights. Good night, Sweet Jane."

Jane smiled in the dark at her mother's unconscious use of her father's pet name for her. He was still with them, even this far from home. Comforted, she drifted off to sleep. The movement of the ship causing her to slip into a sweet dream of a sunny day long ago, when her father pushed her back and forth on the willow tree swing in their garden.

+ + +

"Psst, Nate!" came a call in the dark. Both James and the boys were awake in an instant, recognizing Clancy's voice from the ladder.

"What is it, Clancy?" James answered nervousness in his voice.

"Ah, James, sorry ta wake ya man," Clancy said. "I was just lookin' fer Nate, is all. I ken how much he likes to see the whales you see, and I've spotted some off the Hector's port bow."

"What about the captain?" James asked quickly.

"He's abed, sir, so it is quite safe," Clancy assured him.

James could see both Nate's and Sgian's eyes shining in the darkness of the hold. "Well, go and wake Willie and be off wit' ya then," James said, yawning. "Mind Clancy now and doona linger ower long, aye?"

"Yes, sir," both boys mumbled, as they were already clambering over to Willie, causing much cursing as they stepped on people clumsily in the darkness.

"Ow, ya raggedy arse clot-heid!" Ian's voice could be heard from nearby.

"Go on wit ya, ya wee rattens!" A female voice barked shortly thereafter, that James recognized as Janet McLeod's. The three boys were soon clattering up the ladder in a none-too-quiet fashion, so James decided to follow them and make sure that they caused Clancy no grief.

"Are ya awake, a luaidh?" James whispered to Mary.

"Aye," came her tired answer, "and now so is William," she sighed. The mewling of a hungry infant stirred the air between them.

"Sorry, my love," James said, leaning down to kiss her in the dark, and finding her warm lips on the first try. "I'm going up with them. Are you and the babe all right?"

"Aye," she answered, with a rustling of clothing and then the sound of an infant suckling eagerly. Her milk and her strength had increased somewhat since the addition of the worm soup to their diets, much to the relief of both he and her friend, Janet. She and George had been invaluable to James during these last hard weeks by helping him care for the bairns and helping him nurse his weakened wife. Janet now spent as much time with his bairns as she did with her own and George's little boy, Hector. The McLeods and the McDonalds functioned as one family now.

"I will be back soon, love," James said, with a parting touch on her cheek.

"Umm," she answered dreamily, already falling back to sleep.

James crept up the ladder and found his way in the starlight to the port bow by following the strange sounds coming from the water. He could see Clancy's large silhouette against the water by the starlight and the boys' smaller ones next to him. It was chilly in the night air, but the sky was extraordinarily clear, the stars sparkling brilliantly in the cool night sky.

As he got closer, he could see the huge wet bodies sliding in graceful arcs out of and back into the water beyond the ship. Great hisses of air and water would often accompany their surfacing and strange calls echoed off across the night. The nearest ones were at least as large as the Hector herself. James was mesmerized by their sheer size, but he felt no fear. "Why, they're nearly as big as Ben An!" he whispered.

One of the boys turned to him in the darkness. It was Sgian and he motioned his father silently forward to stand near him at the rail. Nate stood at his other side and James slid quietly in between them. "Aren't they beautiful?" Nate sighed, without taking his eyes from them.

"Aye," James answered, "I ha' never seen their like."

They stood in silence together as the whales effortlessly paced the ship. All that could be heard in the silence was the sound of a soft wind in the Hector's sails, the slap of water against her hull and the watery noises of the whales nearby. The occasional call echoed from beneath the waves as the beasts moved with a grace that seemed unreal, considering their size.

Finally, Nate broke the silence again, "we should see them soon."

"See what soon?" James asked.

"The fairy lights," Nate breathed, reverently.

James did not know what to think, so he stayed quiet and waited to see what Nate had meant.

"There they are!" Nate said, in an excited whisper.

James squinted in the starlight in the direction of Nate's pointing finger. There was some sort of green colored lights moving sinuously in the water below. It was the oddest thing he had ever witnessed in his life. He felt the hairs on his arms stand up in gooseflesh. "What are they?" he found himself asking, like a boy himself in his curiosity.

"Nate says as they are lights made by fairies that live in the depths," Sgian whispered.

James turned to Clancy for explanation, but he had discreetly left them alone at the port rail. "What makes you think they be fairies, lad?" He asked Nate.

"I doona ken, I just think tha' they mun be," Nate said, eyes wide and shining in the starlight, but pinned on the mystical sight of the fairy lights. "They're always near the whales, like magic, ya see. I think they live wit' the whales, as they always seem ta follow 'em."

"So you ha' seen these lights before?" James asked.

"Aye, always with the whales nearby," Nate answered, "except the once." He clapped his hand over his mouth as soon as the words were out, eyes large in the as he looked straight at James, fear evident on his face even in the starlight.

"What is it lad," James asked, suddenly frightened after all. "C'mon, ye can tell me, whatever it may be." He turned Nate toward him gently and stared into his face in the meager light. His eyes looked frightened all right and he could not imagine why.

"The night that..." Nate began slowly and stopped.

"It's all right, lad, now tell me," James encouraged him.

Nate took a deep breath and began again. "The night that the first bairns were buried at sea during the pox," he spat out quickly. "I saw them then and wondered if they were lighting the way home for the poor dead babes, like they do for the whales."

With a rush of emotion, James understood what Nate was trying to say and why it had been so difficult. This tender hearted boy was not afraid of the lights, he was afraid of hurting James by forcing him to remember the death of his stepson and the other children. "I see," James said, trying to keep the waver from his voice. "I think that is as good an answer as any," he said, meaning it with all of his heart. He pulled Nate into a quick hug to reassure him and then he watched the fairy lights as the whales seemed to be a part of their eerie glow. His throat was tight, but his heart soared high above the sails. The thought of these beautiful lights accompanying those sad little bodies into the sea gave him a strange kind of comfort.

As if reading his thoughts, Nate spoke again, "I meant to tell Mary, I mean Mother," he corrected himself. "I thought she might like the idea, but then..." he trailed off, unsure of himself.

"Aye, it's all right, lad. I ken why you didna wish ta tell us just yet, but it's glad I am that ya told me the noo," James said to him. "Mary and ta others may ha' been in no mood ta hear o' it at the time. It was wise that ya let time do her work, before tellin' how ya felt aboot what ya seen."

"Aye, sir, I mean Da," Nate whispered back, punctuated by a relieved sigh.

Sgian and Willie had remained quiet during this exchange, but now Sgian spoke.

"Do ya think it true then, Da? Do ya think the fairies of the sea showed the bairns the way hame?" Both he and Willie's expectant faces shone up at him, reflected stars dancing on the watery hope there.

James swallowed against the renewed strain in his throat. "Aye, I do. I canna imagine a better way for the Almighty ta guide home any poor souls lost at sea, can you?" He asked them gently.

The boys shook their heads vehemently. The kindness of the dark hid any stray tear that might betray their private grief to their friends. James surreptitiously wiped at his own face as they continued to watch the whales and the luminous green glow in their wake. The cold wind was dying down now and the whales moved on ahead of them, impatient to be about their own business. The man and the boys watched until they could no longer hear their strangely musical calls across the water, nor see the greenish glow sparkling on the water.

Without another word between them, James led the boys quietly back to the warmer quiet of the hold and the sweet forgetfulness of their dreams.

George was awake when James returned with the boys. He was always awake lately, it seemed. He slept in the same place he had since they had left Ullapool, between the McLeods and the McDonalds and near the ladder, with his Hector in his arms. It had been a satisfactory arrangement, at least until the onset of his feelings for Janet. Now it was sheer torture to be so near that he could smell her skin and not be able to draw her to him. He could pick out her sweet smell, despite the crowd of unwashed bodies around him. He knew that he could find her even in the darkness, if he had to, and that was some small comfort to him.

Good Old Hugh was still between them, rock solid in his habitual protectiveness, along with her three children. Not that he mistrusted the two lovers; Hugh was just doing what he saw as his duty. Those, along with George's and Janet's own proprieties and the close quarters in the hold, made Janet's virtue a certainty. Yet, he often found himself wishing it were not so, especially in the lonely hours of the night.

George had been married before and understood the nature of his wanting, but it did nothing to make it any easier to bear. Nor did it help him to have the newlyweds so near in proximity. He liked Ian and Margaret very much. However, the giggling, kissing and playfulness of their newly married status were making him think less than charitable thoughts about them lately.

He recognized his jealousy for what it was, and he would wait until they reached Pictou and a proper preacher. He had no choice in the matter. But it did not provide him with any comfort during the long cold nights of wanting Janet to himself, his body aching with months of unmet needs. More than that, he yearned just to hold a woman in his arms again, whispering love thoughts to her as he drifted to sleep at night, as his friends Ian, James and Davy did. Not just any woman would do either; he wanted Janet McLeod with a ferocity that surprised him. Her bright spirit and her warm brown eyes had lifted his spirit to a higher place where it seemed that any grief could be borne.

When he could not be with her, his hungry eyes followed her about on her daily rounds of caring for her family or tending the sick and the hungry. She had a smile or a kind word for everyone and was on the move from dawn until dusk. His love and respect for her grew steadily with each passing day, but it surged forward at great speed when she favored him with a stolen moment alone, or a touch of her hand.

Janet never wavered in her care of others, especially the petite and over burdened Mary McDonald. The two of them had become fast friends and he knew that her constant care was at least partly responsible for Mary having survived so far. The other part of that equation was Mary's equally resilient soul, one that found a kindred spirit in Janet McLeod. George had been glad to see the blossoming of their friendship, as he hoped to maintain the connections between both families in the years to come.

James had become his own closest friend, the only one he had ever had as an adult. Certainly, he considered him the most trusted friend he had ever had or could ever hope to find. George had married his wife, Rose, when they were very young and he had spent most of his time trying to find enough work to keep a roof over their head. When his son, Hector had come and then later when his wife Rose had gone, he had little time to spare for cultivating friends. That very solitude had been a major factor in his decision to come onboard the Hector and make a fresh start.

George had been luckier than most young men, having found a good apprenticeship as a carpenter. He had never had to see his family suffer for the want of food or shelter. Not like he had, as a child himself. Those long ago days had left their marks upon his body and upon his soul and he rarely revisited them, except during the occasional nightmare.

Hector stirred restlessly in his arms and George repositioned himself to accommodate the little boy. It was too dark to see him, but Hector's warm, solid little body was a comfort to his wide awake mind. He could bring his face to mind from memory and he easily found his way there now. The little boy definitely had his mother's sweet smile, but other than that, George fancied that he could see more than a little of himself in the boy. Although, Hector was so much more playful and joyful than he remembered being himself at that age. He supposed that that had come from Rose, as well.

George's thoughts turned another direction, shying away from thoughts of Rose. Willie had been so gentle when he had crept over them to go back to sleep earlier and it made him feel warm to know that the lad respected him enough to stay quiet. Now, he found himself wondering what sort of man the younger Hugh had been and what sort of father he had been. He frowned in the dark as he also found himself curious as to what sort of a husband he had been to Janet. Not wanting to be jealous of a dead man, he tried to imagine a younger version of Old Hugh. George found those thoughts even more disturbing, as Hugh still cut quite a dashing figure, even at his advanced age.

He rubbed his eyes wearily and closed them tightly, wishing all thoughts away and praying for sleep to take him. After what seemed an eternity, he opened them again, as awake as ever. The first soft rays of dawn were lighting the pink and lavender sky, beyond the open door to the hold above him. George sighed. There would be no sleep for him after all, since the dark hours of night were reaching their bittersweet end.

"Land, Ho," the sudden cry came from high above the ship, "Land, Ho!"

Dozens of people sat up in the gloom of the hold. The air buzzed with a hundred questions and muted conversations. The mumbling turned into a low thunder that rippled palpably through the crowded hold.

"Land, Ho," the unmistakable and welcome cry came again. The entire ship erupted in a chaos of cheers and cries both above decks and below. In the hold itself, it was near deafening as children startled from their slumber began to wail, and the frightened goats began to bleat, in contrast to the joyous and raucous cheers of the relieved adults.

Clutching a whimpering Hector to his chest, George was the first passenger up and out of the hatch with James and Ian close at his heels. They scanned the horizon on the port side and Ian was the first to spot the small, dark shape of land in the distance. "There it is! It's land!" Unable to contain their joy, the three men danced an impromptu jig around the sleepy little boy, as he stood in the center yawning and rubbing the sleep from his eyes, timidly looking around to see what all the noise was about.

"Three cheers for the Hector," Clancy cried. "She got us through agin'!"

"Hip-hip-hoorah, hip-hip-hoorah, hip-hip-hoorah," bellowed the sailors to the echoed accompaniment of those still below in the dark.

"Hip-hip-hoorah," a pink-faced little Hector imitated, in the ensuing silence.

Clancy was nearby and overheard him. He reached down for the little boy and swept him up onto one of his broad shoulders. "And three cheers for her good luck charm here. This here wee laddie, is her namesake, Hector, lads! Let's hear three more cheers for 'im!"

"Hip-hip-hoorah, hip-hip-hoorah, hip-hip-hoorah for wee Hector," they bellowed, as Clancy made his way around deck with the little boy on his shoulders, both of them smiling ear to ear. George stood back watching with a bemused smile on his face as the sailors paraded Hector around deck, but ever watchful of the little boy's safety.

The celebration was cut short by the captain's abrupt arrival from his quarters in the stern. All hands quieted down and looked toward him expectantly. He took the looking glass offered to him by Dewey, the first mate, and put it up to one eye as the other squinted shut in order to focus. He fiddled with it for a long moment and then stared into, dragging out the moment of his answer until the crew grew restless enough to mutter, then he said "aye, land it is," he confirmed to the crew at large.

"Huzzah!" They crowed.

"Now then, let's find out what piece of land she is. Meet me in my quarters and unfurl the charts," he ordered Dewey who took off at a run. "And be careful with 'em ya wee lout!" he called, as Dewey tripped over himself in his haste.

The deck exploded with laughter at Dewey's expense.

The captain scanned the deck for his ship's officers and spied Clancy with the tot on his shoulder. "What are you doing with that tot, you buffoon," Captain Spiers snapped at Clancy. "Put him down and shag your arse up to my quarters. You too, McSorlie."

A somewhat red-faced Clancy handed Hector back through the seamen to George's waiting arms. Seamus McSorlie joined him as they ascended to the rear deck behind their captain.

+ + +

The Hector bobbed back and forth on the swells, her sails down along with her anchor as everyone awaited word from the captain as to their whereabouts. The land off the port bow appeared to be only an island as they had come closer and there was a great deal of muttering and disappointment among the crew. The sun was warm on James and George's back, but the wind was cold from the direction of the island. Little Hector had been returned to the hold shortly after he had been returned to George and several of the men had come on deck in his place to await the news. Among them were Old Hugh and Davy McLeod, Ian MacGregor, Charles Fraser, Janet's father Robert Innes and Alex Ross, John Ross' brother.

After what seemed an eternity, Captain Spiers and his men returned from his quarters and stood at the rear upper platform rail. It was his preferred position when he was making a formal address to his crew. Everyone on deck surged toward the rear deck, anxious to hear what he had to say. Captain Spiers took his time, adjusting his hat and buttoning his coat with an air of propriety, drawing out the moment of his address, much to the annoyance of the impatient crew and passengers. Finally he spoke, "after consulting my charts, I have determined that this is, Sable Island," he said indicating the island with a flick of his hand. "We are very close to the mainland and right on course, men!"

"Huzzah!" the men cheered once again.

Captain Spiers immediately silenced the cheers with a disapproving frown and a downward signal with both of his palms. "I am not finished. Please restrain yourselves from further outbursts until I am finished speaking," he growled.

Silence reigned aboard the expectant Hector.

"Now, as I was saying," Captain Spiers began again, "this is Sable Island. As most of you know, that means that we are close to our destination. However, we must still sail north around Cape Breton and that means that we are still a few days away from Pictou River, depending on the prevailing winds."

Murmuring began amongst the crew again. One brave fellow stepped forward at the encouragement of his mates. "Excuse me, Captain Spiers, sir," he stammered.

"Yes, Ranes, isn't it?" Captain Spiers asked the man.

"Yes, sir, Murdo Ranes, at your service, sir," Ranes replied, shifting his weight nervously from one foot to the other.

"Well, what is it, man?" the captain asked impatiently.

"Thank you, sir." He looked over his shoulder at his mates who nodded in encouragement. "Weel, some of us were wonderin' if'n mebbe we could put in ta Halifax for provisions afore we sail on for Pictou, seeing how we are sa depleted, sir," Ranes finished nervously.

Captain Spiers face screwed up his face into an expression of extreme disapproval. "No, we will not!" he exclaimed. "We will sail on north to Pictou, as previously arranged, since we are already behind schedule. A few more days will be no great inconvenience."

Jane Forbes and her mother, Mary Jane, had come out of their cabin to listen to the news and now Jane stepped out into plain sight, shrugging off her mother's restraining hand. "I beg your pardon, Captain, but you call a few more days with no food no great inconvenience?" She asked angrily. "I believe it is a great deal more than an inconvenience to continue in this manner for even one more day!"

"Miss, with all due respect, this is none of your concern. Kindly, return to your quarters at once. This is no place for a woman," the captain said, with a dismissive wave in her direction.

Jane would not be put off so easily and approached the captain before anyone could stop her, to stand face to face with the captain. "Captain Spiers, must I remind you that this ship and her passengers' welfare are your responsibility? There are people near death from starvation on board this ship!" Her fair cheeks were now stained a vivid pink from her rising anger.

Captain Spiers leaned menacingly toward her, "And must I remind you, Miss Forbes, that I am the captain of this ship?" He roared. "No one questions my orders aboard the Hector, especially not some spoiled slip of a girl!" He raised his hand as if to strike Jane with the back of his hand.

Now Mary Jane quickly jumped bravely forward and placed her small but determined body solidly between them both. "Captain Spiers," she said angrily, "you shall not lay one finger on my daughter or I shall have you arrested the instant that we reach port," she said with a quiet, but unquestionable fury and indignation. "If you ever manage to make port, that is," she added sarcastically. "Your conduct thus far is definitely not impressive for a ship's captain, nor does your manner speak very highly of your character as a man."

Captain Spiers attempted to regain the upper hand, feeling it slip quickly away under the interested gaze of his crew. "Mistress, I..." he began loudly.

Mary Jane interrupted him with intentional rudeness, shaking her finger in his face as if scolding an unruly child. "No! I will not be spoken to in this utterly rude and uncalled for fashion, nor shall I allow you to speak so to my daughter. And we shall not return to our cabin as there are people in need of tending below. As paying passengers, we shall do as we please." She erased all pretenses, betraying the true motives of their actions during the trip in that one statement, but was she was now far too angry to care. "If you try to hinder us further, we shall see what the local magistrate shall make of your actions. Mark my words, sir! Come along, Jane," she ordered, with a final and formidable stare into the captain's face, daring him with her angry glare to stop their progress.

With her basket already over one arm, she pulled a surprised but amused Jane along with her as she flounced haughtily down the rear deck steps and onto the main deck. "Excuse us," she said, more of an order than a request, as they stepped into the group of men at the bottom of the steps with her head held high and proud. The crowd of bemused seamen parted politely for them as they stepped through them, then the sailors closed ranks again to face their captain. No one dared laugh or even smile, but many sets of eyes sparkled with good humor at their fierce captain being bested by this feisty little woman.

"Let them pass," Captain Spiers said, belatedly trying to regain control after they had long since made their way forward to the hold's hatchway. He had no wish to be detained in Pictou for questioning, having seen what passed for a civilized settlement there. Their lack of amenities, most notably women of loose morals, made the thought of an extended stay there most unattractive to him.

Old Hugh offered Mary Jane his gnarled hand to lean on as she began her descent. She smiled at him gratefully, but her color was still high and her eyes sparkled dangerously. Hugh eyed Mary Jane Forbes with appreciation. He had always admired strong willed women. He whispered, "ya took the wind out'n his sails, Mistress, that ya did," then he winked at her and inclined his head to indicate that she go on below with her daughter. She grinned then triumphantly, making her face appear almost girlish again, and then disappeared into the darkness below. Her surprised daughter, Jane, followed her, seemingly unable to speak, but grinning proudly. Hugh overheard the curious chatter and questions greet the two women as they reached the bottom of the ladder. He stood slowly back up, his old back creaking as he did so, not even bothering to remove the smug and satisfied grin from his face. He took his place again next to the other men from below and crossed his arms, waiting with interest to see what would happen next.

Captain Spiers cleared his throat and then spat obnoxiously upon the deck, "Women," he muttered with disgust. "As I was saying, before I was so rudely interrupted, we will continue to sail north 'round the cape. I expect to be in sight of the Northumberland Straight and the Pictou River by tomorrow or possibly the day after. Drop all the sails, men, and let's be on our way."

The sailors dispersed, each to his duties, many of them nimbly scrambling up the masts and across the yardarms to let down the huge sails. Captain Spiers took his place near the ship's wheel. He rechecked their heading with his compass and gave orders to the first mate, as the Hector gracefully turned so that the wind would be at her back. The many yards of canvas sail snapped to attention as they dropped and filled out, slapping and groaning as they strained against rope and wood as if longing to fly free in the wind.

The group of men from the hold watched as the island slipped by off the port side and was soon behind them. "Weel, I guess we had best go below and hand oot the rest o' the worm soup," Hugh said finally. "We'll have ta make the best o' it the noo, lads."

"Aye," James and George answered, sighing wistfully as the only piece of land to be seen swept slowly out of sight behind them.

"Doona despair, lads," Ian said. "We are verra close now and our journey is nearly done. Soon we will be on solid ground again and off this accursed sea."

"This sea is not cursed," Davy argued, admiring the beautiful blue of the North Atlantic Sea. "Our captain is our only curse." A man of few words, he always made them count and the other men laughed in appreciation of his candor and humor.

"Aye, and soon we shall be rid o' him, either by reaching the end of our voyage, or by Mary Jane Forbes hand," Hugh answered laughing. "Let's go below and spread the good news."

The men followed him down the steps into the gloom of the hold below. George, always hating the dark confines of the hold, was the last to go below. He took one last longing look at the curve of Sable Island disappearing behind them and then ducked down the ladder into the hold. The waiting arms of Janet and his son waiting below were his only consolation.

Chapter Twenty-two

Love's Rich Rewards

Nate lay awake in the dark predawn hours, worrying about his new mother, Mary. She was sleeping nearby as she had been doing for the majority of the last week or two. She rose only to eat and use the necessary pot and feed the babes. The rest of the family had been quietly taking turns caring for the younger bairns. Janet McLeod and young Jane Forbes had been keeping busy tending the many who were weak and ailing from the lack of food, but Janet always gave Mary as much of her attention as she could spare. She and Jane had made several draughts for Mary, trying to revive some of her former strength, which had only shown limited success. Nate also had seen Jane give Mary and many of the youngsters, including him, food that he knew to be her own.

His young mind turned as restlessly as his body did on the hard planking. He could not keep the thought from his mind that he might have to lose a second mother. The mere thought of it, made him feel as cold and worn out as if he had been keel-hauled all night below the Hector, instead of resting warm in her belly as he had been. Sgian and Katy stirred next to him, as his shifting disturbed their sleep. Not wanting to bother anyone, he rose as quietly as he could and stepped over the prone bodies of his new family and made his way to the ladder.

Once he was out on deck, he paused to check for nearby activity and swiftly made his way to his favored spot at the rail on the port bow. He saw nothing in the ink black waters except for the reflection of the moon staring back up at him. He followed the path of the moonlight as it swept across the dark waters and terminated at the place where sky met sea. He had no idea how long he stood there at the rail as his mind floated aimlessly, worrying at one thing or another, as a dog worries at a bone. The moon sank lower in the sky until she sank out of sight below the distant horizon. The sea changed color and began to appear more blue than black, while the rising sun colored the skies a shade of pink that reminded Nate of a woman's cheek. He had not prayed in many years, but he reached out now.

"Dear God, please keep my new family safe. Please bring us safe ta harbor," he whispered out loud. Feeling inadequate he began again. "Heavenly Father, please watch over my new mother, Mary McDonald. Keep her strong and help her ta live. Please doona take her," he pleaded, his young voice cracking as the tears rose in his throat. "Ya already ha' my mither and sister, please let me keep this one for my ain," he said awkwardly wiping at his now wet face. "I ken I am no deserving and I am bein' selfish, but her ain bairns need her too," he added, desperately searching his mind for a better prayer. "I promise ta be the best son tha' I can be ta the McDonalds and ta always be kind and obedient. I wull ne'er talk back, nor shirk my chores, nor misbehave in any way if you will only let her live. Amen." He stopped and crossed himself as he remembered his mother doing, hoping desperately that he had done it properly.

A large hand on his shoulder startled him and Nate stumbled against the rail. He was caught and pulled around to face a teary eyed, but smiling James. James pulled him fiercely into his embrace kissing his blonde brow as he did so. They embraced, eyes closed, for long minutes in the silence of the approaching dawn. Nate sniffed loudly and James released him to look into his eyes and emphasize the importance of the words he wanted to say to him.

"Nate, my son that was the loveliest prayer I have ever heard, even from the mouth of the finest priest at kirk. Do ya ken why tha' is?" James asked.

Nate shook his head. "I doona ken if I've even done it proper."

"It was more than proper, Nate. It was sa verra fine, because it came straight from your heart. A heart tha' has proved itself ta be true from the verra first time that we met. God willna fail ta answer a request as sweet as tha' one was. I thank you my son, with all of my heart, for the love you have given sa freely to my Mary, your mother." James stared with love and wonder at the boy who had become every bit his own son during their voyage. "I love you, Nate, never doubt tha'."

Nate's eyes gleamed with the deep emotion that swelled in his young chest. His blue eyes appeared lavender in the rosy glow of the early morning and they reflected back all the love that was being given, withholding no part of his bruised young heart. "I love you too, Da," he croaked.

A movement over Nate's shoulder caught James' eye. A group of large sleek fish was pacing the ship a short distance away. James smiled and turned Nate toward them, pointing them out.

Nate's breath caught. "Dolphins!" he exclaimed. "We must be near shore!"

"Aye, that is what yon beasts are called?" James asked.

"Aye, I have seen them before. Playful beasts they are. They make the oddest chirps and squeals as if talkin' ta one another when they are at play." Nate said, the tears having been quickly replaced by excitement with the resiliency that the young enjoy.

"Fast wee buggers, aren't they?" James commented, wiping away the last of his own tears.

"There is naught faster that I ha' ever seen," Nate agreed, his blonde head bobbing up and down as he watched the bodies jump in perfect arcs in and out of the ship's wake as if a part of the waves themselves.

Strange noises echoed up to them from the shining grey bodies in the sea below, mainly clicks and whistles and strange squeals. "Sounds like Mary when she gets to clicketing real fast and the needles knock together," James said with a laugh.

"Aye, and mayhap a few giggles and squeaks like little Lizzie," Nate agreed. "Do ya think...?" Nate began to ask.

"I ken what ya mean, no need for another word. I shall fetch Sgian and Willie directly and send them up to see the Dool-fins," he said, awkwardly trying to pronounce the new word.

Nate nodded but his eyes remained fixed on the dolphins. He had seen them often enough to know that their groups were seldom too far out to sea. He tore his eyes away from them for a minute and scanned the horizon his blue eyes sharpened by their squint betraying his true bloodline for a moment. Upon sighting the shadowy outline of land in the distance, they immediately softened again to their clear sky blue. He smiled. He felt the elation rising, like a warm bubble in his breast. It was a feeling that could only come after surviving an arduous ordeal and he dissolved once again into tears. He dared believe now that they would make it.

He closed his eyes for a moment in thanks then opened them again to reassure himself of what he was seeing. Now he could see the dark outlines of land approaching on the port bow and he knew instinctively that they were indeed approaching port. The ship was beginning to wake around him, as the hands started calling loudly back and forth to each other between crow's nest and yardarm, and yard arm and deck. Excitement filled the air as Sgian and Willie came to his side at a run, whooping and hollering. As if in answer the dolphins began calling to them, nodding their smooth noses at them and dancing gracefully backward across the water their huge tails supporting them as they chattered with shared joy.

The boys called back to them, attempting to imitate their odd sounds. They were rewarded with several dazzling back flips and more of the strange backward dances across the calm waters. The boys leaned over the rail to watch the dolphins as they tried to race the ship, skimming daringly close to the bow as the Hector plowed through the water.

"Look at that, will ya?" Sgian exclaimed, his gaunt face alight with fascination. "They are trying ta race the Hector!"

"Aye," Willie agreed, "I ha' seen them once whilst fishing with my Uncle Davy and my Da, but never have I seen 'em as large as these and jumping sa high!"

"Aye, alla fish seem sa much larger on this side o' the Atlantic," Nate said, knowingly. "I heard tell of great schools of fish here that stretch as far as the eye can see!"

Willie nodded eyes wide with wonder. "I ne'er saw 'em bigger, tha's for sure, nor sa many." The dolphins were chasing teeming groups of smaller fish. "Why this mun be the grandda of all fishing spots! Wait until my Uncle Davy sees this!"

The older men had quietly come up behind the boys after hearing the news of land sighting, grateful to finally be reaching their long awaited destination.

"I see it, lad, and it's the finest fishing anywhere, just like I've heard," Davy agreed. "The kind of fishing I allus dreamt of," he sighed.

"Aye," Old Hugh agreed, "the kind of fishing to keep a family properly fed, it is, the way things used ta be near the Broom. I believe we ha' made a good choice, lad, despite our losses." Hugh put his arm around his only son as they both eyed the waters that seemed so full of fish as to nearly be able to walk across the water upon their backs. Davy's bright eyes clouded over at the remembered loss of his small son, Alex. Hugh saw it and gave his son's shoulder a sympathetic squeeze.

"I ken what you are thinkin', lad, it's an awful shame that wee Alex didna survive the crossing ta see it. But, the new lad or lassie tha' is coming wull and sa shall the ones yet ta be made. Sa take heart, my son."

Davy nodded, bravely trying to put the future ahead of them into the forefront of his thoughts.

George and Ian moved to the rail to scan the approaching land masses for any sign of life. The foliage was past its high summer shades of brilliant green and bright color splashed here and there across the hills, but the forest was still lush and abundant. Small rocky beaches could now be made out on the port side.

The ship's bell rang out and sailor's crowded to the port rail as well, shouting to one another that people could be seen. The men squinted and could now make out dark shapes that were obviously human, scurrying along the water's edge. Ian suddenly darted back in the direction of the hold, leaving both James and George to stare after him in confusion. James shrugged and he and George continued watching the water's edge with the boys along side the other men.

Captain Spiers was up on the rear deck, his looking glass up to one eye, staring in the same direction. He said something to the first mate, who then passed the word quickly down to the nearest man, where it swept across the sailors to the passengers, like a wave across the water. "It's Indians the captain says!"

"Indians?" the boys exclaimed, half out of excitement, half out of fear. They had heard tales of the sometimes ferocious people who lived wild in the Americas.

"Wull they attack us, Da?" Sgian asked, instinctively placing his hand at the ready to grab his knife.

"I canna say, lad, but my ain gut tells me no," James answered.

George stared at the shoreline curiously, but now with a new wariness in his gaze.

Ian suddenly returned with both the pipers in tow. He was flushed, panting and out of breath, but smiling widely. James looked at him with one eyebrow raised in question. "Are ya planning a ceilidh already then, laddie?" he asked with a laugh.

"Nay, more like a welcome, mo' brathair," he answered with a grin.

Both William McKay and Colin MacGregor, their bagpipes across their shoulders, began playing joyfully, each his own tune and yet strangely harmonized. Cheers from below rocked the ship as the bagpipes loudly proclaimed their arrival.

The Hector was now close enough to make out the people ashore. They were dark-skinned and wore strange conical hats adorned with feathers and animal skins cut into garments that were very different from their own. They stopped moving along the shoreline as the sounds of the bagpipes drifted across the water to them. In moments, they were fleeing, disappearing quickly into the nearby trees. Dismayed, the pipers abruptly stopped playing.

Captain Spiers rough laughter could be heard from his place on the platform at the stern. "Even the savages dislike that squawking and wailing that you people call music," he called across the ship to them.

McKay and MacGregor looked at the captain with undisguised anger for his insult to their beloved bagpipes. Ian also took exception to his insult, but wisely stayed quiet.

However, the nearby Tom Mandler jumped at the opportunity to curry favor with his captain and joined in the insults. "Aye, now you've done it! Scared away the onliest people we've seen fer months with your filthy noise," he sneered.

Ian stepped forward, "the only filthy thing I see hereabouts, is you Tom, why, I can smell ya from here!" He wrinkled up his nose with distaste.

The other sailors guffawed at Ian's quick-witted rebuttal and Tom's obvious embarrassment.

In a flash Tom was on Ian, but Ian had been braced for it and nimbly sidestepped him, laying a harsh blow across the back of his head as Tom stumbled by. Tom sprawled across the deck on his face, as the crew howled with laughter.

Tom shook his head to clear it and then charged Ian again. Ian put one knee up to block Tom's forward momentum and then laid him out with a skillful uppercut under his jaw. Tom was not so quick to rise the second time, but the anger was still smoldering on his grimacing face.

Ian backed towards the port rail as the men stepped away to give the pair room.

Tom charged suddenly from a crouch in an attempt to take Ian off guard. Ian was ready and stepped neatly to the side again as he delivered a robust blow squarely into Tom's nose, then he quickly grabbed Tom by both the collar and the seat of his pants simultaneously and tossed him neatly over the Hector's rail. A dumbfounded Tom Mandler clumsily scrabbled at the air for as he fell with a great splash into the ocean below.

"Man overboard," Clancy cried, smiling widely. "Heads up to the aft, an' fish him oot lads," he called. Lines were hastily dropped over the side and Tom surfaced and grabbed frantically for one as the stern of the Hector slid by him. Several laughing seamen hauled on the ropes and a wet and bedraggled Tom was pulled adeptly back on deck.

He lay there panting and shivering from the cold water as the captain's booted feet appeared near his bloodied nose. "Get up," Captain Spiers growled.

Tom hastily scrambled to his feet before his captain, wiping gingerly at his broken and bleeding nose, as humiliated tears of rage rolled unwanted down his leathery cheeks along with the icy seawater.

"You are lucky that you grabbed that rope, seaman. I would have left you to swim for shore or drown, rather than waste any more of my time on the likes of you. When we return to Scotland, your services will no longer be required. If, you make it back at all, that is," he hissed menacingly.

"But, Captain, Sir," Tom begged, "it wasna my fault! That MacGregor has been spoiling for trouble since we left port!"

"Quiet!" Captain Spiers bellowed. "I'll not hear another word about it, or I'll have you keelhauled into port in Greenock and you can have a real taste of salt water. Is that understood?"

"Aye, sir," Tom swallowed and hung his head. He did not like to admit it, but he was beaten. He knew that anything else he said or did would only make his journey home a bigger misery than it already would be. He stalked off to pout gingerly feeling his swelling nose.

Ian wisely went below with the boys and the pipers before the captain's wrath would be turned on him, but not before being the recipient of surreptitious praise and pats on the back from other sailors for besting the unpopular Mandler.

Davy and George met the anxious Maggie and Janet, respectively, at the foot of the ladder sweeping them into their excited embraces. "We made it!" George yelled as he spun around holding Janet, unable to contain his excitement and relief any longer. Willie held Finlay and Elspeth held Hector's small hand as they stood alongside her Grandpa Rob, laughing with joy. The hold boomed with chatter and cheers as everyone began laughing and crying at once, rejoicing and hugging each other in overwhelming relief.

Davy just held Maggie close as they cried private tears of both pain and happiness. Old Hugh encircled them both within his arms and wept all the tears he had been holding back.

Ian swept Margaret up like a small child and spun her in a circle, her splinted leg sticking out awkwardly and eventually bumping into the nearby Sgian with it. "Ow," she exclaimed, though still laughing, "put me down, Ian, before ya break my good leg too!"

"You should ha' seen Uncle Ian, Margaret," Sgian began excitedly, "he and tha' Tom Mandler got into a rare stramash and Uncle Ian gave Tom Mandler a thrashin' and threw him overboard!"

"What?" Maggie began, looking at Ian fearfully.

"Later," Ian growled at Sgian as he silenced Maggie with a sound kiss. Sgian whooped and began to make kissing noises, teasing his uncle's boldness.

"Off with ya, ya wee poolie, or I'll throw you in the drink as well," Ian growled with mock anger toward Sgian. Sgian jumped out of his uncle's reach, laughing.

James sat down near Mary, whose head rested in Katy's lap and took her small white hand in his. He gently brought her hand to his lips and kissed it, and then he leaned over and kissed her thin lips. "'Tis over, mo mhurninn, we're in sight of shore." She weakly tried to rise, so he helped her to sit up and drew her into his own lap and his warm embrace. Katy, along with little Lizzie hugged them both close from behind as tears ran freely down their faces.

As if feeling left out, the babes, Alasdair and William, both began to squall and the girls expertly picked them up, including them in the family's relieved embrace. Nate and Sgian joined them, each taking a babe from their little sisters and began telling them about the dolphins and the Indians as their parents enjoyed a moment alone.

The two girls' dark eyes grew wide as the boys regaled them with tales from the world above, that they had so rarely seen during the voyage. At once, feeling sorry for them and sensing their parents needed the time alone, the boys put the now content babies back into their baskets and grabbed their sisters by the hand. They wanted them to see their new land as they approached. Motioning to Lizzie for silence, they crept away and up the ladder, but not before motioning to Willie to join them. He caught on quickly and followed with his sister, Elspeth.

Mary turned to James, hope shining in her brown eyes. "It's true then, and we shall be in port this day?"

"Aye, my jo, 'tis true," He answered, nodding surely. "The waters here be full of fish and the land looks rich and green beyond the shore, just like we were told."

Mary smiled up at him. "We did it, my love. We really are here." She put her hands together and whispered a prayer of thanks. "Then I need not ha' any more of that soup poured down my throat?" she asked, giving him a saucy wink that was more like her old self.

James laughed, "Nay, love, no more of that soup, I promise. The first thing I will do when we reach land is hunt us some real meat! If the fish I have seen are a rule to measure the game by, the deer and rabbits here shall be as big as a house!"

"Well then, I shall grow as big as a house myself then with the eating of them," she joked, though the thought of red meat was almost too incredible to imagine.

"Not as big as the house tha' I shall build for us, my jo. It wull make our cottage in Loch Katrine look like a shanty, I promise ya tha'," he said, sealing the promise with another resounding kiss.

"Achh! I doona need a big house, just one with you and the bairns inside o' it."

"Weel, and since I am doin' the building of it, I guess you'll ha' no say in the matter," James teased her.

"We'll see aboot tha', won't we?" Mary replied, teasing him back. The sparkle that he had fallen so deeply in love with was still there in her deep brown eyes, despite the weakness of her tired undernourished body.

James did not reply. Instead he silenced her with a longing kiss that left her wide awake and with wanting in her eyes for the first time many days. "Aye, tha' we wull and as soon as we can too," he said to her warmly.

"Why, James McDonald," Mary said, breathlessly. "You've gone daft, man."

"Aye, daft and ower the moon for ya, as allus, lass," he whispered into her dark curls. It had been a saying between them for many years and it still had the same effect on them both. They stared lovingly into each other's eyes, both wishing for a more private place to express their love, but content with each other's arms for now.

Small feet rumbled down the nearby ladder and soon they were enveloped with excited children all talking at once about Indians, dolphins and all manner of sea life. Mary and James smiled at each other over the children's heads and Mary shrugged. They would have their long awaited time alone very soon now.

"I saw a Dool-fin and a silkie, Momma!" Lizzie shrieked, wiggling excitedly between them.

"You did?" Mary asked, with mock surprise. "And what do they look like then? Do they have big teeth to bite you with, like this?" Mary pretended to bite at Lizzie's bare neck succeeding in kissing and tickling her, causing a fit of giggles.

"No, no, no!" Lizzie cried out as she laughed and squirmed away, rubbing the ticklish spot on her neck. She sought refuge on her father's lap. "Da, have you seen a Dool-fin or a silkie before?"

"Aye and the silkies had sleek black hair like your sister Katy," he teased Katy, lovingly picking up a lock of her black curls between his fingers. She smiled and giggled shyly. Both their girls looked pink and lovely from the fresh air and he was relieved to see it. Elspeth also looked better, her skin pink and glowing and her red hair gleaming even in the gloom of the hold. She smiled up at James and wordlessly pitched in to help Katy with the babes. He gave the boys a grateful look and a thankful nod, which they acknowledged with broad grins in return, before hurrying away again.

"I'm going back on deck my love, ta see our new hame. Would you like ta come with me?" James asked.

"Aye, if you wull help me, I would like nothing better; except perhaps a bath in a cool stream." Mary replied, wistfully.

James lifted her into his arms, trying not to think about how very light she had become as they made their way to the ladder. It was time to see the place they had sacrificed so much of their own flesh and blood for. They, along with the other passengers had paid a price much higher than they had anticipated to reach this new land that was, by all accounts, filled with so much unlimited opportunity and unrealized potential. This was the day they had been striving for and he had an overwhelming need to share it with his beloved, Mary.

Jane Forbes and her mother, Mary Jane, stood next to the starboard rail waiting, as the Hector positioned herself to enter the bay at the mouth of the Pictou River. James put Mary down beside them and she leaned on him for support as they watched the tall ship come around gracefully. The sailor's busily changed the sail configuration in order to head her into the harbor at a more southerly angle. Ian and Margaret, George and Janet, and Davy and Maggie stood on their other side next to Old Hugh. They all watched, transfixed, as they drew into the bay, hoping to catch sight of the town and other people on shore.

Soon several smaller boats came into view on a graveled shoreline that was backed by a small main street and a cluster of rustic buildings. More houses could be seen to each side of the town and scattered across the rock strewn and wooded hills beyond it. The town was small but the bustle in the streets showed it was definitely inhabited.

"Ha' ya e'er seen anything sa lovely," Hugh sighed.

James laughed, "wull she is small, but she be dry, sa it'll do," he teased him. The town was arguably no more than a rustic settlement, but it looked like an ethereal paradise to the battered and starving passengers of the Hector.

A flurry of movement began near the shore as people could be seen running about. Homey smoke hung in wispy layers in the air above the town from all the fires lit inside the shops and cottages. A small launch pulled away from shore rowing out to meet them. It looked to have several men aboard.

"Look," Ian exclaimed, "the Indians have returned!" He pointed excitedly to a point beyond the port bow and the approaching launch. People who were dressed in the same unusual fashion as the Indians on the other side of the point had been, appeared out of the trees above the rocky shore and began cautiously picking their way along the shore toward Pictou. They appeared to have overcome their previous fears and pointed at the approaching ship excitedly, as they steadily approached the town.

Captain Spiers approached the rail from his place on the rear platform to officially greet the boatload of men.

"Ahoy!" A man called from the gently rocking skiff when they pulled alongside. "What ship is this and what be your business here?"

"Ahoy," Captain Spiers replied, "We be the ship Hector, arriving from Scotland!"

The men muttered excitedly amongst themselves and then the man who had addressed them stood up in the rocking boat. "Greetings, Ship Hector, we ha' been expectin' ya for many days and thought ya lost! Welcome to Pictou!" he hollered past his cupped hand. "You've no ill persons or animals on board, have ye?"

The captain glowered briefly toward the small group of passengers that stood at the starboard bow. His eyes caught James and held them insolently for what seemed like an eternity.

James sucked in his breath, realizing with a jolt that Captain Spiers had not been as easily fooled as they had all believed. "Dear Lord," he muttered softly, hoping the captain would say nothing of the deaths of their children. They could ill afford a delay in making port. Many more might die of starvation while they waited in quarantine out in the bay; notably, his beloved Mary.

After what seemed like an eternity to James, the captain finally broke his stare and addressed the boat below. "Nay, none sick, just many hungry folk. Our rations have long since run out," he yelled back.

James exhaled, only then realizing that he had been holding his breath.

"Aye," the man called nodding sympathetically, as he spied a sailor unconsciously put a shipworm into his mouth and chew it with relish. The man watching swallowed visibly. "Make her secure then and begin your unloading, afore the tide changes. I wull send oot some empty boats ta assist ya." The skiff neatly turned, as at his command the men rowed on just one side. The man reclaimed his seat as they began rowing in earnest back toward the docks.

The captain ordered the large main sails pulled up as the large anchors dropped into the harbor waters with twin splashes. With an ironic bow toward James and a small smile playing about his lips, he ordered the final instructions to secure the Hector in Pictou Harbor.

James nodded back, acknowledging what both men knew. The crossing was behind them now, in every way that mattered most. James hugged his petite wife to his chest. He had every reason to believe that all would be well now. They stood in the crisp early fall sunshine for a few more moments, taking in the welcome sight of the town of Pictou, their new home. Then, it was time to return to the hold one last time and collect their bairns and their belongings.

Chapter Twenty-three

The Hector's Arrival - Pictou, Nova Scotia, September 1773

Colin Charles McCain waited anxiously on shore to greet the returning launch. Wisps of his long black hair escaped its neat cockernonny to blow in the breeze against his worried young face. The mayor, Mr. Kenneth Linset, was retuning to shore with some fishermen in a small rowboat. He had gone out to ascertain the ship's identity as she prepared to make port. Colin, mangling his hat in his hands worriedly as he approached Mayor Linset, cleared his throat to gain the man's attention.

"Ah, Mr. McCain," Mayor Linset said, as he acknowledged Colin. He hastily straightened his clothing and checked the set of his wig after disembarking the small boat, before he grasped Colin's hand politely. "You wull be pleased ta know that yon ship is, indeed, the Hector. Your wait is over it seems," he said beaming.

The whole of Pictou knew that Mr. McCain had been waiting for his bride-to-be and her mother to arrive on the Hector. The ship had been overdue for several weeks now and Colin had been seen hovering near the shore in all sorts of weather, watching the bay. Mayor Linset felt he knew both ladies in question already, being that he had spoken to the worried young man about them every day now for weeks.

"Is she well then? Did you speak to her yourself?" Colin asked anxiously. He had been overwrought at the thought of the women being lost at sea and had been blaming himself for their untimely demise.

Mayor Linset laid a calming hand on the younger man's arm. "Nay, lad, I didna, but there is no reason ta think that she is not well," he added, seeing Colin's stricken look. "The captain himself assured me that none aboard are ill, just hungry from their being sa late making port. They have run oot of rations, he said." Kenneth Linset did not wish to add to the kindly young man's guilt by telling him that they had looked beyond hunger and nearer starvation to him. He would see that for himself all too soon.

"Of course, of course, how foolish of me," Colin mused, more to himself than to Mayor Linset. "They would be out of rations by now, wouldn't they?"

"Aye," the mayor said slowly, eyeing the look in Colin's eye speculatively.

"I shall return, Mayor Linset," Colin replied as he took off at a run, sprinting away and up onto Main Street, clattering noisily up the stairs of the small boarding house, the Pictou Inn. Several shopkeepers popped out of their doors, curious to see what all the noise was about in their normally quiet little town.

Mayor Linset shook his head smiling in amusement and scratched at a place under his powdered wig, tipping it askew as he did so. "Ah, the enthusiasm of youth," he commented philosophically to a nearby fisherman as the man tied up the skiff.

"Yes sir," the somewhat confused looking fisherman replied, "whatever ya say, Mr. Mayor, sir."

Mayor Kenneth Linset shaded his eyes with one hand and noted the Hector's position. It would take her at least another half hour to secure the ship and begin to unload passengers into smaller boats to be brought ashore. He followed the path that Colin had taken to the boarding house, but at a much more dignified pace that was more befitting of his position.

Once inside, he found Colin talking animatedly to the Inn's cook, Benjamin Foulds. Benjamin's face looked amiable enough, but his eyes betrayed his rising panic at being completely overwhelmed by the list of requests from this young, but most important guest. Colin had rented not one, but two rooms at the Inn for the last few weeks. Everyone knew that McCain Mercantile was a prominent import and export business that dealt in all manner of merchandise from overseas and from up and down the coast. This lively young man was their lead merchant, and represented Martin McCain himself. The tiny town of Pictou needed all the shipping connections it could obtain, so they had done their very best to accommodate Mr. Colin McCain and make him feel welcome during his extended stay with them. Mayor Linset approached the two men and joined the conversation just as it was wrapping up.

"And their must be some sort of pastries made up for dessert. Something that would go well with the hot broth and beef," Colin added.

"I ha' some dried prunes tha' I could make some tarts wit'," Benjamin added thoughtfully. "Bein' oot ta sea sa long, they'll be needin' some fruit," He said, nodding knowingly.

"Of course, of course," Colin agreed, pouncing on the idea, "to prevent the Scurvy. Yes, make as many of those as you can, as well. Spare no expense, there is a shipload of hungry people coming in and I intend to feed every last one of them today!"

Turning his attention to the lady proprietor, Mrs. Helen Foulds, he asked her several questions in rapid succession. "How many people can you seat at one time? Where can we get some more dishes and maybe some blankets for seating outside? Can you get some locals to help serve? Can we get some peppermint candies from the Banks' store for the children? It is warm enough for a picnic style luncheon, don't you agree?"

Recovering nicely from the rapid assault of questions she replied, "Aye, a picnic would be best as we can only seat a dozen or so in the main room here. I wull go and fetch some lassies ta help me and we will be aboot your requests straight away, don't you fret, Mr. McCain." She bobbed into a brief curtsy and then hurriedly removed her apron, flinging it across the room expertly to flutter down and drape neatly over a stool while she hurried out the front door. Her hoops got stuck momentarily and she tugged on them impatiently, before she freed herself, looking somewhat like a ship at full sail herself, as she seemed to float up the street on unseen feet.

"How may I be of assistance?" Mayor Linset asked the near frantic Colin. "Perhaps, I should ring the church bell and call in some of the people from the outer edges of town ta help with this rather large, er, endeavor of yours?"

"Yes, yes, that would be very helpful, thank you. Perhaps you could alert the rest of the townspeople, that we have half-starved people arriving and ask them to help any way they can." Colin answered, looking distracted, as he patted his pockets. "I must get something from my room, but I shall meet you on the shore to greet the Hector."

"Yes, sir, luckily it has been a good year's fishing. Until then," Mayor Linset touched his hand to his wigged forehead and bowed slightly in a gesture of respect and then turned and stepped out the door of the Pictou Inn.

Colin was up the small staircase to his two adjoining rooms before the mayor had even reached the street and was rummaging madly through his valise. Finding what he had been looking for, he placed it carefully in the waistcoat pocket over his chest, patting it twice to be sure it was secure. Outside, the church bells began tolling, alerting everyone in the area that there were doings in the town. Colin dashed back out of his room frightening a chamber maid that was just backing out of another room as he bumped into her in the tiny hallway. She jumped out of his way with a squeak and he apologized on the run as he clattered back down the steps and out of the Inn.

Noticing a shopkeeper grinning at him in amusement as he passed, he self-consciously slowed his pace to a more leisurely stride, only to break into a run again as soon as he was around the corner and out of the shopkeeper's sight. His heart was pounding and he felt that he had gone quite mad, but he was much too excited to care. The woman that he had agreed to marry had survived the ocean voyage and he was about to meet her and her mother for the very first time. He was sweating and shaking and he tried desperately to compose himself. He had tried to prepare himself for bad news for the last week, as the Hector became long overdue, and had only succeeded in making himself more anxious as the bay remained ominously empty.

His father, Martin McCain, had insisted on this match and Colin, having had few eligible ladies to choose from in the colonies, was agreeable. Now that she was actually arriving, he was as nervous as a schoolboy. Would she be as pretty as she had been purported to be? Would she think that he was handsome, or would she regret her choice? Would she be kind and intelligent, or would she be one of the women of a type he detested; the ones who fawned and preened and were utterly useless in a conversation other than as decoration.

His mind raced with a thousand questions but one rose over all of them. Would they be a good match, or had they both made a nearly fatal mistake? He felt that he had been asleep while he had waited and the idea had then seemed very distant and obscure. Now suddenly, she was so very near and he felt more wide awake and alive than he had ever felt before. The minutes to their face-to-face meeting flew past him now, like the wind he faced into as he ran.

He reached the shore and came to an abrupt halt next to Mayor Linset, who had donned a different coat and hat, apparently sprucing himself up for the Hector's arrival. The mayor eyed him bemusedly. The young man was obviously highly excited and his cheeks were ruddy from rushing around the town. Mayor Linset raised one eyebrow and nodded at the younger man's waistcoat and hair, indicating politely the dishevelment that needed his repair.

Quick to pick up on small cues after years of trade, Colin quickly felt of his hair and his half undone buttons and made some minor adjustments to his person. He looked up at the mayor, asking the question silently with pleading eyes.

"Aye, ya look fine now lad," Mayor Linset answered with a knowing smile. "She will think herself quite the lucky lass when she sees ya," he assured the nervous Colin with a confident nod.

"Thank you, sir," Colin said. "I realize that I am behaving like somewhat of a fool, but we have never met you see, and I..."

"I understand, Mr. McCain, I was once a young man a courtin' my ain self," the mayor said patting Colin on the back. They both stopped talking as they noticed a group of the friendly MicMaq Natives approaching them. "Well, I'll be..." the mayor trailed off watching them as they warily, but curiously watched the approaching ship. "This is the first time I ha' seen them sa interested in a ship," Mayor Linset commented.

"Is that so?" Colin answered. "They are not hostile, are they?" he asked worriedly.

"Nay, never, yet, I wonder wha' has made them sa curious this time?"

There was a loud splash as the Hector dropped her huge anchors into the bay several hundred yards out. Bagpipe music began to play from the ship's deck and it floated eerily across the water, washing over the town like a tidal wave. In a flash, the MicMaq's were racing back down the beach the way they had come, obviously terrified.

Mayor Linset and Colin McCain looked at each other, faces twitching with amusement, and then they burst out laughing. As the crescendo of the piper's music grew, the MicMaq's ran faster and faster glancing fearfully behind them, as if hell itself were pursuing them. The men on the shore laughed and guffawed until tears ran down their faces and they were supporting each other to keep from falling into the water in their mirth.

"Ah, the poor buggers, they ha' ne'er heard the bagpipes. We shall have some explaining ta do ta their chieftain, I'm afraid," Mayor Linset said wiping the tears from his eyes.

"Aye, I have rarely seen anyone run faster," Colin agreed as his laughter died away to the occasional uncontrollable chuckle. "You would think the Donas himself was on their backside."

"Douglas," Mayor Linset called out to one of the men gathering dockside. "Let's send some of the men out to start unloading the Hector's passengers and bring them ashore."

"Aye," Douglas answered. He gestured at several of the men and boys and they immediately stepped forward and began to untie their boats, launching them toward the Hector. She now floated peacefully, bobbing atop the gentle waves, seeming to rock to the rhythm of the joyous bagpipers' tunes. The fine morning mist had lifted and the sun shone through it, a white disc glowing in the mist, its warmth burning away the chill damp in the coastal air.

In a short time, people were being loaded aboard the small boats, most carrying small sacks, various possessions and children in their arms. One group of passengers in particular caught Colin's eye immediately. It was a young well dressed woman with golden curls piled high upon her head in the latest fashion. She was accompanied by an older woman and looked like the description of his intended. She also seemed to be visibly irritated by the attentions of an older man. His heart jumped, knowing this young lady was likely to be his betrothed.

"I say, is that the captain, Mayor Linset?" Colin asked, pointing out the man helping the ladies get settled into a boat with a great deal of luggage accompanying them.

"Yes, it is. Captain Spiers, he said his name was when we hailed her," Mayor Linset answered.

Colin's eyes darkened for a moment as he saw the young girl pull her arm away from the captain's obviously unwanted attentions. The girl said something to him and then turned her back on the man rudely to take a seat next to her mother in the small dinghy. Even at this distance he could see frowning dislike on her face. He noticed that she held something tightly against her chest with one hand and he wondered about its significance. Colin politely pushed past some men and moved closer to the water's edge, his curiosity growing as the boat containing the two women began to row toward shore.

The sun shone on what could be seen of the women's hair beneath their bonnets, one head golden, and the other silver. They sat erect and proud in the small boat as if it were a carriage and not an old fishing dinghy that had seen better days. He knew instinctively that this must be them and his heart began to rise up into his throat in anticipation. He hoped that his own nerves would not cause him to act foolishly or misspeak himself in front of his future bride and mother-in-law.

Colin took a deep breath and found that all that it did was cause him to feel slightly dizzy. A steadying hand came out of the crowd behind him and grabbed his shoulder before he could tip forward and into the water that rocked against the shore and receded with a hiss. Regaining his composure, his shocked senses back in place, he turned to find Mayor Kenneth Linset's reassuring face behind him as he held fast to Colin's coat and shoulder. Colin smiled and nodded at the older man gratefully, as the ground quit tilting beneath his shaky legs.

"We don't want you ta meet your bride-to-be as you are being hauled from the water soaked ta the skin now, do we?" Mayor Linset asked.

"No, thank you kindly, sir," Colin said sincerely. "That would not do at all."

"Well and here they are," Mayor Linset said as the boat reached the shore and was pulled as close to shore as possible by the waiting men.

Colin rushed forward to be the first to extend his hand to Jane and her mother and assist them from their boat. Other boats were coming in behind them, but Colin's attention was firmly held by the young woman whose slim hand he now held in his own as she accepted his help to shore. She looked up at him with eyes that were bluer than either the sky or the sea and he felt her intense gaze unlock the door to his heart. "I am Colin Charles McCain," he said, the sureness of his voice belying his pounding pulse. "And you are?" he asked hopefully.

"I am Jane Isobel Forbes," she replied with a sweet smile and a melodic voice. "And that is my mother, Mrs. Mary Jane Forbes," she added, as he gallantly helped her mother up and out of the rocking dinghy.

The women reeled a little and he immediately inserted himself between them, taking them each skillfully by the arm, his own recent dizziness forgotten in his concern for their welfare. "Careful! It is hard to get accustomed to solid ground beneath your feet after so long at sea." He handed several boys some coins and indicated that they should retrieve the ladies' belongings and follow.

"It would certainly seem so," Mary Jane commented as they both staggered a little and leaned heavily on him trying to reacquaint their legs to the forgotten feeling. "Why, I feel as though I've had one too many glasses of port wine!" She looked thoughtful for a moment, "perhaps that is why they call it port," she joked with a nervous but charming giggle.

Colin laughed, delighted with her unexpected good humor after their obvious ordeal. "I cannot tell you how grateful I am for your safe arrival! We have been so very worried since the Hector did not make port on schedule," Colin said to them both, but he found that he could not pull his gaze away from Jane's for long. Jane displayed an appealing mixture of strength and vulnerability in her expression. She remained silent, just staring into his face, until he became uncomfortable. "Is everything all right?" he asked her somewhat nervously.

"Oh, I do apologize," Jane exclaimed. "I am afraid my manners have become quite dreadful on this journey. I do not mean to stare," she added looking down at the ground suddenly shy as they walked onto Main Street.

"Not at all, my dear, I just hope that all is, er, well?" Colin asked, also at a sudden loss for words. He glanced down and noticed that what she had held so tightly to her chest on the boat trip to shore was a small frame which she held face down against her stomacher. He swallowed the lump that rose in his throat as he wondered jealously whose portrait it was that seemed so very dear to her.

Jane noticed his glance and smiled up at him with tears in her eyes. She pulled the tightly held portrait away from her breast and offered it to him. He glanced down at it, bracing himself for what he might see. A slow smile of surprise bloomed on his face when he realized what it really was.

"Why, it is a portrait of me," Colin said with genuine surprise.

"And who else would it be?" Jane answered with a mischievous edge to her tone.

"I am sure I don't know," he said. Seeing her look of confusion he quickly amended, "what I meant was that you caught me off guard is all. I am most pleased that you would be carrying my portrait," he added sincerely.

Suddenly Jane's eyes rolled back and she slumped limply against him. He deftly caught her before she could fall into the dirt.

"Oh, dear," Mary Jane exclaimed reaching for Jane's pale hand. "I'm afraid she has not eaten well in many days. I think she was giving most of her rations to the children, you see," she began to explain to Colin.

He noticed for the first time how very gaunt both women looked, their dresses no longer fitting as they likely had when they were sewn for them in Scotland. "Of course, how very foolish of me," Colin said matter-of-factly as he swung Jane up into his arms. "Are you all right, Mrs. Forbes? Shall I call for help or can you walk on your own?" He asked Mary Jane, eyeing her with genuine concern. "Our rooms are just there and I have hot food being prepared," he indicated with a nod of his head toward the Pictou Inn.

"I am quite all right now that we are off of that dreadful ship," Mary Jane waved away his concern. "Please just get Jane inside."

He obeyed with prompt efficiency and she had to scurry to keep up with his purposeful stride. Mary smiled a secret smile to herself. Despite Jane fainting she was very pleased with this first auspicious meeting of her son-in-law to be and with his take charge attitude. She breathed a sigh of relief, realizing she felt as though she had been holding her breath for the entire voyage and worrying about this meeting.

James carried Mary off their launch to a large grassy knoll near shore that was beginning to fill with the new arrivals. Katy hurriedly spread a blanket on the ground for her frail mother. He placed Mary gently on it and then he put the babes beside her and Katy and Lizzie. "I mun go and retrieve our things, mo mhurninn," he said softly to her, not wanting to leave her side, but knowing he must secure their few precious belongings.

"Aye," she answered, "I willna be going anywhere," she said with a weary grin. "And don' ya be forgettin' my spinning wheel or my rocker pieces," she reminded him.

"Ian has them already, my jo; you just rest here with the lassies." He glanced with meaning at Katy and Lizzie who moved closer to their mother protectively. Alasdair sat up in his basket, looking curiously around at the new surroundings.

Nate and Sgian followed James back to help retrieve their goods, but could be seen looking back over their shoulders through the crowd occasionally, concern in their eyes.

The McLeod women came next and made a place for themselves next to the McDonalds. As soon as Janet settled her own children and belongings and helped Maggie tie up the goats to a scruffy bush nearby, she came to tend to her friend Mary. Margaret, Ian's new wife, joined them walking gingerly across the gravel on her own, using the cane that George had made for her to support her mending leg. Seeing her casting about for a task to do, Janet sent her off in search of food. Despite her splinted leg, she made quick time limping in the direction of the odor of cooking food. The smell of fresh bread and broth now filled the air and many hungry people were licking cracked lips in anticipation.

A sudden scream from shore accompanied by a male shout of triumph caught everyone's attention. Little Jane Gibson was being hoisted out of her delivering boat by a huge red-haired man. She held their newborn babe in her arms and her husband Angus held them both above his massive frame, roaring with his elated surprise. He carried them both as if they weighed nothing and set them down on shore, only to seize them again in another exuberant embrace.

Jane Gibson's brother, Charles Fraser, still stood in the boat tired and weighed down with bags and parcels and looking somewhat forlorn. Angus rushed back, to retrieve the young man and the luggage, carrying them in the same offhand gleeful manner that he had his wife and new daughter. Charles' face reddened as those nearby laughed at his being carried by the bigger man, like a bairn. Mary and Janet watched from there place, laughing heartily at the spectacle. It seemed that their little Jane and her new babe were receiving a rousing welcome.

Margaret returned with Mary Jane Forbes, who had not forgotten them. Between them they carried a whole pot full of soup and a huge basket of oatcakes and another filled with pastries. Janet stared at her shaking her head with wonder, at her seemingly magical gifts. Seeing her look, Mary replied with a shrug, "It seems my son-in-law to be has anticipated our needs quite nicely. The townspeople are aware of our circumstances and are being most hospitable preparing food for everyone. Even the Natives have come into town bearing baskets of berries and nuts! Apparently, they believe we are some sort of deity after hearing the bagpipes playing from the ship," she said, her eyes shining with amusement as she relayed this bit of information to Janet. "I, for one, am not about to dispel them of their notions as long as they bear food!" she added with a chuckle.

"Nor am I," Janet said, laughing as she quickly handed out some oatcakes to the children. The children wasted no time in hungrily dipping into the hot soup with the bread. Quickly, she took the wobbly tray full of china cups that a worried looking Margaret was using all her effort to balance with one hand. "And china cups, as well. You really are a wonder," Janet remarked to Mary Jane.

"They belong to the Inn," Mary Jane said, "I believe they would give Colin McCain every dish in the place for the asking. Why, he has them running around him in circles," she added with a grin.

"Tis true," Margaret added, "I have never seen such a hurly-burly," she remarked wide-eyed.

"So, Miss Jane seems happy with her husband-to-be then?" Janet asked, eyeing Mary Jane shrewdly. She had come to care for the girl during the voyage of the Hector and wished her all the happiness that she could find.

"Aye," Mary Jane laughed, "more than happy, ecstatic even. I have never had the pleasure of so much silence from her," she said with irony.

Janet laughed. "Well, that is well then. Do you think we shall meet the man in question?"

Mary Jane smiled broadly. "I think it is safe to say that you will see them at their wedding, along with all of Pictou, within the next day or two if Colin has his way."

Both Janet and Mary hooted with laughter. "So that is the way of it then, eh?" Janet remarked, winking at Mary knowingly.

Janet scooped a cupful of the soup into a china cup and helped Mary to sit up, encouraging her to drink some. Mary took a sip or two tentatively and then swallowed the rest in a few hungry gulps and reached for some bread.

"This is the best soup I ha' e'er had," Lizzie remarked her pink lips rimmed in broth. Everyone nodded in agreement, too enraptured with the hot food to speak further. Mary Jane had even thoughtfully brought some cow's milk in a small jug for the babes. Finlay, Alasdair and William all drank some of the cool rich milk, staring in surprised wonder at their new surroundings over the rims of their china cups. The girls could not stop laughing at the way they looked as they drank from the fancy china cups. Little William had struggled at first, but once he got the taste of the rich milk, he drank it greedily from the cup, as long as someone held it. The tide began to come in slowly, shushing soothingly along the pebbly shore as small rocks tumbled lazily against one another in the surf. Peace settled on the embattled group of survivors along with the warmth of the early autumn sun.

In the meantime, the men and boys returned with the rest of the belongings and they gratefully partook of the hot food. They were careful not to overeat, despite their extreme hunger, and risk losing the wonderful meal to overburdened stomachs that had not known such plenty in many days. Nate's skillful nose was the first to discover the prune tarts made by Benjamin Foulds and he crowed with delight. After tasting one, he was quick to shove one into the hand of each of the other children and knelt down beside Mary to present her with a large one, as if it were a precious jewel. "Here Mistress, please eat this for the bairns," he cajoled, seeing her reluctance. "The fruit wull help strengthen ya after bein' at sea."

Now sitting up and looking a little stronger, Mary nodded in agreement. "On one condition," she said to Nate.

"Name it," he said earnestly.

"That you cease calling me Mistress and call me Mither this instant!" she said with mock anger that dissolved quickly into a shaky, tearful smile.

"Yes, Mistress... I mean Mither," Nate said with a widening grin. Looking over her shoulder at the Hector floating safely out in the bay, he finally felt free enough to say it and mean it. His father, or Captain Spiers, as he preferred to think of him now, had not even bothered to bid him farewell. It was the final severing blow to their tempestuous relationship and it had served its purpose well. He now felt no regret in leaving behind the only father he had ever known, only relief.

Sgian looked on, feeling no jealousy. He knew his mother's heart well, and she had plenty of love to go around. He had only gratitude in his heart for this adopted brother.

Willie looked on as well, as proud of Mary McDonald as he was of his mother, Janet; their strength and their willingness to help others had made it possible to endure the awful crossing. He knew that she would never be one to boast about it, but without her aid many more would have died during their journey. He walked over to her and kissed her tenderly on the cheek.

She looked up at him surprised. "Why, Willie, what ever was tha' for?"

Willie shrugged and then leaned in and whispered, "I love you, Ma." He grinned at her sheepishly and then hopped up to run off his boyish enthusiasm. The three boys, now possessing full bellies, were anxious to explore their surroundings and stretch their young legs. The nearness of the MiqMaq's was a sight they could no longer resist. With a tap on Nate's shoulder by Sgian, the three were off, breaking into a run as they nimbly climbed over and around the huge rocks that sheltered the beach toward the town.

"Doona wander too far, ye wee heathens," Janet called after them laughing.

Maggie and Margaret were sitting down together in the shade by the goats, talking companionably about children and animals as the goats grazed contentedly on the green grass. Maggie smiled a private smile as she fondly stroked the beginnings of a bulge on her belly. She held a sleeping Finlay over one arm and finally looked more hopeful than sad. Davy, Rob Innes, and Ian MacGregor stood nearby, earnestly discussing the fishing prospects and the lay of the land, respectively. Replete, all the infants soon settled down to sleep, finally content with full bellies. Little Alasdair even smiled fleetingly as he slept, as if dreaming of even better times to come, much to the delight of his watching sisters.

Elspeth boldly took Katy by the hand and tried to pull her away to play. Katy balked, looking to her mother for permission, which she granted with an encouraging nod and a smile. She let Elspeth lead her to the nearby shore where they busied themselves happily collecting the small shells and colored pebbles that lay here and there like treasure. Elspeth squealed and exclaimed loudly when she discovered some lovely purplish ones, her favorite color. She ran back to show her mother and then was off again in a flurry of excitement.

Not to be out done, Lizzie took Hector by the hand and tried to follow suit, only to discover Hector was more than willing to follow her, but he stubbornly refused to be led by the hand. With a small shrug of her little shoulder, she tossed her auburn curls at him defiantly and flounced ahead of him to trail the older girls. He followed her, but at his own stubborn pace.

George and Janet watched this little exchange with amusement and George slipped an arm quietly around Janet's waist as they watched the children at play. She knew some might not consider it quite proper, but it felt so right that she dismissed all thoughts of propriety and leaned against him companionably. George eyed the huge stands of pine behind the small town, every bit as hungry to get his hands on some wood as he had been to get them on some food. "I'll be startin' a house for us just as soon as we sort out where our parcels of land lie. A large one with a few bedrooms I'm thinking, mebbe more?" He let the question dangle expectantly.

"Aye, mebbe more," Janet said with a saucy grin, flirtatiously lowering her eyelids. She turned toward him and rose up on tiptoe to kiss his lips quickly, leaving him with a frozen pucker and a stunned look on his face. Then his grin burst free like the sun from behind winter clouds. "Perhaps we should be finding a priest of our ain soon?"

"Aye, tha' we should, George love, tha' we should," Janet replied hugging him close, her heart buoyant with expanding happiness.

Old Hugh and James sat on the blanket near the peacefully sleeping Mary, saying nothing of George and Janet's embrace, just smiling with proud satisfaction, as if they had made the match themselves. Around them, the ship's passengers were being greeted warmly by the sympathetic townspeople and served food and drink as each relieved boatload arrived on shore. All around the McDonald's and the McLeod's they gathered, to rest from their ordeal. Hugh closed his eyes for a moment and thanked God and Flora for their safe deliverance to dry land. When he opened them again, he found James staring thoughtfully at him.

"What is it, lad?" Hugh asked, wondering at his suddenly serious expression.

"I was just trying ta think of a way ta repay you and your family for everything ya have done for me and mine. I canna think o' anything grand enough."

"Achh, ya ha' done as much for me and mine," Hugh said. "Besides, all I expect ya ta do is ta make good on your promise of friendship. We canna build neither a new life, nor homes here without helpin' each other oot, now can we?"

"A charaid, ya have my friendship and aught else I can give ya, man," James said, putting his arm around Old Hugh.

"Weel then, may I impose on ya ta hand me my walkin' stick there? The bairns arena the only ones who need ta stretch their legs a bit; I am right tired of squatting aboard yon ship!" Hugh said, with a rueful nod toward the Hector where she bobbed in Pictou Harbor. "Care ta join me for a stroll? Mebbe find the mayor and see which part o' this wild land is ta be ours? I ha' a promise ta keep ta my Flora," he said, thinking of her final warning concerning preparations. He did not intend to be caught off guard.

"Aye," James answered, as he covered the now peacefully sleeping Mary and the bairns gently with a blanket. "George?" he asked nodding in Mary's direction.

"Aye," George answered with a nod, knowing the question. "We'll stay right here and watch o'er the lot o' them." They had all been together so long now, that they could nearly read each other's thoughts and finish each other's sentences. "Bring tha' mayor back wit' ya when ya find him. I've many a question about yon timber." He added his eyes bright with anticipation. His nostrils flared taking in the sweet earthy scents of the lush woodlands nearby, while his eyes scanned the lush tree line, longingly.

"Aye, and I've many a question about the fishing hereabouts," Davy called from across the way. He had been listening to the last of their conversation and he nodded respectfully at James, silently acknowledging his own promise of friendship along with that of his father's.

James grinned as he helped Old Hugh to his feet. He was thinking about how close they had all become and he felt tremendous gratitude for such a fine group of friends. He could not have chosen finer, had he hand picked them himself. It occurred to him that fate had a funny way of dealing out her lots. They were now no longer alone, none of them. In fact, they had a larger extended family now than the one they had left behind.

Each man and woman brought with them their own skills and as a whole they formed a formidable group. Even though they were in an unknown land they still had their family and trusted friends to lean on. They could take on the rugged wilderness and more if need be.

The ordeal had tested their strength as it had their bonds and they had survived. With the horror of the voyage finally behind them, James felt a renewed faith that they could now face anything that was in their unknown future. With his feet planted on solid ground, he felt every bit the hunter and farmer that he had always been. Confidently, he squared his shoulders and straightened his clothing in preparation to meet the local town leaders. Much still needed to be learned and many promises waited for fulfillment. James meant to see that their land was secured before the day was done.

Hugh McLeod leaned on his walking stick for support, but he still cut a proud figure beside James. The sea birds called and flapped their wings overhead, reminding Hugh of the eagle he had seen as such a fortunate omen over Loch Broom. He smiled to himself, thinking of the green hills of his past as he and his new friend James McDonald walked toward the rustic settlement of Pictou and the greener hills of their future.

Afterward

History has not recorded how many of the original passengers of the Hector remained in the Pictou area, or how long they may have stayed. It is certain that many of these intrepid souls remained in Pictou, where their descendants still live to this day. Others moved on, to more settled parts of the province and eventually explored even further. Today, a full-scale replica of the Ship Hector floats proudly in the harbor of Pictou, Nova Scotia honoring her passenger's contributions to Canada's rich history.

Like their journey, things were not simple for the people of the Hector even after surviving their arduous ordeal at sea. The land was raw and rugged and needed a great deal more preparation and work than they had been led to believe. Nor were the promised provisions set aside for them for that important first year, let alone the approaching winter. The people of the Hector and the many immigrants that followed them in later years had to rely on their own ingenuity, hard work and their sense of community to carve new lives out of the wilderness. In our modern world it is all too easy to forget the great hardships these people endured and the monumental sacrifices they made, while building the foundations of a better future for their children and grandchildren.

The people of the Hector were not the first Scots to settle North America, but they were the first large group of many more to follow. In the ensuing one hundred years, over 20,000 people from Scotland sailed into Pictou Harbor and by the late 1800's more than ninety percent of the mainly rural population of Pictou possessed Scottish surnames. Many thousands of Canadians and Americans of Scottish decent can trace their ancestry directly back to these brave early settlers.

Thanks to the Town of Pictou, The Ship Hector Foundation and Hector Heritage Quay in Pictou, visitors can explore the ship and appreciate the people of the Hector, their rich culture, their inspiring music and their strength of spirit. That resolute spirit survives not only in Nova Scotia, but anywhere that people gather to remember and honor their ancestral roots.

Although, the characters in this story are fictional depictions, since only their names remain, they were created with as much attention to available historical detail as possible. Their story is a testament to courage and strength and one that begged to be told to a broader audience. History should never lose sight of all the courageous immigrants that sailed away from the countries of their birth with bravery, fortitude and hope in their hearts. Many souls were lost in the risky ocean journeys, yet people continued to have faith in their dreams as they sailed toward unknown horizons.

Glossary of Terms: Toward the Horizon

This is meant as a guide for reading the aforementioned novel. It is, by no means, a replacement for a detailed study of the intricacies of the Gaelic language. If you are interested in the study of Gaelic, please refer to the references in the Bibliography.

A: *Gaelic* - 1) oh/o 2) from, out of
A bhalaich: *Gaelic* - o boy
A beannachd: *Gaelic* - o my blessing
A boireannach: *Gaelic* - o woman
aboot: *slang* - about
a' catching: *slang* -1) contagious
A charaid/caraid: *Gaelic* -1) oh friend
Ach/Achh: *Gaelic* - 1)but, however 2) literal noise of disgust/denial
agin: *slang* -1) again
ague: *slang* - 1) influenza 2) colds 3) general illness
ain: *Scots slang* - 1) own
A leannan: *Gaelic* - 1) sweetheart 2) endearment in regards to female or infant
allus: *slang* - 1) always
A luaidh: *Gaelic* - 1) o dear
amiss: *Gaelic* -1) gone wrong 2) awry
an: *slang* - 1) and
anither: *slang* - 1) another
arena: *Scots slang* - 1) are not
arse:*Scots slang* - 1) literally ass or butt
askin': *slang* - 1) asking
a'tall: *slang* - 1) at all
aught: *slang* -1) none 2) nothing
auld: *Scots slang* - 1) old
auld gommerel: *Scots insult* - 1) old idiot
auld mumper: *Scots insult* - 1) old bugger
aye: *English & Gaelic* - 1) yes 2) affirmative

bairn: Scots - 1) baby/infant 2) child
bairns: *(plural) Scots* - 1) infants 2) children
balach boidheach: *Gaelic* -1) beautiful boy
beggin': *slang* - 1) begging
ben: *Scots* - 1) mountain or large hill
bloody: *English/Scots* - profanity 1) damned, etc...
blowzabella: *Scots slang* - -1) whore 2) easy woman
bodhran: *Scots/Gaelic* -1) small circular celtic drum - beaten with a two-headed stick
braw: *Scots* - 1) strong 2) healthy looking
brew-ha-ha: *slang* - 1) mess 2) skirmish 3) riot
bum: *slang* - 1) butt 2) rear-end
burn: *Scots* - 1) stream or creek

caithris: *(archaic) Gaelic* - 1) a ceremony for the deceased 2) a funereal lament
canna: *Scots slang* - 1) can not
canty: *Scots slang* - 1) sly, mischievous 3) spry, lively
ceilidh: *Gaelic* - 1) celebration, usually with food and music 2) visit
ciphering: *English (archaic)* - 1) doing sums 2) mathematics
clarty: *Scots slang* - 1) dirty
clicket: *Scots slang* - 1) knitting
clot-heid: *Scots insult* 1) *clot*-head 2) idiot
clouts: *Scots slang* - 1) diapers
cockernonny: *English (archaic)* - 1) men's "ponytail" hairstyle:tightly wrapped at nape
cuimhnich/cuimhne: *Gaelic* - 1) remember 2) memory

D

daft/dafty : *Scots slang* - 1) stupid 2) feeble-minded 3) mentally ill
darena: *Scots slang* - 1) dare not
darlin': *slang* - 1) darling
dearie: *slang* - 1) dear one
didna: *Scots slang* - 1) did not/didn't
dinna: *Scots slang* - 1) did not/didn't
doesna: *Scots slang* - 1) does not
doldrums: *English (nautical term)* - 1) calm seas with no wind
don': *Scots slang* -1) do not/don't
Donas: *Scots* - 1) the devil

doona: *Scots slang* -1) do not
dowsing: *English (archaic)* - 1) an ancient method of locating water
drammach: *Scots* - 1) a watery form of oatmeal cereal
draymen: *English/Scots* - 1) men who drive long carts and hauls heavy loads
dysentery: *English (archaic)* - 1) severe symptoms of diarrhea and/or vomiting

enoogh: *Scots slang* - 1) enough

foundling: *(archaic) slang* - 1) an infant that has been magically replaced by a fairy child
fortnight: *(archaic) English* - 1) a period of two weeks or literally fourteen nights
fash: *Scots slang* -1) worry 2) bother about

gaol: *Scots/English slang* - 1) jail/prison
glen: *Scots* 1) valley
gory: *slang* - 1) golly!
gowk: *Scots slang* - 1) clumsy fool
g'wa: *slang* - 1) go away

ha': *slang* - 1) have
hame: *Scots slang* - 1) home
hangit: *slang* - 1) to hang or be hung by the neck
hant/ha'nt: *slang* - 1) haunt 2) ghost
hasna: *slang* - 1) has not/hasn't
healin' airts: *slang* - 1) the ability/knowledge to heal 2) witchcraft
heid: *Scots slang* - 1) head
hoy: *nautical term* - 1) hello
hurly-burly: *Scots slang* - 1) fight, row 2) tempest 3) ruckus

idjut: *slang* - 1) idiot
isna: *slang* - 1) is not/isn't

𝔍

K

keelhauled: *(nautical–archaic)-* 1) to be drawn under the ship/through its wake by ropes

kelpies: *Gaelic/Scots-* 1) mythical water horses

ken: *Scots-* 1) know/understand

kent: *Scots-* (past tense) 1) knew/understood

kin: *Scots-* 1) family, relatives

kine: *Scots-* 1) cattle

kirk: *Scots-* 1) church

knivvle: *slang -* 1) beat upon

L

lad: *Scots-* 1) young male (plural): lads or laddies

lass: *Scots-* 1) young female (plural) lasses or lassies

lest: *English (archaic)-* 1) unless 2) or

loch: *Scots-* 1) lake

luaidh: *Gaelic -* 1) dear

M

marrit: *slang -* 1) married

mebbe: *slang -* 1) maybe

milady: *English slang -* 1) my lady

mither: *slang -* 1) mother

m'dearie: *slang -* 1) my dearie

Mo': *Gaelic -* 1) my

Mo' brathair: *Gaelic -* 1) my brother

Mo' cridhe: *Gaelic -* 1) (Male version) my heart

Mo' cridheachan: *Gaelic -* 1) (Female version) my heart

Mo' luaidh: *Gaelic -* 1) my dear

Mo' mhurninn: *Gaelic -* 1) my darling

Mo' nighean ban: *Gaelic -* 1) my fair-haired girl

mun: *slang -* 1) must 2) much

my jo: *slang -* 1) personal endearment

naught: *English (archaic)* - 1) none/nothing 2) not at all
nay: *English (archaic)* - 1) no
ne'er: *English slang* - 1) never
nip: *Scots slang* - 1) small sip or drink
noo: *Scots slang* - 1) now (usually used with "the" - i.e. the noo)

o': *slang* - 1) of
onecet: *slang* - 1) once
oot: *Scots slang* - 1) out
out'n: *slang* - 1) out of
ower: *slang* - 1) over
owermuch: *slang* - 1) over much 2) overly

philtre: *(archaic) English* 1) *potion/medicinal mixture*
pox: *slang* - 1) contagious diseases characterized by small red pustules on the skin
pur: *slang* - 1) poor

quaich: *(archaic) Gaelic* - 1) small wooden bowl/cup with a handle
quay: *English* - 1) bay or inlet

rush lights: *(archaic) English* - 1) swamp plant stalks dipped in grease: used for lighting
rioghal: *(archaic) Gaelic* - 1) royal

sa: *slang* - 1) so

saft: *Scots* -1) rainy/wet 2) dumb - i.e. "saft in the heid"

sark: *Scots* - 1) long, loose shirt

sealg: *(archaic) Gaelic* - 1) hunt

sgian dubh: *Gaelic* - 1) black knife 2) sm. sock knife 3) Andrew McDonald's nickname

shag: *English slang* - 1) get 2) have sex with

silkie: *Scots slang* - 1) seal 2) mythical seal/person

simples: *(archaic) English* - 1) herbs, oils, tinctures and basic medicinals

slainte: *Gaelic* - 1) health: as in a toast

sommat: *slang* - 1) somewhat

so's: *slang* - 1) so as

sporran: *Scots* - 1) small pouch/purse worn at the front of a man's waist

S' Rioghal mo Dhream: *Gaelic* - 1) Royal is my race 2) MacGregor clan motto

stramash: *Scots* - 1) fight or conflict

swivet: *Scots* - 1) excited 2) upset

ta: *slang* - 1) to

taing: *Gaelic/Scots* - 1) thank you

tchaa: *Scots slang* - 1) get going 2) derogatory noise

teuchter: *Scots slang* - 1) term used by lowlanders for highlanders 2) derogatory term

tha': *slang* - 1) that

'tis: *slang* - 1) it is/ it's

tuld: *slang* - 1) told

twa: *slang* - 1) two

'twas: *slang* - 1) it was

tannasg: *(archaic) Gaelic* - 1) spirit or ghost

tha'll: *slang* - 1) that will/that'll

uisge: *Gaelic* - 1) water 2) rain

Bibliography – Toward the Horizon

<u>Art</u>

Cover art graciously supplied by David MacIntosh from his original painting – Dave is currently the summer resident artist at Hector Heritage Quay Museum – for more information on Dave's work contact the Pictou Recreation, Tourism and Culture Department, 40 Water Street, Pictou, NS – BOK 1HO or www. townofpictou.com

<u>Book Resources</u>

Book - *A Midwife's Tale – The Life of Martha Ballard based on her diary 1785-1812* – published by Random House – written by Laurel Thatcher

Book - *Gaelic – A Complete Course for Beginners* – Teach Yourself Books, trademark of Hodden & Stoughton Ltd. – written by Boyd Robertson and Iain Taylor

Book - *MacBain's Dictionary – An Etymological Dictionary of the Gaelic Language* – Published by Gairm Publications, Glasgow Scotland – written by Alexander MacBain

Book – *Nova Scotia* – from the "Discover Canada Series" – by Jim Lotz

Book – *Scotland* - written by Conrad R. Stein

Book- *Scottish Witchcraft The History and Magick of the Picts* – published by Llewellyn Publications - written by Raymond Buckland

Book – *The Best Baby Name Book - in the whole world* – by Bruce Lansky

Book – *The Outlandish Companion* – published by Delacorte Press – written by Diana Gabaldon

Book - *The Scottish Clans and their Tartans* – published by Chartwell Books – by Wordsworth Editions Ltd. 1992

Internet Resources

Article – *A History of Birth Control Methods* – www.plannedparenthood.org/ news-articles-press/politics-policies-issues/birth-control-access-prevention/bc-history-6547.htm

Article – *Ancestors Unlimited* – Nov-Dec 1986 Newsletter by the Southwest Nebraska Genealogical Society

Article – *Before the Ullapool We Know Today*, from website: http://www. ullapool.co.uk/history.html reprinted there with permission from the author of "A Guide to Ullapool" by K.J.B.S. MacLeod

Article - *Cetaceans of the North-east Atlantic Fringe* by Anna Moscrop, from the website: http://www.gpuk.org/atlantic/library/biodiversity/moscrop5.html

Article – *From Old Scotia to Nova Scotia* – from website: http://www.ullapool. co.uk/hector.html reported by Andy Mitchell

Article – *Highland Clearances* – from the website: http://www.rootsweb. com/~pictou/clearncs.htm and written by Iain Kerr

Article – *Journey of the Ship Hector* – from website: http://members.tripod. com/~suzmac/journey_hector.html

Article – *North Pacific Right Whales (Eubalaena japonica*)* by J. Scarff - from the website: http://www.dnai.com/~jscarff/js/RTWHALES/nprightw.htm

Article – *Pictou County Reminiscences – Early Years* – reprinted with permission on website: http://rootsweb.com/~pictou/earlysg.htm - written by Stanley Graham

Article - *"The People of The Ship "Hector" – 1773* - from http://www.execpc. com/~haroldr/hector.htm reprinted there with permission from the author, Henry Beer

Article – *Ullapool's Fishing Industry* from website: http://www.ullapool.co/ fishing.html and written by Joan Britten

Assorted Articles from the website: http://electricscotland.com

Multiple Articles and Images - The Nova Scotia Museum and the Nova Scotia Museum of Natural History official websites: http://museum.gov.ns.ca/ & http:// museum.gov.ns.ca/mnh

Multiple Articles, Images and Inspiration - The Town of Pictou, Nova Scotia, Canada official website: http://www.townofpictou.com/

Map Resources

Maps - Early Pictou map from website: http://www.rootweb.com/~pictou/earmap.gif

Maps – *The counties of Perth and Clackmunnan* circa 1783 by James Stobie, *Map of the county of Renfrew* circa 1796, and *Early Maps of Great Loch Broom and Little Loch Broom*, all courtesy of The University of Edinburgh, Scotland at: http://www.ed.ac.uk

Miscellaneous Resources

Excerpts from *Pictonians at Home and Abroad, Chapter 1* – courtesy of The GenWeb Chignecto Project - from website: http://www.rootsweb.com/~nspictou/Pictonians_ch_1.htm

Folk Songs, articles and traditional lyrics from website: http://www.contemplator.com

Gaelic to English Dictionary at: www.taic.btinternet.co.uk/dictionary.htm

Gaelic and Scots language resources at: www.rampantscotland.com/gaelic.htm

Glossary of Terms list - *Nautical Terms Index* from the website: http://www.sailorschoice.com/Terms/scphrases.htm

Glossary of Terms list – *Nautical Know How – Boating Basics Glossary of Terms* – from the website: http://www.tcmall.com/nauticalknowhow/GLOSSARY.htm

Guidance from "Kezza" Kerry Guy and the great people at Loch Broom FM 102.2 found at: www.lochbroomfm.co.uk & www.lochbroomfm.internetradio.co.uk

Interesting Gaelic information from: www.savegaelic.org/

Interesting Scottish resources: http://living.scotsman.com/books.cfm

Invaluable information from the website: http://www.highlanderweb.co.uk/culloden.htm

Nautical Terms and their origins – Nautical Know How from: www.boatsafe.com/nauticalknowhow/terms0101.htm

Newsletter - *Twin Ports Genealogical Society* – dates and author unknown – covering archaic medical terms to aid in deciphering old death certificates.

Prayer - *The Selkirk Grace* (traditional) from website: http://www.siliconglen.com/scotfaq/5_11.html

Passenger List(s) of the *Hector --- 1773* (attributed to Squire William McKay or one of his sons) from the website: http://www.rootsweb.com/~pictou/hector1.htm and also from: http://www.rootsweb.com/~pictou/mainpass.htm

If enjoyed Jeanne MacGregor Lahn's *Toward the Horizon,* may we also suggest some other titles from our catalog...?

The Path of Our Destiny
by Calvin Louis Fudge

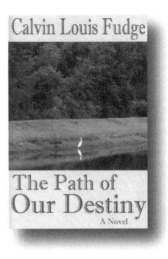

Growing up is never easy, and Calvin Louis Fudge has written knowingly in The Path of Our Destiny of the pains of twelve-year-old Hunt Hews' living with a mother dying of cancer and an alcoholic father. Set in small town El Dorado, Arkansas beginning in the 1950s, Hunt tells his story of a difficult adolescence, made bearable only with the help of an understanding teacher, Mr. Ash and his wife.

Hunt meets temptations in junior high school as he deals with the problems of coming of age: first love, his first sexual experience, and losing his parents. Through all his troubles, business problems, and frustrations of love, Hunt never forgets his roots in his first real home in El Dorado.

You may order online at www.bluewaterpress.com/destiny or by mail:

BluewaterPress LLC
2220 CR 210 W Ste 108 Box 132
Jacksonville FL 32259-4060

Name: _____

Address: _____

City, State, Zip: _____

Phone number: _____

Email Address: _____
(All information kept in the strictest confidence)

Please send me Calvin Louis Fudge's *The Path of Our Destiny*. Cost is $16.95 per copy. Shipping & handling is $3.95 per book for one copy, $6.95 for up to seven of any titles, and $1.15 per book for any combination of more than seven.

Number of books _____ x $16.95 = _____

Shipping and handling = _____

FL residents, please add sales tax for county of residence = _____

Total remitted = _____

We gladly accept payment of your choice: check, money order, or credit card.

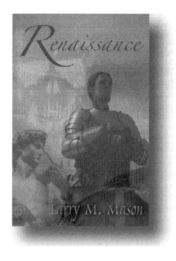

Renaissance by Larry M. Mason

Lorenzo Demarco, his mother would have him be a priest, his father wanted him to be an artist; he would try both but be neither. Relying on agility, wits and guile, Lorenzo would fight, love, and live his way into the lives of the famous – Michelangelo, Leonardo da Vinci and Machiavelli – and the infamous – Savonarola and Tommaso Bramante – in this epic tale set in Florence Italy at the height of the Italian Renaissance. Lorenzo finds adventure with his best friend – a German mercenary, Johann Holper. "Back-to-back, Johann and I fought the enemy, 'Well, you wanted to engage the enemy in a great battle in a combat to the death,' I barked over my shoulder. 'Yes, I did,' Johann shouted back. 'Glorious isn't it.'"

You may order online at www.bluewaterpress.com/renaisssance or by mail:

BluewaterPress LLC
2220 CR 210 W Ste 108 Box 132
Jacksonville FL 32259-4060

Name: _____

Address: _____

City, State, Zip: _____

Phone number: _____

Email Address: _____

(All information kept in the strictest confidence)

Please send me Larry Mason's *Renaissance*. Cost is $15.95 per copy. Shipping & handling is $3.95 per book for one copy, $6.95 for up to seven of any titles, and $1.15 per book for any combination of more than seven.

Number of books _____ x $15.95 = _____

Shipping and handling = _____

FL residents, please add sales tax for county of residence = _____

Total remitted = _____

We gladly accept payment of your choice: check, money order, or credit card.

A Portrait of Grandma's Dog
by Janet Ward

War is a terrible thing, but sometimes miraculous stories spring forth from the tragedy. Such is the case of *A Portrait of Grandma's Dog.* Although a work of fiction, Janet Ward based this warm novella on the actual story of her mother-in-law, Erna Ward.

In her story, Ward captures and presents the emotions of a woman who transitions from childhood in the war torn Germany of World War II to a time of old age and grandchildren. There is the fear, the hatred, and the loss of hope that is a part of every story from the Second World War. There are also great stories of dreams that will not die and new hopes born of those dreams.

You may order online at www.bluewaterpress.com/dog or by mail:

BluewaterPress LLC
2220 CR 210 W Ste 108 Box 132
Jacksonville FL 32259-4060

Name: _____

Address: _____

City, State, Zip: _____

Phone number: _____

Email Address: _____

(All information kept in the strictest confidence)

Please send me Janet Ward's *A Portrait of Grandma's Dog.* Cost is $10.95 per copy. Shipping & handling is $3.95 per book for one copy, $6.95 for up to seven of any titles, and $1.15 per book for any combination of more than seven.

Number of books _____ x $10.95 = _____

Shipping and handling = _____

FL residents, please add sales tax for county of residence = _____

Total remitted = _____

We gladly accept payment of your choice: check, money order, or credit card.